SEA HAWKE

SEA HAWKE

TED BELL

BERKLEY
NEW YORK

BERKLEY
An imprint of Penguin Random House LLC
penguinrandomhouse.com

Copyright © 2021 by Theodore A. Bell
Penguin Random House supports copyright. Copyright fuels creativity, encourages diverse voices,
promotes free speech, and creates a vibrant culture. Thank you for buying an authorized edition of
this book and for complying with copyright laws by not reproducing, scanning, or distributing
any part of it in any form without permission. You are supporting writers and allowing
Penguin Random House to continue to publish books for every reader.

BERKLEY and the BERKLEY & B colophon are registered trademarks of Penguin Random House LLC.

Library of Congress Cataloging-in-Publication Data

Names: Bell, Ted, author.
Title: Sea Hawke / Ted Bell.
Description: New York : Berkley, [2021] | Series: An Alex Hawke novel
Identifiers: LCCN 2021026571 (print) | LCCN 2021026572 (ebook) |
ISBN 9780593101230 (hardcover) | ISBN 9780593101254 (ebook)
Subjects: GSAFD: Spy stories. | Suspense fiction.
Classification: LCC PS3602.E6455 S43 2021 (print) | LCC PS3602.E6455 (ebook) |
DDC 813/.6—dc23
LC record available at https://lccn.loc.gov/2021026571
LC ebook record available at https://lccn.loc.gov/2021026572

Printed in the United States of America
1st Printing

Book design by Laura K. Corless

I would dearly love to thank the love of my life for her unwavering support, her keen intellect and love of good storytelling, her megawatt smile, her unfailing good humor, her style, her gracious demeanor, her keen wit, and the way she laughs, as cheery as church bells on a sunny Sunday morning! God love you, girl, because I know I do!

THE VOYAGE

'Tis not too late to seek a newer world.
Push off, and sitting well in order smite
The sounding furrows; for my purpose holds
To sail beyond the sunset, and the baths
Of all the western stars, until I die.
It may be that the gulfs will wash us down;
It may be we shall touch the Happy Isles,
And see the great Achilles whom we knew.
Though much is taken, much abides; and though
We are not now that strength which in old days
Moved earth and heaven; that which we are, we are;
One equal temper of heroic hearts,
Made weak by time and fate but strong in will,
To strive, to see, to find, and not to yield.

—ALFRED, LORD TENNYSON

SEA HAWKE

PROLOGUE

L ord Alexander Hawke, a tall and rather attractive chap in his mid-thirties, a bit of a dandy, was, on this particular evening, even some-what resplendent in his regal purple Chinese silk pajamas, his bare feet clad in Chinese red leather slippers. Lord Hawke—or simply call him Alex, as he vastly preferred not to be addressed by his title—was alone at last.

You were most likely to find him in the library of his comfortable two-hundred-year-old gated manse in the heart of London's Mayfair. He looked about this gracious high-ceilinged room, his eye alighting on treasured mementos from the course of his rather dramatic life. And, naturally, the splendid portrait of his late, beloved mother, Katherine, known as Kitty Hawke. He was a bit surprised to suddenly find himself more content than any man had a right to be. And what was his lordship's plan for the evening stretching out ahead?

That remained to be seen.

The weather outside was hellish, and, having walked all the way to Mayfair from his office, MI6 HQ at 85 Albert Embankment, he was now soaked to the skin and chilled to the bone. His usually curly black hair was plastered on his forehead, and he felt very much like the proverbial drowned rat.

Upon reaching his front door and entering the warmth of the foyer, he'd breathed a sigh of relief, as he was only just now thawing out. He'd kept his permafrosted hands jammed deep into the lambswool-lined pockets of his trench coat all the way home.

It had gotten so bad out, he'd momentarily considered popping round the corner to the Duke of York, his trusted neighborhood pub, for a pint or three or four of the best bitters before heading for home. But, upon consideration, he had thought better of it. His new plan?

Straightforward enough. It was to simply sit here in the quietude of his book-filled library before the crackling fire on this cold, windy, and rainy night whilst nursing a smallish tumbler of Haig Pinch whiskey. He sank down suddenly into his favorite chair—a large red leather club chair, which Pelham had thoughtfully tucked in close to the hearth. It was well worn to the point that it now fit him like a glove.

The fragrances of numberless very old leather-bound books cheered him considerably. How he loved the hours spent alone with his books. He had once been widely quoted in an article about men's libraries in the Sunday *Times* Lifestyles section as saying, "The gods do not deduct from the allotted span of men's lives the hours spent in reading."

Also in the air tonight was the scent of spilled brandy from a distant century on the faded rose-pink cushions of the Queen Anne sofa just inside the bay window that overlooked the lush, now sodden, back gardens.

Other scent memories rushed in: sunrise camping at the foot of Mount Kilimanjaro; lush vineyards on a hillside on the isle of Madeira; a beloved parent, holding a mug with steam gently rising while he snuggled deep within the folds of his blanket; a fresh apple pie, still warm, now cooling on the windowsill of some busy matron's kitchen in Kensington Mews; the early-evening streets of Istanbul; the clouds of cherry blossoms bursting forth in full bloom in at the Shinjuku Gyoen garden in Tokyo.

All these, and countless more images and pungent olfactory sense memories, cascading and never-ending as the recollection of fragrances, suddenly brought the whole world into focus, and into him.

The warmth of the fire made him drowsy, and he was happy to allow sleep to overtake him. It had been an extraordinarily rough day. Two of his trusted colleagues, intelligence officers at MI6, had turned up dead in a back alley in Beijing early that morning.

He dozed off, apparently, but upon waking to the howling wind ratcheting up to a still keener pitch, now whistling around the eaves and chimneys, with the rain, steadily turning to ice, pricking and clacking, clacking, clacking at the paned windows, he leaned forward and eagerly picked up the prize he'd treated himself to that very afternoon: an exceedingly rare book he'd stumbled upon at his go-to Piccadilly bookseller, Pimms & Co.

The Haig Pinch tasted delicious, but to get the full effect, he lit a cigarette. Not Morlands, mind you, which had created a secret tobacco blend just for him code-named "Hawkeye," but his new brand, Marlboros. He looked at the glowing tip in his left hand and shrugged his shoulders.

He had, after all, never smoked because he thought it was good for him. And if cancer had any fancy ideas about killing him, it would just have to take its place at the back of the queue and wait its turn, goddammit.

Earlier today, haunting the tiny bookshop in Shepherd Market, with its low ceilings and tightly spaced aisles, for an hour and then spying the familiar name of a well-known Chinese historian on the cover of these old and rare diaries, he could scarcely credit his astounding good fortune!

A seemingly original work by the master Han Xin? Detailing the decades-long and bloody history of the infamous Tang Dynasty! In very, very good condition? It was a miracle. And now it was all his for the perusing!

Bloody hell. This was one phenomenal find! The newest mission of his friend and superior at MI6 entailed learning everything he could about the Tangs, the villainous twins he'd battled with in the Bahamas the previous year—and then circling the globe to root them out wherever they should be found.

Tommy and Tiger *Tang*!

If ever there'd been an enemy worthy of Hawke's keen attention, his tradecraft, his knowledge of the Great Game, his formidable warrior skills on the ground, in the air, and on the sea, and his full-throated roar of courage as the battle raged, it was this pair of full-blown sociopaths (and Tang *Twins*, no less, twice the criminal for the price of one!).

He'd been engaged in a study of the history, past and present, of the Tang Triad, one of the oldest and most powerful of the Chinese crime dynasties. As he and his wingman, one Stokely Jones, Jr., had discovered in the Bahamas on a personal mission for Her Majesty the Queen, the Tangs' worldwide criminal empire now stretched around the world and back again.

A monstrous enterprise it was, too.

He'd recently gone to Washington for a meeting at the CIA with his old friend CIA director Patrick Brickhouse Kelly, or "Brick," as he was known, as well as senior members of Hawke's own counterespionage team at MI6, London. The meetings were all about bringing that empire down and thereby saving the fabric of society in the multiplicity of nations where they operated.

The subject of Han Xin's battered, dusty old tome was none other than General Deng Xi Tang himself!—the mysterious and shadowy ancestor of the venerable Tang Dynasty and father of the Tang Twins. The Tangs' origins dated back five hundred years and more. Hawke, since the joint task force meetings in Washington, had learned a good deal about the intricacies of the Tangs' worldwide operations. The Tangs, whilst never publicly acknowledged by the powers that be in Beijing, basically operated with both immunity and impunity and were wholly outside the law as the de facto criminal arm of the CCP, the Chinese Communist Party.

As Lord Alex Hawke was soon to embark upon a lengthy navigation of the globe with his young son, Alexei, he'd spent the preceding weeks in Tang-oriented briefings, noting the locations of their strongholds throughout the far-flung corners of the earth. Now, in both Washington and London, he was gathering as much information as he possibly could before he set sail.

Hawke turned the thin, crumbling pages with a delicate hand and began to read the general's musings, philosophic meanderings, and crystal clear observations. He'd struck gold, all right . . . God only knew what pearls of wisdom he might find here . . . When Hawke saw that the title page of the book was headed "Shanghai Diaries of the Tang Dynasty, 1932. By General Han Xin," he almost screamed for joy at his jolly good fortune.

The Tangs, he thought, it's about the bloody *Tangs*, for heaven's sake! Talk about a massive stroke of luck . . .

He paid for his prize, raced out into bustling Oxford Street where Pelham was waiting with the "Locomotive," his 1953 Bentley Continental. He yanked open the rear door and jumped into the backseat, where he could start thumbing through the pages.

"Whistles and whirligigs, m'lord!" Pelham exclaimed, peering back over his shoulder at his employer. "Lobsters and lollipops! Celery and soup bowls!"

Hawke looked up from his book. "What's that you said? Something about whistles? Lobsters? Celery?"

"Ah, that. You see, I've started reading C. S. Lewis again. Starting with the Chronicles of Narnia."

"And?"

"One of my favorite characters is always spouting off things like that. I find it terribly cheery. Don't quite know why, for the life of me. Loopholes and lariats, indeed!"

"Well," Hawke said, glancing up from his much-prized book, "try not to make a habit out of it, won't you, dear fellow? There is a limit, you know, to one's eccentricities."

———

"Ah, here we are, m'lord," Pelham said twenty minutes later whilst easing the Locomotive to a stop in front of 28 Ashburton Place in Mayfair close to Green Park. "Spot of rain, I'm afraid. I'll let you off here at the entrance door and—" But Hawke had already bolted and flown inside the house, racing down the corridor to his library with his prized possession clutched tightly in his grasp. He collapsed into his deep red leather chair by the fire, his pulse racing as he began to read . . . the pages seemingly afire.

And so, although he did not yet know it, another violent and storied chapter in the epic saga of one Alexander, Lord Hawke, versus the Evil Empire of China would now commence. Hawke, as he sipped his watery whiskey, the rain beating against the windowpanes, the reassurance of a crackling fire beside him, was almost giddy as he began to read in earnest. He turned the page . . .

————————

"As is always the case at this season," the first entry in Han Xin's diary began, and Hawke was off to the races. He began soaking up the tale, knowing the information within would yield countless clues to help him safely navigate the dangerous waters ahead. Perusing this remarkable volume was like having the other side's playbook well in hand ahead of the football championship matches.

"Cool evening breezes," Hawke read, "are drawn over the city from the sea, moving onto the warm landmass of China; here, where in old Shanghai, embroidered yellow silk draperies billow out from the glass French doors of the veranda of large house on Avenue Joffre in the French Concession. For the last few centuries or so, the great house has remained the sacred home of the Tang family. Tang is a known quantity here. The centuries-old Tang Triad Society still strikes fear into the heart of the populace, now, then, and forevermore, as it has always done. The violence, when it erupts, is terrible to behold, grievous to fall victim to."

But as Hawke had now read in some detail, the current chieftain of the clan was not a man prone to torture, rape, and murder. No, no. The man was a retired military officer, a mild-mannered fellow vastly more likely to be found here at home, reading Proust in his book-filled library, playing Chopin preludes on his Steinway grand, but spending the preponderance of allotted time left to him in the study and maintaining these diaries, and, of course, absorbing modern applications of future military strategies in the ancient Chinese board game known as Go.

CHAPTER 1

Hawke, lighting yet another Marlboro, lay back with his curly black head resting against the red leather cushion, pausing to digest what he'd read so far. He closed his eyes and allowed himself to fantasize about that first meeting coming up. The one wherein all the MI6 lads from the third floor would be summoned to C's conference room to be debriefed on all the available intel on the Tang Dynasty known to man. And when they'd wrapped it all up, Hawke, ever the hero to the rescue, would arise at the table and, smiling, would begin to debrief the lads from the third floor!

He read on, deep into the rainy night. And deep into the murky mists of times long past.

Now General Deng Xi Tang withdrew a white stone from his lacquered Go ke and held it lightly twixt the tip of his middle finger and the nail of his index. Passing strange how cool to the touch the smooth stones always felt. Some minutes passed in silence, but his concentration was not on the game, which, in its 176th gesture, had begun to concrete toward the inevitable. The general's dark and deep-set eyes came to rest on his handsome young opponent, who, for his part, was completely absorbed by the patterns of black-and-white stones on the pale yellow board.

General Tang found himself distracted and conflicted. He had decided, sadly, that the young boy, his dear son and the brilliant legitimate scion of the Tang Triad, must be sent away to Japan as soon as possible. Preferably to Kyoto, where his Japanese mother had gone home to her family estate to live out her remaining days before the cancer finally triumphed in the epic battle raging within her frail person. In a stroke of luck, General Tang had once more been ordered into combat. The Japanese were coming. An invasion was coming. War was coming. Tonight, his dear son, Tommy Tang, would have to be told of his own imminent departure.

But not just now. It would spoil the flavor of the game, and that would be unkind because, for the very first time, the young man was winning. He would be told the news after supper, after he'd had a chance to savor his victory at the 2,500-year-old game of Go. Tommy would depart on the morrow.

———————

After the game, despite emerging victorious, Tommy found that he was unsettled; something in his father's darting eyes and restless hands had raised alarms. Secrets were being kept in this house. Tommy was peering through the curtain at shifting shadows of things he could not see. Things were not at all as they seemed. He'd been sensing all this for some time now. He needed fresh air. This vast old house full of musty furniture and dusty draperies was all too much with him. He needed to be out among his street friends. Out of the house where he sometimes suffocated and into the evening melee where he thrived and breathed and breathed!

After his mother had fled to Japan to die in the bosom of her family, young Tommy Tang, age twelve, was put at the mercy of a series of English nannies who followed one another through the household, so English joined French, Russian, and German as the languages of the crib, with no particular preference shown, save for the general's expressed conviction that several languages were best for expressing certain classes of thought. One spoke of love and other romantic trivia in French; one discussed tragedy and disaster in Russian; one did business in German; and one addressed servants in English.

Because the children of the servants were his only companions, Chinese was also a cradle language for the boy, and he developed the habit of thinking in that language alone, because his greatest childhood fear was that his mother could read his thoughts—but, being Japanese, she knew no Chinese! And thus, the many secrets in the dark chamber of the boy's heart remained his alone.

"I'm going out for a walk, Father," he said suddenly, not pausing to kiss his father's cheek as was his usual wont whenever he left the house. Beyond, the sounds of the streets beckoned to him, calling him out into the real world of movement and vivid color and rank smell and harsh reality. He pushed out into the world and was soon lost within it.

The more practical aspects of young Tang's social education—and all of his fun—came from his practice of sneaking away from the house and wandering with street urchins through the narrow alleys and hidden courtyards of the seething, noisome, noisy, and even noxious city.

Dressed in the universal loose-fitting blue overblouse, his close-cropped hair under a round cherry cap, he would roam alone or with friends of the hour and return home to admonitions or punishments, both of which he accepted with great calm and an infuriating elsewhere gaze in his bottle-green eyes as he endured the lash reluctantly wielded by his father.

Down at the docks, young Tang watched sweating stevedores dogtrot up and down the gangplanks of metal ships and wooden junks with stra-bismic (in modern usage, cross-eyed) images painted on their prows. In the evening, after they had already worked eleven hours, chanting their constant, narcotizing *hai-yo, hai-yo*, the stevedores would begin to weaken, and sometimes someone would stumble under his load. Fall. Then the Gurkhas would wade in with their blackjacks and iron bars, and the lazy would find new strength . . . or lasting rest.

The perceptive child had quickly learned to recognize the secret signs of the "Greens" and the "Reds," who constituted the main of the world's largest secret societies and whose protection and assassination rackets extended from beggars to politicians at the very top. Chiang Kai-shek himself was a Green, sworn to obedience to the gang. And it was the Greens who murdered and mutilated young university students who at-tempted to organize the Chinese proletariat.

Tang was by now a keen observer. He knew how to tell a Red from a Green simply by the angle at which a fellow held his cigarette, by the way he snapped his fingers and whistled when he walked, and even by the way he spat.

And so it goes and so it went. During the long days of his seemingly endless boyhood, he had learned from a succession of piano teachers and the endless tutors hired at great expense by his father: mathematics, classical literature, and philosophy. In the evenings he learned from the streets: commerce, politics, enlightened imperialism, and the humanities—and the mysteries of relative moralism.

And at night, in the days before she had left him for Japan, he would sit beside his mother. To his eyes, she was always a glittering ornament in this grand house, as she floated from room to room and entertained the cleverest of men, who controlled Shanghai. She'd picked up top secret information from them and then wrung them all dry! Got them tossed out of their clubs and the commercial houses of the Bund. What the majority of these men thought was a radiant shyness in Tommy Tang, and what the brightest of them thought was mere aloofness, was in fact stone-cold hatred for the British, for their insufferable shopkeepers, their merchants and merchant mentality in general.

And then, at last, in its imperceptible fall, the loitering sun sank low, and from glowing white changed to a dull red without rays and without heat, as if it were about to go out suddenly. Stricken by the touch of gloom brooding over the lives of those below, it finally set behind the French Concession, on mainland China.

Lanterns were lit in the old walled city, and now the smell of thousands of cooking suppers filled the narrow, tangled streets. Along the banks of the Whangpoo River and up the meandering Soochow Creek, the sampan homes of the floating city came alive with dim lights as old women with blousy trousers tied at the ankle arranged stones to level cooking fires on the canted decks, for the river was at low tide and the sampans were heeled well over, their bloated wooden bellies stuck fast in the yellow mud.

Even Sassoon House, the most elegant facade on the Bund, seemed stuck in the mud. Built on profits from the opium trade, it had finally been demoted to the mundane task of housing the various headquarters of the occupation forces. The greedy French, the swaggering British, the pompous Germans, the craven, opportunistic Americans—they were all gone. Now the Japanese were coming.

Above, a strikingly pretty girl with lustrous black hair and flashing dark eyes sat in an opened window, barely balancing on the sill, but whilst she was hanging out of an opened second-floor window of the once-grand building, she smiled and heartily wished the young man standing below a very good evening.

"What's good about it?" Tang asked, pausing for a moment, hands on hips, to stare up at her. "Shanghai is now under the control of the Japanese," young Tang added with a sharp pinch of anger in his voice. "We're at war! Or hadn't you noticed as much from your ivory tower?"

He saw how her face fell and at once regretted his spitefulness.

"Oh! Sorry!" she said, her soft voice barely audible now.

She clasped her hands to her lovely face and dropped back into the shadows of her candlelit rooms, wounded by the beautiful boy whom she'd admired for months now but had never dared approach before.

Unseen, she peeked through the window and watched him disappear into the morass of seething humanity. She felt a chill shiver up her spine. The thought that she might never gaze upon him again had seized her mind and held it in a death grip.

Any passerby, upon encountering him, would have thought that he looked very young for his twelve years. Only the frigidity of his too-green eyes and a certain firm set of his mouth kept his face from being too delicate, too finely formed for a male. A vague discomfort over his physical beauty had prompted him from an early age to engage in the most vigorous and combative of sports. He trained in classic, rather old-fashioned jiujitsu, and he played rugby with the international side against the sons of the British taipans—or merchants of death, as his mother had called them—with a stoicism and effectiveness that bordered on brutality, not to say cruelty, such was his disposition toward them.

Although he understood the stiff charade of fair play and sportsman-ship with which the British have historically protected themselves from real defeat, he much preferred the responsibilities of victory to the com-forts of losing with grace. In truth, he did not really like team sports, preferring to win or lose by virtue of his own unique skill set and tough-ness. And his emotional toughness was such that he almost always won, purely as a matter of will.

It was 1935. War was in the air. War was on the wind. War was in the light at the windows, leaving on the evening tide, and all along the hum-ming wires strung between vast forests of poles. It was in the eyes of the children, the citizens, it was in the dark hearts of the Japanese soldiers intent upon taking Shanghai, in the wakes of the Japanese warships as they delivered payloads of death and moved on farther up the Whangpoo.

That night was the only time Tang had a brush with death. When the squadrons of Japanese Nakajima bombers came roaring overhead, he was with other street urchins in the district of the city's two great department stores, the Wing On and the Sincere, when one of the common "mis-takes" brought the enemy bombers in a steep dive, now way too low over the densely packed Nanjing Road. It was the supper hour. And the mill-ing crowds were thick when the Sincere received the first direct bomb hit, and one whole side of the Wing On was cleaved away in a brutal instant.

Ornate ceilings caved in upon the faces of people staring up in horror. The occupants of a crowded elevator screamed in one voice as the cable was sheared in two by an explosion, and it plunged six floors down into the basement. An old woman who had been facing an exploding window was stripped of her flesh in front, while from behind she seemed un-touched. The old, the lame, and children were crushed underfoot by those who stampeded in a blind panic.

Tang, who had remained outside in the street below, paralyzed with horror, looked at the boy who'd moments ago been standing next to him. Now he grunted and sat down heavily in the middle of the street. The boy was dead; a chip of stone had pierced his chest. As the thunder of the bombs and the war tide of collapsing masonry ebbed, there emerged through it an unbearably high-pitched scream from thousands of voices, hurled up into the heavens, unified in human desperation.

At the Wing On, a stunned shopper whimpered and sobbed as she searched through shards of glass that had been a glittering display counter. She was an exquisite young woman clothed in the Western "Shanghai" mode: an ankle-length dress of emerald green silk, provocatively slit to above the knee, with a stiff little white collar standing around her curved porcelain neck.

Her extreme pallor might have come from the pale rice powders fashionable with the daughters of rich Chinese merchants, but it did not. She was searching the debris not only for the ivory figurine she had been examining at the instant of the bombing, but, yes, also searching in vain for the severed hand in which she had been holding the pretty porcelain figure.

A young girl in the bloom of health!

It was heartbreaking. Tommy Tang turned away to banish the horror of the moment and disappeared into the milling throng of the terrified mob.

Suddenly, he missed his father, and the solidity of his home. He was a strong runner, and now, pushing himself to the outer limits, he ran for home as fast as ever he had.

"My son, my life, come here to me," the general said as he entered the hall, gesturing to him with a beckoning finger. "We must talk." The general began to collect his stones and return them to the Go ke. "What do you say to a cup of tea, boy?"

His father's major vice was his habit of drinking strong, bitter tea at all hours of the day and night. In the heraldry of their affectionate but reserved relationship, the offer of a cup of tea was the signal for a chat. While the general's batman prepared the tea, they walked out into the cool night air of the veranda, both wearing yukatas. The garment was a casual version of the kimono, purple in color and made of cotton wrapped loosely around the body.

Now the sky was black to the east, and purple over China. Out in the vast floating city, the orange and yellow lights were winking out as people made up beds on the canted decks of the sampans heeled even farther over in the mud. The air had cooled on the dark plains of inland China, and breezes were no longer being drawn in from the sea.

The general found himself thinking of the boy's mother. She had found emotional shelter in the lee of the general's strong, gentle personality. He had found spice and amusement in her flashes of temperament and wit. Between the general and the woman—politeness, generosity, gentleness, physical pleasure. Between the general and the boy—confidence, honesty, ease, affection, mutual respect.

After a silence during which the general's eye had wandered farther out over the city, where the occasional light in the ancient walled town indicated that someone was celebrating or studying or dying or selling herself to the highest bidder, he asked the boy, seemingly apropos of nothing, "Do you ever think about the war?"

"No, sir. War has nothing to do with me. Until today, I mean. Now I have something to do with it."

"Always remember, my son. War is never about who is right, but about *who is left.*"

Ah, yes, the egoism of youth. The confident egoism of a young man brought up secure in the knowledge that he was the last and most rarefied of a line of selective breeding that had its sources long before tinkerers became Henry Fords, before coin-changers became Rothschilds, before merchants even dreamed of becoming Medici.

. "I am afraid, Tommy, that our little war is going to touch you after all." And with this entrée, the general told the young man of the orders transferring him to the front lines, into combat, and of his plans to send his son to Kyoto, Japan, to comfort his dying mother, who lived in safety behind thick garden walls and round-the-clock security. Despite the enmity between the two countries, war could not shatter the strength of her lifelong family ties.

"There you will meet my oldest friend, Otake-san—whom you know by reputation as Otake of the Seventh *Dan.*"

"I realize that, sir. And I am excited about learning from Otake-san. But won't he scorn wasting his instruction on a rank amateur such as me?"

"Scorn is not a style of mind that my old friend would ever employ. He is the soul of kindness and gentility. But, come, let us speak of other matters. Your finances."

"As you think best, sir."

"Your mother has very little money, as it turns out. Her investments were scattered in small local companies, most of which collapsed upon the eve of occupation. The men who owned the companies simply returned to Britain with our capital in their pockets. It appears that, for the Westerner, the great moral crisis of war obscures minor ethical considerations. There is this house we live in . . . and very little more. I have arranged to sell this house for you. The proceeds shall go an account to be used for your maintenance, instruction, and education."

"As you think best, Father."

The general let a soft sigh escape his throat. The hour was late. He was very, very tired. And the morrow held much in the way of getting the boy off to his mother and Japan. And in the way of getting his aged old carcass off to war once more.

He would miss this beautiful child. He saw enormous power seething behind the fulsome stare of those green, green eyes. Yes. He would be a force in this world—fiercely intelligent, great physical beauty, curious about the world and all that was in it. Like the poetic fuse that through the green stem drives the flower, as he liked to think about it. Yes. With every generation, a Tang always rose to drive the future of the family forward, to keep it whole and strong, to keep it at the top while still leading the way . . . To each and every one of them was given the same time-honored name.

Tiger.

That, then, was to be the boy's future. That was to be Tommy's calling. The boy they all called, with good reason, "Tiger."

His whole life, his entire existence, would become but a preparation for what would be his momentous rendezvous with Destiny.

CHAPTER 2

"Why, the Queen would have me in bloody chains!"

Black's Club, London, SW1

B last!" Hawke exploded, running up the broad white marble steps at the entrance of his St. James's men's club, Black's. Located at 37–38 St. James Street, London's oldest club for high-born gentlemen, with its formidable Palladian presence, is a Grade I listed building. Founded in 1693, its notable former members have included Beau Brummell, Baron Rothschild, actor David Niven, and King Edward VII. Current notables include Lord Conrad Black, Baron Black of Crossharbour, the Prince of Wales, and Prince William, Duke of Cambridge.

So, there you have it.

Hawke was angry with himself because he was late again for yet *another* luncheon appointment with his legendary boss at MI6, former Royal Navy admiral Sir David Trulove. Trulove was not a man easily rattled. But one thing he could not abide, among many things, was tardiness. And this was the second time this week that Alex Hawke, his senior counterterrorist officer, had been late for an appointment!

Hawke, dashing inside the club, looked with disbelief at his trusty steel dive watch, an old Rolex. Could that hour possibly be correct? Had the aged thing actually finally ground to a stop? It was a dive watch he'd inherited from his father, Admiral Lord Hawke, upon his tragic death at the hands of drug pirates in the Caribbean.

The murder most foul of both of his beloved parents was a slaughter.

Horrifically, the just-turned-seven-year-old boy had been an up-front eyewitness to a hellishly grisly abomination—and the child had forever lost his innocence that cruel evening.

A stamp of the true power of evil had been branded forevermore on his heart and inscribed deep within his soul.

His stalwart spirit forged and buttressed forevermore by the heinous event, he would commit the balance of his life to avenging the deaths of his beloved parents by using his own vast resources, his immense strength of will, and his courageous heart to protect and succor the weak, all whilst wreaking havoc upon evil and terror when and wherever he found it. He'd been only a mere boy, but he had grown into a knight errant, a fearsome warrior down to his bones. A man of whom his father had pronounced on the eve of his squalling birth, "A boy born with a heart for any fate."

He possessed an innate quality, one inherited from his father's side of the family. Unpleasant to some, but to his father, a godsend:

Ferocity.

This ferocity became obvious to his father shortly after the nurses began to notice that deafening thunder overhead and blinding flashes of lightning exploding inside the nursery in a blaze of blue-white light only served to make the baby boy smile and giggle and squeal for more!

Lord Alexander Hawke, a much-decorated airman in the skies over Afghanistan whilst serving in the Royal Navy, once had this to say about war: "Wartime consists of long periods of intense boredom punctuated by short intense periods of fear and trepidation." This apt description of British military life on the square under a drill sergeant was really meant to apply to the regimental routines of trench and billet.

The deep fears generated by the wicked violence and ghastly horror that is modern warfare seem inescapable at the time. But, truly, all war is itself a test in self-discipline and will. And all hardened warriors know that a good deal of the boredom can be easily avoided by the intensely satisfying hazards of saboteurs working like malevolent devils behind enemy lines.

Hawke had heard his grandfather speak of his wartime escapades behind German lines with his good friend Commander Ian Fleming. "It is a time," Fleming had said, "when visible and personal blows can almost daily be struck against the foe." Fleming and Hawke had spent a good part of the war as saboteurs, a two-man team working secretly behind German lines under the direction of the Lion of Britain, Prime Minister Winston Churchill.

"My Lord Hawke," the liveried club staffer said with a slight bow and a smile of recognition of the famous member, Lord Alexander Hawke, a dashing gentleman spy who just happened to be one of the most admired men in England. His exploits in the service of the Crown were legend.

At least half the women in London had gone stark raving gaga for his lordship, and Porterfield, the club's majordomo, could well understand it. But, really, what was the attraction?

Women at the highest strata of London society had some time ago coined a secret nom de guerre for his lordship. "What shall we call him, then?" one exasperated dowager had said to her luncheon companions at Harry's Bar one spring afternoon.

"Well," one spoke up, "I for one think he's positively Byronesque! If that's any help. How about 'Lord Byron'?"

"Perfect, darling," they all said in unison, glad of the opportunity to not tax their brains any further with this puzzlement. And so London High Society would thereafter and henceforth privately refer to him as "Lord Byron."

It should be pointed out that, for whatever the actual reason, meeting, wooing, and bedding beautiful women had never been much of an issue for our Lord Hawke. He was, as some would say, a ravishingly attractive man.

Byronesque, even.

And masculine beauty was only one of his many considerable assets. Another was the fact that he was one of the wealthiest and most admired men in all Britain, according to the Forbes annual list. He'd fought desperately for years to keep his name out of the papers and, certainly, off that bloody list, but, sadly, to no avail. Luckily, he'd long ago had the solicitors at Hawke Enterprises build a firewall around his banking and international business and personal affairs.

Yes, he was tall enough, well north of six feet, with a full head of unruly jet-black hair, finely modeled features—some would even say "sculpted"—and a strong, straight, imperious Roman nose. And those damnably clear blue eyes that one London gossip columnist had famously described as "two pools of frozen arctic rain."

Lord Hawke was, quite simply, the kind of man other men want to stand a drink—and whom women much preferred horizontal.

It may also be said, albeit indiscreetly but verifiably, that Mr. Porterfield had quite an eye for masculine beauty himself.

"My dear Porterfield," Hawke said, smiling back at the man. "Sorry, can't chat, bit of a hurry, you see! Late for luncheon with the boss. As usual, I'm afraid!"

He dashed inside the august, if rather gloomy, interior of London's most exclusive gentlemen's club, handing off his soaking wet Burberry and wilted brown fedora to the happy old chappie at the coat check closet.

He took the wide, curving main staircase three steps at a time until he reached the third floor. The Men's Grille, as was usual on the Saturday, was a logjam of ebullient humanity jostling for position at the horseshoe bar. This humming beehive of upper-class, Savile Row–clad humanity bobbed and weaved beneath a hazy gray cloud of pungent tobacco smoke.

Augustus Porterfield prided himself on being something of an amateur psychologist. Now, standing with the lovely Lila, a platinum blonde, full-breasted cocktail waitress and handsome ornament of the club's bar scene, he opined on the state of mind of Sir David Trulove this afternoon. As a card-carrying member of the club's key staff and a father confessor to many of the members, Porterfield knew quite a lot about all of them. He turned and whispered to Lila, "You know that terrible stuff that Sir David drinks when he's in one of his moods? That Algerian red wine that the wine committee will no longer even allow on the wine list? Well, Sir David explained to me once that in the Navy, they used to call it

"The Infuriator" because if one drank even a soupçon too much of it, it used to cause a chap to fall into a blind rage. Make no mistake, Lila, something hit, or is going to hit, Sir David quite hard this morning."

"Like what, do you suppose?" Lila said.

"Well, let's just say I heard a rumor swirling round the bar that Lord Hawke requested this lunch in order to submit his resignation from the Old Firm."

"Well," she said, "whatever the case may be, I don't envy Lord Hawke, stepping into that lion's den, Infuriator or no Infuriator!"

"Never you mind his lordship. Our Lord Hawke is the golden boy, the chosen one. All these years, I've never seen a cross word between the two of them. They're very close socially, you know, since their country estates are practically next door to each other's in the Cotswolds."

Wading into the huddled masses was not an option for Hawke, as Trulove was on the far side of the room at his usual table beneath the towering windows, great golden shafts of sunlight streaming downward through the dusty air to the worn Oriental carpets below. Hawke, who knew every other man in the room, could take an hour saying his hellos, and so he skirted the outer edges of the throng and arrived, slightly worse for wear, in the presence of the old man himself.

Sir David Trulove, the man whom they all knew by his MI6 code name, "Tanqueray," was already feasting on his meager luncheon—a grilled Dover sole followed by the ripest spoonful he could gouge from the club Stilton. And, as usual, he sat by himself in one of the window seats and barricaded his personage behind the *Times*, occasionally turning a page to demonstrate that he was actually reading the thing, which in point of fact Hawke well knew he actually wasn't.

Hawke remained on his feet, staring down with some idle curiosity at the turned-away profile on the other side of the round table covered with a spotless white linen tablecloth and two place settings of sterling silver in the Francis I pattern the club had possessed for a couple of centuries. There was no welcome greeting. He sensed trouble.

C's snow-white head was sunk down into his stiff turned-down collar in an almost Churchillian pose of gloomy reflection, and there was a hint of bitterness at the corners of his lips. He swiveled his torso around to face Hawke and gave him an appraising glance, as if, Hawke thought, to see that Hawke's old-school tie was straight and his curly black hair properly brushed back off his high and aristocratic forehead, and then he began to speak—rather fast, biting off the succession of sentences as if he wanted to be rid of what he was saying and, quite possibly, Hawke, as quickly as possible.

Then he went silent again. Not another peep out of the old boy.

Hawke uttered a mild cough to announce his presence. He thought perhaps the man had dozed off behind his *Times*. And he barely managed to suppress his insane notion to bend down and whisper in the sleeping man's ear, "Mr. Gorbachev, tear down that newspaper!"

But finally, down came the paper wall Tanqueray had been hiding behind. "Ah, there you are, Hawke! You did pick a date in the month of March, the first Tuesday, did you not? I was beginning to think I had my dates mixed up. Hmm," he added, glancing at his cheap watch. "Time flies, what?"

"Terribly sorry, sir! Couldn't be helped, I'm afraid. You see, I was just about to come onto Piccadilly right by Fortnum's, when this bloody lorry pulled out in front and I was stuck behind—"

"Oh, please, spare me the prattle, Alex," the famous ex–Royal Navy admiral said. "Just sit down and order a damn drink, for God's sake! I'm not your schoolmaster, for the love of heaven. I don't demand a bloody note from your parents to explain your perpetual and, some might say, deliberate tardiness!"

Deliberate, had he said? What in hell did he mean by that assertion?

Hawke smiled at that, for it was spot-on when it came to his feelings for the old man at times like this. No one intimidated Hawke, really, but the old man, with his clear, cold blue eyes, came closest. "Sorry, sir," Hawke said, picking up the drinks menu. "What is that concoction you are having?"

"A good glass of the Algerian red wine, if you must know. Drank it whilst on station in the West Indies aboard HMS *Hesperus*. Good for what ails you. It could turn the most mild-mannered of men into rabid dogs,

red-eyed and with saliva looping from their fangs! Good prep for my
men going into battle on the morrow, was always my view. I could use a
good flagon of it right now, as a matter of fact . . ."

"Are *you* going into battle tomorrow, sir?" Hawke said, the question
coming out as more disingenuous than he'd intended.

C didn't look up. "We are not amused," he growled.

Then he swiveled his proud head, searching for the damnable waiter
who'd also kept *him* waiting.

"Shall I fetch your wine from the barman?" Hawke asked.

"It's coming. That is, it may well arrive sometime before the middle
of next week. Where is that bloody waiter? Oh, here he is at last!"

The stiff-backed waiter bowed from the waist, served Sir David's gob-
let of dark red wine, which, to Hawke's sensitive nose, exuded an odd,
unpleasant odor. Like something one would use to clean a small, low-
horsepower lawn mower engine if no kerosene was available. The waiter
turned to Hawke and intoned, "And for you, your lordship? The Algerian
wine is delicious!"

"Hmm. No thank you, Charles. I fancy a restorative of some kind.
Perhaps a G and T? No. A spicy Bloody Mary, no ice, Carson. Chase
Vodka and American V8 juice with a wedge of lime."

Hawke sat back and surveyed the scene for a moment, gathering his
wits about him for the coming encounter.

"How've you been?" Trulove said, eyeing his senior counterterrorist
officer from stem to stern. "You're looking rather well for a man your
age . . . Alexander the Great. That's what they call you in the secretarial
pool. Did you know that? How do you suppose that came about? Hmmm?
Rumor has it you've been spreading yourself rather thin as of late . . .
among the lilies of the field."

Hawke didn't rise to that juicy bait. He sat back and regarded C with
a wry smile. Sir David Trulove, ladies and gentlemen, master of the well-
honed barb. Hawke still had the deep-water tan he'd acquired during his
most recent exploits down in the Bahamas, and his nut-brown hide hid a
myriad of sins.

Those sins consisted largely of late nights and long liquid lunches just like this one, to be brutally honest—despite the advice of his physician at King Edward VII Hospital in Bermuda to limit his daily intake of cigarettes to ten a day and his alcohol consumption to three drinks per day, max.

When his physician inevitably had asked, "How's the drinking these days, Alex?" Hawke had replied, "Fabulous, thank you for asking, never better!"

———————

"Looking well, am I? Oh, I don't know about that," Hawke said. "But I want to thank you for making some time for me at the last minute. Rather important ground to cover today."

"Nothing too momentous, one hopes," said C, taking a delicate sip of his infuriating wine while peering steely-eyed over the rim of his glass at his prize counterterrorist operative. "You're not getting married again, are you? God help us! Say no."

"No, no, nothing to be alarmed about on that front, sir. Just a rather significant request on my part, Sir David . . . One that I deeply hope you'll look upon favorably, actually. Rather a pivotal, life-changing moment for me, to be honest . . ."

"I see. Well, I've already heard the swirling rumors from Porterfield, so spare me the melodrama. Do not for one moment even *think* that you want to tell me that you are resigning from Her Majesty's Secret Service, Alex. The Queen would have me in chains, a permanent resident in the Tower of London. Don't even think about it, Alex. I don't care about your reasons. I will not even consider—"

"No, no, sir! Stop. Whatever gave you that idea?"

"I just told you—a rumor I heard from Porterfield, who followed me on my way up the stairs."

"Well, don't listen to him; listen to me. I'm not now, nor am I ever, resigning from the service, sir. It's my honor and duty and privilege to serve my Queen and Country. Not to mention you yourself."

"Then, what in heaven's name kind of trouble *are* you in, Alex? At least you're not getting *married*, for God's sake. You've not had much luck in that department, have you? Tell me something. Have you ever considered celibacy? Saves one a good deal of trouble . . . no woman wants a celibate man as a husband! Trust me. Women will scatter to the four corners of the earth upon hearing that word."

"Certainly not, sir! Though I may well have gone completely off the rails in the marital department more times than I care to remember! I'll not walk down another aisle; not in this lifetime, certainly. With the possible exception of looking for my seat at a revival performance of *The Mousetrap* at Ambassadors Theatre in the West End."

"Then forget your meager attempts at humor and spit it out. Spill the bloody beans, for all love, my boy! Whatever is the matter?"

"Ah, well, Sir David, therein lies the tale," Hawke said.

CHAPTER 3

"The blood flows like wine, m'lord."

Black's Club, London, SW1

Hawke took a deep breath, composing himself.

"Well, you see, sir, it's like this. I want perhaps a year off, perhaps a bit less, depending on where the wind and tides take me, Sir David. Unpaid, certainly."

"An entire year? To do what, exactly?"

"Well, Sir David, to be honest, I've been thinking about a Tennyson poem."

"Of course. Which one?"

"The one that, if memory serves, goes something like this . . ." Hawke said, and then recited from memory:

'Tis not too late to seek a newer world.
Push off, and sitting well in order smite
The sounding furrows; for my purpose holds
To sail beyond the sunset, and the baths
Of all the western stars, until I die.

"'The Voyage,'" Sir David said, noticeably pleased with himself and his still-powerful memory. "One of my absolute favorites!"

"And mine. And it neatly captures some of the essence of what I envision pursuant to this grand adventure."

"How so?"

"Well, six months to a year or so at sea. I was reflecting on something my dear father said to me once. We were on his yacht in the Caribbean, just a few short days before, as you well know, my parents were murdered. We were up on the foredeck, having just returned from a long swim to the sandy beach and back. I remember we were lying side by side on our bare backs, the warmth of the sun above, and the sun-warmed teak decks below felt bloody marvelous. Suddenly, he sat straight up and smiled at me.

"'Are you happy, son?' he asked, the look in his clear gray eyes filling me with love and wonder.

"'Yes, Papa,' I said, and, truly, it was the happiest time of my young life, crashing through the blue waves with him on his beautiful snow-white schooner round the Isle of Man. She was named after my mother. That boat was called *Kitty Hawke*, and believe me when I tell you that, by Jove, she was *yar*.

"Dad said, 'I'm going to tell you something, sonny boy, and I'm only going to tell you this once, so pay attention and remember it. It's something your grandfather said to me when I was about your age.

"He said, 'Any man, or boy, lucky enough to be aboard a fine sailing yacht on a beautiful, sunny day is lucky enough.'"

"A fine and noble sentiment," Sir David said. "And one worthy of your dear father, Alex. I have many happy memories of him. As you well know, we served together aboard the HMS *Ardent* in that bloody Falklands affair."

"Thank you, sir, I do know that. So, his advice triggered the following thought: I vowed to find time to spend a year at sea with my son, whom I dearly love but see precious little of. As you know, I've had a new sailing yacht under construction up in Holland for quite some time. She's nearly ready for her sea trials and a shakedown cruise off Rotterdam."

"Yes, yes, you mentioned that. You were searching for a good name for her, as I recall. What did you come up with?"

"She's to be called the *Sea Hawke*, sir. I'm naming her in honor of my dear father. His favorite yacht, in the years after *Kitty Hawke*, was to be his last boat. She was called the *Sea Hawke*. And she's the boat he died on whilst single-handedly defending her against murderous drug pirates. He lost his life that night, as did my mother. So I think it's fitting . . ."

"Splendid name, *Sea Hawke*, by Jove! Carry on!"

"You see, sir, I want to take Alexei on an epic sea voyage and teach that boy how to sail. How to bend, reef, and steer by the stars. How to become a man, a proper gentleman. How to summon courage when needed and how to take the harder path ahead when the easy way out beckons you. How to ground oneself in modesty when one's position in the world can lead to a grandiosity of manner that is wholly unwarranted, unbecoming, and denigrating. I want to talk to him about girls he will meet and what to look for and look out for in a woman, at some point. And how to shoot twenty-five clay pigeons without missing a single shot. And how to hit a three-iron into a life buoy at a hundred yards off the stern, and—"

"Yes, yes, yes," Trulove interrupted. "All well and good. But, Alex, an entire year? We at Six are at a challenging period. This bloody China business, not to mention Russia and Iran. This pandemic of Beijing's was apparently merely phase one. China is rising phoenixlike from the ashes they've created around the planet. China's rise must be put in check. We are working, as you well know, with the CIA and Interpol on this threat to our Western hegemony. So. Why a *year*, and why now?"

"As I mentioned, I have had a boat built. At a yard in Holland. Rotterdam. A rather large sailing yacht. Two hundred feet long, fifty feet of beam. Armored, stem to stern. With state-of-the-art gunnery and exotic laser defense systems. She's about to go to sea trials and a shakedown cruise off Rotterdam. I intend for Alexei and I to encircle the globe. I have both a primary and a secondary motive for this year abroad, sir."

"Pray tell. I'm listening."

"Well. This nasty Putin puppet and paid assassin—Mr. Smith, as you call him so generously . . . even though his given name is far more descriptive of his nasty nature . . ."

"Yes, yes? What about him?"

"Putin has set him after me once more. A two-billion-ruble bounty with the stipulation that my head be served to the president at a state dinner at the Kremlin on a sterling silver platter. Without question, that's what's riding on me. The last time I saw the Russian president, at his dacha outside Moscow, he told me that I had betrayed him for the last time. That I should know that neither I, nor my family, should consider ourselves under his protection. None of us was safe.

"As you well know, he demonstrated this with his merciless and dangerous kidnapping of Alexei from the ski gondola in St. Moritz, Switzerland, Christmas before last. I was most fortunate to rescue him at the last moment after Putin threatened to kill him. Next, he sent his Mr. Smith to Bermuda. Not just to the island, but to my own residence, Teakettle Cottage. You already know some of this, but let me remind you of how vicious this Smith fiend truly is. He forced his way inside my home, despite the strongest possible resistance by my dear octogenarian valet, Pelham, and insisted on Pelham getting me on the blower and summoning me back to the cottage lest he be cut open and gutted like a fish!"

"Tell me what happened, Alex."

"So, I arrive at the house, which is suddenly plunged into total darkness as I approach it. I enter through the rear, hear mournful sounds coming from behind the bar, and discover Pelham lying atop a pile of broken glass with a deep gash in his hand from which, as he said to me, "'The blood flows like wine, m'lord . . .'

"A moment later, I hear stealthy movement in the room, and suddenly the vile beast is behind me with that bloody bowie knife of his! Without a word, he slices my belly open. It's a fairly severe, deep and wide, according to the doctors at King Edward VII, thus allowing my entrails to exit the cavity. Basically, disemboweled. At that point, with my guts in plain sight atop the bar, I assumed neither Pelham nor I would survive to witness the next sunrise."

"My Lord, Alex! All I knew was that you'd suffered a fairly major injury but would recover with time reset! Had I known how ghastly the wound was, I should never have let the Queen railroad me into cutting short your complete recovery with that sketchy business of the missing prince."

"I appreciate the kind sentiments. But as it happened, I healed much faster than the doctors at King Edward VII thought possible. That night, whilst Pelham and I were both being admitted to hospital, Smith returned unseen to the scene of the crime after the police had left. There he found Sigrid Kissl, with whom I was engaged in an affair of the heart. He tortured her with a cattle prod and then cut her to ribbons. She crawled out onto the terrace and died. But not before using her own blood to scrawl her murderer's initials onto the paving stones:

"*S* . . . *S* . . ." Hawke intoned aloud.

"Shit Smith," C said sorrowfully, but with utter distaste. One could only imagine the mother who would saddle her child with such a moniker . . .

"Indeed. And now, having disappointed Putin once more, you can assume that Mr. Smith is prowling the world in search of one more go at me . . . and my son."

"I'm sure you're right. What do you intend, Alex?"

"I intend to find him before he finds me. And I will send that monster deep into the fires of hell if it's the last thing I do. I will scour the earth, utilizing all of the networks of intelligence officers at Six, as well as CIA and Scotland Yard, to aid me in my search.

"If I may ask a favor, Sir David?"

"Anything at all, so long as it's within my power."

"*Sea Hawke*'s first port of call after we've taken on fuel and provisions at Madeira will be Bermuda. I would like a certain piece of disinformation to fall deliberately into KGB hands, using one of our codes that we know they have previously broken. The message should come from Six to the head of British affairs at our consulate in Hamilton, Bermuda, advising him of the *Sea Hawke*'s arrival at the Royal Bermuda Yacht Club on the seventeenth of March and instructing that his staff should provide me and my crew with protection for the duration of our visit there."

"And how does that serve, Alex?"

"I will arrive in Bermuda on the tenth of March. I will have eyes and ears at every last port of entry into Bermuda. The airport, the cruise ship docks at the royal dockyards, every marina, every hotel lobby, and so on. The only way the man might actually elude me is if he's bold enough to attempt a HALO night drop into the mountains from a passing plane.

"When I say 'we,' I refer to the hardened warriors among my crew, who will be ready for our Mr. Smith. If we have our way, he'll never know what hit him . . ."

"What I like about your plan is that you're taking Smith off the board at the very beginning of your worldwide voyage. So he will not be a distraction to you, chasing you through hell and high water for the duration of the voyage."

Hawke nodded in the affirmative.

"Precisely my intention, sir. So, a voyage to reconnect with my son. To get closer to him. And that's my primary motive, sir. In shorthand, of course."

"And, your second?"

"Of course. As you well know, my recent time in the Bahamas was spent looking into the disappearance of the Queen's grandson. This mission gave me a front-row seat to China's strategic policies, throughout the Caribbean and elsewhere. First, the spreading of Chinese political influence worldwide. Second, the CCP's fervent wish to destabilize the world's democracies through monetary policies, bribes, the spread of pandemic disease, drugs, sexual trafficking, crime, political murder, and advanced weapon development, such as a new secret weapon now under final testing—which, apparently, can take out a ten-billion-dollar American aircraft carrier in one blow . . ."

"Alex, I'd like to know more about these bloody Tang Brothers. They play a major role in all of this, do they not?"

Hawke said, "Indeed, they do. Their hands are on the controls of the entire worldwide empire. Everything I've learned about them suggests that their criminal empire, worldwide, is a cover for the Chinese government's subversive criminal and political activities. Things are reaching dangerous levels of threat to Western civilization and stability. I'm thinking that my cover story, with proper false documents, as a wealthy Englishman and his young son sailing around the world on holiday, will allow me to dig deeper into the Tangs' operations and report my findings back to you and my friend Brick Kelly at CIA.

"In addition, I intend to render any damage I can to their enterprises, wherever I may find them. I'm taking my kickass mercenary friends, Thunder and Lightning, along for the ride. The boat will be a warship disguised as a rich man's toy, with hardened commandos disguised as common sailing crew. But we will be well protected and we will be lethal. I could go on, but—"

Tanqueray was smiling.

"Request granted," he said, and he polished off his cocktail and picked at his fish a bit. He opened today's *Times* and turned to the Sports section.

"Sorry?" Hawke said, somewhat astounded.

"Take your year," Trulove said, already turning the pages of his newspaper. "Your timing is absolutely perfect!"

CHAPTER 4

"On what meat doth this our Caesar
feed that he is grown so great?"

Black's Club, London, SW1

M y timing? Perfect, you say? How so, sir?" Hawke said, somewhat
stunned at Sir David's tepid reaction.

"We're scheduled for one of our meetings with the Prime
Minister at Bletchley this weekend. China is going to be topic A in that
discussion. Your grasp of the situation matches my own. China has targeted the UK and America and all of our smattering of European allies
and other allies around the world. We are going to feel China's wrath,
that's for certain. They are out to negate us, to take us out of the worldwide political equation so that they rule the earth and all that is in it for
the balance of this century and on into the next. That, however, is only
part of the Communists' new master plan to conquer the world, according to our and the CIA's sources in Beijing. You've been included on a few
of my memos regarding something called the Red Star?"

"Yes, sir, I have. But they were all rather 'Stay tuned, more to come'
as opposed to informative, if you take my meaning."

"Correct. And now the time has come. The highly secret Red Star
Movement or the Red Star Brigade or the Red Star Alliance is how it's
described in top secret, eyes only internal communications."

"And what is it again?"

"Simply put, it's a proposed 'Grand Alliance' of all the Communist and socialist nations on earth."

"Good God."

"Let's hope he's on our side, too, Alex. This is perhaps the gravest threat to our way of life. Certainly the worst since World War II. The Chinese are selling advanced weapons to Iran. Iran, in turn, is selling nukes to Venezuela, of all places! Sharing stolen intellectual property with Russia, or F-35 fighter jets to North Korea? And, that, my boy, is just the tiniest tip of a monstrous iceberg."

"Unimaginable, sir," Hawke said, his words laced with shock.

"A month ago, I would have agreed with you. But, now, knowing what I do, I can imagine it all too well."

"Where do we stand now?"

"I'll tell you. But first I need to ask you a question. Is there any possibility that your voyage will take you to the Tropics? Or, better yet, to the eastern coastline of Brazil?"

"Yes, sir, it certainly will, and if time permits, and the weather down there holds, I plan to sail down to Antarctica and have a good look around. Our intel on the Chinese at the South Pole made me very curious about China's relation to Cuba these days."

"What sort of activity?" Tanqueray said.

"They're attempting to perfect some sort of laser-based system to blast our military and weather satellites out of orbit, out of the sky, not to mention sinking a few of the US Navy's cruisers and ten-billion-quid aircraft carriers. I'll be all over it, sir. Time and tide allowing."

"That's the best jolly news I've had all week, Alex. I've been terribly worried about that what the hell they're doing down there. Not to mention the fact that the Russians and the Chinese have begun mining on the dark side of the moon! Mining on the bloody moon? Can you imagine what these devils are capable of?

"One assumes they're certainly not building igloos for the poor up there, Alex, under the ever-watchful eye of Jimmy Carter. I'm positive it's all tied up in this unfolding Red Star business."

"And what about Brazil, sir?"

"Same again. Red Star."

"How does Red Star fit into the larger picture?"

"We don't know yet. But I intend to find out. One of the two primary missions I'm going to assign to you very much ties in with Red Star. Code word, for your ears only, is 'Redland,' so, as of now and going forward, you're going to be in the know . . ."

"Hmm, Redland. What OSS used to call the Soviet Union during the Cold War, was it not?"

"Indeed, it was. I called it that at the suggestion of the prime minister. He's nostalgic for that era, as you know. The bad old days were pretty damned good in retrospect, as he says. So. As to Brazil. Our contacts in Brazil have been coming up with intel regarding an upcoming international Red Star conference to be held at a location a few hundred miles inland from the mouth of the Amazon River. The five top Red Star attendees, according to multiple sources, will include China, Russia, and Cuba (the Big Three), followed by Laos and North Korea.

"I'm quite sure you're aware of this, Alex, having spent some time in prison over there, but the North Korean government doesn't consider itself Communist, even if most world governments do. Instead, the Kim family has promoted its own brand of Communism based on the concept of *juche*—self-reliance."

"Any idea who's organizing this shindig?"

"Yes, Cuba may well be behind it. I need you to find out. It is all part and parcel of the way this jumped-up General Castro is going to expel the conservative right-wing government. Or plans to, at any rate. That's our take on the damn thing. And speaking of Cuba—any chance I can convince you to make Havana one of your ports of call?"

"I adore Havana, sir. Been there many, many times. Why?"

"It seems that General Castro plans to have a joint trilateral meeting with both Russia and China at some point in the near future, on an island thirty miles off the south coast of Cuba called Isla de Pinos, or Isle of Pines. It's where Fidel spent nearly fifteen years in prison after a failed coup. When we first heard this, we had no way of knowing what that meeting was about. Now we know exactly why he's doing it. It's a plan-ning meeting. The three countries in attendance will be there to discuss the method by which they will create their Grand Alliance."

"Namely, Red Star," Hawke said.

"Indeed. I assure you of one thing: None of this Red Star business is idle speculation. It is happening, and soon. We have been receiving con-firmations from our friends in every single one of the attending nations. We know who all the major bad actors are. Oh, and one other thing you should be aware of is just in. As I mentioned, it appears that the COVID-19 pandemic was known in Beijing's highest circles as phase one."

"As in a trial run?" Hawke said.

"Indeed. They wanted to see how the world would react to the escape of a deadly man-made virus. Would America take a Chinese pandemic as an act of war and retaliate with nuclear missiles launched from their fleet of submarines in the Pacific? Or would America and her equally damaged allies around the world do what Xi Jinping and his CCP cohorts fer-vently believed they would do—turn the other cheek?"

"Well, they got their answer."

"Indeed, they did. And so they now roll out their global plans to elim-inate any challenge to their burgeoning wealth, prestige, and power, and to pave the way for their new Red Star allies to continue their pursuit of world Communist dominance in this century and the next. You, my dear boy, are going to be the tip of our spear in the coming struggle.

"You and the crew of the *Sea Hawke* shall represent our challenge: the Anglo-American challenge to China for dominance in this century. You will sail your yacht-cum-warship and your crew of soldiers of fortune up the Amazon and spoil their bloody party. You will take the fight to them in Brazil, and wherever else you find them, and you will let them know that England does not bow down to China, nor do our American cousins, nor the rest of our European allies. Be it Hong Kong or Antarctica, or deep in the darkest Amazon rain forests, ere they go, ere go you."

Hawke said, smiling, "Well, sir, I must say, it's a relief to find us both on the same page here. I was expecting something else entirely in your reaction to my proposal."

"Such as?"

"Oh, I don't know. Outrage. A summary dismissal from the Service. Firing squad. Something along those lines occurred to me, to be honest."

Sir David's eyes softened, and he smiled with such rare warmth as to make Hawke's eyes water . . .

"Alex, we've known each other a very long time. You well know that my dearly departed Grace and I never had the good fortune to have children of our own. And so, since first we met, it's always been you I've imagined in that role. The man whom I've seen as a surrogate son since that long-ago first meeting at the little pub in Berkeley Square, when you were fresh out of Dartmouth Naval and the Royal Navy Air Corps and looking for a job. Something about the innocence in your eyes, and the kindly manner of your speech, and the Sheffield tempered steel courage I could sense in the stiffness of your spine. Got that from your father, of course. It was then, if I may be so bold, that I knew that, as long as I should live, in both heart and mind, you would forever be the son I never had . . ."

"Sir, I never knew. I never—" Hawke was nearly speechless. "The Infuriator," that Algerian wine of C's that, according to Porterfield's account, had the capacity to send him into blind rage, and which normally rendered him unconscious, had now turned the old man into a jellylike substance.

"Sir, please, let's order a pot of hot coffee. I didn't sleep at all well last night, and I think that cocktail of mine has left me a bit tight, sorry to say. Must be age. Can't hold my liquor anymore." And, with that, Sir David had his head thrown back and was snoring loudly enough to be audible down in the traffic on St. James.

Hawke caught the eye of Porterfield, who was passing by, and directed his attention to Sir David, now happily ensconced in Dreamland.

Porterfield looked at the man, shaking his head.

"Not again. Second time this month, m'lord," he said to Hawke. "Give me thirty seconds and I'll put him right again, m'lord."

Hawke ordered the coffee, black and hot—not to mention immediate.

"Right away, sir."

"Thank you, Porterfield. You know, I was unaware of this current addiction. I believe, having witnessed the effects personally, that I'll have a word with the food and beverage manager about the possibility of removing the Infuriator from the club wine list. Please inform him that I'll stop by his office after we get Sir David safely into his car and have his driver take him to his country place straightaway."

Porterfield raced off to the kitchen.

Hawke made sure his superior at Six got at least four cups of the steaming beverage down the hatch.

He blinked a few times, and then his eyes popped open wide and he looked around to see where he was.

"Oh! Good Lord! Must have nodded off. Now, where was I?"

"Something about Cuba, a third Castro brother, and Red Star, sir."

"Yes, yes. But what about them?"

"Not sure, sir. You'll recall that I had to make a dash to the loo right in the middle of our conversation." He lied to spare the old fellow embarrassment.

"Yes, I remember. But now that I've had gallons of coffee, it's beginning to come back a bit. I was telling you about my expectations for your upcoming voyage, I believe. Yes, that was it. Hit China first. And hit them hard. That's what we need to do."

"I expect you're right about that, sir. But how do you envision we proceed? You said you wanted me to stop by Cuba, as well as a location somewhere up the Amazon and Antarctica."

"Yes. First, we will provide you with a summary of our investigations into potential or existing Chinese criminal hot spots around the globe. Once you've called in successfully at my top three targets, you may do with it as you wish. Prioritize them by order of danger—or another way, as you see fit. But these are all myriad places, scattered across the oceans, that could stand on-site assessments by an officer such as yourself in the field. Your reports will be invaluable as we assemble the means to take down China's plans to destroy her enemies worldwide without firing a shot."

"China seems to feel invulnerable. I wonder . . . As Shakespeare said,

'On what meat doth this our Caesar feed, that he is grown so great?' *Julius Caesar*. Act 1, Scene 2."

"Listen to me, Alex. I'm telling you that China will throw everything they have at you should they discover your true identity and your real mission against them. You and your men will be tested as never before—and, I pray, found not wanting for courage under fire or under sail.

"But I also know your strengths and your sense of honor, duty, and country. And I know in my heart that, despite all odds, you will not only survive, but you will prevail. And you will smite our foes wherever you may find them, and you will show them that we shall never surrender to them, nor will we and our American allies ever even entertain the merest idea of defeat. They've awoken our secret weapon, my boy."

"Moi?" Hawke said with his trademark grin, trying to lighten the old boy up a wee bit.

"Yes, dear boy, that would be you."

CHAPTER 5

Lenin's Tomb is a vast monumental structure. It incorporates some elements from ancient mausoleums, such as the Step Pyramid, located northwest of the city of Memphis in Egypt, or the Tomb of Cyrus the Great and, to a lesser degree, the Temple of the Inscriptions. It is, in fact, an imposing piece of architecture and, in its own way, possessed of a certain degree of funereal beauty few crypts can rival.

Vladimir Lenin's remarkably well-preserved body has been on display here for well-nigh one hundred years, ever since his death in 1924. One rather grande dame visiting from London in the late thirties leaned over and peered at him through the thick glass with her monocle, shook her head, and said to her friend, "Hmm! He is aging rather well, don't you agree, Mavis, dear?"

"Well, my dear, let's be honest. He was never a looker, you know," her friend Mavis said dryly. "All he ever had going for him was that batshit crazy brain of his."

"Mavis, please! Such language!"

"What, 'batshit'? Don't be a hypocrite. You say it all the damn time, don't you? Shit. Shit, shit, *shit*!"

"Oh, hush up, will you? Do put a sock in it, Mavis."

There is a narrow, twisting street, actually more of a crooked lane, on your left just a hundred yards beyond the tomb itself. Take it. At the end of the lane stands a large, imposing building, formerly a grand hotel, but in the twenty-first century it is now a VIP brothel called Madame Or-lov's. It was wildly popular from day one and patronized by high-ranking Kremlin officials, including President Putin, who can usually be found in the mahogany-paneled bar just off the lobby.

He is there today, having invited Colonel Igor Kolobanov, new head of the FSB (formerly the KGB and still called that by Putin himself and many, many Muscovites).

Natasha and the two men were seated on a tufted red leather ban-quette, sharing a tin of Imperial Russian Malossol caviar and a bottle of Beluga Gold Line vodka—Putin's drug of choice, recently. The noble spirit had just been delivered, nesting in a crystal bucket full of crushed ice. And that first icy sip had brought a smile to the face of the most pow-erful man in Russia.

"Well, Igor, good of you to come," Putin said, raising his glass. "I know how busy you are over there on Lubyanka Square. How is that new location working out for your team? Are you all settled in?"

The imposing building, which had been the former KGB headquar-ters, had stood vacant for years after the new, incredibly modern FSB HQ had been built and occupied across the river from the Kremlin. When Putin had first envisaged what he liked to think of as a shadow intel op-eration cloaked in secrecy, he had the notion to make the building Kolo-banov's KGB2 headquarters. Igor, who reported only to Putin, was perhaps the president's closest confidante. In their private conversations, both men slyly referred to their shadow service as KGB2.

"Yes, Mr. President, all settled in," Kolobanov replied. "And I can't thank you enough for your making such a grand space available for us. The Lubyanka building has a great historical significance that we all re-spect, and for a group such as ours, top secret and off the radar, it couldn't be better. We've reopened the museum on the ground floor, and some days in summer, we're overrun with tourists. Our offices are all on the upper floors as in days of old. And, of course, we still keep the prison closed to the public."

"A pleasure to see that lovely old ruin put back to good use, Colonel,"

Putin said, leaning back and sipping his "little water," as Russians call their precious vodka. "Any news on our new friends in the East? Are they willing to speak to me? I suddenly have a strong sense that our two celestial bodies are coming into alignment once more."

"I'm working on that, sir. My highest priority right now is Beijing. There have been preliminary exploratory conversations at the lower levels. Some were even productive. My guess is that, at some point in the near future, your new friends will be happy to come to the table. It has been made abundantly clear to them that it is a conversation which can only benefit both sides equally."

"Yes, precisely," Putin said, "A Grand Alliance of Russia and China to counterbalance the West is what I have in mind. I'm laying the groundwork for it even now. I even have a third party who has expressed a very strong interest in brokering the deal."

"Who is it? I can't imagine!"

"And you won't believe me if I tell you, Comrade."

"Try me, Excellency."

Putin smiled across the table and motioned for the man to come closer so that he might whisper the answer in his ear.

"His name is Castro."

"Castro? He's been dead for years!"

"Not this Castro. He's very much alive and kicking."

"You cannot be serious! There's a *third* Castro brother? Saints preserve us!"

CHAPTER 6

Putin smiled broadly and pulled back to regard his friend. He took great delight in being one of the very few on earth who knew the actual secret the left-wing Cubans were keeping to themselves for the time being.

"There's a third Castro brother," Putin said casually, as if saying it was the most normal thing in the world. "Someone whom the world knows nothing about."

"No! I don't believe it! Are you saying Fidel is still alive? Impossible."

"Believe it. The youngest of the three children the Castros produced. Fearing her baby would be discovered and killed by Batista's anti-Castro thugs, she smuggled him out of the country and raised him in total secrecy as to his name. He has now returned to Cuba to overthrow Washington's puppets, the right-wing fascist government in Havana. He calls himself General Castro. It is a great secret. Never say his name again. I want you to go to Havana this very week. I will use our sources there to arrange for a secret meeting with General Castro to discuss our common enemy."

"I am honored that you place such confidence in me."

"Excellent! Keep up the pressure. If we succeed, the future is ours, Comrade Kolobanov."

"To the future!" Kolobanov exclaimed whilst recklessly raising his full glass, causing countless heads to swivel and eyes to stare.

Putin kept his voice low but commanding. "Comrade, discretion, as they say, is the better part of valor. You must never breathe a word of any of this, not a word!"

"Yes, but of course not, so sorry, sir."

"You said you had some interesting news about our friend at MI6. Is he well? Say no. I should hope not. Rumor has it that Hawke was murdered on the island of Bermuda."

"I should say that he is definitely not dead, as I briefed you last month in your office when we had him followed upon his return from the havoc he wreaked upon our friends the Tang Brothers in the Bahamas. He's been quite the busy boy lately. Not spending a great deal of time at the office, apparently."

"Don't tell me he's taking early retirement. That would ruin all the fun."

"No, not retiring. He's built himself a very sizable new sailing yacht. She measures well over two hundred feet. A motor-sailer, actually, with an enclosed wheelhouse. As I say, she's about seventy-five meters . . . perhaps more. According to our boys in Amsterdam, she's heavily armored and packs a mean punch. Some weapon systems are run by AI, including a new laser-based missile defense system. And she's rigged for ASW, anti-submarine warfare. She may look like a rich man's toy . . . but she's a warship of the first order. He's somehow managed to re-create himself as a one-man navy."

"Then he's definitely up to no good. If I had to guess, I would say he means to cause more trouble for our new friends. They are most certainly not happy that he blew up their secret submarine pen in the Bahamas, as well as their massive heroin laboratories. Where is he going? Do we have any word on his plans for this voyage?"

"We do. One of our Dutch agents at the Russian consulate in Amsterdam is also a well-known naval architect and engineer. He has been working on Hawke's massive boat at the DeGroot Yard since the day her keel was laid. He says it's a circumnavigation, or even an epic sea voyage—more of an expedition than a pleasure cruise. All our man says is that Hawke is looking for something . . . 'new,' I suppose, is the word. He's seeing himself as some new twenty-first-century explorer. The new Admiral Byrd, all sleds and dogs to the South Pole! Mush! You huskies! Or, Hush! You muskies! Or something along that order."

"I don't buy it, not a bit of it. It's trouble Hawke's looking for, Igor, trust me," Putin said. "He's spoiling for another fight, and not just one. If this new yacht of his is anything like *Blackhawke* or the previous two, you're looking at a state-of-the-art battleship neatly disguised as a rich man's toy."

"Nature of the beast," Kolobanov said, before draining the remains of his drink. "We've dealt with him before. Say the word, Mr. President. I've now got half of the lads who participated in the Chechen death squads under my command. And, believe me, sir, they, too, are spoiling for a fight."

"I will certainly keep that in mind. They are well trained? Armed and dangerous? Ready to spill blood?"

"At a moment's notice, Mr. President!"

"We shall say more about this. Keep me in the loop. What's she called, this new toy of his? I want our naval commanders at sea to be able to recognize her and take whatever military action presents itself."

"He's not saying a word about the name. He tells everyone who'll listen that they will find out her name when it's painted on the transom when she's launched and not before. Something to do with bad luck, I believe. Meanwhile, he's begun to assemble his crew. A leader, Hawke himself; his new captain, a fellow named John 'Jack' Horner; and his new second-in-command, a chap by the name of Lieutenant Ballantrae—a Scot, obviously. And, finally, an ex–Navy SEAL, apparently. Gentleman by the name of Jones. Served in Afghanistan as the leader of SEAL Team Seven."

"Ah. So Stokely Jones will be aboard. Formidable, actually. All right, then. Who else?"

"Well, he's recruiting potential crew members now. So far, he's got a captain to run the boat, a first officer, a ship's navigator, of course, first engineer, second engineer, ship's surgeon, a geologist, a meteorologist, cooks, carpenters, and a host of able seamen and deckhands."

"What's the code name of our man in Amsterdam? A Spaniard, as I recall."

"Yes, sir, that's correct. From Seville. He likes to be called El Toro, but his real name is Fideo Chico. Which means, oddly enough, 'Little Spaghetti,'" Kolobanov said with an odd little giggle.

"Were it me, if my name was Little Spaghetti? I'd stick with El Toro!" Putin said.

"All right, listen to me now," he continued. "I want you to arrange for our most trusted agent to fly to Amsterdam tonight to meet with this fellow Spaghetti. Let Fideo Chico know someone is coming from Moscow to see him. A courier with a message from President Putin. And make sure that this Señor Spaghetti gets signed on board as a crew member. No matter what it takes, I want you to ensure that he's signed on as crew and equipped properly. By that I mean he gets a small but very powerful encrypted device to communicate with you here in Moscow, at KGB2, no matter where the route may take him.

"He will be instructed to contact you at least once every forty-eight hours. He will then give you the yacht's current location and new destination and estimated time of arrival at each destination. Understood, my dear Igor?"

"Unequivocally, Mr. President. Is there a problem with this impending voyage?"

"I never cease to be surprised at your incredible gifts in understatement, Colonel. Are you quite sure you don't have some British ancestor sitting atop your family tree?

"But to your question—yes, you might say there was a problem with this impending voyage. A very big fucking problem, in fact! Our paid friends at CIA say that his lordship once more is planning to stick that aristocratic nose of his into places where it doesn't belong. You remember the notorious Tang Brothers, of course? The Evil Twins, I call them. One's bad, the other's worse."

"Who could forget them?" Igor said with a smile at Putin's little joke.

"Well, certainly not our friend Hawke. Apparently they got on his nerves when he discovered the Chinese had managed to build and conceal an underwater nuclear sub pen in the Bahamas, not a hundred miles from Miami. So he called in the US Navy carrier fleet, the aircraft carrier USS *Theodore Roosevelt*, and destroyed the sub base, two of the subs, and, to add insult to injury, much of the Tang Brothers' Bahamian empire. And now he's vowed to go to global war with the Tangs, as well as with those CCP members who do their bidding all over the world. They are convinced that China has become the whole world's crouching tiger."

"A little late for them to reach that stunning conclusion, sir, no?"

"Watching the Yanks, the Brits, and the French try to stay on the same political page with one another is like watching someone herding cats!

"And that is the true, undisclosed mission of this great adventure he's planning. He's out to set fire to the Tangs' international empire, and thus poke a sharp stick in the eye of the tiger. This is what they've been up to. They hammered this out during endless meetings with the State Department, the Pentagon, and the White House. Hawke is set to search the whole globe and run them all to ground, wherever they are and whatever they may be hiding. Send the CCP in Beijing a strongly worded message—that is the Allied strategy." Putin paused and said to Natasha, "My dear, I'm sorry. I know how boring this must be to you. Why don't you excuse yourself—go for a walk or find someplace upstairs where you can lie down and get some rest?"

She gave Putin a winsome smile, got up gracefully, and made a perfectly poised exit that brought a smile to the president's face. Igor watched his leader carefully. He was in love again. But then, he was always in love again.

He turned to Putin and leaned in so there would be no chance of being overheard.

"Is this mission a well-known secret in Beijing?"

"It is now. I made sure of that. They'll be hosting an official welcoming reception for our Lord Hawke wherever he storms ashore. I expect, knowing well our Chinese friends and their fondness for fireworks, that things might get explosive . . . should he put a foot wrong."

"How much of this should I reveal to our Spanish colleague?"

"Spare me, Igor! No. Of course not! None of it. Not a word of it. I wish to get information from him, not provide it, and I will be—"

"So sorry, Excellency!" the maître d' said, bowing from the waist. "There is a young lady at the bar who says that you are expecting her."

Putin craned his head around and surveilled the lovelies in attendance. Seeing no one who caught his fancy, he waved the man away and returned to the topic at hand.

"Another thing, Igor. The Chinese think that because of the leaked Wuhan pandemic, they've got the Americans right where they want them at the moment . . . weak, frightened, hopeless. 'On the ropes' is, I believe, the Yankee expression. Some kind of boxing reference."

"With all due respect, Mr. President, in 1941, the Japanese believed the exact same thing about the Americans. The outcome was predictable. China may also find itself all alone on a rocky road to ruin."

"A rocky road, perhaps, but alone? No. They will be our brothers in arms. Together, we shall become invincible! And others will follow our lead."

The colonel smiled at this riposte and took a healthy swig of his ice-cold "little water." He had never, he thought, seen the great man in such a positive, almost ebullient, state of mind. He found it most edifying, both morally and intellectually.

"*Prosit*, excellency! To your very good health!"

"*Spasibo!*" Putin rejoined, and got to his feet. "Sorry, Igor, I have to rush off. I have a very important meeting with a certain young lady up on the third floor in about five minutes. She scolds me for being a naughty boy if I'm late! And sometimes she doesn't stop there . . ."

He moved to the staircase and started upward.

Igor tipped a soupçon of chilled Beluga Gold Line vodka into his glass. He sipped and smiled, watching the highly polished black shoes of the great man disappear up the wide marble staircase as he left to end his long day the way he always did: with a smile a mile wide—and a mile high.

CHAPTER 7

"Fifteen men on a dead man's chest."

Amsterdam Palace Hotel, The Netherlands

Papa! Papa! Wake up!" Alexei said, shaking his father's shoulder.

"What? What's the matter?" Hawke said sleepily.

"Wake up! I've already ordered our breakfast from room service! Blueberry pancakes, your favorite, Dad."

Alex Hawke rolled over and saw the golden glare of the sun streaming through gaps in the heavy velvet draperies that hung in every window of the palatial bedroom. He cracked an eye at his watch and said, "It's not time yet . . . Go back to sleep!"

"Papa! Today's our big day—a day to remember, you said."

"The big what day?" his father mumbled into his goose-down pillow, still groggy with sleep. He'd been working with the engineers and crew at the shipyard until 4:00 a.m., calling the hotel and speaking to his son's Scotland Yard royal protection officer, Lacey Devereux, every hour or so to apologize to her for the lateness of the hour.

His brand-new first engineer, a stone genius from Spain named Fideo Chico, wasn't happy with the way Elon's new and highly complex laser cannon on the bow had been mounted. Fideo had insisted that the carpenters, machinists, and metalworkers be recalled to the yard to remount the super secret weapon before the first engineer would sanction the voyage and declare the ship officially seaworthy in time for tomorrow morning's launch.

As a result, Hawke had not crawled into bed until just shy of 5:00 a.m.

"It's my birthday, too, Papa!"

Hawke looked again at his watch. He'd certainly overslept—and Alexei was right. Today was not only his son's eleventh birthday but the day they would finally launch the good ship and begin their epic adventure. And tomorrow, after today's shakedown cruise out in the wild and woolly North Sea, out around Bonaire Island and back, he, Alexei, Stokely Jones, Jr., and the rest of his goodly crew would hoist the sails and make a westward dash across the Atlantic for the gloriously colorful, charming isle of Bermuda, with a brief layover at Hay's Wharf at the Port of London to take on fuel, food, and supplies.

The very first port of call on the big yacht's global voyage would be the Royal Bermuda Yacht Club on Hamilton Harbor, home to Hawke's most favored bar on the island. It was not quite four thousand miles from the Port of London to Bermuda. If his new yacht could manage to average twenty knots an hour, he could make landfall at Bermuda in roughly eight days.

The huge bed had been part of his sleep problem for the entire month that they'd been guests at Amsterdam's most exclusive hotel. The hotel beds were just too damn comfortable. You felt like you were being consumed in a heavenly swamp of goose down. And still he awoke exhausted every morning. He'd been spending twelve- to fifteen-hour days every day for the last month out on the water in gale-force winds and heavy seas. Sea trials. Sea trials and tribulations was more like it, he said to himself, getting to his feet with great resolve. And, for a moment, he reflected on what had been on his mind these last weeks—namely, the downside of designing, constructing, and launching, not to mention paying for, a multimillion-pound sailing yacht with some of the most complex and advanced technical systems afloat. One of the greatest challenges was posed by an extremely advanced sail rigging on four towering masts that were operated automatically, using signals from wind sensors monitoring even the slightest increase of diminution of or shift in direction of windage twenty-four hours a day, every day. On any other vessel that would be one of the primary concerns—on any vessel that didn't also include a weapon of a certain type three times more powerful than anything the Chinese had come up with.

It had been designed specifically for the new vessel and expressly for this dangerous global expedition by Hawke's new friend and the smartest man on the planet since Edison: Elon Musk.

The high-tech weapon, which Hawke had dubbed "The Jolly Green Giant," now successfully remounted, was hidden up on the bow, completely covered by a massive, polished stainless-steel superstructure that was operated hydraulically should the damn thing be needed in any conflict or military emergency. When one of the crew got curious and asked him what was lurking under that shiny cover, *Sea Hawke*'s owner told them, "It's a harpoon gun. For whaling in the Atlantic. You know, like Ahab." They stopped asking him about things on the ship that they didn't recognize after a while.

What it *really* was, was one of the world's very first laser cannons. How powerful was it? Capable of blowing a giant ten-billion-dollar aircraft carrier out of the water, no matter the tonnage, or blowing an enemy spy satellite out of the sky, no matter how high the orbit. Sir David Trulove, at their last meeting at Six, had managed to convince Hawke that if China ever got wind of Hawke's true mission of rooting out systemic Chinese corruption and criminality, Beijing would throw everything they had at him. And more.

He slid out of bed and padded into the bathroom, turning on the shower and waiting until it was steaming hot before he stepped under it. A hot shower followed by a cold one was the only way he could wake up these days . . .

He'd gotten lucky in one department. He'd managed to convince Fideo Chico, the yard engineer who'd been responsible for nearly all the truly complicated systems, to sign on with the crew as first engineer, hiring him away from Elon by doubling his salary, much to the latter's chagrin.

When Hawke, Alexei, and the boy's newly arrived royal protection officer, Scotland Yard Sergeant Major Lacey Devereux, arrived at the DeGroot Shipyard for *Sea Hawke*'s launch that morning, you would have thought the yard had turned out to welcome some kind of conquering heroes home from the wars. Brightly colored flags and pennants snapped from every pole in the freshening breeze, and red and white bunting was strung everywhere you looked.

A small military brass band had been turned out and the chorale was just launching into the always-popular "God Save the Queen" as the proud owner and his very excited son made their way to the platform just under the soaring prow, the place where the speeches would be given, and then, finally, where Alexei would christen the new vessel and send her sliding down the slipway until she was floating by herself. Amazing, the treatment you got dealt your way when you dropped a hundred million quid in some lucky chap's lap!

A beautiful old classic mahogany launch from the 1920s ferried the crew members, along with all their remaining luggage and supplies, out to the yacht riding at anchor. She was being held in a single position to overcome the swiftly running tide by two powerful tugboats, one moored to the bow cleats, the other tied off at the stern of Hawke's new pride and joy.

Before they'd left the hotel suite, Hawke had explained the mysteries of a ship's christening ceremony to his young son, using an empty bottle of Perrier to show him how to smash a champagne bottle against the bow to break it while he said the magic words that would give the new vessel her formal name. "Are you ready to do this, son?"

"Oh, yes, sir. It'll be a breeze, Dad."

At this point, the small chorale that had launched into "God Save the Queen" now broke into their rendition of Psalm 107, with its special meaning to mariners in the UK and throughout the world.

> *They that go down to the sea in ships;*
> *That do business in great waters;*
> *These see the works of the Lord, and His*
> *wonders in the deep.*

The big moment had finally arrived. Hawke took the podium to accept the comments of the mayor of Rotterdam, his naval architect, the owner of the shipyard, and his top engineers. When Hawke took the microphone and said, "*Goedemorgen! Goedemorgen!* Good morning!"

There was an instant eruption of sustained applause from the attendant spectators, Dutch Navy senior personnel, and the friends and families of the departing crew members. There was, too, the moment when Lord Hawke placed the palm of his hand upon Alexei's luxuriant head of curly jet-black hair, gleaming a shade of blue-black in the brilliant sunlight of the day. He put the bottle of brut champagne in his son's hand and whispered, "Remember the words to say, darling?"

Alexei looked him in the eye and said, "Of course I do, Papa! I remember everything you tell me! I mean *everything*!"

"What will you say when the bottle breaks on the bow of the boat? Before she slides down into the sea?"

"'I christen thee *Sea Hawke*! May God always protect and keep her, and all who sail upon her!'"

Hawke pulled the beautiful boy to him and hugged him to his breast until he felt his proud heart would burst within him.

He had lost his mother and he had lost his father and he had lost the boy's wonderful mother. Alexei was all he had left. But Alexei was all he needed for his happiness now. And, that morning, his mood lifted, for he found himself happier than he had felt in a long, long time. He and Alexei would return to London this very afternoon and make all the necessary arrangements needed to leave house and home for perhaps as long as six months or longer.

It had been prearranged that crew would sail the *Sea Hawke* southward from the Netherlands, ultimately mooring at the East London docks to take on fuel, water, and fresh supplies of rum and vittles. Hawke and Alexei would meet the boat there, and Lord Hawke would, in a few days time, be at the helm of his beloved sailing vessel!

Three days later, excitement was welling in both Hawke's and Captain Horner's hearts as Hawke took the *Sea Hawke*'s helm for the very first time. He began to navigate his way down the Thames, knowing he had a good, sturdy ship beneath his feet once more and the wind at his back. He had to tread lightly though, because, as had been usual for centuries, the Thames was chockablock with marine traffic of every kind.

Nothing on earth was easier for a man who had, as the saying goes, "followed the sea" with reverence and affection than to evoke the great spirit of the past upon the lower reaches of the Thames. The tidal current still runs to and fro in its unceasing service to seamen and tradesmen alike, crowded with memories of the innumerable men and ships it has delivered to the peaceful rest of homecoming or far abroad to the stirring naval battles of the sea, from which countless thousands of them were never to return.

The Thames has known, and served, all the men of whom the British nation is most proud, from Sir Francis Drake to the Arctic explorer Sir John Franklin, knights all, titled and untitled— the great knights errant of the Seven Seas. The Thames has borne them all, the ships whose very names still gleam like jewels flashing in the dark night of time, from the *Golden Hind* returning home with her rounded flanks full of treasure to the *Erebus, Dauntless,* and *Terror,* all bound on other grand conquests, sadly never to return.

Hunters for gold or pursuers of fame, they had all gone out on that swift stream, wielding the sword, and often the torch, messengers of the might and power that lay within the emerald isle, bearers of a spark from the ancient and sacred fire . . . the dreams of men, the seed of commonwealths, the germs of empires . . .

And now, onto this brilliant voyage into whatever awaits, whatever mysteries, whatever hellish dangers and earthly delights awaited them out there on the seas, he would bind the son to the father and make them as one. He would impart to him all of his hard-earned knowledge of the sometimes wicked ways of the world. He would fill him with wonder at the sights they would see and make him come to love the sea as his father and grandfather and great-grandfather had before him.

Alexei would learn how to reef, knot, and steer by the stars. To revere nature and be able to name from rote the grand panoply of stars, and the birds and the fish and the flowers and the trees. To read the great adventure books together deep into the night, the father sitting beside the son's bunk in his amidships cabin.

"Are we going to read your favorites, Dad? I mean, from when you were just a little kid?"

"Oh, absolutely! I'll give you a few titles to whet your whistle, boy."

He began with *Treasure Island, Two Years Before the Mast, Kidnapped, Moby Dick, Kon-Tiki, Mutiny on the Bounty, Huckleberry Finn, The Call of the Wild*, and Sir Joshua Slocum's epic, *Sailing Alone Around the World*. And so many, many more . . .

Hawke intoned each and every book title slowly and with profound pleasure, returning to the magic time that was his childhood. A book, his father had told him back then, was in fact a vessel that could carry you far, far away!

"Can we read Harry Potter, too, Dad? And the Adventures of Tin-Tin?"

"We can read anything your perfect little heart desires, son. As long as you let me throw in a few classics now and then . . ."

That said, he cracked open *Treasure Island* and sang out when he reached that memorable song of the sea, much loved since his own childhood: "Fifteen men on the dead man's chest—Yo-ho-ho and a bottle of rum!"

CHAPTER 8

"Avast, ye scalawags!
There be sharks!"

They had been at sea for six glorious, sun-filled days, the big, gleaming white-hulled boat, polished to a glassy ivory perfection, heeled over on a beam reach and making a good twenty knots, wind out of the NNE, barometer at 30.90 and dropping. And, now, running seas, having left the Thames and the Port of London far astern, the crew of the mighty *Sea Hawke* made their way boldly out into the vastness of the wider world.

This morning, since an early breakfast with Pelham, Hawke's valet and lifelong friend, and his new ship's captain, John "Jack" Horner, a mountain of a man, on whom, upon his arrival, Hawke had welcomed aboard and instantly bestowed the honorific of "Hornblower," Hawke and Alexei had been sitting on cushions atop the teak decks at the bow, enjoying the sunshine. The brisk iodine bite of the sea, inhaled with the crystalline air, filled Hawke's lungs with oxygen and his mind with a keen sense of returning strength and good health after the grievous wounds he and poor Pelham had suffered that horrid night at Teakettle Cottage, left for dead at the hands of Mr. Smith on Bermuda.

Looking forward over the bow pulpit at some porpoises frolicking just to port, putting on their splendid acquatic ballet, he saw that the sea and sky were welded together without a joint, and in the luminous space, screeching white gulls and shrieking storm petrels wheeled and hovered about in the dome of clear blue skies vaulting overhead.

Hawke had been patiently introducing his son to the most essential knots every sailor should know how to tie. Namely, the bowline (pronounced "boh-lin"), the most useful and crucial knot anyone will ever learn as a sailor. Used since ancient times, it forms a fixed noose at the end of a line that cannot run or slip. It is mainly employed for attaching the halyards and sheets to the sails, but it is an all-purpose knot useful for a myriad of purposes.

Once Alexci had mastered the bowline, Hawke moved on to the clove hitch, the stopper knot, the reef knot, and finally the cleat hitch. Captain Hornblower came forward to check on the boy's progress. He said, "Hello, lads. How's he doing, Skipper?"

"Quite well, I think, Cap'n," Hawke replied. "I remember going through this process with my own father. I remember the admiral being rather testy about my difficulties with some of these damn knots. But Alexei seems very taken with the process . . ."

"Well, I leave you to it, then, sir," Hornblower said with a snappy salute. Then he saw something that gave him pause and moved over to the starboard rail, raising his binoculars to his eyes and scanning the horizon. "Bit of a weather front coming in, either tonight or early tomorrow morning; nothing we can't handle, I assure you, but just so you know, we may be in for a bit of a sleigh ride. Not to fret. The front is moving south and west and we may miss it entirely . . ."

Hornblower turned away and continued scanning the horizon.

Hawke affectionately watched his back as Captain Hornblower stood in the bows, now looking seaward with his sun-washed blue eyes. He had the frame and face of a prizefighter and the disposition of a fallen angel. He had perhaps the deepest deep-water tan Hawke had ever seen on a man. On the whole of this ocean there was nothing and no one that looked half so nautical as did the *Sea Hawke*'s newly minted but already beloved Captain John Hornblower.

To Hawke, he resembled a harbor pilot, which to any true seaman means trustworthiness personified. Hawke counted his blessings, knowing that with Hornblower in command, should anything untoward befall he himself, the *Sea Hawke* would be left in the best possible hands for the full duration of the voyage. It took one old salt to recognize another, and Hawke knew him for what he was: a man of honor and steely integrity; a good hand in a fight and a great leader of men; a man with an intimate knowledge of the ways of the sea.

After a cheery luncheon served below, with Pelham serving Hawke, the captain, Alexei, and Sergeant Major Devereux a delicious buffet of Scottish salmon, potato salad, and fresh greens with vinaigrette in the small dining room that adjoined the owner's stateroom, Hawke and his son slipped away to the small walnut-paneled library next to Hawke's quarters. It was a lot of historical fiction, to be sure—sea stories, spy stories, nature volumes, accounts of daring expeditions—and old classics (Hemingway, Conrad, Melville, C. S. Forester, Patrick O'Brian, and Jack London), as well as the complete *Encyclopedia Brittanica* and other books that Hawke always had nearby.

He reached over to retrieve one of the books he'd put in the footlocker with the rest of his possessions. It was, of all things, Fidel Castro's autobiography, a book that had been highly recommended by Brick Kelly, not to mention Sir Richard Trulove, when both men requested (read: *ordered*) that he make a call at the Port of Havana.

There was tremendous unrest there these fateful days, rumors of a leftist coup to take down the right-wing, pro-American, pro-democracy, pro–freedom of religion government now in power. They both wanted Hawke to gather as much intel about the situation as he could. Another rumor swirling about Havana these days, according to two CIA officers working the American desk at the Swiss embassy, had it that some kind of alliance between the Communist bloc nations was being considered.

Nothing could have displeased Washington, the Pentagon, and the CIA more than a new global political entity composed of China, Russia, and possibly even Cuba, not to mention those other two towering bastions of peace and freedom, Iran and North Korea.

So the two men had said, "Read everything you can get your hands on regarding the late Fidel. Or, we should say, the late, unlamented El Jefe is the key to everything political going on in Cuba right now."

No one had any interest in seeing a return to the bad old days of Communism, atheism, starvation, and Russian missiles targeted at the US—a situation that had come within an eyelash of starting World War III. Hawke's mission was to find the Communist insurgents behind this attempted coup and take them off the board, permanently.

On an oval mahogany table in the center of the walnut-paneled room, beneath a great brass chandelier and beside a small fire crackling on the hearth, were beautifully framed old maps of the world that Hawke had collected since childhood. He and his son were looking at them now, studying them with great interest, when Hawke looked up at his son and said:

"Now, Alexei, when I was but a wee little chap like yourself, I had a passion for maps and sea charts. I would look for hours, hypnotized by South America or Africa or Australia and lose myself in all the glories of exploration and expeditions then and now. At the time of those old maps, there were still a few blank, uncharted spaces remaining on this earth, and when I saw one that looked particularly inviting on a map (but of course they all look like that), I would put my finger on it and say aloud, 'When, and if, I grow up, I will go there!' The North Pole and the South Pole were two of those places then, that I remember. Other places were scattered about the equator, and in every sort of latitude all over the two hemispheres.

"Well, Alexei, I haven't been to all of those places yet, and I shall not try it now, unless there's a very good reason to do so. The glamour's all worn off.

"I have spent a goodly amount of time in some of them, mind you, and, well . . . we won't speak of that—But there was one yet—the biggest, the most blank, so to speak—that I had a hankering after. True, by this time it is not a blank space anymore. It has gotten filled since my boyhood with many rivers and lakes with names. It has ceased to be a blank space of wondrous mystery—a vast, empty canvas in his mind for a boy to dream gloriously over. It had become a place of mystery and darkness.

"But there was in it one river, a mighty big river, that you could see on the map, resembling an immense snake uncoiled, with its head in the sea, its body at rest curving afar over a vast country, and its tail lost in the depths of the jungle. I looked at the map in the shop window on St. James Street; it fascinated me as a snake would a bird—some silly little bird . . . Anyway, I've always wanted to sail up this River of Doubt, as I call it. In my view of places of interest to us on our voyage, it ranks high, Alexei. Mainly because, lo these many years, great explorers have gone up it in search of El Dorado, the Lost City of Gold—sadly, never to return. But we shall see what we see, shall we not?"

"Oh, yes, Father. I want to see this River of Doubt. See where it goes, where it leads . . . to a City of Gold! Oh, can we do it? What is it called, Papa? This great river?"

"It's called the mighty Amazon. If Cap'n Hornblower believes we can safely navigate her treacherous shoals and rapids, then we shall."

"I would give anything to see it all, Father," Alexei said.

"And so you shall, son. Soon!"

CHAPTER 9

We shall speak of it again. Now, I think you've been in the sun long enough. It's two o'clock—time for you to read. If you fall asleep, I'll ask Miss Devereux to wake you in time to bathe and get ready to have our supper and watch the sunset up on deck. Supposed to be a fiery one tonight. So don't miss it, boy. Also, Pelham and Chef Auguste are cooking up something special for you, you'll see."

"Spaghetti, Papa?"

"Hold your horses! You'll see soon enough!"

Next day, walking the warm teak decks barefoot in the brilliant late-afternoon sunshine and cool ocean breezes, Hawke was back up on the bow with his son, going over the new knots he'd learned so well the day before and now introducing him to a kind of hitch that was more sophisticated and so more of a challenge. "The Monkey's Fist! Go! Now!" he said to his son.

He heard footsteps on the teak deck and looked up to see his second officer, the ship's doctor and ex–US Navy fleet surgeon Dr. Savannah Merriman, approaching, a worried look on her face. Lacey Devereux, Alexei's royal protection officer, was matching her stride for stride. When the boy saw Devereux, his protector, but also his tutor for the duration of the voyage, he jumped up and ran to her, hugging her and laughing at something she said as she ruffled his hair.

Hawke was immensely relieved to see how well they were getting along. It had not always been so. SP4, a special branch of Scotland Yard, was notorious for hiring ex-Army officers now retired and in their sixties who were no match for the children they were charged with protecting.

These formerly high-ranking officers had spent their lives ordering men around, dressing them down, expecting the troops to comply immediately. Instant obeisance! That was the ticket! Children were frequently a mystery to these retired warriors. These men, who thought that they had seen all the worst the world has to offer, now had to confront a dangerous new force to be reckoned with:

Little boys.

They had a bad habit of instantaneously disobeying any rule you laid down the moment you let your guard slip. The little buggers were oftentimes free spirits, independent, pint-sized carpet monsters capable of little, if any, adult behavior. They ran when they should be walking and walked when they should be running. They woke when they should be sleeping and slept when they should be awaking. And trying to march them in tight formation? Might as well try herding cats.

"Skipper," the second officer said, "the first engineer has asked that you join him ASAP up at the stern masthead. Someone has been tinkering with the settings you two programmed into the early warning radar sensors."

"What? Who on earth would do that?"

"No idea, sir. It's rather bizarre, to be honest. He's up there now, but he needs your input to make sure everything is just where you want it to be."

"All right. Make ready the bosun chair. I'll go right up. Sergeant Major Devereux, would you mind putting Alexei down for his rest period? You two can get started on his reading assignment in the owner's stateroom till I return. If you finish early, please give him the Old Bermuda book on my desk, *A History of Paradise.* I'd very much like it if he could possibly finish it before we sail into Hamilton Harbor.

"He wants me to start reading C. S. Forester's Horatio Hornblower books to him, now that he's officially a sailor man. Meteorologist says we're entering a low-pressure zone for the next few hours—lots of thundershowers overnight, apparently. Good reading weather for fathers and sons."

"Certainly, sir. I'll take him down below now. Would you mind if I started the lesson with *Treasure Island?* Boys of every generation have a love-hate relationship with black-hearted pirates. Excuse me for yawning, sir. I got some kind of stomach virus and didn't get a wink of sleep last night."

"Of course I don't mind. It's wonderful to see you two getting on so well . . ."

"Thank you, sir. He's an adorable child. You must be very proud of him. Oh, and by the way, I believe he missed lunch today. Would it be all right if I asked Cook to make him a sandwich?"

"Certainly. I'd appreciate it."

Hawke smiled and got to his feet, stretched his back, and started aft to see what the bloody hell was going on with his early warning systems. He put the newfangled wireless earbuds into his ears. He hated the way they made his whole crew look like they were wearing earrings, but by God, they made instant communication with every man aboard possible!

As soon as the ship's second officer had strapped him into the canvas bosun chair and hauled him sixty-some-odd feet up to the top of the stern mast, Hawke went over the possibilities of this troublesome news about one of the ship's key defensive weapons: a radar-tracking anti-ship missile system. There was a word knocking around at the back of his brain, but it was so beyond the realm of probability, he tried to ignore it. The mere word was unthinkable at a moment like this:

Sabotage.

Unsayable, but there it was, and he could not escape it nor will it away . . . But who? But whom? Every man, woman, and child aboard had been vetted to a fare-thee-well! But the notion persisted, no matter how he tried to reason himself out of it.

There was a traitor aboard.

His new first engineer, the handsome Spaniard, Fideo Chico, reached down his hand and helped the skipper scramble up out of the chair and get both bare feet planted securely on the massive wooden spar high above the scrubbed teak decks far below. So long was the spar that it projected well out over the water to both starboard and port. As was the rule of the sea, "One hand for the ship and one hand for yourself," Hawke reminded himself. He got a tight grip on one of the sturdy steel stays that rose up from the deck below and kept all the towering masts rigidly in place and upright.

"What have we got here, Fideo?"

"A mystery is what we've got here, sir. Damned if I can make heads or tails of it. You'll remember how much time and effort we put into getting this unit properly set up. Now it seems wholly inoperable. Down on the bridge, I noticed we were getting no signal from this thing on the systems readouts and came up to have a look. I thought you should see this for yourself. I can repair it, of course, but the question remains, who the hell would do something like this? It leaves us very vulnerable to an attack of any great magnitude!"

"Drop the front panel and let's have a look inside. Maybe we forgot something when we closed it up."

"Sure," Fideo said, pulling a Phillips screwdriver from his utility belt and spinning out eight screws.

Half an hour later, they'd gotten the thing powered up and seemingly working again. Fideo said, "Suggestion, sir?"

"Anytime."

"Well, until we look into this more, I suggest the captain might want to post two guards up on deck every night. That way, we'll be able to discover who the hell is—"

There came a loud and terrifying shout from the deck below—

"Man overboard!"

"Man overboard off our stern! Full stop!"

The big ship shuddered and gradually slowed to a stop. A crewman at the stern rail had his finger pointing at someone splashing about in the water off to starboard. Life rings were being heaved over the rail, splashing down here and there . . . launch boats were being lowered away . . .

Hawke followed the line the pointing man was indicating and saw a lot of splashing around going on, and then his heart stopped. There were a large number of shadowy sharks in the immediate vicinity of the swimmer, their dorsal fins slicing through the clear blue water. And they were starting to encircle the victim, closing in on the little boy, who was plainly terrified . . . His blood froze.

It was *Alexei*!

"Fideo! Attach that halyard to my leather belt! Now! Give me that bloody knife of yours. I might need it down there."

"Aye, aye, sir!"

"Get on the radio. Tell the strong-arm crew at the stern to haul us aboard the instant I've got my arms around him! I want sharpshooters with M60 rocket-propelled grenades lined up at the stern rail discouraging the sharks from attacking! Do it now!"

The man raised the two-way radio to his lips.

"Attention, stern crew! The skipper's going into the water to rescue the victim. He's got the halyard secured to his belt. Uncleat the other end and haul him aboard the second he's reached the victim and got him under control. Get some rifle shooters down there, too! Get those effing sharks the hell away from that child and this boat!"

Hawke let go of the steel cable and kicked off his worn old Top-Sider boat moccasins, letting them plummet to the deck far below. Then he shed his favorite Sea Island cotton shirt and, bare-chested, walked surefootedly out to the end of the polished mahogany spar that stretched out over the water. He took a calming breath, clenched the razor-sharp bosun's knife twixt his teeth, went up on his toes, and dove arrow-straight down into the froth of the shark-infested waters below.

Alexei's pleading cries for help were ringing in his ears when he hit the water . . .

"The sharks! The sharks are coming for me, Papa! Please save me! Don't let them get me, Papa, don't let them get me . . . *Please!*"

Hawke, desperation seeping in, started clawing furiously at the cold water, his powerful legs working as hard as they ever had in his lifetime.

Please, dear God, protect my son and keep him safe from all harm . . .

CHAPTER 10

"A nosy, toothsome sonofabitch!"

At sea

Hawke immediately looked upward into the sun-splashed seawater above his head. Yes! Just above him, backlit by sunshine on the surface of the water, perhaps twenty or thirty feet below the spar he was standing upon, up in the rigging, he saw Alexei's wildly pumping feet, his hands clawing at the water, treading water as he struggled to keep his head above water. The silent sharks had circled almost imperceptibly closer to his son since he'd dived from atop the spar.

There could be no doubt about their intentions: They were curious. They didn't know what kind of animal was disturbing the surface around it. Their innate instincts, millions of years in the making, had taught them to take a swift bite out of any strange meat to determine whether or not it was worth eating. At any moment, one of them would surge forward and take a chunk of flesh out of his son.

Sharks could distinguish between small prey and large prey. Nine times out of ten they'd go for the smaller of the two, knowing it would offer the least resistance.

He had not a second to lose!

Hawke kicked his powerful legs even harder and closed the distance quickly, getting his left arm around his son's torso and plucking the viciously sharp bosun's knife from his teeth with his right hand.

A nosy and very toothsome sonofabitch had suddenly caught sight of the new arrival, flicked his tail, and turned in Hawke's direction to have a closer inspection of this interloper; this fresh meat.

Hawke, motionless, stared at the brute, letting him think there would be no resistance. Sharks much prefer it if you play dead when they move in for the kill. Hawke found himself whispering in his mind.

Come to Papa . . . Come to Papa . . . you sonofabitch!

When this shark came in for the kill, he would get a big surprise. Hawke was ready. He let the big bastard get to within three feet of him before he struck, but when he did strike, it was with the adrenaline-powered force of a man twice his size. He thrust his right arm out straight, straight and true, to give his attack all the momentum he could muster underwater, and drove the pointed tip of the razor-sharp blade directly into the shark's left eye, scooping the eye out and then repeating the action on the right eye.

Then he slashed and hacked viciously at the animal's gills in an effort to shut down his breathing. He finally put paid to the beast by bringing down the heavy ivory blade handle as hard as he could on the creature's snout. They really don't like that one bit. A marine biologist he knew in the Royal Navy, an expert in all things *Selachimorpha*—the subclass all sharks belong to—had told him that a harsh blow to the snout of a shark, even with a clenched fist, was as excruciatingly painful as a world-class soccer player bringing his bony knee up to bear on your family jewels.

He paused and waited to see if the man's theory was accurate.

The wounded beast turned tail and swam away.

———————

As Hawke had hoped, a good many of those sharks still threatening his son now raced after their injured comrade, roiling the bloody water around him and taking huge chunks out of his hide. An injured prey spewing blood is far more desirable to sharks than an unknown foe who might fight back. Only one shark now remained nearby, and Hawke put his body between that shark and his boy.

This last fellow clearly had not been paying attention to what had just happened to his mate. He, too, stuck his nose where he shouldn't have, and with two lightning-fast jabs, Hawke quickly plucked his eyes out and dug his blade deep into the shark's gills, literally trying to rip them out in his fury.

Hawke instantly kicked hard for the yacht, clinging to his terrified son's torso. When both their heads appeared, the strongest of the able seamen hauled on the halyard with all of their combined might and grim determination. They had hung a ladder off the stern rail, and as soon as he was able, Hawke grabbed one of the lower rungs and hauled himself and Alexei up to two of the waiting crew. He waited until they had taken Alexei from his hands. They then both grabbed Hawke's hands and forearms and easily lifted the exhausted survivor up and over the ship's rail and laid him side by side with his son on the deck in the shade of the mizzenmast to catch their breath.

The ship's surgeon, Dr. David Dickens, was waiting there, and he and Savannah quickly evaluated the two of them for any injuries they may have unknowingly received. When she looked up at all the men surrounding her, she smiled and said, "Not a mark on them!"

The crew responded most heartily, cheering and clapping as hard as they could.

"Savannah, have you seen Lacey around?" Hawke said.

"Yes, spoke with her briefly. She was scouring the ship in a holy terror. She'd left the stateroom to fetch a bit of lunch for Alexei in the galley, and when she returned two minutes later, the steward making up your stateroom told her the boy had said he was 'Going up on deck to see the whales . . .'"

There were shouts and applause and a good deal of laughter and backslapping of father and son as Hawke stood up, then bent to pick his son up in his arms and start forward to the staircase leading belowdecks.

"I think you've had quite enough excitement for one day, laddie," he said to Alexei. "So have I, frankly. You and your father are going for a good rest before supper. All right with you?"

Hawke heard his son quietly sobbing and looked down at his face, only to see his beautiful blue eyes swimming in pools of tears. Hawke could see that the little boy's heart was full to bursting with gratitude. He reached out and drew the boy close to his chest, patting his shoulder.

"It's all right, son," he said. "They can't hurt you now."

Alexei looked up at the face of the man he loved beyond measure and said, "You saved me, Papa. You *saved* me!"

"No big deal, son. It's what fathers do for their little boys. You'll do it, too, one day."

"I would do it, too, Papa. I'm quite sure of it."

"Now, listen to me, son, and pay careful attention. Miss Devereux is on this ship for any number of reasons. Number one: She's here to tutor you and help you with your lessons so you won't fall behind your class when we get home to England and you return to Eton. But the biggest reason is this: She is here to look after your safety and see that no harm ever comes to you. But it almost did just now, didn't it?"

The boy cast his eyes down at his feet.

"Yes, Father. I'm sorry."

"You left our stateroom without waiting for her and asking her to go with you or, at the very least, telling her where you were going. She's probably down in her cabin crying her eyes out right this moment. I'm quite sure she blames herself for the near tragedy we had just now."

"She feels real bad, doesn't she, Papa?"

"Yes, she does. But she shouldn't. She did nothing wrong, unlike you. What happened was not her fault. It was yours. You knew when you left without telling anyone and ran up on deck to see the whales that you were not doing the right thing, didn't you? You knew she'd come back and not know where you'd gone, didn't you? And she'd be worried. Scared to death. Tell the truth."

"Yes, Papa. I'm sorry . . ."

"What should you have done?"

"Waited till she came back with my lunch and asked her if I could go see the whales. Or asked if she wanted to come with me?"

"Correct. Now, we're going down to see her and see if we can cheer her up. And what's the first thing you'll do when you see her?"

"Apologize?"

"Yes. And then give her a big hug and tell her what happened was *not* her fault. It was all *your* fault. And it was, wasn't it?"

"Yes, sir."

"In the future, you will never, ever go anywhere or do anything without asking for Miss Devereux's permission. It's her job to never let you out of her sight. That's what she gets paid for. That's her job. Your job is to always be a gentleman, always do the right thing even when the wrong thing sounds like more fun, always tell the truth, no matter how much it hurts. And have respect for people like Miss Devereux, who are only here to protect you. Okay?"

"I'm very sorry, Papa. Please forgive me?"

"I do. I know you're a good boy, a brave boy, with a good heart. There's not a mean bone in your body. If anything should ever happen to you, I don't think I could go on with my life. You remember that, too, son. You're all Daddy's got in this world. You, me, and good old Pelham? We may be a small family, but we're a family all the same. Families stick together. Right?"

Tears filled the little boy's eyes as he ran to his father and leapt up into his strong and waiting arms.

Family.

That's all there was.

Family.

CHAPTER 11

Madame Orlov's Brothel
Red Square, Moscow

Natasha Irina, Putin's current honeypot among his bevy of busty, leggy secretaries, cracked open his office door, poked her pretty little upturned nose into his office, and said in a sugary voice, "So sorry to disturb you, sir. But Colonel Igor Kolobanov's office just rang and said the colonel would very much like to meet you this afternoon around five. At the usual place, they said. Apparently, he has some very good news that he wishes to share with you, Mr. President. Some recent good news coming out of China."

"Good news, eh? That's something that's been in short supply around here lately, what with the bloody Americans swooping in and taking over our very profitable space taxi service up to the International Space Station. Something must be done about this Elon Musk and SpaceX. He's too clever by half, and he's fast becoming America's most dangerous secret weapon. Whoever he is, he's making a habit of leaving us in the dust when it comes to space-age technology. Hmm. Perhaps we could arrange for him to have a reversal of fortune? Or an unfortunate accident? Within the realm of possibility, I would say . . ."

"What shall I tell Colonel Kolobanov, sir?"

Putin considered. "Tell them that the president would be delighted to meet with Colonel Kolobanov." The man was just back in Moscow after a diplomatic trip to Beijing. A meeting there with Foreign Minister,

Wang Yi. Putin said they would meet sometime around five this afternoon.

She smiled at him in that certain way and slipped out of his office. He picked up the phone and speed-dialed her extension.

"Natasha Irina," she said cheerfully. "How may I direct your call?"

"Direct it to yourself," Putin said, and, for the first time all day, he actually laughed. Christ! I need a bloody vacation, he thought, and I need it now. I'm stale. I'm tired. The world keeps spinning, and nobody moves an inch. Everything old is old again and there's nothing new under the sun. Fuck. I am depressed . . . You know you're in the shit when you're the richest man on the whole damn planet and you're ready to shoot yourself . . . Oh, well, maybe the news out of China would serve to buck him up a little.

"I'm sorry?" Natasha said, "I don't understand . . ."

"It's me, darling girl. I want you to direct my call to yourself."

"Oh. Well, here I am!"

"And there you are. Listen. I've had a thought. I think this meeting with Kolobanov this afternoon needs to be carefully documented. Call Madame Orlov's and book a quiet table in the back for three. I want you to be there and take notes. Then we can go up to my suite at the Metropol and have a nice quiet drink after he goes back to his office. Sound good?"

"Sounds divine. Should I go home and change into something more . . . appropriate? The undies you bought me in Paris, perhaps?"

"Yes, you should. The pale pink ones. But don't be late. He'll be there at five sharp, and we should be there at four thirty. How about the red Oscar dress I bought you in Paris? Or the pink Dior?"

"Perfect! Either one. Bye-bye!"

True to his word, at half-past four, Putin and Natasha were seated in a dark, smoky corner at a very quiet table with strict instructions given that no one else be seated in the area. Three of Vladimir's heavily armed "security boys" (read ex–Chechen death squad thugs) were seated nearby to make sure the president, his guest, and his "secretary" were not disturbed. A large tin of Imperial Russian caviar and a bottle of Beluga vodka, the president's favorite, were nesting among crushed ice in a sterling silver wine cooler awaiting his arrival. He'd decided he need not wait for Kolobanov and was happily dipping into the caviar whilst sipping at the frozen nectar and playing footsie under the table with "Miss Russia," as he liked to call her when they were alone.

Also in the category of "under the table" was Natasha's left hand on his right knee, inching ever so slowly upward until she finally found the object of her affection. It was a "game" they played all the time. A game in which he always reciprocated.

———————

At five on the nose, in walked a uniformed and heavily bemedaled Colonel Kolobanov, a living picture of Russian pomp and circumstance fit for a tsar. Putin looked at his new Patek Philippe wristwatch, a birthday gift from a grateful Natasha Irina. She loved to surprise him with very expensive gifts, because he never, ever failed to respond in kind. He trusted her implicitly, and she returned his affection with equal enthusiasm. It was exactly five, which was a trait of the colonel's that Putin himself had never managed to master. "I don't wait for people," he had once said. "People wait for me."

A waiter rushed over and pulled up a chair for the man whose face was almost as recognizable as the president's. Powerful men, especially those who engender fear, expect to be recognized and take it for granted. The colonel took his seat and stretched his hand across the table to Natasha first, of course, and then his good friend the president of Russia.

After all the niceties had been exchanged, Putin got right down to the business at hand. Namely, the good news from the Chinese. All of his top secret suggestions to them about meeting to discuss forming a major alliance had thus far been rejected out of hand.

"Let me guess, Igor," Putin said with a wry grin while he poured the colonel a small vodka. "They turned down our latest offer. These bastards in Beijing are starting to get on my nerves again. You remember our last outing with them in Hong Kong, I'm sure. Started badly, ended badly, with our worthy Ambassador Stolkin doing a face-plant in his chicken

Kiev. I wonder if we're not just wasting our time with those people. All they do is make frivolous demands and give conciliatory signals, all the while demanding respect from Russia. Jesus Christ, as the Christians say."

Putin, who was determined not to enter into any alliance until he had secured the Chinese committment, had even gone so far as to send a personal letter of invitation to Xi Jinping. The man had not even been extended the courtesy of a reply. Nothing.

Igor sipped his drink, then leaned forward over the table and smiled at the boss. He put his index finger to his lips to indicate that this conversation was going to be quiet and appear as casual as they could achieve. He nodded at Natasha, her cue to begin taking notes. Then he lowered his voice and began to speak to the president.

"Ready for some good news at long last, Mr. President? The Chinese have finally agreed to a first meeting."

"This better not be a joke, Igor. I'm not in the mood for it."

"This is no joke, believe me. They are now willing to meet. They will go as high as their foreign minister for now, but no further until they've had a chance to examine how we really execute this secret alliance to our mutual benefits. If one side gets more than the other, they will pull back from any further negotiations at all . . ."

"Did you give them my personal letter to deliver to Xi Jinping?"

"Of course I did. I told them it was our collective opinion that the world will suddenly tilt significantly in favor of both of our interests should we go forward with the alliance plan we propose. To wit, the facts as they stand: China is a superpower. Russia is a superpower. But America is a not only a superpower, but a megapower. And the only way to correct that global political imbalance would be for our two nations to form an unassailable alliance. Militarily, politically, economically, and culturally, we would bring a united front to bear on the world's current megapower. We would leave them no choice but to accept the new world order. Together, acting in concert, we could change the course of history for the balance of this century and on to the next if it can hold."

Putin stared hard at the colonel. "And his reaction to all this?"

"Positive, sir. Almost giddy, I would say."

Putin smiled and said, "Please, continue. How do they think Washington will react to a formal Sino-Russo alliance?"

"We continue to stress that America must never learn of this potential alliance until it is too late. During these negotiations, we will continue with our efforts to reassure American leadership that China is content with the status quo of the three nations. Iran is the sole dissenter."

Putin smiled. "What did the foreign minister have to say about that, specifically?"

"As regards the status quo with the US, Wang Ji had this to say: 'Some friends in the US might have become suspicious of our recent visits to Moscow or even wary of an economically growing China. I'd like to stress here again what I've said publicly, that China never intends to challenge or replace the US or have a full confrontation with the US. What we care most about is to improve the livelihood of our people. That is our official position, and we do not intend to deviate from it during these negotiations.'"

"Good, good," Putin said, and clearly he was pleased. "So, what are our next steps?"

"Ah, here's the good part," Kolobanov said. "Wang Ji has agreed to a secret meeting in Bermuda aboard the Russian president's yacht *TSAR*. Theirs will be a seven-man delegation: two security officers, two secretaries, and the foreign minister's personal chef. And his, um, girlfriend. Is that acceptable?"

"Of course. Whatever makes him comfortable. I might bring along one of my own if it will make him more comfortable. What did you tell him?"

"I told him exactly what you told me to say. That there were reasons, good reasons, why the president's yacht will be in the harbor at Havana for the meeting. That there are momentous events occurring offstage in Havana that will have very fortuitous consequences for both of our nations. There is soon going to be a change in the Cuban government, and Cuba is very eager to join forces with both China and Russia to rid Cuba of the Yankee devils, starting with Guantanamo Bay. And that we can be prepared to meet at a time most convenient to his schedule. I told him the itinerary. That we would make some ports of call in the Caribbean, but that our final destination would be Nassau and that we could arrange for the Russian president's private aircraft to ferry the minister and his entire contingent back to Beijing."

"Well done, Colonel," Putin said, raising his glass. "We are finally on the road I've envisioned for the last five years. You've done a fine job of negotiating for our side. I'm proud to call you my friend and colleague."

"Spasibo!" Kolobanov said. *"Prosit!"*

"Prosit!" Putin returned. "And now, Natasha and I must get back to work. It never ends, does it? Can you see yourself to the door, Colonel?"

"But of course," the man said, getting to his feet. "I wish you both a very good afternoon!"

When he turned to leave, Putin leaned over to kiss Natasha on the cheek. When he did so, her left hand left his right knee and moved slowly upward . . .

Putin smiled. His mood was, not so miraculously, improving rapidly. It was Natasha. Natasha and the eternal dance, the timeless old ways of this wicked old world.

All just as it should be.

CHAPTER 12

"Go to Heaven if you want, I'd druther stay here!"

Somewhere off Bermuda

*S*ea Hawke was making the best of the bad weather that had been forecast by the numerous stormy petrels they had seen high above the masthead. These lovely seabirds are always a harbinger of a storm in your immediate future. The sailing vessel had just emerged from a squall full of driving rain and wicked high winds. She had been heeling hard over for some time now, her lee rail buried in the frothy seas as she surged ahead at speeds Hawke had never seen a sailboat of his achieve. Now the dark purple clouds were moving on to the south. The skies were clearing as the sun loitered on the horizon, about to bow out for the day and to make welcome the rising moon.

All aboard ship was just as it should be. Hawke and Fideo Chico were sitting in the stern cockpit nursing cocktails—Dark 'n' Stormy for Hawke, Irish whiskey for the first engineer. They'd finally shed their foul-weather gear, and the order of the day was Top-Siders, khaki shorts, and navy blue Izod polo crew shirts with the name *Sea Hawke* emblazoned in red across the chest.

Fideo had found Hawke reading in a chaise up on the bow. "May I have a word, Skipper?"

"Of course. What's on your mind, Fideo?"

"That damn cannon of Elon's, sir. What the lads have taken to calling 'the Green Monster.'"

"Ah, that monster," Hawke said. "We have so many, you see?"

Fideo, unaccustomed to the yacht's owner having a bit of fun with him, said, "I'm sorry, sir. We do? I'm only aware of this one."

"What seems to be the problem, Fideo?"

Fideo was much relieved to finally be having this conversation with the owner of the boat. He'd been having a devilish time getting a feel for the laser cannon mounted on the bow. He knew he was punching above his weight when he went toe-to-toe with Elon Musk. It *was*, after all, an extremely complicated piece of futuristic weaponry, capable of blowing heavy bombers out of the sky, battleships out of the water, and enemy combat sats in orbit five miles above the earth, and even of tracking and destroying any incoming enemy missile getting inside a twenty-mile defensive perimeter of the big yacht.

Fideo's problem was this: In the event the ship was attacked by an enemy vessel, or from the air, or even an enemy satellite, a certain number of crewmen needed to know exactly how to fire the damn thing! This, he'd explained to Hawke, was an untenable position for him to be put in. But, as Hawke said, what the hell could they do about it?

"I've been thinking about just that, Skipper. I've gone over some of the charts around the Florida Keys, some of them going back over a century. Here's what I found. A lot of people are unaware of this, but those waters were infested with U-boats during World War II. A lot of them were sent to the bottom, some of them half buried in the sand but completely intact. Then there are the freighters that plied these waters for decades. A lot of them were lost, disappeared, either sunk by U-boats operating off the Florida Keys or, having run aground in some hurricane, still hung up on the reefs in the area.

"I found one I like. She's a big mother, all right. Approximate deadweight of 220,000 tons, measures about 1,504 feet long by 200 feet wide. She's about as big as Chicago's Willis Tower and weighs about as much."

"What's she called?" Hawke asked.

"The *Sea Hawk*. Named after the vessel in *Captain Blood* starring Errol Flynn, back in 1935."

"All right, mate, you've got my attention. Now what?"

"Simple. We use sunken subs and freighters or tankers for target practice. How does the cannon perform with submerged targets? How does it impact a huge freighter hung up on a reef? Totally obliterate it, or just blow the damn boat in half?"

"Right. Good thinking. But the damn cannon didn't exactly come with a book of instructions, did it?"

"No, sir. It did not."

"It's also very problematic in a lot of serious ways. The length of time it takes to recharge before firing again is going to be a huge problem in the midst of battle, as is the fact that you are the only one who knows how to operate it."

"And there's really only one man on the planet who has the answers to our questions . . ."

Hawke said, "Elon Musk."

He looked hard at Fideo. He was starting to have trust issues with this man. There was something unsettling about the way his eyes darted when confronted. And if it was a heavy conversation, Hawke had noticed that it instantly produced a sheen of perspiration on both his face and his hands. Fear sweat, Hawke was sure of it.

Hawke got to his feet, ready to head below. "All right. I'm all in for a hot shower and some fresh clean clothes. We'll continue this later. I've an idea. Not sure I can pull it off, but pretty sure I can try."

He paused for a minute as if he were considering his next words carefully. "What's our ETA at Bermuda this evening? Any word from the captain?"

"He says we should be moored or anchored by nine o'clock p.m., latest."

"Good, I'll let you know how my plan works out."

"Yes, sir. Buckets of luck to you, Skipper. We're going to need it."

CHAPTER 13

South Atlantic, north of Bermuda

Hawke went down to his stateroom and stretched out on the bed. Then he rolled over, picked up the satphone, and dialed the private number Elon Musk had given him for his home.

"Hello?"

"Hello. This is Alexander Hawke calling for Mr. Musk, please. He knows who I am. He designed all the weapons systems for my yacht, *Sea Hawke*."

"Just a second. Please hold. I'll see if he's available. If not, can you leave a number where you can be reached?"

"Of course. Put me on hold."

Elon picked up a second later.

"Alex! How are you? Where are you? Happy?"

"Never better. Thanks for picking up. Sorry to disturb you, but I'll be quick."

"My time is yours, my friend."

"You remember Fideo Chico? Chap who worked with us on the weapons systems, defensive and offensive. He says he's not confident in his ability to utilize the laser cannon to its optimum effect. I think we need someone to come to Bermuda for a few days of hard-core training. Do you have any suggestions?"

"I certainly do. As it happens, I'd recommend two of the laser cannon specialists who installed the first weapons of its kind on that US Navy

Arleigh Burke destroyer. They spent a month at sea on that destroyer, teaching the US Navy gun crews how to aim, fire, and maintain the cannon. We call these tech/spec boys the 'Silver Surfers' around here. Both first rate and experts with the gun. One's name is Owen. The other is called Wilson."

"God, I was hoping you'd offer that! Listen, I'll send my plane to pick them up in LA, fly them to Miami for a few days of training, then return them to Los Angeles. Plenty of bunk room for them here on the boat, but if they prefer landside accommodations, my club here, the Fisher Island Club, is one of the loveliest spots on the island.

"Just let me know and I'll make all the arrangements. By the way, congratulations on the SpaceX rendezvous with the ISS. I hear Putin is spitting bullets over the loss of his lucrative space taxi service! I was riveted for the duration; never took my eyes of the screen. You could feel the pride all over America swelling. You brought America back to one of her most triumphant decades, Elon."

"It went off pretty well, didn't it?"

"Understatement of the century."

"Listen, these guys can teach Fideo and his gunner mates more in forty-eight hours about the laser cannon than anyone else other than me. So they're all aboard for this mission. Please give your pilots this number and have them contact me regarding their pickup at Private Aviation, LAX. All right?"

"Can't thank you enough. See you again soon, I hope."

Hawke rang off and went back up on the main deck, where he found Fideo standing at the rail, waiting for the approaching launch.

"Elon Musk's sending two US Navy specialists, who will be in Miami to begin training you and the gun crews on the cannon," he said casually.

"Seriously?"

"Absolutely. You going into town? Couldn't help but notice the pink linen blazer."

"Yes. I have a date, as it happens. A lovely Bermudian girl I've been seeing off and on for years."

"Lucky you. Well, have fun. We're going to be very busy around here for a few days . . ."

"Aye-aye, Skipper," he said, stepping down into the cockpit of the yacht club launch.

When the sun had set, Fideo Chico stood in the bows, ramrod straight, facing forward all the way to the RBYC docks where the launches were moored. He was smiling like the cat who ate the canary. How easy could this be? That afternoon he'd gotten an encrypted message from Moscow telling him when and where he was meeting his contact here in Bermuda. A certain "Mr. Smith," who was staying at the Hamilton Princess, right on the harbor and only a few blocks from the Royal Bermuda Yacht Club. Mr. Smith would be waiting in the lobby bar. The message continued:

Smith will be expecting you at 9:30 p.m. Tell him whatever the hell it is he wants to know, including future destinations. Remember, he reports directly to me. Has for a few years now. A bit strange, but a very effective enemy of mine enemies . . .

Fideo entered the nearly empty bar and saw a darkly handsome man dressed all in black sitting at a table in a quiet corner, waving at him, a large black Stetson cowboy hat on his head, and on his feet, gleaming black cowboy boots polished to a fare-thee-well and almost blinding.

"Mr. Smith?" Fideo said, approaching the table.

"Bet your ass, son. Sit down and talk to ole Shit here for a spell."

"What do you want to know?"

"Everything, Fideo. Tell me all you know about this goddamn Hawke and this new boat of his. Can you do that?"

"I can," Fideo said. And, for the better part of an hour, Fideo did.

Smith leaned forward to make his point. "VP wants you to keep me abreast of anything and every darn thing that goes on aboard that boat that you think he should know about. He wants us to stay pretty much in constant contact."

"No problem."

Smith said, "What's the name of his boat, anyway? Lemme guess. The *Silver Spoon*? 'Cause that's what he was born with in his mouth, rich bastard that he is."

"Not *Silver Spoon*," Fideo told the cowboy. "She's called the *Sea Hawke*."

"What's his next move?"

"What do you mean?"

"Let me try this in English. I *mean*, Fideo Chico, when's he leaving Bermuda, and where's he headed next? Capisce?"

Fideo held his tongue for a moment, considering his next move . . . This condescending dickhead with the crooked yellow teeth was as full of it as his stupid name suggested.

"Well. I'm not exactly sure of our date of departure. It's a moving target. There's a serious mechanical problem requiring parts to be shipped in. Weather is always a factor when you're planning to leave the harbor for an extended period—or simply as the situation aboard changes due to unintended consequences. I know that one current idea of the owner is to put into Miami for stores, fuel, and maintenance, but Horner, the ship's captain, didn't confirm that when I asked. I'll do some digging around and get back to you with the latest info, sound good?"

"You've got my number," Smith said, then stood up and left the bar without even a thank-you or a word of good-bye. "Use it," he said, under his breath.

Dick. Where the hell did Putin find these people? Scum.

CHAPTER 14

Teakettle Cottage, Bermuda

B right and early the next morning, Hawke leaned forward and said
to the Bermudian taxi driver, "Next turning on your left, sir. You've
got to be looking for it. It's pretty well hidden."

"Is it a big house, Papa? Teakettle Cottage?" Alexei said as the taxi
driver turned into a narrow drive, a white sandy lane, barely visible from
the road, that led up to the cottage proper.

"No. It's a little house. A beautiful little house beats a beautiful big
house every time."

"Do you get to Bermuda much, sir?" Lacey said.

"Not nearly as much as I'd like to. This island is where I'm happiest. My
favorite American author, Mark Twain, stayed here all the time. He absolutely loved it. Once, near the end, when he was deathly ill, a friend of Twain's
suggested he return to his home in Hartford to live out his days. Twain
smiled and said, 'You go to Heaven if you want to, I'd rather stay right here!'"

The sandy white lane twisted and turned all the way up through the
dense jungle that was Hawke's property. It was filled with an incredible
spectrum of wildly colorful tropical birds and tropical flowers—flowering
orchids, lady palm trees, elephant ears, breadfruit trees, crotons, star
fruit, and many more. If you didn't know there was someone living at the
end of this narrow path, you'd never believe it . . . just the way he liked to
live. Private, off the grid, and off the beaten path.

Hawke paid the driver and they all climbed out of the minivan. Sergeant Major Devereux stood at the walkway to the front door with her mouth hanging open . . .

"You like it, Lacey?"

"Like it?" Lacey said. "Why, it's the most charming house I've ever seen! And so aptly named, too. It looks exactly like a teakettle!"

Pelham opened wide the front door, and they all pushed inside. As he always did upon returning from an extended absence, Hawke let his eyes roam about each and every room, alighting on objects, paintings, exquisite ship models from the nineteenth century, ceramic lamps, and such, looking for something either amiss . . . or missing.

But it all looked just the way he'd left it the day he took off to the Bahamas to find the Queen's grandson—also his godson—Prince Henry.

"Pelham, would you please go into the kitchen and see if we have anything to eat or drink? I think there's bread, butter, and bacon in the freezer . . ."

Alexei reached up and grabbed his father's shirtsleeve.

"Papa, where is the secret escape hatch you told me about?"

"It's in my bedroom. Want to see it now?"

"Oh, yes!"

"After you. Miss Devereux, you might get a kick out of this, too!"

They all moved to the rear of the house, where the master bedroom had grand views of the pinkish-white sand beaches and the big rollers stacked up out from shore, waiting for their turn to make landfall.

"Is that what I think it is, Papa?"

"Alex, what in the world is that?" Lacey said.

"Oh, that old thing? Just a fireman's pole I bought in Chicago years ago."

"A fireman's pole?" she said. "Seriously?"

Alexei took one look at the thing, let out a whoop, and raced right over to the shiny brass pole that went from the ceiling and through a hole in the cedar floor, all the way down into a deep green pool of ocean water that opened onto the Atlantic Ocean itself. Hawke had originally designed it so he could roll out of bed naked and slide directly down into the water for his morning swim.

And, once or twice, it had saved his life. A fiendish Chinese assassin had chased him through the house when he'd dashed inside his bedroom, slammed and locked the door, grabbed the pole and slid down, then swum away from the house underwater and undetected. One of his better getaways, he'd always thought.

The Chinese assassin had been sent by the late General Sun Yung Moon. In the intense heat of battle, with his men under withering fire and taking casualties, Hawke had grabbed a sniper rifle and taken the old boy out at about 2,500 yards—an event that had poisoned the general's daughter, China Moon, against him. "It was war, China. People die," he had told her.

Alexei, wearing a Coral Beach Club polo shirt and his brand-new bathing suit, said, "Here I go, Papa! Watch me!"

And with that he leapt up, got both hands round the pole, and dropped from sight, making a good loud splash that echoed up into the bedroom. Hawke turned to the boy's protection officer and said, smiling, "Want to have a go?"

She laughed. "I don't think I'm dressed for the occasion."

"No, I, uh, didn't mean in that. There is a closet just by the loo with a vast collection of ladies' swimwear. I'm sure you could find something in there to your liking . . . If you want to, I mean."

"Well, it does look like fun. And I'm dying to get in that water . . . I'll be right back."

"I'll leave you to it, then. I'm going to see if I can scramble up some breakfast for this crew."

Hawke went back into the sitting room at the front and turned on the Sonos system, which immediately started blaring out some old Bob Marley favorites of his: "No Woman No Cry," "Is This Love," . . . and on and on . . .

"Okay," he said to himself. "Now let's see to breakfast."

He strode passed the beautiful Monkey Bar, trying to forget that it was there that he and Pelham had spent that fateful night, clinging to life with little hope they'd see sunrise. A happier memory of the bar was the tale about Hemingway, who'd rented the cottage just after the war. It was sitting at that very bar, the Monkey Bar, that he put the finishing touches on *The Old Man and the Sea*—which, of course, got Papa a Nobel.

The first thing he saw upon entering the kitchen gave him pause. He didn't know what it was, but he was pretty damn sure it wasn't good.

It was a large white envelope, sealed, with the word HAWKE scrawled in red, in childish handwriting. He snatched it up and collapsed into one of the two red leather club chairs by the hearth.

"All right, what have we here?"

He ripped it open.

A thick piece of white paper with more of the childish scrawl. Hawke had a sinking feeling deep in his gut. It was from Smith, he just knew it

He read it aloud.

"Welcome Home, Lordship! So sorry I missed you! But don't you worry none 'bout that. I'm sure we'll see each other again, and real SOON! I'll drop back by some other night when I know everybody's home. Your ole pal, Shit Smith."

Hawke picked up the antique Bakelite phone on the bar and called his dear friend Chief Inspector Congreve of Scotland Yard. Ambrose and his wife, Lady Diana Mars, had finally arrived at Shadowlands, their estate in Bermuda, and now he had his best friend and golf buddy to hit the links with at the Mid-Ocean Club, his favorite track on Bermuda.

"Hullo?"

"Ambrose, it's me."

"Alex. You don't sound like yourself. Are you quite all right?"

"I'm at the cottage, and the short answer is no, I'm not. I just found a threatening letter from our Mr. Smith. He's come back! Back on the bloody island once more. Somehow, he knows we're all here. Bloody hell! Who could provide that information?"

"Lurks there a spy among us?" Ambrose said, only half joking.

"God knows. I was planning a few lovely days here at the cottage, on the beach and in the ocean with Alexei and his royal protection officer, Lacey Devereux. But I don't see any way to do that now, not with that monster lurking about with his blade of steel. We can't stay here at Teakettle, that's for sure. It's too easy for him to track our comings and goings. And, as he proved once, too easy for him to get inside."

"No. And, even beyond that, I don't think you can stay here on Bermuda. This killer of Putin's is highly motivated—by bloodlust and filthy lucre. And somehow he's getting information about your movements. Maybe he's got a tail on you. Have you seen any evidence of that?"

"None."

"I'd go back to the RBYC, to *Sea Hawke.* That's where you're hardest to get to and hardest to harm. You've got RBYC security men everywhere, as well as heavily armed mercenaries aboard. He comes anywhere near *Sea Hawke* and you just blow him out of the water. But listen to me—get as far away from this island as you can, as quickly as you can. What's your next stop?"

"We're bound for Miami early tomorrow morning. I'm expecting two tech specialists sent by Elon Musk to train us on how to use and maintain the laser cannon up on the bow. They're flying nonstop to Miami. And I'll also be there to take on stores, supplies, and fuel."

"Miami? I've always loved Miami . . . even though I've never been. Would you mind having a stowaway on board?"

"Are you kidding? I'd love it, Constable. But what about your beautiful bride?"

"Not here. Flew back to London to be with her darling mother, who's taken ill, I'm afraid."

"So you're free as a bird. Pack a duffel and meet me in the yacht club bar. We'll have a spot of lunch and then set sail. I'll alert the crew to prepare for departure. I want to weigh anchor no later than two p.m. We'll make short work of the crossing, with any luck. The winds are predicted to be in our favor. And the bigger the boat, the faster the boat. On this brute of mine, I'd say we can make it there in about three beautiful days, if we stay lucky."

"Sounds idyllic. You've no idea how much I need this break. I've been hunkered down in my small study at Shadowlands for over a month, editing like a fiend. I'm burned out!"

"Well, just take a deep breath of the lovely sea air, lay back, and close your eyes, and I'll have someone deliver your favorite frosty rum potion. How does that sound, old boy?"

"Heavenly. Thank you, Alex."

CHAPTER 15

At sea

Sea Hawke was making a good fifteen knots through the light chop of
the Atlantic off Miami Beach. The sun god was radiant on this day,
beaming down on one and all. And Hawke, for one, was glad of it.
The breezes were balmy. This last day at sea had been the kind of day an
old salt like Hawke lived for. He called such weather "days shot through
with blue." The tangy scent of salt in the air, vaguely akin to iodine, the
crystalline sunlight . . . Bliss.

The weather had held and their luck had held. The two techs Elon
had sent from LA were arriving aboard Hawke's G700 Gulfstream the
next morning.

In preparation for their coming live-fire exercises, Hawke and Fideo
had been boning up once more on the Miami charts, on the Florida Keys,
on the trip across, looking for sunken subs and huge freighters hung up
on reefs. Hawke was happy to see that targets for their practice firing
were in plentiful supply, including a U-boat resting comfortably and
peacefully on the sandy bottom in about two hundred feet of water.

As the two men worked the charts, carefully noting latitudes and
longitudes of intended targets, Fideo told him he thought two or three
days practicing off Miami or somewhere out of the way down in the Keys
would be sufficient to get the gun crews ready for action.

A gunnery officer, in Hawke's view, must usually be a US or Royal
Navy officer, one who has formally had general charge of the care and

maintenance of the massive batteries, ordnance materiel, and ammunition of a warship. He superintends all gun drills and directs the gunnery training of the newly arrived crew.

As *Sea Hawke* made her stately way up the channel toward the Port of Miami, loads of people lined both sides of the channel, having seen news reports about the huge mega-yacht arriving today from England. People were shouting, waving their hands, and tooting their horns along the "parade route." Alexei stood on the bow with Miss Devereux, both of them waving and smiling at the spectators.

Since Hawke knew he would be tied up with meetings with Stokely and Congreve, he'd made arrangements for some fun sightseeing for the two of them. This afternoon they would take a tour of Vizcaya, an amazing Italianate estate built by some fabulously rich industrial baron (who made his fortune selling tractors in south Florida). It was so rich in beauty and art and incredible gardens that Hawke always tried to make a visit whenever he was in Miami.

He rented a huge black Cadillac Escalade for Miss Devereux's use whilst touring with his son. He ordered the car hire people at Miami International to have the windows blacked out.

An hour later, the big yacht was riding at anchor in open waters outside the breakwater of the South Beach Marina.

Whilst they waited on the arrival of the two new crew from California, the staff had set up two chaises on the bow for the owner and his guest, Chief Inspector Congreve. Both men were content: Hawke, with the book he was reading, *Heart of Darkness* by Joseph Conrad (one of the finest writers in the English language, who just happened to have been born in Poland and spoke not one word of English when he'd arrived in the UK). Congreve was reading an edited manuscript of his own book, believe it or not, which he'd just received from his publisher, Penguin Random House, in London. The quintessential Sherlockian, the chief inspector had penned what he hoped would be his masterpiece.

Moriarty and the Phantom Spirit it was called, although Alex had told him he thought the title gave too much away. "How about just plain old *Phantom?*" he'd said. "Much more intriguing title, in my humble opinion.

Titles need to be short and smart, easy to read, easy to remember. And, of course, have a bit of wit about them."

Hawke had recently read a spy novel with the one-word title *Patriot*, about a British spy and a Russian spy. Readers in English think the hero is clearly going to be the Brit. But in the end, it turns out that both men are the true heroes of the book. Both are patriots, just with different political points of view. That's the wit of the title.

"There's never anything remotely humble about your opinions, Alex."

"Point taken."

Congreve looked over at his friend with the color in his cheeks rising at an alarming rate.

"Gives too much away? You've got some nerve, boy, especially as someone who's never published a book in his entire life, much less cooked up a killer thriller title, and still decides to belittle his best friend by ridiculing the title that his own wife and his editor have both declared is nothing short of genius! Genius, they say! Anybody ever called you a genius?"

"Only my late father, on the occasion of my being officially trained in the masculine ways of the world . . ." Hawke let it go. You were tiptoeing on dangerous ground whenever you openly criticized a man of whom it was oft said was the brainiest, most brilliant chief inspector in the long and storied history of Scotland Yard, by God!

"Hullo," said a beautiful auburn-haired Irish lassie with an angelic face, her voice so soft and warm, her eyes so bright and clear, her figure one that would strike a fire of lust in the heart of any man.

"Hullo yourself, Devereux." Hawke turned and replied with his trademark smile, a wide white grin that did little to ease the pain of the nascent author's creative literary decisions. "Ambrose, where are your manners? Stand up, man, there's a lady in our presence!"

Congreve bit his tongue and stayed put.

"Hope I'm not disturbing something . . ." Lacey said in her lilting Irish brogue, sensing she'd stumbled into a bit of a row.

Hawke jumped to his feet and said, "Good morning, Sergeant Major. Lovely day for it, is it not?"

"You mean going for a tour of Miami?"

"No, no. Sorry. I just, uh . . . balmy weather, that's all."

She smiled at Ambrose and said, "Chief Inspector, good morning to you. What are you two boys plotting for today? The racetrack at Hialeah? Alexei's champing at bit for a visit to the ponies."

"Something a little bit less fun than Hialeah, I'm afraid. We're going out to blow up some old sunken relics of World War II, courtesy of our host over there. Nothing Hawke here likes better than blowing things up. This manuscript of mine? He just H-bombed the whole bloody thing!"

"Oh, Constable, do calm down. You'd better have thicker skin than this if you plan to jump into the literary pool with all the sharks . . ."

"Oh, please. Haven't you heard, Alex? When I get into the pool, the sharks get out!"

Lacey laughed out loud. "Good one, sir!"

"Where's Alexei now?" Hawke asked the woman. "He's got cabin fever. He needs fresh air and a place to run around. Vizcaya is perfect. By the way, Ambrose, there's just been a change of plans. I'm going to put Fideo in charge of training our gunners with the two demolition techs from Elon Musk. I've just had a call from Stokely. He wants the two of us to come out to his home on Key Biscayne. Harry Brock has just returned from a week or two in Havana on CIA business. Apparently, he's got vital intel from there to share with us. Brock thinks we need to get to Havana and have a look round for ourselves. Seismic events in the offing down there, it seems."

"Sounds intriguing."

"Oh, it is, I'm sure. I've never heard Stoke so excited about intel before. Miss Devereux, where's my son now?"

"Having a cooking lesson down in the galley. I'm on my way there now to retrieve him. And then we're off to Vizcaya. I googled it. You're right, it's stunningly beautiful! Well, that's it then. Will we see you at dinner? Chef's doing broiled lobsters and corn on the cob. Yummy!"

"Well, I'll run down to the galley and say good-bye to Alexei. Ambrose, please wait here and get on the mobile to our first mate. Tell him to have my car brought up from the toy store and offloaded up onto the pier. We're going to need it here in Miami, I think."

"Certainly, Alex."

Ambrose had begun calling the acquatic deck storage area Hawke's toy store because it was chock-full of them. Not just Jet Skis and mini-subs, either. He had his new (to him) Mark VI Bentley, metallic gray, down there, as well as *Top Gun*, a forty-one-foot fire-engine-red Cigarette Nighthawk racing boat.

He was obsessed with the damn car; couldn't leave it alone. He'd not gotten round to installing the Amherst Villiers supercharger, but that had pleased young Ian, his mechanic. The Irishman had this to say about "blowers," as he called superchargers. "Best do without all those useless bits and bobs, sir," he'd said. "All they do is suck, squeeze, bang, and blow. Who needs it?" Hawke had to stifle a laugh as he remembered the mechanic's aphorism. Who indeed?

To extract the vehicle from his toy store, one only had to press a button and a large section of the hull opened upward. Then the steel floor under the desired toy extended out over the water and was elevated to the desired height to be removed from the yacht.

Hawke, in a hurry to hear what Stoke and Brock had to say, sprinted down two decks to the brightly lit, spotless, stainless-steel galley. He saw his son and his chef standing side by side at the big range, both dressed in their chefs' whites and a toque blanche. He was startled to see that his young son now stood a full head taller than the pudgy little Frenchman, Auguste Lamieux.

"Chef!" Hawke said, walking over to join them. "What magic are you imparting this morning?"

"Bonjour, Monsieur! *Mais oui! La magie!* Witchcraft! I am teaching ze boy all ze finer points of ze perfect grilled cheese sandwich. No easy feat, unless you know what ze hell you are doing!"

"Hi, Dad," Alexei said, flipping a sandwich on the griddle. "The secret is you cook it at very low heat, letting the cheese melt perfectly and both sides get golden brown . . . like this!"

He stuck a spatula under his masterpiece and flipped it onto a plate.

"C'est parfait! N'est ce pas, monsieur?" Auguste said, leaning over to inspect it more closely.

Not a minute after Hawke left the galley, Ambrose was ending his call to the first mate when he was mildly surprised by two men, identical twins, who could rather easily be identified as card-carrying residents of the state of California. Brown as two nuts, both had long, sun-bleached blond hair pulled back in ponytails, surfer dude baggy shorts cut off just below the knee, leather necklaces of shark's teeth, flip-flops, and matching T-shirts boasting "You better Belize it!"

"Yo," one of them said to the chief inspector, sticking his hand out.

"Yo, yourself," Ambrose said. "I'm a friend of the owner of this boat. Your employer, Mr. Musk, was kind enough to offer us your services. My name is Congreve, by the way. Chief Inspector Congreve of Scotland Yard. Are you two going to share yours?"

"Our what, man? Hope it's not reefer, dude. We fresh out."

"Yeah, dude, we got busted at LAX."

"Bummer," Congreve said.

"Tell us about it," one of them said.

"No, not your weed, dudes, your names?"

"Sure, dude, whatever. I'm Owen. He's Wilson. Our father's a famous movie director in Hollywood. He named us after his favorite movie star. Pretty cool, right?"

"Must have missed that one, sorry. Hey, Wilson, welcome aboard. You guys have all the equipment you need for today?"

"Yeah, man, and it's all right up here," he said, pointing at his noggin.

Ambrose finally spoke up. "And there are two of you for the price of one! Even better!"

"Nice boat you got here," Owen said to Congreve, whistling under his breath.

"Thanks." Congreve smiled. "She didn't come cheap, believe me."

"Dude, I believe you!" Owen said. "I mean, holy shit."

"You boys wouldn't happen to be surfers, would you?" Congreve said.

"Naw, man. Surfing's for pussies. Candy asses. We're geniuses."

"Ah, what a coincidence." Congreve smiled. "Me, too!"

"Awesome," the two of them said in unison.

CHAPTER 16

Vizcaya, Coconut Grove

ergeant Major Devereux had no idea what to expect while driving along a very shady road, a tunnel of green, really, through a tropical jungle. If the stalker chose to close in on them, ram the Escalade from behind, and hop out with guns, no one would be there to see or to help. She slowed the big black Escalade as she approached the imposing main gates at the entrance to the Vizcaya estate. She was a bit uneasy and trying not to show it. It was probably nothing serious, but there'd been a car following them closely, way too closely, on the MacArthur Causeway ever since they'd left the parking lot at the South Beach Marina.

The fact that the vehicle was armor plated and had three-inch-thick bulletproof glass all the way around gave her some confidence. Still, she'd kept her eyes glued to the rearview mirror.

The driver of the gray, nondescript sedan was lying back, trying to blend in. He obviously had no idea whom he was up against. Sergeant majors at Scotland Yard had veritable degrees in the fine arts of escape and evasion, not to mention the situational awareness to pick up a tail that not one in a hundred might spot.

Entering the quaint little village of Miami's Coconut Grove, she'd considered parking in the small area adjacent to Vizcaya's gatehouse and going inside to have a quick word with the security guards.

But upon further reflection, she'd decided to hell with it. She'd take the thing head-on, if that's where this was going . . . She wasn't one to be bullied; quite the opposite, in fact.

She slowed, signaled a left-hand turn as the heavy wrought iron black gates swung open, and drove through them at a normal speed. Keeping her eyes riveted to the rearview mirror, she saw the gray car, with a middle-aged man behind the wheel. Long, dark hair, a thick black mustache and sideburns, and the chiseled profile of the evil villain in a bad cowboy movie. Say, Jack Palance, for starters.

She held her breath, hoping he wouldn't follow them inside the gates. He never turned his head to see her, though, just kept on going, traveling at the posted speed limit in Coconut Grove.

At the last moment, she changed her mind again about speaking with security. She pulled over and parked in the shade of a huge banyan tree and climbed out into the dense heat.

"Come along, Alexei, we're going inside that little house and talk to some policemen."

"Good. I like policemen. They're cool."

"I'm a policeman, you know."

"No, you're not."

"Well, a policewoman, anyway."

"I like policewomen. They're cool, too."

"Why thank you, Alexei. I like you, too. You're cool."

There were two uniformed officers inside, both armed. They were very relaxed, with pleasant smiles and a friendly demeanor. The senior man, tall, tanned, and extremely blond, got to his feet. She knew that smile. He was going to flirt with her. It happened. She'd been blessed with a stunning figure and a sweetheart of a face with wide-apart brown eyes, a straight nose, and full red lips. Her hair, a luxuriant auburn mane, framed her face perfectly. So it goes, so it goes . . .

"Please excuse me, officers. I've a favor to ask."

"Certainly, ma'am. How can we help? I'm Officer Taylor, by the way . . . You're new around here, aren't you? Just arrived in Paradise. Hey, listen, if you'd like somebody to show you around, why, I'd be pleased as punch to—"

"Knock it off, Taylor!" the senior man barked. "I'll write you up for insubordination quicker than you can say 'Billy be damned!'"

"Yes, sir. Sorry, sir!" The chastened Taylor walked outside and lit a cigarette.

She reached into her handbag and pulled out her Scotland Yard red leather wallet, with both her picture ID and her gold shield, placing it on the counter. The senior man studied the foreign object with keen interest, obviously never having seen such a rare specimen of police identification.

"Sergeant Major Devereux, welcome to Vizcaya. We're here to help you in whatever assistance you require. My name's Lieutenant Armstrong. Sorry about that unfortunate business with—"

"Thank you, Lieutenant, but if you knew how many times a week that happens, you'd go a little easier on him. As you can see, I'm a royal protection officer attached to Scotland Yard. We primarily attend to the members of the Royal Family, or, in some cases, like mine, attend to members of the extended Royal Family. This lovely little boy is the only son of Lord Hawke, one of the Queen's favorites. Tell the nice man your name, Alexei."

"Alexei," he said, offering his hand across the counter. "A very great pleasure to meet you, sir."

"And you, as well, son," Armstrong said. "What seems to be the problem, ma'am?"

"Well, there are certain forces at work, criminal and political and otherwise, who have repeatedly attempted the kidnapping of this young man. His father, a very well-known figure in Britain, has somehow managed to rescue him more than once. But we are determined to prevent any further action against my client's son. That's what I'm here for. We're aboard my client's yacht, at the beginning of a worldwide voyage. I'll be aboard the *Sea Hawke* for the duration.

"But here's thing. I picked up a tail pulling out of the public parking at South Beach Marina, where the yacht is currently moored. I kept my eye on him, of course, and noticed him pulling back when he got too close, as well as other troubling clues. I got a look at him passing by your gates there. Gray sedan, ordinary rental. Driver appeared to be in his early forties, long dark hair pulled back into a ponytail, a thick mustache, and heavy sideburns. Looked a bit like the villain in a bad cowboy movie."

"You say he continued on."

"Yes, somewhat to my relief. But my thought is perhaps he intentionally wanted me to relax my defenses.

"If he's a local, he probably knows this is a famous museum and that we will probably be here for quite some time. So he either lingers outside the gate, waiting for us to emerge so he can pick up the chase, or he could simply bide his time and come through the gates a little later, buy a ticket, park, and try to find us somewhere on the grounds on foot. Neither of those options sound good."

"I understand completely, ma'am," said the officer.

"Thank you. I want to write down my mobile number for you. If you see the car and the driver I've described enter the grounds, please let me know. If I do encounter him and he is acting in a threatening manner, I'll immediately text you that he presents an imminent danger. And you in turn will alert all available security to be on the lookout for this man. He is wanted for heinous crimes all over the world, including by Interpol. If you do intercept him, please notify me immediately. Alexei and I will try to find some safe place to shelter and wait for you to sound the all clear."

Armstrong smiled in a reassuring way. "You made the right choice, Sergeant Major. If he enters these premises, we'll have him subdued and arrested by Miami-Dade police officers. They maintain a small station on the property."

"Well, what can I say? I feel much better. Thank you for your help. I just hope we don't need it!"

"One question, Sergeant Major Devereux?"

"Of course."

"Are you armed?"

She smiled and said, "Bet on it, Officer."

Somewhat reassured, she and Alexei returned to the Escalade and followed the signs that led to the various parking lots, all hidden from

sight somewhere in this subtropical labyrinth of gardens, the entire property encompassing over forty acres. It was muggy making their way from
the distant lot over to the villa. Make that muggy and buggy. But it didn't
slow Alexei down. That morning at breakfast, having seen pictures of the
spectacular interiors of the Deering mansion, she had said, "Alexei, do
you know what a knight is?"

"You mean, uh, like, um, when it gets dark outside?"

Devereux looked at the clever boy. He was sorta kidding, sorta not.
You could never be sure with him. Chip off the old block, she thought.

"No. That's night . . . n-i-g-h-t. Like in a book: 'It was a dark and
stormy night.'"

"Is there another kind of night?"

"Yes. Spelled with a K. So, 'knight.'"

"Oh. Sure. Camelot. The Round Table knights. King Arthur's Knights
of the Round Table. Sir Lancelot is my favorite! Sir Galahad, too, but not
as much."

"Exactly so! Well, guess what? A long time ago, when the knights all
decided to retire from the Round Table, a lot of them moved down here
to Florida. And just so you know, inside the house where we're going, a
lot of those brave knights can still be seen if you carefully—"

"*Really?* C'mon, you're kidding."

"No. Really."

And that did the trick. Once they got inside that Italianate Renais-
sance of beauty and splendor, all Alexei cared about was discovering the
suits of armor hiding in every nook and cranny of the downstairs hall-
ways. But, she, too, was excited. The villa was impossibly posh, though
dated, and it was one of the most enchanting interiors she'd ever visited.

She'd grown up visiting the great country houses of Britain with her
parents. But Vizcaya? It was a hidden jewel, a realm of splendor and gran-
deur and almost decadent beauty. Unlike anything she'd ever seen. She
wanted to linger in every room and savor every detail of what had been
created here by the Dunning family in 1914, when south Florida was
primarily comprised of the Everglades, alligators, small fishing camps,
and the tribal lands of the Seminole.

As they explored further, she made a concerted effort to keep one eye on the ebb and flow of the visitors as tour groups moved with the current from room to room and floor to floor, looking for anyone suspicious.

Alexei wanted to hold her hand, and that suited her just fine.

Descending the main staircase, they came upon an especially fine-looking knight, and she dubbed him "Sir Lancelot." As a girl, she'd rather fallen for him. One of the greatest knights in Arthurian romance, he was the lover of Arthur's queen, Guinevere, and was the father of the one true knight, Sir Galahad.

"Wait! Who is this knight?" Alexei asked.

"The greatest knight of all," she said. "Sir Lancelot, of Camelot."

"My favorite! Is he still in there? I mean, you know, inside the armor? I mean, he's dead, right? So—"

"Hmm, yes, he is quite dead. But he left this suit of armor behind when he died so that the world would never forget him—how he never failed in gentleness, courtesy, or courage. Or in his prowess on the battlefield . . ."

"I want to be a knight," Alexei announced, and then said, "Can we go outside now? I want to see that big red Cigarette boat by the pool. Dad has a boat that looks just like that!"

When they finally emerged into the sunlight, she noticed that the temperature had dropped considerably. Hawke had said something about an approaching cold front that might keep them in port for an extra day or two. She welcomed the cooler temperatures, especially as the dense tropical gardens were well known for their bugs and heat and humidity.

They walked out across the broad marble terrace that overlooked Biscayne Bay. You would have sworn you were in Venice, gazing out at the Grand Canal. A massive pool in the shape of a Venetian gondola beckoned the weary, overheated masses with open arms. Alexei wanted to dive right in, but it was clear that the pool was not open to tourists.

And so on to the legendary gardens, located on the far side of the palazzo. Designed by Europe's most revered landscape architect, Diego

Rivera, they were reminiscent of gardens created in the seventeenth and eighteenth centuries in Italy and France, and truly beautiful.

It pained her to keep her grip on the little boy's hand. He was desperate to break free, to run and jump and play. But these mazelike gardens were designed to entice and seduce, and she was not unaffected by their attractions. She tried to keep him interested in the multicolored tropical flowers, only slightly overshadowed by the presence everywhere of colorful birds in mass profusion . . . She saw an incredible gardenia bush and put the Leica up to her eye and bent to photograph a huge white blossom . . .

And then her mobile rang.

"This is Sergeant Taylor. We haven't seen your gray rental. I guess he's not coming."

"I guess so. Thank the Lord I was wrong about him."

"Well, yes, ma'am. But we'll be here for another hour, so we'll call you the second we see anyone fitting your description."

"Thank you so much," she said, trying to hold on to Alexei whilst swatting at a pesky bee that was encircling her head with a vengeance.

"Shoo!" she cried. "Get away from me, you little pest!"

And that's when the bee alighted at the tip of her nose and stung the hell out of her. The pain went through her nervous system like a jolt of electricity. She had to let go of Alexei to protect herself, to try and swat it away, but the little monster kept buzzing about her head. The sting had caused her eyes to water, and she was dizzy from spinning around . . . having trouble seeing . . . she stood stock-still and reached for Alexei's hand . . .

And . . . he wasn't there. He must have darted into the thick shrubbery. Her heart was racing!

And then her heart stopped.

The man in black. He had grabbed Alexei while she was momentarily distracted. Alexei was yelling at him, pounding his arm with his considerable fists.

He held her young charge by the wrist and was dragging him toward an opening in the solid green wall of jungle thicket. It didn't look like any charming garden pathway, either. It was black. It looked like the yawning maw of an entrance to hell. The boy was calling out for her, begging her to rescue him. She had to act now or it would be too late.

She screamed at the top of her lungs. "You there! Stop! Let that child go! Now!"

He stopped dead in his tracks, but didn't turn to face her. He stared straight ahead, grinned a bloodlust grin dripping with malice, and said, "You gonna make me, little girl?"

"No, but if you don't let go of him in five seconds, I'm going to kill you."

"Yeah? And how you planning to do that, bitch?"

"Well, let's see. I've got six hollow-point .357 magnum slugs in my revolver. I could kill you six times if you piss me off, cowboy. How's that sound?"

"Lying bitch. You ain't got no gun."

"Turn around and you'll see if I do, you creepy bastard."

He whirled around. He wore a long, faded, black Australian rancher's dust coat that came down way below his knees. He stuck his free hand inside and came out with a huge knife in his left hand—more like a sword than a knife. That's when he saw the silvery Colt Python .357 magnum revolver emerge from her handbag, pointed directly at him.

"Drop the knife and let the boy go."

"Ain't happening, little lady . . ."

"Okay," she said calmly. Then she aimed and fired, putting a round in his shoulder, causing him to howl in pain and exploding the man's upper arm into tiny slivers of bone and cartilage.

"You're lucky, Smith. I only winged you. I'm a policewoman and a crack shot. Where do you want me to shoot you now?"

Sergeant Taylor was saying something on her mobile she couldn't quite make out. "Sorry, Sergeant, you're breaking up! I'm sorry. Bit of a tense situation here. We're being held at knifepoint."

"Got two men on the way, ma'am. Pulling up to the station house right now. I'll send them your way directly."

"Alexei, stop that! Leave that man alone. You hear me? Right this very second!"

Alexei did not like being told what to do; he didn't like it one little bit. So he just stared back at her and nodded his head. The next second he'd moved in close so swiftly and with such fierce determination that there was precious little she could do about it. The boy sidled over into the vicinity of the bad man, nonchalant, just walking around, pretending to be looking at the flowers. But then he planted his foot and spun around, now facing Smith head-on. Without warning, he lunged forward and kicked his tormentor square in the kneecap. Smith staggered backward, almost losing his balance. Alexei had nailed him. Hit him as hard as ever he could. Something he'd learned in judo at Eton.

And Smith raised his knife.

"Don't you touch him, you monster!" she screamed at Smith, who was gathering himself up. "Get back here, Alexei! You're too close to him! Run to me! Now!" There was fear in her voice now, and it was well placed.

"Yes, ma'am," Alexei said, racing over to her and embracing her. "Sorry."

But he wasn't the least bit sorry. He saw that the cowboy was totally distracted by this beautiful Irishwoman. He couldn't take his eyes off of her. Watching every move she made. And *not* watching Alexei.

Alexei saw his moment and made his next planned move.

It was the work of an instant. Alexei darted forward as soon as the man turned his head away to look at Miss Devereux, grabbed the monster's wrist, twisted it viciously, and brought his hand up to his mouth. He leaned forward, his jaws wide open, and bit down on the soft, fleshy part of the man's hand like a starving lunatic, taking a huge bite out of the biggest, juiciest fleshburger ever.

Smith was screaming, waving his hand about over his head, spraying himself and the boy with his blood.

Even then, Alexei was not satisfied.

He opened his mouth wide once more and chomped down to the very bone before he let the killer's mangled hand go.

Devereux said, "Last chance, cowboy. Drop the knife!"

She fired the Python once more, putting the second round through the crown of the black cowboy hat on his head and scaring the crap out of the villain. She could see the sun's light in the bullet holes.

"Pretty good shooting, huh? But I bet your hair looks better now that it's parted right down the middle . . . Throw that bloody knife on the ground and get out of my sight! Now, Mister! Right now!"

"Kiss my ass, bitch."

Smith had hesitated a second too long, and the cowboy saw her raise the pistol and this time aim it at his crotch. He watched in slow motion as she pulled the hammer back and began to squeeze the trigger . . .

"Don't shoot!" Smith screamed, and grabbed Alexei once more. Smith was whipping his head to and fro, looking for his best route of escape.

Smith suddenly had the bright idea to put Alexei in front of him, standing between Devereux and himself.

"Let him go or I swear to God I will put the next bullet right between your eyes. I'll give you five seconds to release him. One . . . two . . . three—" And she stopped counting. Smith had freed her charge and shoved him toward her.

Alexei smiled at his guardian, racing toward her, throwing his arms around her as he said, "A-B-T-H-T-G-Y. *Always bite the hand that grabs you . . .*"

"Now the knife, Mr. Smith!" she called out. "I meant what I said, you bastard. Drop the knife."

"Nope. You want my knife, you gotta come take it away from me, sugar britches."

She took dead aim at him. His eyes went wide when he saw that she was once again aiming at his crotch.

"Well, have it your way, cowboy. I guess you'd rather have that big knife of yours than keep another important body part . . . even if it means you'll never again be a real man nor a threat to any woman or child . . . Wait for it!"

"No!" Smith cried, but it was too late.

She'd raised the muzzle up from his knees and fired again, this time putting a round right between his upper thighs, barely an inch below his genitals.

She could have blown the knife right out of his hand had she wanted—hell, she could have blown the tiny diamond stud cuff links right out of his cuffs, had the sonofabitch been wearing any. There were a few things she could not do, but taking dead aim and shooting straight and blade true was not one of them.

He still clung to his big-boy knife.

"Last chance, Hopalong," Sergeant Major Devereux said, pulling back the hammer on the pistol and aiming at his remaining shoulder.

"Ah, shit," he said, knowing by the fire in her eyes that she'd pull the trigger in a heartbeat, and angrily threw his knife to the ground. He was desperate to find an escape route. He wasn't seriously wounded, but when he made a run for it, he moved faster than any human being she'd ever seen run.

She returned the pistol to her bag, then turned to Alexei, who was plainly disappointed in this latest development. He had, more than anything, wanted to run over and throw the wounded man to the ground and pulverize his face. Devereux took him into her arms and ruffled his curly black hair.

He whispered, "Thank you, Miss Devereux," into her ear and smiled at her, his cornflower-blue eyes glistening with tears now that it was all over.

"For what?" she said. "You did a pretty good job of it all by yourself."

"Just following orders," Alexei said with a wry smile.

She cradled her iPhone between chin and shoulder and dialed the guard station.

"Taylor," a voice said.

"Sergeant Major Devereux," she said. "Smith is here on the grounds. He found us in the garden. He grabbed the child. I shot him before he bolted."

"Is he dead?"

"No. Just one bullet, in the right shoulder, and one round right through his big black cowboy hat for good measure.

"I threatened to blow out the other shoulder if he didn't drop his weapon. He finally did. Now he's trying to get away. He's moving very fast. Sorry, but I can't tell you exactly what direction he's heading in now. My guess would be he was headed for the bay. He disappeared down a path through the jungle in that direction."

"Don't worry, ma'am. We'll throw everybody at this. We'll seal up the perimeter and find him."

She took a deep, calming breath.

He wouldn't get far, anyway, not with the entire Vizcaya security staff after him.

"Thank you, Officer. We've had more than our share of excitement. I think it's time for us to call it a day."

"Be safe. We'll be in touch if there's anything else you need to know."

She returned the mobile to her bag.

"We're going back to the boat now, Alexei. I'm sure your father is wondering where we are."

"Is the bad man gone?"

"He's gone, all right. Gone for good, I should think."

"I hope . . ." she whispered to herself.

As they were making their way through the gardens to the parking lot minutes later, her mobile rang again. It was Sergeant Taylor.

"Got some bad news, Sergeant Major," he said. "He escaped the noose. Some tourists told one of our officers that they'd seen a man, bleeding prodigiously from a severely wounded hand, making his way out to the Vizcaya docks on the bay. There was a big red Cigarette race boat docked out there, waiting for him. He climbed aboard and they roared away, heading due south for Key Largo, or other points south, the tourists said."

Lacey remembered what Alexei had said about a red Cigarette boat out by the docks. "Did they see a name on the transom?"

"Yes, the wife did. She said it was called *Top Gun.*"

"Dammit," she said to the officer, although another, stronger word had come to mind as she ended the call.

They found a stone bench out in the open near a splashing fountain spewing glittering diamonds into the sky. She sat down to regroup. "I'm going to call your father," she said, "and tell him about this."

"Good idea," Alexei said.

She quickly dialed the number.

"Hawke," she heard her employer say at the other end.

"Yes, sir, Devereux here. We've had a bit of a nasty incident here at Vizcaya, I'm sorry to say . . ."

"What? Tell me. Anybody hurt?"

"Yes, but neither of us. Rather a long story. I'd prefer to tell you in person, if that's all right?"

"How's Alexei?"

"He's fine, sir, don't worry. Unscathed. Shall we come right back straightaway to the *Sea Hawke*?"

"No. The chief inspector and I are at a meeting at the home of one of my colleagues on Biscayne Bay. Have you got a pencil? I'll give you his address. Bit tricky to find, actually. On a little island called Lost Key. There's a small bridge from the mainland . . . Oh, and bring your bathing suits. It's a pool party, thank God. You can give Alexei another swimming lesson . . ."

"I'm ready, sir, and we will. The address?"

He gave it to her and said, "Can you put my son on?"

"Certainly," she said, and gave her phone to the boy.

"Dad?" Alexei said.

"You're all right, son?"

"Yes, sir. I'd say Miss Devereux and I definitely got the best of a bad situation. We're coming over to Stokely's to see you, right?"

"Yes, you are. I love you, buddy. Somehow, God knows, one day I'm going to make this world safe for you, no matter what it takes."

"You already do, Dad. Knowing I've got you, and Pelham, and Mr. Congreve, and Stokely, and Miss Devereux looking out for me? Makes me feel pretty darn safe already, sir."

Hawke, relief flooding in, deeply moved by the rising maturity he saw in the boy, took a beat and managed to choke out, "See you soon, darling," before he clicked off.

Whatever had happened didn't matter.

His son was safe.

CHAPTER 17

Villa Encantada, Lost Key, Miami

W here in the name of God is this damn place, Alex?" Ambrose said. He felt like they'd been driving in circles around Key Biscayne for hours.

Hawke sighed and said, "I know, I know. I've been here twenty times and I still have a hard time finding it. It's deliberately difficult to find for security reasons—a tiny little island surrounded by mangroves and tropical vegetation. Place called 'Hidden Key.'

"Stoke lives in some splendor these days. His wife, as you well know, is a very successful nightclub fado chanteuse from the Cape Verde Islands. I gave you one of her LPs for Christmas once. She inherited this estate from her wealthy late husband, who built the house as a wedding present for her.

"Fancha had met the two-bit mobster from up in Tampa when he was just out of charm school, as Fancha called the Florida State Penitentiary. He rather fancied himself as the Italian Jackie Gleason. He wasn't. He was about as funny as terminal herpes.

"He got himself whacked on the table at a strip mall massage parlor down in Homestead called the Happy Ending Club, just across the road from the US Air Force base. He'd been shot in the head, in flagrante delicto, apparently, while in the capable hands of one of the spa's younger but uglier hostesses. The end? Well. No surprise there. It was always going to be something like this, as Fancha had long imagined. Her husband was phony to the bone."

When Fat Tony wasn't doing his lousy impression of Jackie Gleason in the bar at the Fontainebleau, he liked to think of himself as Tony Montana in the movie *Scarface*. He wasn't. But he'd watched those damn movies—*Scarface*, *Goodfellas*, and all the Godfathers—over and over again in order to learn how to look and act like a goombah, like a made man.

He didn't. He was barely five feet tall and had a stunning male physique—not of a Greek, but of a penguin. He waddled like one and looked like one. It was not a good look. One night on Fancha's birthday, after abusing her, he passed out on the kitchen floor, snoring loudly, his mouth wide open. She wasn't sure how the idea occurred to her, but she went to the fridge and got a fresh flounder she'd bought at the fishmonger's that day. She stuck it in his mouth and took some hilarious photos with her iPhone. She'd shared some of them with her closest gal pals, who hated him almost as much as she did. Someone leaked them and they went viral.

Ouch.

But it had been worth it. The miserable little shit had to divorce her now! Right?

But he didn't. Tony was Tony. Deal with it.

But it was the twenty-first century, she'd told him on countless occasions. "Nobody wears those paisley shirts with the huge collars anymore, Tony. Nor those god-awful Beatles boots, nor the stupid bell-bottom trousers . . ."

So, on the morning when Greyson, Fancha's courtly butler, brought her breakfast tray and the *Miami Herald* and *New York Post* late the Sunday morning after Tony's timely demise, she grabbed the paper and opened it to the front page.

And there he was.

For better or for worse.

It was even worse than his flounder shot. It was a crime-scene shot they'd published of her late hubby, laid out in his birthday suit on the table in a tacky massage parlor in Homestead. He had dried blood spilling out of his mouth and ears. It was not a particularly good portrait to accompany an obituary.

But Fancha, a beautiful woman who'd suffered more than her share of years of gratuitous cruelty behind closed doors, abused at the tiny hands of the mini-me, as she called the mini mobster behind his back, could hardly stifle the guffaw that came out of her at the sight of the *Herald*'s headline emblazoned above the farewell photo:

MOB BOSS RUBBED OUT!
Gun violence at Homestead's Happy Ending Spa
Fat Tony, mob bigwig from Tampa, dead at age 53!

Meanwhile, back in the Bentley, Hawke said, "Wait a second, there it is!" He'd finally found the aging simple stone arch over the water up ahead and the sandy lane to the residence disappearing into the dense green jungle. "Okay, yes. I knew that bridge was back here somewhere . . . and there it is. I hope it's sturdy enough to bear the weight of the old Locomotive. Christ."

Hawke's favorite car was a steel gray 1953 Bentley Continental R that he'd bought from the previous owner, one Ian Fleming. Fleming had done massive amounts of modifications on the engine, the suspension, and the steering, and the old girl was capable of stupendous acceleration and top-end speeds. It was Fleming who nicknamed her "The Locomotive." Hawke's late grandfather, long a friend of the famous author's, had always liked that name, and so he kept it when the car passed to him, as did Lord Hawke when it passed to him upon the death of his father.

"It well may be hard to find," Ambrose said, "but it's genuinely beautiful back in here. My Lord, these bloody flowers, and the unbelievable birds. Magnificent."

"You ain't seen nothin' yet, Constable," Hawke said, in a poor attempt to mimic a Southern good old boy accent, and he meant it. Stoke's house was out of this world. It was a carbon copy of one of those magnificent Palm Beach palaces built in the twenties in the Mediterranean style by the architectural genius of the age, former Hollywood set designer Addison Mizner.

Stoke, Hawke would remind him, had come a goodly way from his West 196th Street origins in New York. And no one deserved it more than Stoke, one of his oldest and closest friends.

They managed to cross the tiny bridge without collapsing it into the brackish drink and found the long, curving drive that leads up through thickets of tropical vegetation to the manse at the top of the hill.

Minutes later, they came to a twelve-foot-high black wrought iron fence, including the main gate, and Hawke rolled up to the speakerphone and pressed the button.

"Yes? May I help you?" a disembodied voice said.

"Yes. This is Alex Hawke and Chief Inspector Ambrose Congreve. I believe we're expected?"

"Indeed you are. Mr. Jones says please come down to the pool when you arrive. We can valet your car if you'd like."

"That would be lovely," Hawke said as the gates swung wide.

"Good Lord," Congreve said as the massive edifice hove into view above them. "That's quite something, all right."

It was a crystal blue day in South Florida, and it tinged the white stone house in shades of pink and gold. A vast sweep of perfectly manicured green lawns swept down from the hilltop where stood Villa Encantada. A liveried valet parker was waiting at the front entrance. The two friends emerged from the vehicle and made their way to the colossal polished oak doors and rang the bell.

"Welcome to Villa Encantada, sirs," said the staff member who'd opened the doors and now stepped aside.

They found themselves inside a very breezy, wide, vaulted corridor with polished red tiles on the floors and hand-painted Portuguese tiles of every kind of design climbing the walls to a ceiling painted in dark blue with a smattering of stars. At the far end, Ambrose could see daylight and a sparkling Biscayne Bay beyond.

"Right this way, gentlemen," the butler said, and they followed him along the corridor, which emerged out again into the brilliant sunshine, where the rolling lawns swept grandly down to the water's edge and the countless pearls of sunlight danced across Biscayne Bay.

In the near distance, a squadron of dinghy sailors was rounding the marks, each one helmed by a ten-year-old. In the far distance were yachts aplenty, a variety afloat. Mini yachts, yachts, and mega-yachts were all headed home, steaming north for Miami, up from a week or so deepwater fishing, to be moored down at the lovely old Ocean Reef Club, still an exclusive destination after all these years.

A blue slate path ambled down to the pool. Stoke had been a busy boy, Hawke saw. Since his last visit, a year or two ago, a beautiful pool house had been added at the far end of the pool. It was in the English garden style, white, with a gabled rooftop and a big trellis billowing with peach-colored roses to either side of the wide entrance.

As they got closer, Hawke saw Stoke holding court at the bricked BBQ pavilion, grilling steaks while a sous chef was tossing what looked to be a Caesar salad in a big wooden bowl and shucking mounds of fresh corn. Hawke hadn't realized how hungry he was.

The breezes off the bay were rustling the clacking palm fronds in the trees that lined the walkway. It was not at all humid here on the water and the temperature was hovering in the seventies. He was looking forward to hearing what Mr. Brock had to say. But he was also looking forward to marinating in the salt air, swimming in the pool's clear blue water, and spending an afternoon brushing up on his deepwater tan.

"Stoke," he said, coming up behind him.

"Bossman! You made it in time for lunch. I was just getting worried."

"Never worry. Waste of energy," Alex said, embracing his old friend with genuine affection.

"How you doing, boss? You feeling good?"

"Never better. Say hello to Constable Congreve. Came aboard at Bermuda. Permanent crew aboard *Sea Hawke* now. Offers the skipper, me, the rare opportunity to boss the old boy around for a change . . . do him good."

"Hello, Stoke," Congreve said, ignoring Hawke's jibes and extending his hand. "You're looking well."

"Yeah, well, you know, nothing like my good old dark melanin to hide a whole damn multitude of sins, you know. You white folks sure missed the boat on that one, I'm just sayin'. I think God was taking a day off when you white guys showed up."

Congreve and Hawke both laughed.

"Where's the good Mr. Brock, Stoke? Really looking forward to hearing what he has to say. What's this all about?"

"Well, here's the thing. Harry just got back from a month in Havana. Down there on company business. From what I've heard so far, what's going on in Cuba right now is downright unbelievable. Except it ain't.

"What he's going to tell you is the absolute truth. We're having lunch in the pool house. Fancha and Harry are in there setting the table. You're going to get an earful at that lunch—I promise you that, compadre."

Hawke heard the voice of his son calling out from up at the top of the walk.

"I'm down here!" he shouted back. "Come get your bathing suits on. You've just got time for a short swim before luncheon is served, boy!"

"You okay?" Hawke said to Miss Devereux as she approached.

"Barely. But, yeah, okay, I guess."

"Let's take a walk down to the water. Alexei, Miss Devereux and I are going for a stroll around the property. There are changing rooms inside the pool house. Get your suit on. That water looks too good to be true. You should hit the pool before luncheon, buddy boy."

"Sounds good, Dad," he said, and disappeared inside to change.

Harry Brock emerged from the pool house and made a beeline for Hawke.

"Good afternoon, sir!" he said cheerfully. Hawke was a bit taken aback. It was the very first time in living memory that he could remember Brock ever using the word "sir" when addressing him.

"Harry," Hawke said, and shook his hand. "Looking forward to hearing what you have to say about your recent visit to our friends in Havana."

"Well, you may not be after you've heard it, sir. But I guarantee you will find it more than interesting. Beer? We've got Heineken on ice."

"Sounds good. Ambrose?"

"Yes, Harry. Can I get a gin and tonic?"

"Absolutely. Gordon's all right with you?"

"Perfect."

Harry served the beverages, and Hawke and Devereux strolled down the wide sloping lawns. "Tell me what happened," he said.

"Yes, of course, sir. Well, I picked up what I thought might well be a tail leaving the marina. A generic gray hired car. Stayed too close all the way to Coconut Grove. I signaled for a left into the Vizcaya property, and the driver just kept going. I thought I'd been mistaken. We toured the house and then moved out into the gardens. There were plenty of tourists, but most preferred to remain inside, where the air-conditioning was."

"And?"

"We were walking across a small open field between two formal gardens. A man in black appeared out of nowhere and grabbed Alexei—"

"In black? *Smith?* Good God!" Hawke said, dumbfounded. "How in heaven's name would he ever know where we went after leaving Bermuda?"

"Absolutely no idea, sir," Devereux said. "But it was him, all right. None other. I hadn't seen him approach because a bee had just stung my nose. I was dizzy with pain, and my eyes were full of tears. I yelled at him to stop, and he did, but he did not let go—he just stared straight ahead and did not turn around for a second or two. Hey. How much of this do you want to know? It's not pleasant."

"All of it," Hawke said. "I want to add fuel to this fire before I finally get around to him."

"Well. When he turned around, with his machete now in hand, I'd pulled my service weapon and told him to let go of Alexei. When he refused, I instantly shot him, deliberately winged him, blew out his right shoulder. He started to crumple to the ground. That's when Alexei grabbed the man's wrist, raised Smith's hand to his mouth, and took a huge bite out of the soft fleshy web between his thumb and forefinger. A stout gush of blood erupted, and yet Smith regained his viselike grip on Alexei. And then he put Alexei right in front of him, between the two of us, using him as a human shield.

"I told him to throw down the blade and let the child go. He refused to do either.

"I fired again and put a hole right through his black cowboy hat. That got his attention, all right, but he made no move to comply. I was getting bored with him.

"'Last chance, cowboy,' I said. 'This next shot is going to relieve you of your manhood, such as it is. Do what I say or I'm going to change your life. And not for the better.'

"I lowered my weapon and took dead aim at his crotch. His eyes went wide at that, and I think he realized I was dead serious about shooting him, let's say, for the sake of propriety, below the belt. I gave him five seconds to disarm and release Alexei.

"'Jesus,' he said before I got to five, 'you win, all right? I'll let him go as soon as you lower your weapon. I swear.'

"'And the knife, Hopalong,' I said. He threw it to the ground.

"I lowered my weapon. Alexei bolted straight for me and ran around behind me, holding me around my waist. He was breathing hard, still terrified. Smith stood his ground. He was whipping his head to and fro, searching for the best avenue of escape. Suddenly, he was gone. I've never seen anyone move as fast as he did. I called security to let them know what was happening. I told them I thought he'd run down a narrow, sandy path in the direction of the bay.

"Security forces were out in strength, but somehow he managed to evade them. Tourists told the cops later that they saw him boarding a waiting red Cigarette racing boat moored at the lagoon docks on the bay. They roared away, headed south toward Key Largo or points south. Who knows?"

"That's it?"

"That's it."

"Bloody hell, Devereux. Again. How the hell did Smith know we were headed to Miami from Bermuda? I told no one save the captain that information."

"Couldn't say, sir. It's all very odd."

"Did you think about putting one through his heart?"

"Yes, of course I did."

"And?"

"It would have been cold-blooded murder, sir, not self-defense. I'm not authorized to execute assassinations."

"Of course not. Let's head back up to the pool, shall we?"

Twenty minutes later, luncheon was served. Fancha had sliced the beautiful New York strips into pinkish-red slices, the yellow corn was steaming, the melted butter applied with a basting brush, and the fresh green salad cold and crisp. Delicious, all.

Hawke ate hurriedly, eager to go up to the main house with Stoke, Brock, and Congreve. He was dying of curiousity about the CIA agent's month in Havana, especially since he'd been ordered by Sir David to drop anchor in Havana Harbor en route to Jamaica. Now there was some serious political trouble brewing there—potentially a Communist coup ousting the right-wing, pro-US government that had succeeded the Castro brothers. Trulove and MI6 intel were pushing him to have a look round Havana and see what he could see. Take the temperature, so to speak.

The four men met up at the house in what Stoke called his den, though it was really more of an English paneled library. Before lunch, Hawke had put in a call to Fideo Chico to get a report on how the gunnery training had proceeded with the two Elon Musk employees, whom Chief Inspector Congreve now referred to as "Elon's Surfer Dudes." Fideo reported it had actually gone exceptionally well. He said he was confident that *Sea Hawke* was now prepared to defend herself from any attack on land, sea, or air—even incoming ship- and land-based missiles, tracked since launch with the boat's Anti-Missile Defense radar and locking on the laser cannon when enemy missiles were still miles outside the perimeter.

"Right in here, gentlemen," Stoke said, pulling wide the heavy wooden door and revealing a large sun-filled room with vaulted ceilings.

There were various comfortably worn leather club chairs scattered around the room and a big bay window flooded with sunshine and a view toward the south to lower Biscayne Bay, Key Largo, and the northernmost of the Florida Keys.

Brock pulled his chair forward into the center of the group, smiled, and said, "How many of you guys are aware of the fact that there is a *third* Castro brother?"

"*What?*" Hawke said, leaning forward. "Harry, a third Castro brother? C'mon, fess up, have you been at the psychotropic drugs again?"

Harry winced, remembering the time Hawke had walked in on him and his girlfriend dropping acid.

"Uh, a third Castro brother?" Brock said, recovering. "What? Nobody's ever heard about him? Really? Just kidding, just kidding. It seems, unbeknownst to the entire world for decades, that Mrs. Castro had a baby boy, Diego Ruz, a decade or so after she gave birth to Fidel in 1926 and then Raúl in 1931, both in Oriente province.

"According to sources I spoke with in Havana, the two brothers were intensely jealous of the baby because the mother no longer paid attention to them. Later, she would discover that the older boys were physically harming the baby in the middle of the night, placing a pillow over his face in the crib and breaking smaller bones in his hands and feet. She righteously threw the two of them out of the house.

"She thought they would surely kill little Diego if she didn't interfere. And she couldn't tell her husband, because he always sided with the boys against her. Always."

"Good Lord!" Congreve said. "*Another* Castro? You've got to be kidding, Harry. Haven't we had enough Castros for one century?"

"I told you this was going to be interesting," Brock said with a smile. "Wait. It gets even better. Or worse, depending on your point of view . . ."

CHAPTER 18

Villa Encantada, Lost Key, Miami

W e're listening," Hawke urged, waiting for Harry to drain the balance of his beer and continue with his Cuban adventure.

"Sorry. Well. Where to start?" he said.

"Gosh, I don't know," Congreve said. "How about the two older Castro boys are about to commit infanticide? That might be rather interesting . . ."

"So his mother, Lina Ruz González, had been a maid to Ángel's first wife, María Luisa Argota, at the time of Fidel's birth. By the time Fidel was fifteen and Raúl was ten, his father dissolved his first marriage and wed Fidel's mother. At age seventeen, Fidel was formally recognized by his father, and the baby's name was changed from Diego Ruz to Diego Castro.

"Lina was terrified, paralyzed with fear for her incredibly vulnerable baby. Finally, she came to the only possible way out. She packed a bag for herself and Diego and stole away from the house in Oriente. Then they both disappeared for the next fifty years.

"She had a friend drive her to the Havana airport, where they spent the night huddled together on the cement floor. They caught the first flight out the next morning, a dawn nonstop down to Buenos Aires. She had a sister there, Carmelita. They moved in and stayed out of sight, fearful that her husband might have sent one of his men down to look for her.

"That is, until decades later, when Diego, who now went by the name

of Ruz, was fully grown and a high-ranking officer in the Argentine military, finally decided he'd had enough with the antics of the so-called regime that had replaced the Castros. The right-leaning government was flirting with capitalism, edging ever further away from its Communist origins, not to mention Cuba's strongest two allies, China and Russia. It was time to act or forever hold his peace.

"Rumors swirling around had it that he planned to smuggle himself secretly back into Cuba along with his burgeoning force of New Revolution soldiers. Some believe that, like his brother Fidel, one of their options might be going high up into the Sierra Maestre mountains. From there they could execute daring attacks on the government forces and begin to forge and train a powerful guerrilla army that could rain death upon the current regime.

"General Castro, née Ruz, had also secretly spent a lot of time in high-level meetings in Beijing and Moscow with the leadership of both countries. I learned from a CIA informant in Havana that he had a plan. His stated aim, apparently avowed, was to cancel out the United States as a world power for the balance of this century and well into the next. It would be, he said, obviously in all three of their best interests.

"Cuba would become the genesis of the new global leftist revolution. The flashpoint nexus of the New Communism that Castro urgently believed in would soon be sweeping across Latin America, eradicating anything or anyone who stood in their way. Russia and China would become Cuba's closest allies in the renewed fight against the hated Americano fascists. In return, General Castro would allow both of his new allies to build and operate shipping ports and naval bases along the southern coast, as well as secret airfields and submarine pens.

"General Diego Castro, a tall, imposing figure who had superb logistical and military instincts, exuded a commanding presence and a legendary ability to bend others to his impervious will. So it was Castro who was able to convince the Chinese to give the Iranians a four-hundred-billion-dollar cash influx to shore up the government, and, as an added benefit, provide a whole new market for China, Russia, and Iran to sell their weapons throughout the region, thus destabilizing it even further

and threatening Iran's regional neighbors, the Saudis, the Israelis, the UAE, and all the rest. That would preoccupy the Americans, keep them looking the other way while Castro laid the groundwork for the 'Tri-Partite Committee,' as they now styled themselves.

"The TPC's single-minded aim? A violent coup that would throw out Cuba's right-wing status quo, reeducate the populace in the study and implementation of a Communist doctrinaire government and political leaning, and install Ruz, who was now openly going by the name General Castro, into the presidential palace and inaugurate him as prime minister—the first one since Fidel rose to that august position in nineteen fifty-six."

With that, Harry paused to get his wind back and down the rest of the ice-cold can of Bud. He smiled. "With me so far?"

"Keep talking," Hawke muttered, not bothering to look up. He was paying extremely close attention to Harry's story, trying to assimilate all of the pieces and begin the process of figuring out some way to stop Castro dead in his tracks before he could do any more damage to the West by taking down a powerful ally in the Caribbean.

He knew one thing. He would not be sailing for Jamaica when he departed Miami on the morrow aboard *Sea Hawke*. He was going to divert the boat to Havana first, see what he could see, hear what he could hear, and report back to MI6.

He had the benefit of the most powerful warship in the Caribbean outside of the US Navy's Atlantic Fleet. A boat that presented a profile as nothing but a rich man's toy just might lend itself to their advantage and make this the perfect opportunity for what could well be the lovely boat's combat shakedown cruise.

Action at sea could commence as early as dawn tomorrow.

The thought made him smile as he dozed off. Brock's tale of tropical intrigue had finally made him realize that he was spoiling for a fight, and had been for quite some time.

He had a fierce need for combat.

CHAPTER 19

En route, Miami–Havana

Hawke awoke in the predawn light the next morning to the sound of the wind howling fiercely in the rigging towering above the owner's stateroom. *Sea Hawke,* having safely navigated the storm-tossed Gulf Stream, was also heeling hard over to starboard, maybe a good fifteen degrees or even a little more. What the hell's this? he wondered. The much-vaunted high wind from Jamaica? Wasn't even on the bloody charts!

There'd been zero reports about any storm system moving up to Miami, either from NOAA, the Weather Channel, the *Miami Herald,* or anyone else, for that matter. He reached up and turned on the small weather radar monitor that hung directly above his bed.

What he saw forecast was not good news. But for an able-bodied seaman like himself, it was not necessarily all bad. It would be a test, not just of himself, but of the boat he'd designed to be impervious to anything nature could throw at him, save a perfect storm.

What the hell, he thought, a boat tested in calm seas has not been tested, as they used to say in the Navy. He swung his long legs over the edge of the bed and sat up, looking at the bronze Tiffany alarm clock that Sigrid Kissl had given him for his birthday, a few days before she herself was brutally murdered by the monster known as Mr. Smith.

It had just gone 5:00 a.m.

He shrugged his broad, muscled shoulders, ran a hand over the whiskers on his chin, and picked up his faded but trusty well-worn Royal

Navy T-shirt. He was about to go to his closet for a pair of trousers but saw his khaki shorts puddled on the floor where he'd dropped them last night and decided, hey, what the hell?

He was on a boat, right? Nobody cared what anyone wore aboard a sailing yacht, with the possible exception of his friend the very tweedy Ambrose Congreve, who always made note of what you were wearing and later made comments intended to help the less stylish in his circle to see the light, fashion-wise, but which usually ended up being soundly insulting.

This from a man who proudly drove a hellish lemon-lime-colored Morgan Plus Four roadster and wore his bright orange tweeds to Sunningdale, Hawke's golf club, when his purple ones were at the dry cleaner's.

Just this Christmas, Congreve had given Hawke a lurid yellow golf sweater with fire-engine-red golf balls and tees scattered front and back. It was from Harrods, of course, and Hawke returned the nightmare apparel first thing in the morning on Boxing Day. And who did he run into at the returns window?

Congreve, of course, in the queue to return Hawke's sarcastic gift, a half dozen pink boxer shorts monogrammed with Congreve's initials. Tit for tat, Hawke had always said. He'd given what he'd got, by God!

He'd been somewhat shocked when the chief inspector had made a grab for his Harrods shopping bag and tried to pry it open to see what Hawke was returning. "Of all the nerve," Hawke said, ripping his bag away from his former best friend. "Show me what's in your bag and I'll show you mine!"

It was a standoff. Hawke shrugged his shoulders and made for the escalators. He paused, looked over his shoulder, and said, more than loud enough for all to hear:

"Merry bloody Christmas to you, too, Constable! And to the bloody horse you rode in on!" Hawke uttered out of the side of his mouth.

———————

Hawke left the owner's stateroom and raced topside to the bridge to find Hornblower. They'd agreed to meet first thing on the morrow to go over the charts, looking for the fastest route to Havana, which was two hundred nautical miles distant. But still, on this rocket ship of a boat, he was thinking two, maybe three days at sea headed down there, max.

The combat comms officer emerged on the bridge and breathlessly informed him that sonar had picked up a sub to stern, stalking *Sea Hawke* at very close quarters. They clearly were not at all worried about the big sailing vessel becoming aware of their presence.

"Cuban?" Hawke said. "I'm not aware that they have any submarines."

The good-looking young ex–US Navy kid with the tight blond crew cut smiled.

"They don't, sir," he said. "At any rate, according to sonar, her screw signature? She's definitely not Cuban—or Russian, for that matter."

"Ah. Well, then, son, spare me the agony. So what the hell is she?"

"She's Chinese, sir. A boomer, sir, nuclear. The new Jin-class Type 094."

"Chinese? I thought we chased them the hell out of the Caribbean after that little dustup at the Dragonfire Club in the Bahamas."

"We did, but, well, I think they're back, sir."

"Obviously. What is she, this Chinese boomer?"

"She is China's first credible sea-based nuclear deterrent. Global security.org claims that a Type 094 patrolling just northeast of the Kuril Islands would be able to strike three-quarters of the contiguous United States, whereas launching missiles from Chinese coastal waters would barely reach the Aleutian Islands."

"What's your name, sailor?"

"Jones, sir. Lieutenant John Paul Jones, Commander." He saluted smartly, and Hawke returned the favor.

"Related?"

"Direct descendant, Skipper. My mates call me J.P., sir."

"Is that a fact, J.P.? And I understand you're a graduate of the Naval Academy to boot. Played football for Navy and beat Army three seasons in a row. I know all that because, for years, I attended all the Army-Navy games at West Point with Director Kelly of the CIA. Well, welcome to *Sea Hawke*, son. I'm glad to have you aboard." Hawke handed the young officer a sealed envelope bearing the legend "EYES ONLY!" "Deliver this message to CIA Director Patrick Brickhouse Kelly. But I also want you to read it to him ASAP over the encrypted satphone. Write this down: 'Hawke, aboard *Sea Hawke*, en route to Havana in stormy conditions, has picked up a shadow. Chinese boomer, probably Jin-class Type 094, whilst crossing the Gulf Stream, east-southeast of Miami. Please contact for more info before I have to take evasive action or attack.' Got that, Lieutenant?"

"Aye-aye, sir. Straightaway. Will that be all, sir?"

"Dismissed, sailor," Hawke said, jamming his fifth Marlboro of the day into the corner of his mouth.

Hawke Zippo'd the cigarette as he made his way over to the chart table, where lay scattered marine charts and sat photos encompassing all of the South Atlantic and the East Coast of Florida and the Keys. He didn't like this Chinese sub driver who was deliberately endangering his vessel and all aboard her. He was like a cat, toying with a mouse, and Hawke was insulted and angry and determined to get the better of him.

He was looking for a way to execute a rather complex battle maneuver he'd learned the hard way from his combat flight instructor at Dartmouth Naval as a fighter pilot often engaged with enemy fighters whilst in the Royal Navy.

"If a bogey gets on your tail, immediately execute an inimitable series of radical evasive tactics that allow you to get on the bogey's tail."

"Sir!" said the ramrod-straight sonar officer, coming to attention.

"What is it now?" Hawke said, not looking up from the charts of Cuban waters. "More bad news? Speak up!"

"I believe this Jin 094 poses a direct threat to the safety of the boat and crew, sir. Behaving in a very aggressive way. Sticking with us. Crowding our sea room. Almost as if she's been ordered not to let us get anywhere close to Havana. Any ideas how to shake her, sir?"

"Yes. Ask Captain Hornblower to join us in the comms room immediately."

"Right away, sir."

Hawke rose and strode across the bridge to the port side where the ship's communications center was located. The captain entered moments later.

"Morning, sir!" Hornblower said. "Understand we've got company. Someone along for the ride."

"We do," Hawke said. "Instruct the helmsman to go to max RPMs. Full throttle, full speed ahead. Let's get a wide berth between us and that bloody sub. Put a lot of water between us. Wide as possible. Jones! What's her speed over the ground?"

"She's making fifteen knots over the ground, sir."

"Helm! Increase her speed twenty-five knots!"

"Aye, sir. Speed at twenty-five."

Hawke said, "Helm! Ten minutes out, peel off to starboard in a wide, sweeping circular arc. Close the circle as rapidly as you can. Then we'll approach them from behind, coming up abruptly on her stern flank."

"Stern flank, aye. Arm the forward laser, sir?"

"Affirmative," Hawke said. "Threaten her on the radio, Comms. Inform them they need to immediately disengage and vacate this area and give us sea room or we'll send them to the bottom. Her skipper won't buy that, because with eyes on us with the periscope, we're nothing but another fancy yacht en route to Jamaica and points south . . ."

"Understood. He'll think he's calling our bluff . . ."

"Exactly," Hawke said, still thinking out his next move on the deep blue acquatic chessboard. And the move after that. And the move after that.

"Aye, sir," Captain Hornblower said.

"Get Fideo Chico and the gunnery crew in position up on the bow, making preparations to lock onto that sub and fire the laser cannon at a target at a depth of . . . how many fathoms, Sonar? Exactly how many?"

"Fifty fathoms, sir."

"Okay, I'll give him five minutes to go hard to starboard to a course of 060 and get the hell out of our way. If he doesn't, we shall open fire with the laser cannon. And from what Fideo tells me, that weapon will not only blow a hole in that sub—it will leave a hole where the submarine was . . ."

"That should just about do the trick, Skipper."

Hawke smiled and said, "One would hope. I learned a lesson about high-tech gadgetry, rocketry, and weaponry years ago from our age's own Thomas Edison. Put your trust in Elon Musk."

"Got that right, boss."

CHAPTER 20

Somewhere off Havana, Cuba

S onar," Hawke barked into the ship's intercom. "What's the status of that bloody sub?"

"Nonresponsive. Not answering my radio transmissions. No response. They're still right up our arse, sir, forgive my French."

"One last transmission, Sonar. Inform that bloody sub driver that he has less than five minutes to separate from us and give us the safety of sea room, according to International Law of the Sea, before we take him permanently off the chessboard."

"Aye-aye, Skipper," the seaman said. "Combat chief says the gunnery boys are ready in the bow turret. Standing by. I'm ordering them to acquire and target the sub now and fire at will upon your orders, sir."

Hawke was about to agree, but something inside him would not let him. He thought for a few seconds before he replied.

"Belay that order, sailor!" Hawke barked, quickly realizing he knew exactly what he had to do and how to do it. "Ditch the two kids in the turret and let the adults have a shot at this bloody 094, whoever the hell he is."

"Roger that, Skipper. They've been relieved of duty."

"Good," Hawke said, and turned to address Hornblower. "Captain, I'm headed up to the bow now. I'm going up there to personally teach this Chinese sub driver some bloody effing manners!"

"Good shooting, Commander!" J.P. said, smiling at him.

Hawke quickly donned his foul-weather gear, left the bridge, rapidly descended the steel exterior steps to the main deck, and made his way forward. The once-horizontal rainfall had diminished. But out on the open deck, the wind felt like a concrete wall—the wicked east wind that carried with it the leading edge of a Sheffield steel blade.

He found it hard to maintain his balance. The teak decks were slippery as hell due to heavy rain. And the boat was heeling at a significant angle, her lee rail buried, as she sailed right into the teeth of the tropical storm. She was built from the keel up to the gunwales, up to the rigging soaring overhead, to weather any kind of weather, bad, good, or indifferent. This was of the bad variety.

Hawke made it to the bow and quickly hauled himself up into the turret and took his seat. He peered intently at the electronic displays showing the cannon's status quo, the amount of battery charge remaining, the time required to be fully operational, and the relative position of the enemy sub to *Sea Hawke*.

It seemed sufficient, but, according to Fideo and all his practice rounds, this would not be the first time the cannon had run out of gas at a critical moment. The other problem Hawke had with the damn thing was how long you had to wait between charges. There was simply no surefire way to know where you stood. No way of knowing. If your first zap wasn't up to par, you were basically dicked.

Sea Hawke's sonar was locked onto the submarine, now showing it pulling slightly forward of them at ten knots at a depth fifty fathoms below *Sea Hawke*'s starboard forward flank.

"Sir!" he heard Hornblower shout in his headphones. "Hawke! Hold your fire! Enemy sub is surfacing, repeat, surfacing, and she's coming up bloody fast. At this trajectory and speed, we calculate she'll break the surface roughly a hundred yards dead ahead of you! In two, maybe three minutes. Get ready, sir."

"That's good news, Captain. I'm ready for them. I'm going to let them get about a third of her bow out of the water—and before they can complete surfacing, blow that bastard's bow off! The bow will flood instantly, and, before they even know what hit them, that bloody sub driver and his crew will be on the bottom. She'll sink like a stone!"

"I like it, Skipper! Good shooting!"

"Roger that," Hawke said. His blood was up, he was feeling almost giddy, and he had his eyes glued to the monitor displaying the surface of the sea, calm in the moments before all hell would break loose, coldly calculating the Chinese sub's position, angle of attack, and real relative distance once her bow broached the surface.

He was now Hawke the Happy Warrior, and a man with a very itchy trigger finger and—Jesus! The forward tip of the sub's bow suddenly broke the surface, surging up at an impossible angle in the midst of an upward explosion of boiling white water!

Hawke was aghast. The Chinese had obviously been forging ahead dramatically with their latest submarine class. What was this propulsion system? How in hell could something that enormous gather enough energy and upward momentum to possibly do something like that?

It was still rising at that crazy angle for an infinite second, majestic and an awesome thing of beauty.

Hawke waited, forcing himself to hold his fire until there was just enough of the sub's hull up out of the water to put the enemy at their utmost moment of vulnerability before he pulled the trigger.

Five seconds he'd give it, max. He had his finger on the trigger.

"One. Two. Three . . . NOW!"

He saw that he'd actually fired the cannon at the precise moment he'd calculated for maximum destruction. And never had he been happier to see Elon's Green Monster spit out its unearthly green death ray . . . He watched as the sub seemingly paused at the top for that precise moment of inertia, ever so briefly in midair for a horrific few seconds before her upward momentum was exhausted . . . and the Jin 094 sub, along with her skipper and crew, slipped slowly and silently beneath the waves, downward, downward to her eternal resting place on the bottom of the sea.

CHAPTER 21

Somewhere off Havana, Cuba

Hawke reflected that the Chinese sub driver never had a chance to second-guess his decision. He'd most likely died in the act of accepting kudos from the officers and crew for his stout defiance of the British skipper's orders to fall off.

Victory accomplished. And now, for his next act, Hawke was bound for his next destination: a city he loved.

Havana!

Hawke snatched the radio transmitter from the laser cannon's instrument panel.

"Bridge!" he said into the mic.

"Bridge, aye, sir," came the instant response.

"Hard a' starboard, full throttle! We make for Havana Harbor, SSE, under a full head of steam, lads! Bear away, crew! Hoist up the mainsail and storm trysails and set the mizzens as well as her top foresails! We'll sail a close reach all the way, it looks like now!"

When she had sailed out of Miami Harbor that morning, with the wind in her sails and a bone in her teeth, *Sea Hawke* had been bound for Castillo del Morro, the storied lighthouse that had stood guard at the entrance to Havana Harbor for centuries.

Once they had moored the gleaming black-hulled yacht safely in the harbor in Havana, he and Stoke, as well as Harry Brock and Chief Inspector Congreve, planned to venture ashore and have a good look round, trying, as well they must, to blend in with the swarming masses of native *cubanos y turistas* that ranged about the broad esplanade officially called Avenida de Maceo that encircled the bay—the road better known round the world as El Malecón. Hawke had ordered them all to dress as inconspicuously as possible.

Hawke, who had grown a thick black beard over the course of the voyage, would don the pale blue guayabera he'd ordered years ago at Ramon Puig's famous guayabera shop on Calle Ocho in Miami. Matched with worn leather sandals and a dusty pair of white linen trousers, he knew he'd be hard to spot for what he was—essentially the owner of the largest yacht in the Caribbean. Stoke, for his part, was wearing a colorful Jamaican Rasta shirt of yellow, red, and green he'd bought from a Serengeti tourist dive and a pair of faded Levi's. He hoped, he'd told Congreve, to be taken for an African. He then looked the man up and down and inquired, "And what do you hope to be taken for, Ambrose? A plumber from Pittsburgh on a busman's holiday?"

Congreve put on his poshest British accent and said, in the style of Her Royal Majesty, "We are not amused."

Ambrose Congreve's costume, as it happened, was truly another story altogether.

He, of his own free will, had mysteriously donned an outfit that was unmistakably, one hundred percent, pure Ugly American. He was wearing a baggy pair of frightfully loud yellow madras Bermuda shorts, turquoise cable-stitched knee socks, a fire-engine-red XXXL polo shirt with the signature Ralph Lauren polo pony embroidered on the left side, and a well-worn pair of Sperry Top-Siders, salt-bleached boat moccasins that he'd been wearing aboard since they'd left England.

It was a pretty sure bet that nobody, but nobody, would mistake this bizarre threesome for the Kingston Trio, just in from Malibu. That much, at least, was pretty clear to Lord Hawke.

Two and a half days later, having traversed a little over two hundred nautical miles in what Hornblower told Hawke was a new world record for the crossing, the great yacht *Sea Hawke* was breaking records, gaining fame everywhere she went, as she slid majestically past the ancient Morro Castle and, dousing her sails and starting her big electric diesels, sailed into Havana Harbor itself. Big rollers came in from the Atlantic, crashing over the seawall at Punta Brava. The sun was high and bright, its rays dancing across the water toward the famous avenue, *El Malecón*.

Hawke, who'd always had a soft spot in his heart for the ancient Cuban capital—and its perfectly restored American automobiles from the 1950s—found his heart beating a trifle faster. Things in the wind, complicated international political things, threats involving existential dangers for the democracy- and freedom-loving Western allies, were swirling about this tattered old metropolis, and he meant to get to the bottom of it, for Queen and Country.

Like many people in his line of work, Hawke had long wondered in whose pocket Russia's parting gift to the island nation of twenty-five billion US dollars was. Also like most of them, he was pretty sure who had pocketed the money.

El Jefe himself—Fidel Castro. And his brother Raúl. That's who.

The skipper contacted the harbormaster. He was given the precise position of their assigned mooring buoys and told that a launch would be made available to ferry Lord Hawke, his crew, and his guests ashore on an as-needed basis. He could contact the launch service by going to channel sixteen on the radio. The captain decided to remain mum about the fact that his vessel carried four "gigs," or admiral's launches, as they were called in the glory days of the Royal Navy, aboard at all times.

He knew the mere appearance of a huge vessel such as the one he commanded sometimes created feelings of ill will toward those who sailed her. Human nature. No matter how big your yacht is, there will always come a day when a much bigger one will appear in the harbor. And that's when the great green dragon of dreaded envy raised its ugly head.

Hawke had been awake since sunrise.

He was still abed, furiously scribbling notes about questions C had wanted him to pose during his voyage to all and sundry who might be able to answer them. This morning at ten, he, Stoke, Harry Brock, and

Congreve had a scheduled meeting at the Swiss embassy. There, they would find the American desk maintained by the Swiss government as a courtesy to their friends in Washington.

It functioned not so much as a fully integrated embassy but more as a consulate where business could be done and where American tourists in need of help could find it.

At that very moment, Pelham shimmered into his stateroom bearing a white wicker breakfast tray, complete with a small sterling silver vase of tropical flowers, along with his orange juice, two five-minute soft-boiled eggs, and an English muffin served with butter and apricot preserves, as well as today's London *Times*, downloaded off the Internet and printed for him every morning.

"Pelham, there you are at last! I've been up for hours. How are you feeling, young man? I trust you slept well?"

"Indeed, sir. Fit as a fiddle, as they say. You know how the sea air agrees with me. I now believe I should have run away to sea as a young lad and been a sailor in the Royal Navy, messing about on boats instead of spending my entire life messing about in kitchens and pantries—and worst of all, boardrooms!"

"Well. I'm not sure you would have enjoyed what Churchill once described as that military life. He said, 'Nothing in life is so exhilarating as to be shot at without result.' I myself have been shot at for most of my adult life, and I will tell you I have never found it to be even remotely invigorating. It's rather terrifying, to be honest. But, then, of course, I'm no Churchill."

"Well, yes," Pelham said, thinking it over, "I do think you've hit that nail on the head, m'lord. I shan't dwell in my rainy realm of regrets a second longer, sir."

"Hmm. I say, old fellow, is Congreve up and about? I'd love to have a word with him . . ."

"Sorry to inform, sir. I called him about his breakfast order quite early. He said he wasn't feeling like eating anything. He was up all night with stomach issues, he said. He plans to spend the day in bed recuperating in proximity to the nearest loo."

Pelham, having delivered the goods, winked out of the room like some kind of woodland faerie in a C. S. Lewis fable.

Hawke speed-dialed Congreve.

"Hullo?" Ambrose said, picking up. He sounded like the living dead, hoarse and ragged.

"Are you quite all right, Constable? Pelham says you're ill. Stomach issues, the man says."

"That's one definition, yes."

"Well, for heaven's sake, stay in bed. I'll go to the embassy meeting with Stokely and Brock. We'll miss you, of course, but I shall take you through it in some detail upon my return."

"I'll tell you what I would really like before you go, if you don't mind . . . I'm in desperate need this morning. You know the feeling. A feeling not unknown to Bertie Wooster and his man Jeeves, what?"

"Indeed I do know. Fire away, Constable."

"Some kind of restorative? A fortifier, as Pelham, in his infinite wisdom, calls them . . . would you mind asking him?"

"Of course not. I hardly blame you. Know the feeling."

Fortifiers are sometimes referred to as "hair of the dog" and are to be taken when one wakes to learn that one has "screwed the pooch" the previous evening. Hawke knew the infamous "pooch" expression dated back to the American Army in 1935. It derived from a popular slang saying at that time: "Screw the pooch, and sell the pups."

"So, a screwdriver, perhaps?" Hawke continued. "Or one of Pelham's old New Orleans tequila Bloody Marys? The one they purvey at Brennan's Restaurant, I believe. Or, one of my pal Malcom Gosling's impeccable Dark 'n Stormys?"

"The Bloody Mary, please, Alex. And tell him no tequila—vodka. And to make it a double. Stolichnaya, pretty please, with Worcestershire sauce and Tabasco aplenty. Lots of lime juice, and a pinch of horseradish. And throw in an ice-cold beer chaser. Preferably Stella Artois."

"Oh, my," Hawke said. "You are in a bad way."

"You've no idea. Now let me be and go to your meeting. I read on the Internet that Cuba is bracing for a potential military coup. You could have a little excitement today. Stay safe, Alex. And stick that damnable Walther PPK in the back of your britches and under your blue guayabera. Hear me? I know Mr. Brock doesn't go anywhere without his service pistol. But you hardly ever carry yours."

He rang off.

Hawke rose, shouldered into the burgundy silk Charvet robe he'd splurged on during his last stay at the Ritz, Paris, and went into the loo for a speedy shave and shower.

He was anticipating a rather full day.

As it happened, however, he had no bloody idea just how full a day he would have.

And no earthly idea that he would end up in prison that very afternoon.

CHAPTER 22

"Castro really only forgot three things.
Breakfast. Lunch. And dinner."

Havana, Cuba

In the unfortunate absence of the quasi-ill chief inspector, who tradi-
tionally claimed a stomach ailment when, in point of fact, he was all
too clearly suffering from imbibing a wee brandy or two too far on the
preceding evening, Hawke was only too glad of the company of Stokely
Jones, Jr., his self-described "boon companion."

He and Stoke went way back—all the way to the day when Lieutenant S. Jones, NYPD, had saved his life in a burning warehouse in Red
Hook, Brooklyn, where the Lucchese crime family, upon learning that he
refused to let them extort a king's ransom for his own life, had bound him
to a steam pipe in a top-floor solvent closet and left him to be burned
alive. Not exactly the death he'd always pictured for himself—which was
namely falling asleep in the Ernest Hemingway Suite at the Ritz Hotel,
Place Vendôme in Paris, a half-full glass of Napoleon brandy in one hand,
a lit cigarette in the other, and a beautiful old girlfriend from his Paris
years sleeping naked beside him, then finally waking up (or not) dead at
the ripe old age of ninety-five.

Now, that death? He swooned at the thought. That death was called
living!

He realized, with the cool salt spray on his rosy cheeks, coming over the
bow of his Wally boat launch, that he was in an impossibly good mood. He

was happier, by far, than he could remember being in a very long time. He had to give credit where it was due. On balance, despite all the danger he'd been in down in the Bahamas at the Dragonfire Club, he'd found the entire experience of the "Voyage of the *Sea Hawke*" to be, so far, exhilarating.

Alex smiled at Stoke, who was zipping up his windcheater to conceal the Glock 9 in his waistband, and then at Harry Brock. He was utterly amazed to find himself smiling at the fellow, a rather uncouth man to whom he had long addressed his chilliest behavior. A moral relativist of a man, whom Congreve had once described as a man who had "a lively tendency to disobey God."

And now he found that, for some unknown reason, he was doing an about-face on the chap's true demeanor.

"What's so funny, Harry?" he said pleasantly, just loud enough to be heard above the roar of the three 300 HP outboards on the stern.

"What?" Harry said.

"You're laughing at something. What is it?"

"Oh, nothing. Just a joke the senior CIA case officer at the Swiss embassy told me yesterday."

"Tell me."

"Naw . . . I don't think it's up to your humor standards, frankly."

"Just tell it, Harry. I don't even have any humor standards. Or maybe just one. I cannot, even slightly, abide what you Yanks call 'potty humor.' If that's what your joke is, I'll pass."

"No, sir, it's not potty based. It's about Castro."

"What about him?"

"Well, you'll meet Nick Pillsbury at this morning's meeting at the embassy. He's funny, what can I tell you?"

"No idea, old chap," Hawke said. "The joke, perhaps?"

"Right. So. These two Cuban commie secret service guys were reminiscing about the late, great Fidel. And one of them says, 'You know, in hindsight, El Jefe brought a lot to the Party. As in, the Communist Party.'

"'Yeah?' the other guy said. 'Like what?'

"'Well, he really only forgot three things. Breakfast. Lunch. And dinner.'"

Hawke laughed out loud. "Oh, that is a good one, Harry. Look here, you say Havana is full of security personnel, both Chinese and Russian. What's that all about?"

"We don't have a clue. But I'll tell you what Pillsbury will say. He'll say they're all here in advance of some kind of bilateral—or, perhaps, trilateral—summit, if you get my drift?"

"I don't," Hawke said.

"Some kind of major meeting is about to go down. Between the Cubans and the Russians, obviously. We hear that Putin has rented a slip in the marina for his presidential yacht for this time frame."

"You mean *TSAR*? The big red boat? I didn't see her sailing in."

"Yep, *TSAR*. I heard last night that he'd invited a boatload of pretty señoritas to go for an afternoon sail over to Isla de Pinos."

"So, Cuba and Russia—that would be bilateral. If it's trilateral, who the hell's the third party?"

"That's what we're going to find out—whoever is actually putting this meeting together. In other words, the Cuban government, aided and abetted by the left-wing underground. They need this coalition in order to cling to power and stymie the rebel forces. It's got to be them that's brokering this much-rumored but unconfirmed commie convention. It's no big secret that the current pro-American government has fallen out of favor with the starving population. They're growing wistful for Fidel and Che . . . poor bastards."

"Harry, c'mon, use your brain," Hawke said. "We both know that the current Cuban government is far right wing. Why the hell would they broker a deal between two far-left socialist countries?"

"Maybe it's not the *current* government doing the brokering," Harry said slyly.

"No? Then who? Don't tell me the Russians? The Chinese? Who?"

"Well, you'll hear this for yourself in an hour or so. But amidst all the commie secret service guys swirling around Havana, there's also a big fat rumor that's on everyone's lips."

"Which is?"

"Oh, come on, Harry! You and I both know full well that there might be a coup in Cuba's future, that's what. Something like nobody's seen since Castro came down from the Sierra Madre mountains and took out Fulgencio Batista's military junta by founding a paramilitary organization, 'The Movement.' Castro first launched a failed attack on the Moncada Barracks. Many militants were killed and Fidel himself was arrested and sentenced to fifteen years imprisonment on the Isla de Pinos. Batista let him out of the slammer in 1955, thinking he was no longer a political threat. Except he still was. Obviously.

"So, Harry, I'm only going to ask you one more time. Who's behind this mythical coup of yours?"

"It ain't my mythical coup, boss, it's the CIA boys. That's the question my CIA buddies here are determined to figure out. They know about you, obviously. They know you and Director Kelly are tight as two ticks. They know he asked you to divert to Havana en route to Jamaica and help them get to the bottom of this threat to the status quo down here. CIA, and the White House, have zero interest in a new version of Fidel's workers' paradise. I mean *zero*. Right is right and left ain't, is how Special Agent Pillsbury sees Cuban politics."

"How secure is the current Cuban president?" Hawke asked Brock.

Brock said, "Rafael Mendez? Not very. There've been multiple assassination attempts already. One was just last week, when a rebel sharpshooter tried to shoot him getting out of the back of his limo in his driveway. A secret service guy took him out at the last second. But here's the mood at CIA these days: They believe we'll know for certain when a coup d'état is real."

"How will they know?"

"Because President Rafael Mendez will be dead, that's how."

"Got it," Hawke said, extracting a fag from his gunmetal cigarette case and lighting a fresh Marlboro with his beat-up old Zippo.

Hawke had arranged to have a car and driver waiting for them in the marina parking lot. Fideo Chico had recommended a chap named Carlos Munoz as the best driver in all Havana. And Stokely Jones nearly went insane when he caught sight of the car the boss had hired for the next few days.

"Holy shit!" Stoke exclaimed, stopping dead in his tracks and staring openmouthed at the gleaming black vehicle. "Is that what I think it is?"

"Dunno," Hawke said. "What kind of vehicle do you think it is?"

"Well, it can't be what I think it is, because there aren't any of those still around."

"But what do you think it is, anyway?"

"Well. I know exactly what it is. A nineteen fifty-nine Chrysler Imperial. I mean, look at those fuckin' *fins*! Mother looks like a goddamn land yacht, I'll tell ya that much."

"Well, in that case, Stoke," Hawke said, "you ride up front with the driver, Carlos. Mr. Brock and I will bring up the rear."

And they were off.

Stoke looked at his watch and then over at Alex Hawke. "Boss, we got us an hour to kill before our meeting. I'm starving. Can we go somewhere and get some breakfast?"

"Sure," Hawke said, because he, too, was famished. "Any idea of where?"

"Yes. The perfect spot. I know you're a Hemingway fan, and this was Papa's favorite gin joint in *Habana*."

"Not the Floridita?" Hawke said, grinning.

"Exactly the Floridita!" Stoke said. "How do you know so much, man?"

"I read," Hawke said.

Carlos pulled up in front of the landmark saloon ten minutes later. The maître d' asked how many and found them a nice table for three, off by itself and right by the window overlooking the plaza. There were black-and-white pictures of Hem everywhere, Hawke was happy to see, often in the company of American movie stars or famous politicians down from Washington. In one of them, he was seated at the bar with another of Hawke's favorite American scribes, Tennessee Williams. Both men looked three sheets to the wind, of course, for that was Hem down to the bone, and Williams, too, who preferred to be called "Tenn."

"So, Mr. Brock, you know how I loathe surprises."

"I sure do."

Hawke said, "Well, then, please tell me what I can expect to hear from your CIA colleagues at the embassy this morning."

"Right. So, Pillsbury and the other two embassy guys want to tell you the story of the third Castro brother."

"That's aces, but you've already told us that tale."

"They will be happy to fill in all the holes for you. The story is not without its share of drama, that I can promise."

The breakfast being served at the Floridita that morning was, Hawke thought, surprisingly good. Perfectly cooked eggs and delicious sausage from Spain, washed down with an ice-cold pint of Cristal beer, Cuba's finest brew. It was a breakfast tradition started in the 1940s by Papa Hemingway himself. Frequently in need of a little dog's hair the morning after a binge, he'd always order a cold beer for breakfast.

Hawke checked the time and called for the check.

They had a meeting to go to.

He fished his mobile out of his pocket, speed-dialed his new driver, Carlos, and asked him to bring the land yacht around to the entrance of the Floridita. Ten minutes later, the three men climbed out of the car and up the steps to the entrance of the Swiss embassy.

CHAPTER 23

Havana, Cuba

Commander Alex Hawke, as I live and breathe," the big, muscle-bound CIA special agent with the mandatory Trumpian blue-suit-white-shirt-red-tie wardrobe said. He spoke in a Kappa Alpha frat-boy Southern accent, getting to his feet, smiling as Brock and the other two men entered his office. He stuck out his large, gnarly hand, his hard blue eyes never wavering. "The man, the legend . . ."

Hawke smiled. "Oh, come on, Pillsbury. Don't be ridiculous. Say hello to my colleague Stokely Jones, Jr., former NYPD, former New York Giant. You know Agent Brock, of course; everyone seems to. I prefer to call him Agent Bane, actually."

"Really? Why is that?" Pillsbury replied.

"Simple. Because Agent Brock is the bane of my existence. And Agent Bane is the Brock of my existence," Hawke added, with a furtive wink to Stoke. "Cuts both ways, you see."

Pillsbury nodded at the two Americans, then smiled at Hawke's joke.

"I'm kidding about 'the man, the legend' stuff, sir. But only half kidding. Because at Langley? We've all had our eyes on you for a long, long time. We know, if not everything you've ever done, at least most of it. We know that when you and Putin shared a cell together in Energetika Prison, President Putin seriously tried to recruit you to leave Six and join the KGB. That's not legend, right? I mean, that's the truth?"

Hawke looked at Pillsbury and gave a slight nod of his head.

"And at Balmoral Castle with the royal family over one Christmas years ago, when Al Qaeda military forces stormed the Bastille, namely Balmoral Castle, and took the entire family captive down in a cellar they'd turned into a television studio, they then threatened to behead them all on live TV, one at time, until the Queen agreed to read a lengthy Al Qaeda manifesto to the British nation on live television.

"Prior to the scheduled telecast, the Queen was somehow able to secure privacy in a coat closet she'd described as the loo, actually, just long enough to get an urgent call to you on her mobile. Three hours later, you and your comrades aboard a Royal Navy chopper did a rope drop and made a nighttime landing on the castle rooftops, fought your way down to the cellar, and . . . well, the rest is history, isn't it, Commander?"

"I can't recall. Ask Mr. Jones here. He was there, apparently . . ."

"You were subsequently awarded the Victoria Cross by the Queen in a private ceremony at Buckingham Palace in honor of your heroism in saving the lives of nearly the entire royal family."

Hawke leveled his eyes on the CIA man and said:

"Listen here, Pillsbury. Clearly you didn't convince Director Kelly to send me all the way down to Havana so we could play old home week . . . Alex Hawke's greatest hits . . . whatever rubbish you're pushing."

"Of course, not, sir. It's just that I've been waiting for a long time to tell you how much we all respect the incredible things you've done at the Old Firm. For your Queen and Country, of course. You've been an inspiration for a lot of us over the years . . . So, let's head down the hall to the conference room, shall we? My two colleagues are waiting there. They've prepared a thorough presentation on the status quo of Cuban forces and the threat the current government is facing."

"Let's go," Hawke said, heading for the door. When he entered the small conference room, two men got to their feet.

"Special Agent Frank Conroy," the taller of the two said, and Hawke shook his firm hand.

"And I'm Agent Gunn, sir, Donald Gunn. Honor to meet you finally."

"Nice to meet you guys," Hawke said, pulling up a chair. "So," he added, "who is going to tell me what this is all about?"

"We are, sir," Conroy said. "We've prepared a brief slide presentation to help us take you through the situation as of now. Agent Pillsbury, if you could dim the lights?"

The room was flooded with darkness.

An image appeared on the old-fashioned pull-down screen. It was of a middle-aged, bearded man, paunchy and wearing olive-colored battle fatigues. He had a cigar jammed into one side of his mouth. He looked familiar because he was. He was almost a spitting image of Fidel.

"This, gentlemen is none other than the third Castro brother. Just what we needed, right? Fuck. Another one? At any rate, I'd like to say the Castro gene pool has not improved after all these years. But I'd be lying.

"The General here is smarter than Fidel and Raúl combined. He's got a commanding presence, and he's a formidable military commander who engenders fierce loyalty among his troops.

"Our station in Buenos Aires has picked up that, had he not heard the distant clarion call coming from Cuba, he was rumored to be the next chosen one as president of Argentina."

"Is he still down there, Agent Pillsbury?" Stoke asked. "Hanging with the Argies, I mean."

"No, he's here in Cuba, apparently after a few decades spent staying well off the global radar. We honestly have no idea when he got back. But it was a midnight run, done in blackout secrecy. Fortunately, we now do know exactly where he is. Slide, please?"

Hawke found himself looking at an aerial shot of a verdant green island with a spine of stone mountains right down the length of it. There was a massive abandoned edifice built on the rocky side of one of the mountains nearest the sea.

At the bottom, a white sandy beach spread its arms around a sparkling blue bay of considerable size and depth, it appeared.

"This is the walled fortress Castro had built in total secrecy on the Isla de Pinos while still in Argentina. That other building looking over the sea is Presidio Modelo, the former 'model' prison where Fidel spent over fifteen years after his imprisonment. Batista had him arrested following his failed early coup d'état attempt against Batista, who foolishly believed Fidel was no longer a political threat. He had him released in 1955.

"Fortress Freedom is now the People's Liberation Headquarters, where you will now find General Castro, his officers, and his highly trained militia. Seventy percent of the current force is comprised of mercenaries Castro has recruited from the Middle East. We're talking Al Qaeda, Hezbollah, Hamas, ISIS—all the usual suspects. The other thirty percent is mostly Cuban, with some volunteers from Venezuela and other Latin countries sympathetic to the Communists.

"These Cuban volunteers are sympathetic to the name Castro and the Communist Party, while suffering under a hard right-wing regime that does little for the people save for persecuting them. The Cuban president, Mendez, is a puppet of the anti-Communist Americans in Washington—at least that's what the populace believes about the current government. It's all they ever read in *Granma*, the pro-Communist newspaper Cubans trust most, having lived with it since Castro published the first edition back in 1975.

"Castro's highly trained new army of mercenaries, soldiers of fortune, and such is well armed by both Russia and China, along with Castro loyalists from some of Cuba's best families. And some, the inner circle surrounding the general, are former top-ranking officers of the Fuerzas Armadas de la República Argentina, the Argentine army."

"A formidable guerrilla force," Brock said, directing his comment to Alex Hawke. "Fifteen thousand strong. And growing more formidable by the day . . ."

"Sounds like it," Hawke replied. "This new Castro was smart enough to base himself on an island whose name would resonate with the general public. It summons up the glorious past of his late brother for the common man, I should think.

"What's all this about an alleged coup in the offing?" Hawke then said to the CIA man.

"Nothing 'alleged' about it anymore, I'm sorry to say. We believe it's only a matter of time," Pillsbury said. "They've already had three failed assassination attempts on the Cuban president, Señor Mendez. That will likely be the signal event that triggers the new revolution."

Hawke said, "How does General Castro intend to invade Cuba? He and his revolutionary guards are marooned on a bloody island. Fifteen to twenty thousand troops going for a thirty-one-mile swim? Not bloody likely."

"The invasion troops will make the crossing aboard boats. General Castro has acquired and recommissioned four ancient Cuban Navy warships from the mothball fleet. Two cutters, a destroyer, and a torpedo attack craft. Also, he's acquired a vast armada of derelict fishing vessels that do little more than float. Castro has been hiding his flotilla at a secret location called Revolution Bay. Hard to find, but located near the north side of the island. Also, hundreds of sympathetic Cuban citizens with private boats and yachts are offering up their vessels to help the cause. Anyone left who's got a boat that floats is still making the midnight crossings over to the island with their running lights doused. All to serve the Cause. Think Dunkirk goes Caribbean . . ."

"You'll fight them on the beaches? In the streets and on the sea?" Stoke said. "Reason I ask is, we've got some badass mercenaries ourselves. They will arrive on the Isla de Pinos via a high-altitude low-opening parachute drop from the Green Giant, their private Hercules C-130. They will make their landing in the heavy jungle in the island's interior and make their way to Revolution Bay for the coming fight. Good guys to have on your side in a fight, trust me on that."

"Good," Pillsbury said. "And how many?"

"Twenty or thirty. Maybe more now. Call themselves Thunder and Lightning. World's finest HRT, or, as you know, hostage rescue team. The boys got a big HQ deep in the jungle. A two-hundred-year-old abandoned British colonial fort. Call the place 'Fort Whupass.'"

"You guys are on a fancy armor-plated yacht. What do you need mercenary soldiers for?"

Stoke said, "Going in harm's way, man. Our mission is pretty straightforward. We've been ordered to take down the vastly powerful Chinese mafia criminal operations, some obvious, some hidden, all around the world. Drugs, human trafficking, prostitution, gambling, the whole en-chilada. You guys know all about that shit, right? Beijing is going to be extremely pissed at us."

Hawke jumped in. "T and L has been hired to help us deal with any actions or problems with the Chinese military during the rest of our voyage. We aim to cause some serious damage to China's international criminal infrastructure wherever we find it. They won't like it one bit. The Chinese cross us, though? We're ready to kick some serious ass. You remember that secret Chinese sub base the US Navy's Southern Atlantic Fleet destroyed down in the Bahamas about a year ago?"

"Of course. That was a very big deal."

Stoke said, "Yeah, well, you're lookin' at the three damn dealmakers right here. Me, Brock, and the boss. Hell, brother, we three just getting our bad selves warmed up, man, I shit you not."

"This op of yours got a name, Agent Brock?" Hawke said, dreading the answer.

"Sure does. 'Operation Kickass.' Like it? I just made it up. I haven't run it by anybody yet, but—"

"Thank you for that, Agent Bane," Hawke said. "Keep up the good work!"

CHAPTER 24

"It ain't a mistake, boss, it's a trap!"

Havana, Cuba

"Carlos," Hawke said, going around to the driver's side of the big black Chrysler Imperial, "take us back to the marina. And step on it, chico! We've got work to do."

"*Sí, sí, Señor Hawke!* Hop in."

He and Stoke climbed into the dark and cave-like backseat, while Harry once more sat up front beside the wiry little Carlos. Harry kept his eye on the skinny little guy this time. He had a terrible habit of constantly looking at his cell phone while he was driving. Something about the guy was troubling him, and Harry always trusted his instincts in situations like this.

It was as though he was expecting some big, important call. Like his wife telling him to pick up some milk at the grocery store on his way home. Or, more likely, telling him not to come home at all. He stank, after all. And he had bad hair and worse teeth. He wasn't the type of polished, liveried driver one normally associated with Lord Alexander Hawke, Harry thought.

For some reason, maybe because everyone wanted to be alone with their thoughts, or maybe just because they were all talked out, there was heavy silence in the car, everyone just looking out the windows at a Havana that had certainly seen better days, now rebuilding beneath the fierce tropical sun in the baking heat and humidity.

After ten minutes or so, Hawke leaned forward and tapped Carlos on the shoulder.

"Carlos," he said, "where the hell are you going?"

"The marina, señor. Just like you say."

"This isn't the way to the marina. The harbor is in the opposite bloody direction, for God's sake."

"Señor, I apologize. I'm taking a shortcut. I heard on the radio that El Malecón is at a standstill. Some terrible accident. A bomb on a public bus blew up, killing almost everyone aboard. The police are just trying to get the dead and wounded into ambulances to the hospital. They say the site won't be cleared for a few hours, I'm sorry to say."

"Well, good for you for checking on the traffic first, Carlos," Hawke said.

"I am a professional, señor. It's what I do."

"I think you know one of my crew members, Carlos."

"Sorry, sir. What his name is again?"

"Fideo Chico."

"Sorry, señor, that name, you know, it does not ring a bell."

"He's a crewman aboard my boat."

"Oh, yeah, him. I forgot. I do know him, señor. He is a friend of my boss."

"Well, he's the one who recommended you to me. Said you were a friend of his and the best private chauffeur in town."

"Very kind of him. I owe him a favor, I guess."

Hawke, troubled by the exchange, put his head back against the seat cushion and closed his eyes. He was still in somewhat of a state of shock after his son's shark encounter. Hadn't gotten much sleep ever since. He dozed off in less than a minute.

Moments later, he was shaken awake by Stokely, grabbing his shoulder while saying, "Wake up, boss! Something ain't right with this. We're driving up a dead-end street. Hey, Carlos! What the eff, man?"

"He made a mistake, I guess," Hawke said.

"It ain't a mistake, boss, it's a trap. Look up ahead. There's a windowless white delivery van and three damn Jeeps with Glocks and mounted fifty cals in the rear. Lots of full-camo boys with automatic weapons . . . They ain't government troops, either. Wrong uniforms. They're People's Lib guerrillas. General Castro's storm troopers."

Hawke came alive and snapped into focus. Stoke was right. This was not good.

"What the hell, Carlos? What the bloody hell is this all about?"

"Change of plans, all I can tell you, Señor Hawke."

Then the little Cuban turned around with a 9mm pistol aimed at Hawke's head. "Is that some kind of a problem for you, señor?"

Carlos never saw Stoke's blurred left hand until it was too late. No one ever did. Stoke had lightning-fast reflexes. That left of his had all the speed and power of a hooded cobra. Nothing to rival Muhammad Ali, maybe, but still. The Cuban screamed as Stoke grabbed his hand and the pistol in one ironclad grasp and, with a fierce downward motion, noisily broke most of the small bones in the driver's right wrist.

"Weapons, boss?" Stoke said, pulling his gun as he was about to get out of the Imperial.

"No, Stoke. We save them for later. There may come a time when we might really need them."

"Right about that, chief."

Carlos, howling in pain, slowed down and rolled to a stop within spitting distance of the guerrillas. They closed in on the car on all sides, weapons at the ready. One of them leaned into the driver's window and smiled at Carlos whilst handing him a thick sealed envelope.

"*Muchisimas gracias*," he said. "*Qué bueno, eh, Carlito?*"

Carlito was in far too much pain to celebrate his newfound riches. Stoke had him by the wrist and was sending him a strongly worded message.

He squeezed the little man's broken wrist until the little bastard screamed.

Stoke said, "Think this is bad? I'm going to find you, Carlos. You can't hide. First, I'm going to break your other wrist. And then I'm going to pull the few teeth you've got left and beat whatever's left of your face to a bloody pulp. How's that sound?"

Brock got out of the car first. Two PLA goons slapped a pair of cuffs on him, frog-marched him over to the white van, opened the rear doors, and shoved him roughly inside, slamming the doors. The officer in charge strode over to the big black Chrysler.

"Señor Hawke and Señor Jones, I presume?" the rounded officer said. He was barely five feet tall and waddled like a penguin, which was what he most looked like. "Will you please do me the honor of exiting the vehicle? I would deeply appreciate it."

Hawke climbed out, looked the khaki-uniformed man up and down, and said, "Pretty good English."

"Thank you. I went to the University of Miami when my parents moved there in the time of the Marielitos. Ended up joining the Marines and getting a battlefield commission in Iraq. Came back to Cuba when I learned my country needed me. I now work for General Castro. My name is General Nestor de los Reyes. I serve under General Castro as the commanding officer of the People's Liberation Army, señor."

"Congratulations," Hawke said, smiling at him. "I see you brought along a shiny new van. Where are you taking us?"

"To prison, señor."

"Seriously? On what charge, may I ask?"

"I have police powers, Señor Hawke. I'm arresting you on charges of espionage against the people."

"What makes you think we're in Havana for espionage reasons?"

"Oh, I dunno, señor. Call me crazy. Perhaps the fact that all three of you are spies? Yes? Maybe that has influenced my thinking. Not to mention the fact that you met with CIA officials in the Swiss embassy this morning. What were you doing there?"

"Ah, the Swiss. You did say the Swiss embassy, did you not? In that case, I believe we were discussing one of two or three very Swiss topics. The first being the inner workings of the clock. And the second? The finer points of *fromage*. And, finally, Swiss chocolates, of course."

"Of what?" de los Reyes said.

"No French? *Fromage* is French for 'cheese.'"

"Do not try my patience, Señor Hawke. It is most unwise."

"What are you going to do? Shoot us?"

"Perhaps. It all depends. That will be up to General Castro."

"You know what happens to people who murder British and American policemen when they get to prison? First, they are hunted down. Then, in prison, they are castrated. Then bound and raped by anyone who has a taste for that kind of thing. Then killed. Throats sliced open. Disembowelment. The only ones who suffer more are pedophiles. A lot of them commit suicide the first night in their cells. Hanging. Not a pretty picture."

"You are not a policeman, señor. I know what you are. A counterterrorist officer. You work for British Intelligence. Mr. Brock is a CIA agent."

"But what about him?" Hawke said, pointing to Stoke.

"What about him?"

"He's a policeman, can't you tell? A New York City detective. The NYPD has a standing commitment to find and kill anyone anywhere in the world who kills an American cop. And they will go anywhere in the world to bring them to justice. Where are you taking us in your van?"

"To prison, señor. It is the warden there who will determine your fate, according to the wishes of General Castro, of course."

"Well, let's go, then. I've been in prison before. In Russia. I'm sure it's far more unpleasant there than whatever you have in mind."

"We'll see about that, won't we? Tell your comrade to get in the back of the van."

The jarring ride over rough roads in the van was killing all three of them.

"Where are they taking us?" Brock asked.

They were speeding and bouncing down a badly paved Soviet highway, and the shuddering steel flooring of the van was utter hell. The Russians' idea of paving roads was unmatched in crudity only by the endless acres devoted to featureless Soviet-built apartment buildings. These hideous gray atrocities were collapsing everywhere because there was far too much sand in their flawed concept of concrete.

Hawke said, "To prison. We've been arrested for espionage against the Cuban people."

"How much do they know?" Stoke said.

"Everything," Hawke said. "That's the bad news."

"So. What's the good news?" Brock asked.

"There isn't any," Hawke said. "Prison will be a relief after this bloody van ride. I guess that's something."

An hour later, they felt the van slowing to make a right-hand turn onto another road. Ten minutes later, it came to a stop. The doors were unlocked, and General de los Reyes pulled them out one by one, under the watchful eyes of five armed guards.

"All ashore that's going ashore," the general said, smiling at Hawke. Hawke had the strange feeling that, despite the circumstances, the general would have much preferred having a semifamous British lord join him for cocktails and dinner at the Floridita rather than throwing him in prison to rot. It was something Hawke might be able to use to their advantage, at least.

Blinking in the oppressive heat and the blazing sunlight, Hawke surveilled the scene. They were parked on a dirt road leading to the coast. The shoreline itself was hidden behind the thick green mangroves. There was an ancient wooden dock projecting out into the sea.

White gulls were whirling and screeching high above. The salt air tasted good after the dank smell of the van. Not all bad, he thought. But where the hell were they going?

As he watched, a large, aging fishing trawler, maybe fifty feet on the waterline, hove into view. She slowed, approaching the dock, and the skipper expertly brought her stern near, then her bow, where a man was waiting for a mooring line to be heaved to him. Deftly, he caught the heaved line in one hand, then bent and secured it to the cleat. That done, he moved to the bow and repeated his actions.

"A boat?" Hawke said to the general. "You're full of surprises, aren't you?"

"You've no idea, señor. But we'll remedy that, I promise."

The voyage to nowhere was a pleasant enough crossing. The general saw to it that they had food and drink. They were all seated in the trawler's spacious saloon on the worn couches and wicker armchairs. Hawke inhaled and wrinkled his nose. Apparently, all the air in the room had been replaced with tobacco smoke.

A white-jacketed chap from the galley was at their beck and call. The general, opening a fresh bottle of Johnnie Walker Blue from the bar, poured himself a snoot full and then offered the bottle to Hawke. Grateful, Hawke took it and filled his glass, then passed it along to Stoke and Brock.

If this was truly how the Cuban PLA was going to treat its prisoners, he thought, then things could have been a whole lot worse.

They drank in silence until the general, now deep into his second whiskey, got to his feet and began his oratory, a stentorian lecture on Cuban political history. The captive audience instinctively knew it was best to appear to be fascinated by this wondrous tale. And, to their collective surprise, it was actually rather fascinating...

"There is Fidel, of course," he began, "the towering hero of our tiny country. El Jefe outlasted ten US presidents over the course of fifty years. It's all too easy to forget about Raúl Castro, Fidel's little brother who started tagging along behind him when they were kids ... and seemingly never stopped."

He continued.

"Raúl faithfully followed Fidel to the failed assault on the Cuban army's Moncada barracks, into the harsh prison confines of the Presidio Modelo on the Isle of Pines, thence into Mexico, and back into Cuba onboard a leaky yacht called *Granma*. Then it was up into the Sierra Madres and, finally, into Havana itself, and immense power.

"Earlier, in fact on July twenty-sixth, nineteen fifty-three, Cuba exploded into a fiery revolution when Fidel Castro and about one hundred and forty guerrilla rebels attacked the soldiers at the federal garrison at Moncada. Although the operation was well planned and had the element of surprise, the higher numbers and weapons of the army soldiers, coupled with some remarkably bad luck afflicting the attackers, made the assault a near-total failure for the rebels. Many of the rebels were captured and executed, and Fidel and his brother Raúl were put on trial.

"Castro's transfer to a remote cell revived concern among the faithful that he was still an assassination target. At the next session at the courthouse, Raúl rose to announce at the top of his voice, 'I fear for the life of my brother! They have mounted a dangerous conspiracy to assassinate Fidel! Viva Fidel! Viva el Jefe!'"

"What happened then?" Hawke said, just to jack the man up a bit by appearing to be enraptured by his discourse.

"He was ordered to sit down and shut up."

"And?" Hawke said.

"He didn't. On his feet again, he said, 'Hear me, hear my words. If they kill Fidel, they will have to organize a massacre at the prison and do away with all of us!'

"They lost the battle but won the war: The Moncada assault was the first armed action of the Cuban Revolution, which would triumph in nineteen fifty-nine. Batista had had enough. Fidel was arrested, tried, and found guilty of treason and imprisoned for fifteen years right here on the Isla de Pinos."

General Nestor de los Reyes took the temperature of the room and was pleased to see his audience was with him all the way. So, taking another taste of the Johnnie Walker, he continued with his tale.

"Even a few years ago, Raúl continued to be his brother's right-hand man, serving as president of Cuba when Fidel became too sick to continue. He should not be overlooked, as he himself played important roles in all of the stages of his brother's Cuba, and more than one historian believes that Fidel would not be where he is in history today without Raúl."

"Tell us about Che, General," Hawke said. "Perhaps the most charismatic Cuban revolutionary of that era. Certainly the best looking."

"Good question. Che, for many years, although an Argentine doctor, was the popular face of the great Cuban Revolution, and an idealist to boot. A poster of his countenance appeared in college dorm rooms throughout America. He was the handsome face of *Revolución*!

"Exiled in Mexico, Fidel and Raúl began recruiting guerrillas for another attempt at driving Batista from power. It was in Mexico City that they finally met the young Ernesto 'Che' Guevara, who had been itching to strike a blow against imperialism since he had witnessed firsthand the CIA's ouster of President Arbenz in Guatemala.

"Che joined the cause and would eventually become one of the most important players in the revolution. After serving some years in the Cuban government, he went abroad to stir up Communist revolutions in other nations.

"He did not fare as well as he had in Cuba and was executed by Bolivian security forces in nineteen sixty-seven. Women everywhere around the world who'd spent lonely nights fantasizing about having the beautiful warrior Che in their beds were devastated by his death."

The general, having exhausted his repertoire, drew himself up, smiled, and thanked his audience for their kind attention.

Hawke took the opportunity to applaud the man's performance. Harry Brock and Stokely Jones, Jr., both seeing the look on the boss's face, immediately joined in by clapping loudly. A bit too loud for Hawke's taste, but what could he say? The general was blushing a bit.

He loved all the attention, you could tell.

Hawke mused. De los Reyes had that thin strain of vanity within to believe that real men did not like him—while most men simply did not know him.

CHAPTER 25

Cuba

ood history lesson, my dear general," Hawke said, as the general
seemed to have wound down. General de los Reyes went over to the
bar and poured himself another whiskey and then collapsed into
the worn leather armchair opposite Hawke.

"Thank you," he said to Hawke and took a healthy swig. He burped
loudly and wiped the liquor from his lips with the back of his hand.
"Charming" was the word.

"You're quite welcome, General. And, now, since we're en route to our
rendezvous with destiny, would you please tell us where the hell you're
taking us?"

Instead of answering, the man looked at his watch and said, "We'll be
arriving in the next fifteen minutes. You'll see for yourselves. I'm going
up on deck to make sure this boat captain radios the prison and tells them
our ETA. We need transport to your new hotel . . ."

Harry looked at Stoke and mouthed the word, *"Hotel?"*

The Cuban officer had his back to them, pouring himself another
drink. Plunking in a few ice cubes, he said, without turning around, "I
say, Alex, would you like a whiskey as well? I hate to drink alone."

Hawke politely declined, and the general plucked up today's edition
of *Granma*.

Harry leaned over, whispering in Hawke's ear, "You know what I want to know? I'll tell you what I want to know. Why the hell is the general so nice to you, Alex? I mean, sweet Jesus, really?"

"Because, Harry, you have to understand something about people like that. He's a snob."

"Oh. A snob. I get it. It's the good old 'his lordship' syndrome. Here we go again."

"You should bloody well be glad he's a snob, Harry. He'll treat us far more decently than he would otherwise, trust in that. Cuban prisons are notorious, as you know."

Brock's reply was, "Yeah, they sure are. The Cuban refugees that fled to Miami in nineteen eighty, los Marielitos, called these Cuban prisons 'roach motels' back in Miami. You check in, but you don't check out."

Hawke said, "Look. I suggest you find some way to endear yourself to our new general. In an odd way, he is our host, after all. You, too, Stoke. We can't be too nice to him to suit me. Kind of a life-and-death thing, if you follow me."

"Don't you worry none," Stoke said. "We'll do it. If it means our chances of survival in the joint go way up? Hell, we got to do it."

When they disembarked at the crumbling wooden pier, they saw that they had arrived at some kind of paradise: an island covered with thick green jungle and towering pines. Multicolored floral displays abounded, and brilliantly colored tropical birds flitted about hither and thither.

"So far, so good," Brock said under his voice as they made their way over to a 1950s-era yellow American school bus—their transport to the prison, they all supposed.

"Don't get your hopes too high," Hawke said. "It gets worse before it gets better, Harry."

"How the hell do you know that, boss?" he replied.

"I read. You should try it sometime. You never know when something you've read comes in handy. Like where we're headed for the foreseeable future . . ."

"You know where we're going?" Stoke asked.

"Yep," Hawke replied, "I certainly do."

"How is that?" Brock said.

"Because I've always been fascinated by the life of Fidel Castro. I've read nearly every book written about him over the years. All the biographies of him, his own autobiography, his magazine articles, his speeches, you name it."

As the three men climbed up the steps to board the bus, an old Jeep roared out of the road into the jungle, obviously military, with a young guerrilla at the wheel.

Hawke assumed, correctly, that this was the general's driver. Out of the corner of his eye, he caught sight of de los Reyes climbing into the Jeep. The general motioned for Hawke to join him in the rear seat of the Jeep.

Hawke stuck his head inside and called to Stoke and Brock, "The general wants to talk to me. I'll see what he wants and come right back. Sit tight."

The general's Jeep slowed to a stop beside the bus. De los Reyes beckoned to him again, and Hawke walked over to find out what this old duck was up to now.

"General," he said, "how can I help you?"

"I'd like you to ride with me in the Jeep. It's about a half hour's drive. Good time for us to talk some more about this situation."

"Sounds good to me," Hawke said. "Let me just go tell the lads what's happening."

He mounted the steps and saw Harry and Stokely sitting side by side in the middle row of the otherwise empty bus.

"Okay. Listen. You guys go ahead. General wants me to ride with him. He says he needs to talk with me about our situation. So, I'll see you when I see you, all right?"

He turned and descended the steps out into the bright sunlight once more.

"Oh, fuck me," Brock said, clearly upset.

"What, Harry?"

"Seriously? *What?* We have to ride in this piece-of-crap school bus, which as you may have noticed has no freaking air conditioning, while his mighty lordship and his new bestie take a grand private tour of the island?"

"Harry, stop. You know this is the kind of childish behavior that gets you in trouble with him. You sound like a jealous teenage girl right now. It doesn't play in his league. Now, just sit back and enjoy the ride."

"Enjoy the ride? To prison? In this effing school bus?"

"Shut it," Stoke said and moved to the other side of the bus, turning his face to the window.

———————

Hawke climbed up into the rear of the Jeep and sat down on the bench seat right behind the driver.

"Ready to roll?" de Los Reyes said over his shoulder.

"Ready when you are, General," Hawke said genially. "I assume we're headed to the Presidio Modelo prison. Looking forward to it. Quite the architecture. I haven't been there in years . . ."

"You were in prison here before?" he said, incredulous.

"Oh, no, no. I was here with my former wife. We were just a couple of *turistas*. I'd been fascinated with Fidel for years, as I may have mentioned. I knew he spent fifteen years there, and I wanted to see what all the fuss was about. I'm sure his excellency, General Castro, has done a major re-hab of the building since then."

"Well, let's just say El Jefe left it a little better than it was."

Hawke said to the general, "I wonder about something, General. Is that Cuban Naval Base here on the island still in use?"

"Of course. Bigger and busier than ever. Why?"

"I became quite friendly with the base commander on my visit years ago. Handsome chap whose name is Admiral Mario Mendoza. Is the base on the way to the Presidio? Don't want you to go out of your way. But if it's up and running, I'd like to inquire into his health and whereabouts. If he's still alive and still in Cuba, I'd like to pay him a visit . . . after I break out of prison, of course."

The general smiled. "Well, I suppose we can do that. Why not? We're not in any hurry, are we?"

"I'm certainly not."

They drove in silence another ten minutes, and Hawke could see the entrance to the base off to the right. It was bustling. He suddenly wished he'd brought a camera, the little Minox his father had left him. Back in the day, the Minox had been *the* spy camera. He looked out over the water. Brick Kelly at Langley would love to see this place. There were Cuban warships aplenty, and Cuban submarines as well. But there were other vessels he also recognized.

A Russian Omsk nuclear submarine was berthed next to a Chinese missile cruiser just like the ones he and Stokely had encountered at the secret Chinese Naval submarine pen in the Bahamas.

There was also a powerful offensive presence of the Chinese Navy here at the Cuban base, which was huge—a couple of conventionally powered aircraft carriers, two or three diesel-electric attack subs, and numerous destroyer warships. And the Russian Navy? Ah, Comrade Putin had made sure that he, too, was equally well represented.

"Looks like the Russians and Chinese are putting on a show of force, General," Hawke said. "Under the guise of 'war games.'"

"As a matter of fact, your lordship, since we've announced the worldwide formation of a grand socialist alliance, our Communist and socialist brethren have announced their intention to send naval vessels to join in the war games."

"Really?" Hawke said. "Without spilling too much for your own sake, which countries have stepped up to the plate?"

"Well," the general said, sitting up straight and getting himself all puffed up. "I can tell you that Iran, North Korea, and Venezuela have all signed commitments with General Castro!"

"Impressive!" Hawke was determined to push all the general's buttons at once. "Don't be surprised if you find yourself promoted to a much higher position."

"Really?" De los Reyes beamed, desperate to hear more flattery from the English lord.

As soon as he got off this bloody island, Hawke knew he'd report all this vital intel to CIA and MI6. America and her allies needed eyes in the skies of all this . . . this . . . no other words for it . . . this run-up to World War III.

He turned to speak to the general as the Jeep pulled up to the heavily guarded gates, saying, "You know what, General? I feel like I should be helping my two colleagues get adjusted to prison life. If you'll just pull over, I'll pop into the guard station. I can find out all I need to know from one of them. Is that quite all right?"

"Of course it is. Do what you need to do."

Hawke got out of the Jeep and crossed the road, entering the guard's station. He went to the senior officer and asked him about the CO's whereabouts and his health, explaining that the admiral was an old friend of his. He was not surprised when the man said he had no idea about that and could not be of help. It was fine.

He used all this trivial conversation to cover his move to stand at the windows overlooking the naval station and his quite obvious interest in all the foreign naval ships here assembled in what very closely resembled preparations for all-out warfare in the South Atlantic.

He turned back toward the waiting Jeep. He'd seen all he'd needed to see already.

"Anything else we can help you with, señor?"

"That's fine. No bother. I just thought I'd check up on the old boy. Please give him my regards should you happen to run into him."

He climbed back up into the Jeep.

"Any luck?" de los Reyes said.

"Not a scintilla of the stuff. Doesn't matter. He's probably long dead by now. Rather silly of me, I think."

"Not at all. It tells me that you are a caring friend."

Hawke waved that off and said, "What kind of shape is the Modelo in these days? I recall reading somewhere about a bombing or an explosion."

"You won't even recognize it. I'm sorry your return visit is under such circumstances. But I'm sure you appreciate General Castro's need to find out what you and the CIA are up to this time. This is a delicate period for us. We are trying to maximize our power and force strength. We're a bit behind his schedule. He is anxious to make his move."

"A coup, one imagines," Hawke said, nonchalant about it.

"Is that the reason you're here? You oppose our position?"

"Hardly, my dear general. As the American gangsters used to say in the film noir movies, 'Britain ain't got no beef with Cuba.' It's the Yanks who've had a beef with Cuba for fifty years, not the Brits. We have bigger fish to fry."

"Russia?"

Hawke said, "No, not really. Are they potentially an existential threat to Western democracy? Sure. But the real threat, the showdown in the making? For us and the Yanks, that's China, now and perhaps for the balance of this century. They make no secret of the fact that they'd like to unseat us as the world's biggest superpower. And they're actively trying, through intellectual property theft, hacking, sending students from China to American universities to steal weapons testing, and on and on—the list is endless. Which brings me to this question, General: What's the deal with all the Chinese and Russian security forces one sees on the streets of Havana?"

"Oh, nothing, really. General Castro is a master politician. He sees that any kind of a meeting here with Cuba and the two most powerful Communist governments on earth will send a strong signal to our enemies: 'Beware of the New Cuba.'"

"I don't need any signals at this juncture. I've learned to beware of the New Cuba this very morning, when my colleagues and I were seized at gunpoint."

"Ah, well, things happen. I will do my best to ensure that you and your two colleagues are as comfortable as you can be under the circumstances, Alex."

"I appreciate that, sir. And since we're talking about comfort? I'd like to put in a room request."

"You mean a cell request. That's what we have here. It's not a hotel."

"Of course. A cell request, then."

"I've never heard of such a thing. But go ahead. I can't wait to hear this. I'm listening."

"Cellblock D, cell fifteen."

De los Reyes stared at him in disbelief.

"Fidel's cell? How on earth do you know that? Only our schoolchildren know that!"

"Simple. I read an accounting of his years in this prison in his autobiography. I know he was made as comfortable as he could be under Batista's orders. He didn't want to make a permanent enemy of Fidel. He had other ideas for him when he got out of prison."

"Ah, I see."

"So? As I said, can you please arrange for the three of us to be in D block? Cell fifteen, to be precise?"

"Of course! It's the only cell large enough to accommodate three prisoners comfortably. If not me, then who? If not for you, then for who?"

"You have my eternal gratitude, my dear general. I wonder. Do you ever do any pheasant shooting? I usually have a splendid shoot every fall at my country estate outside of London. Lots of chaps you might enjoy meeting. The King of Spain; various Hollywood celebrities; royals, of course, from all over Europe; and, always, Harald, the King of Norway. American senators and congressmen . . . you know the drill."

"Yes, yes, of course, Alex," General de los Reyes said. "I've been to many shoots all over Europe and Latin America . . ."

"Of course you have, my dear general," Hawke said, smiling at the man. "You clearly are quite the man of the world. Well. For many years, Prince William and Prince Harry would attend. But no more, sadly. Prince William is busy with his family now—the sad loss of Prince Philip—and preparing to ascend to the throne. And, too, Prince Harry, who, for some ungodly reason, has decided to move to Los Angeles. Many wonder if this new woman in his life has not put some kind of evil hex upon him."

The general wheeled around and looked at Hawke.

"Are you serious? Harry and Wills would come to the shoot?"

"Of course I'm serious. Dead serious! I don't scatter these invitations around willy-nilly, my good man. You of all people should know that."

"When is it?"

"Last weekend in October. Shall I put you down as a possible attendee? Pencil you in?"

The general smiled a smile that became a grin.

"I think so, Alex. That is unless, of course, you'd rather face a firing squad at the end of your stay with us . . ."

Hawke was on the verge of laughing when he realized the man might well not be joking. Just when you think you've got someone all figured out? Here he thought de los Reyes was a kindly old soul just trying to survive the political and military chaos that was about to envelop him, that El General just wanted to retire, take his military pension and his savings, and return to Miami. Buy a little casita in Coral Gables. Be with his parents, his wife, Paulina, and his two *preciosas* daughters.

But a voice in Hawke's head told him to rethink that hasty take on the general's true motives.

Kaboom!

You really never know what someone, anyone, is truly capable of. Seriously.

CHAPTER 26

*"The prison looked like something Flash Gordon and Batman might
have discovered on the backside of Mars."*

Isla de Pinos, Cuba

Hawke had forgotten what a massive piece of strangely futuristic pan-
opticon architecture was the Presidio Modelo. It looked like something Flash Gordon and Batman might well have encountered on the
dark side of Mars. It was mammoth; gargantuan; five huge circular domes
with six stories of multiple cellblocks, all overlooking an open dirt courtyard with a skylight of glass for illumination during the daylight hours.

In the middle of the five courtyards were lighthouse-like structures
where all the prison guards were housed and on duty. And the genius
behind building a watchtower in the middle of a giant circle of cellblocks
was that the guards, with 360-degree fields of vision, could watch the
actions of all the prisoners at once without their ever knowing just how
closely they were being watched.

The prison had been built under then-president-turned-dictator Ge-
rardo Machado in the 1920s. The five circular blocks, with cells constructed in tiers around central observation posts, were built with the
capacity to house up to 2,500 prisoners in humane conditions.

Most of the survivors of the rebel attacks on Batista's soldiers were
housed at the Moncada Barracks during one failed attack when the revolutionary leader, Fidel Castro, and his brother, Raúl Castro, were imprisoned by Batista there in the early 1950s.

When Fidel and Raúl Castro were imprisoned at Presidio Modelo, the five circular structures were packed with six thousand men, every floor was filled with trash, the rats were as large as small dogs, there was no running water, food rations were meager, and the government supplied only the bare necessities of life.

After Fidel Castro's revolutionary triumph in 1959, Presidio Modelo remained in operation. By 1961, due to the overcrowded conditions (up to four thousand prisoners at one time), it was the site of various riots and hunger strikes, especially just before the Bay of Pigs invasion, when orders were given to line the tunnels underneath the entire prison with several tons of TNT.

"Well," de los Reyes said, flashing his credentials at one of the guards, "here we are. I hope you don't mind if I don't accompany you. I've got to get back to the mainland, as I have a meeting with General Castro in half an hour. But don't fret, I've already called the warden and informed him about your situation and need for a larger cell to accommodate three men. He said it will be no problem, as the cell is currently empty."

"Well, thanks for the lift and all your hospitality. I assume we'll see each other again, General?"

The general climbed out of the car and into the rear of a shiny black 1955 Cadillac Coupe deVille. Then, just before the vehicle roared away, he stuck his head out the window and said, "Do you mind putting that Jeep of mine back in the parking lot by Revolution Bay? Take that sandy road through the jungle over there to the right. Can't miss it!"

"No problema, señor!" Hawke said, smiling at this fresh break he'd caught, hardly able to grasp his good fortune. He said to the general, "We should communicate about it. I can teach you how to be a proper upland game man . . . make sure you've got all the right kit and artillery."

"Of course, of course! I'm forever in your debt. And I definitely want to hear more about this shoot in England. What kind of firearms do we use?"

"Shotguns, General. Usually double-barreled, twenty gauge. Purdey or Boss are the preferred guns. Also, for the cognoscenti, Holland & Holland. That's the proper weapon. A twelve gauge will tear a bird to pieces. With anything less, say, a .410 gauge, it's too hard to hit them on the fly! So, a twenty gauge is definitely the way to go."

The general smiled, the chauffeur engaged first gear, and away they roared in a cloud of dust, speeding through the very lovely old El Vedado residential neighborhood of Havana. The architecture, though quite aged, was still lovely. And the huge trees and flowery gardens gave it a sense of tranquility not on display in many other parts of *La Habana*.

Everywhere Hawke looked there were small groups of Russian and Chinese security milling about the streets and plazas of the prison complex. What the hell? This must be where they were barracked prior to the upcoming trilateral "conference." Conference, indeed! Or was it a global change in the world order established at the end of World War II?

The latter.

Putin and Medvedev would be here, of course, and the Chinese foreign minister, who, according to intel intercepted in Beijing, apparently had his own personal problems. Pillsbury's intel had indicated that it seemed he was bringing his new Chinese "girlfriend" to Cuba, both of them guests aboard Putin's big red yacht, *TSAR*. She was a woman of Hawke's acquaintance who went by the name of Zhang Tang. Zhang was the beautiful sister of the Tang Brothers. And every bit as dangerous as her siblings.

Mother of God! Hawke had thought when he heard the news. Zhang Tang? *Here?* Now, that would be interesting . . . At the conclusion of their torrid affair in the Bahamas, he'd concluded she was probably a sociopath and a homicidal maniac. And she'd probably try to kill him for choosing the late China Moon over her during those salad days down at the Dragonfire Club in the Bahamas.

The *TSAR* was dwarfed by *Sea Hawke*, and the comparisons drawn between the two yachts would be odious to Putin. It would irritate him to no end, what with his pride and all that masculine "Mine's bigger" nonsense!

Conference, my big toe, Hawke was thinking as he climbed behind the wheel of the dusty Jeep. How damn lucky am I going to get today? he was also thinking.

A man spoke to him; he must have been a warden, as he was dressed in civvies. "May I help you? Are you the one who was with General de los Reyes in his Jeep?" he asked in heavily accented English.

"Indeed," Hawke said. "He just dropped me off."

"Your friends are in D block, cell fifteen. Is that what he told you?"

"Yes."

"Right this way. Please follow me."

"Sorry—first I'm doing a favor for General de los Reyes. He asked me to put his Jeep back in the parking lot where he normally stows it."

"No worry. I'll see you when you get back. We're not going anywhere . . . nor are you."

He turned his back, and Hawke headed for the jungle pathway.

Hawke found an empty parking spot facing the bay, turned the ignition off, and decided to leave the key where it was, in the Jeep's ignition switch.

The general probably did that anyway. He had a very casual way of dealing with life. Not that Hawke was unhappy about that. He was astounded by the sheer number of vessels riding at anchor in the half moon–shaped bay.

Revolution Bay was chockablock with boats, small and large, of every description, just as the CIA boys had told them. He quickly surveyed them all at a distance, looking for the one that promised to be fastest of all. There was a brand-new Chris-Craft cabin cruiser. As luck would have it, Stokely had recently purchased an identical one to keep in his boathouse on Key Biscayne. A few months earlier, he had taken Hawke out for a cruise on Biscayne Bay. He said the new Chris-Craft was bitchin' fast. That the new ones were powered by the biggest diesel engines available, or, at the very least, the biggest ones the designer could cram into the confines of the engine room.

The boat, called *Bandito*, was moored at the end of a long concrete pier. And as luck would have it, it was right next to the fuel pump.

He walked out to the boat, trying not to appear furtive in any way, but determined to instead look as innocent as he possibly could. He looked around to see if anyone was watching him. There didn't seem to be any security guarding these precious vessels, but he knew Castro would not take kindly to someone who tried to steal one.

He jumped down into the cockpit, praying the key was in the ignition.

It wasn't.

He searched about, looking everywhere a man might instinctively hide his key. That's when he remembered Stoke reaching up into a cabinet directly above the helm housing the VHF radio. He reached up and felt around with his fingers.

He had the key.

He switched the power on and checked all the gauges. Fuel, battery power, all of them looked good. He went aft to the stern and scanned the perimeter of the harborage for signs of security, someone watching. Still nothing. What the hell?

He turned on the batteries and cranked the engine. It instantly roared to life.

"All right, all right, all right!" he said to himself. There was, he knew, a storage locker aft in the transom. That's where the mooring lines were stowed. And the center storage space was where Chris-Craft had stowed tool kits designed especially for the cabin cruiser's new owners. He pulled out a small flashlight, a mallet, a flathead screwdriver, a chisel, a ball-peen hammer, and a heavy claw hammer. He managed to conceal all of this gear in the inside of the deep pockets of his bright orange foul-weather jacket. He also found a flour sack full of Romeo y Julieta Cuban cigars. They could come in very handy should he find himself with the need to bribe one of the guards.

Things were definitely looking up.

He returned the precious key, which, after all, was now literally a matter of life and death for all three of them, to its hidey-hole. Then, much optimistic about this turn of events, he started back up the road to the prison. He was whistling "Yo, ho, ho, and a bottle of rum" as he walked in near darkness. The skies were pink and gold now, the sun was almost all the way down, and it was getting a bit harder to see the uneven ground beneath his feet. There was no ambient light out here; no stars, no moon.

His luck was holding. He was holding his breath now, as the warden made a beeline for him. If the man searched him, or had one of the guards do it, he would find the tools stowed in his foul weather jacket. And that would be the end of any plans he might have of escape. The three of them might well rot in here for a very long time.

To his very great relief, not one of the slovenly guards standing watch over him, with their machine guns very much in evidence, had the notion to search him. They were too busy taking swigs from a flask of rum and laughing at some joke or other.

He was going to make it out of here alive, even if it killed him.

Warden Mendez introduced himself to Hawke. His eyes were on the flour sack in Hawke's left hand. "And what's in the sack, señor?" he asked.

"Ah, just my cigars," Hawke said. "I carry them around in this when I'm traveling. Say, would you like one, Warden?"

"Depends. What is the brand? Are they Cuban?"

"Romeo y Julieta, Warden."

"In that case," the man said, "I'll take all of them for safekeeping until you are released."

He then took his new prisoner up five flights of worn stone steps leading to cellblock D. The place suddenly reminded him of all those Hyatt hotels that had popped up like so many mushrooms all over America, back in the day—the hotels where the guest rooms encircle a central atrium six or seven stories high and are created to look like a jungle somewhere. Weird, but it was all the rage back then.

But, the famous Prison Modelo? It might have looked like a Hyatt, but it felt like a bloody nightmare waiting to happen.

Hawke could barely imagine the suffering that had gone on inside this place. Starvation, torture, solitary confinement, execution . . . *"Ah, the good old days,"* General Castro would say . . .

When the warden unlocked cell 15 and motioned him inside, he found Stoke and Harry Brock sitting cross-legged on the floor playing cards by candlelight. No electricity? Hawke wondered. That could definitely work in his favor.

"Is there anything I can get for you, Commander Hawke?"

"I think not, Warden. I'm sure I'll be very comfortable here."

"Very well, Commander Hawke. As much as I am allowed, I wish you three gentlemen a most pleasant evening. I'll inform General de los Reyes that you are all here and that all is well."

"Thank you, Warden," Hawke said.

The guys looked up and smiled. Harry Brock said, "Did I hear him right? He wishes us a most pleasant evening? What the eff?"

Hawke laughed. "What are you playing?" he asked them. "Go Fish?"

"Gin rummy," Brock said. "Pull up a chair and sit down."

"There are no chairs, Mr. Brock. Or hadn't you noticed?"

"They're imaginary," Brock said, deadpan. Hawke sighed. The old Harry was back.

"Boss, heads up. It's more like *bang, bang, shoot* than Go Fish," Stoke said. "Agent Brock makes up the rules as he goes along."

"Where am I sleeping?" Hawke said.

"Anywhere you want to. You're the boss," Stoke said.

"You just missed the banquet, boss," Harry Brock said.

"Oh, I did. What did I miss?"

Brock said, "Lemme think. Yeah, roast prime rib, scalloped potatoes, Caesar salad, and . . . oh, yeah, peach cobbler for dessert."

"Let me translate that for you, boss," Stoke said. "Mystery meat, with a side of mystery veggies, and Jell-O."

"Well, I'm going to grab an hour or so of shut-eye. You lads should, as well. We've got a long night ahead of us, and I want everybody rested and alert. Please wake me at nine o'clock. We've got some work to do tonight, boys."

Hawke went to the bunk bed on the opposite side of the cell from where the two card sharps were hard at it, arguing over whether or not aces were high. He climbed up to the top bunk and pulled the thin excuse for a blanket over him. By the time his head hit the concrete pillow, he was snoring.

———————

"Wake up, boss." Someone was shaking him. He opened his eyes.

"Whassup, man?" Hawke said, cracking an eye, deliberately imitating Stoke's street talk.

"You, I hope. Nine o'clock. You said we had work to do tonight. What kinda work we going to do in here? Besides trying to beat Brock at cards, I mean. That's real work."

Hawke smiled at him. "Oh, I don't know, Stoke. A jailbreak, maybe."

"Jailbreak, huh? I hear you, brotha man. How the hell we gonna do that? I mean, what about the guards?"

"What about them?" Hawke said.

"I'll tell you what. They go cruising by here every half hour, that's what."

"Right. Regular as clockwork," Hawke said. "If those clowns are what passes for guards in this joint, we're good to go."

"Okay, I can dig that," Stoke said. "So now what?"

"I'm going to show you. Let me get down from this window. Oh, and hand me that ball-peen hammer, will you, please?"

Hawke started tap, tap, tapping with the hammer on the rear wall of the cell. There was a window above him, open to the elements, with six iron bars. It looked out over swampy marshland and thick green jungle, which helped to orient him as to his location. He wondered how many men had stood up on a stool and looked at this same view, puzzling over how the hell to escape this fortress of pain.

Tap, tap, tapping on the stone with the ball-peen hammer, Hawke was waiting to hear that hollow sound that would mean he was in the right place. But he came up empty.

"Want some help?" Stoke said.

"Yeah. The sooner we can find it, the better."

"Find what?"

"You'll see, Stoke. You'll see. Here, take this claw hammer and start tapping lightly. You're looking for a deep, hollow sound. If you hear one, let me know. Give Harry this mallet and tell him to do the same."

Twenty minutes later, Stoke said, "Got a live one over here, boss."

Hawke was all over him.

"Let me hear it."

"You got it," Stoke said, and tapped the plastered wall three times with the hammer. "Bingo?"

"Bingo," Hawke said.

Hollow as a bone.

Hawke's smile was a mile wide.

"That's it, Stoke. You found it. Our doorway to the Secret Garden."

"Our doorway to what, exactly?"

"Our ticket to the great outdoors," Hawke said, pulling a chisel out of his jacket and handing it to Brock. "We need to open up a hole in this wall big enough for us to squeeze through. So we start to work now. And the sooner we're out of here, well . . . we don't want to be banging away in here when the sun comes up . . ."

As it happened, with all three of them working feverishly, they managed to create an opening large enough for each of them to crawl through in less than an hour. This was too easy, Hawke thought. Unless someone, say Fidel and Raúl, had long ago plastered it over to avoid detection while they plotted their escape.

"Bring those candles, Stoke," he said. "We might need them. I've no idea how old these torch batteries are. Oh, and do you have matches?"

"No. But Harry has a lighter. That Zippo he stole from you down in the Bahamas?"

"What?" Hawke glared at Brock.

"I didn't steal it, Stoke, f'crissakes. I found it," Brock said. "In the front seat of Zhang's Bentley at Dragonfire. How was I to know who it belonged to?"

"Keep it, Harry," Hawke said. "Maybe it will be a good-luck token for you. All right. I'll go out first to make sure the coast is clear, then Mr. Brock, then you, Stoke."

Hawke clawed, wriggled, and wiggled his way through the handmade escape hatch with the powerful torch in one hand. What he saw next thrilled him beyond measure.

He'd been right. There was a tunnel!

It had a dirt floor and was wide enough and high enough that a man could easily stand up inside it. He turned around and called to his men.

"Mr. Brock, your turn, come on through," Hawke said. "Then you're up, Stoke."

"A tunnel," Stoke said, lowering himself down to the damp red dirt below. "How the hell did you know about this?"

"Yeah," Brock said with a smile, adding, "unless Superman here's got X-ray vision!"

"Plenty of time to explain it later," Hawke said. "Let's move out!"

"Which way, boss?" Stoke said.

"Remember the window on the rear wall? It looks out onto marsh and jungle. So we go this way," Hawke said as he spun around and lit up the tunnel with the other torch he'd found on *Bandito.*

"Where are we going, anyway?" Brock said. "It's a long effing way back to the sea, especially in broad daylight."

"Follow me, Mr. Brock, and ye shall be free, for I am the light and the way," Hawke said, smiling, not because it was so clever but because he always enjoyed giving the cynical, sarcastic Agent Brock a taste of his own medicine.

Ten minutes later the three escapees were outside the prison walls and pounding dirt and each other on the back. They were now as free as three birds. Since the power was out in the prison, the entire structure was dark and foreboding . . .

"All right," Hawke said, "let's get as far away from this place as fast as we can. It's not bloody likely, but you never know whether some guard, bored stiff, might decide to come up and check on us. But we'll be long gone, buddy . . ."

"What's the plan, boss?" Stoke said.

"Just on the other side of this swatch of jungle is a sandy lane. From there, it's about fifteen minutes to our destination. That's where we'll find our new boat."

"New boat?" Brock said. "What new boat? I didn't know we had an old boat . . ."

"All will be revealed, Harry, all will be revealed," Hawke said, laying it on a bit thick.

Sometimes, he just couldn't help himself. Brock brought out the worst in him—always had.

"Free at last," Hawke said to himself, coming through the thicket of trees and seeing the beautiful silver moonlight on Revolution Bay.

CHAPTER 27

"Time to get out of Dodge, boys!"

Isla de Pinos, Cuba

Hawke ran through the jungle, ran like hell through the jungle, sweating buckets in the oppressive tropical heat and humidity, pounding up the twisting sandy road, and the others followed, barely keeping up with him. When they all three emerged out into the open from the thick green tangle lining both sides of the narrow lane, they stopped dead in their tracks. All now saw the bay full of countless boats of every size and description. Lights suddenly went off in their heads as it dawned on Brock and Stoke just how cleverly Alex had plotted out the details of their miraculous escape from the Presidio Modelo.

Hawke said, "Our new boat's moored at the end of that main pier out there. Brand-new Chris-Craft. She's got plenty of petrol and fully charged batteries, and when she gets up a head of steam, none of these other boats can catch her, right, Stoke? We've got about four hours till sunrise, so let's get moving, shall we?"

"You something else, boss," Stoke said, smiling at him with unbridled admiration. "Something else entirely is what you are!"

When they reached the end of the pier, Stoke said, "Damn, that looks just like my boat! *Bandito*, huh? Some name. I like mine better."

"What's the name of yours?" Harry Brock asked Stoke.

"Mine? You kidding me, right, man?"

"No, I'm curious."

"Well, I'm a lotta things, but stupid ain't one of 'em. So what you think I call it, huh? I call her *Fancha*, man. Wasn't no other choice, you want Mama to be happy. 'Cause, least down South, Mama ain't happy, ain't nobody happy."

Hawke smiled at him, then leapt down into *Bandito*'s aft cockpit. He went to the helm and powered up the batteries, then made sure the fuel pump was working, the tanks full of petrol, and the batteries fully charged.

"Let's get out of Dodge, boys!" Hawke said, almost gleefully. "Stoke, free the bow line. Mr. Brock, you get the stern line, then jump aboard." Hawke turned the ignition key, firing up the big diesel in all its thunder. He was secretly dreading what might happen, in the age-old tradition of spy novels and spy movies—which would be the abiding cliché of an engine refusing to turn over no matter how many times the hero or heroine cranked it in sheer desperation to escape some villain or murderous zombie who wanted them dead.

But this was no spy movie. *Not yet, anyway,* he said to himself with a secret smile.

"Boat is free, lines away!" Brock said from behind him as he leapt down into the cockpit with the coiled stern line in his left hand and shoved them away from the pier with his right.

"Hold on to something, both of you. This thing gets up and goes, doesn't she, Stoke?"

"Hell, yeah, boss. She comes out of the hole and gets up on plane before you can say diddly-squat!"

Hawke shoved the twin chromium throttles forward, firewalling them. It was a good thing he'd told his crew to hold on to something . . . because . . . that's when the big Chris-Craft howled and leapt up out of the water, surged ahead, and was almost instantly up on plane.

One of the earliest lessons he'd learned boating with his father had remained with him. "Always remember, Alex," his father had said to him the day before he was murdered by drug pirates aboard his magnificent schooner in the Caribbean. "One hand for the boat, one hand for yourself." It had long stood him in good stead.

Half an hour later, the Isla de Pinos was but a distant memory. And the only excitement *Bandito* encountered? White dolphins had come to join them. A school of nine or ten was patrolling on the starboard side, right next to the hull, while another group streamed along in their wake, thirty yards or so behind the aft, looking, for all the world, Hawke said, like the motorized escort of a head of state or an international film star on an official state visit.

"Harry, go below and see if you can find any bottled water in the galley. Stoke, take the helm. I'm going below to see if I can raise *Sea Hawke*. Get Ambrose on the radio and tell him the jailbirds have some good news and to be on the lookout for a cabin cruiser called *Bandito* to sail into Havana Harbor in a couple of hours or so."

With good fortune and good seamanship, they managed the crossing to mainland Cuba in a little under two hours. Hawke throttled back *Bandito*, slowed her down to about four knots, the posted speed limit in Havana Harbor. He could spot *Sea Hawke* easily in the crowded harbor. Hers was the tallest spar there. Right next to her, another familiar yacht had appeared. The bright red presidential yacht, *TSAR*, belonging to none other than his old friend and current enemy, Vladimir Putin. Well, well, well, he thought. This gets more interesting every day. What in God's name was Putin doing in Havana? Oh, yes, he corrected himself, he's here for the alleged conference.

"You guys in Miami are onto something down here, Harry," Hawke said. "Any idea what?"

"Not yet. But we're on it."

"It's not good, that much I can assure you."

"You got that right, boss. These three bad actors? Definitely up to no good. And I'll tell you one other thing. General Castro? His paw prints are all over this deal."

"Meaning the coup draws nigh?" Hawke said.

"They're all here, aren't they?" Brock said. "Putin, Xi, Little Rocket Man? All right here in Havana. The only one who's not at the party yet is the new commandante of Cuba . . . El Jefe himself."

Hawke nodded his agreement and slowed the boat to idle speed as he approached his big, beautiful, jet-black sailing yacht.

Chief Inspector Congreve, wearing a rather ratty white linen suit and

Ray-Ban aviators, watched their approach to the *Sea Hawke*. He was leaning casually against the mainmast and thoughtfully smoking his pipe.

Hawke, waving at him, called out, "Ahoy, there!" and eased the cabin cruiser portside along the yacht's starboard side, where the crew had hung a mahogany boarding ladder.

"Morning, Ambrose," Hawke called up to him. "Lovely day for it, what?"

"You're early."

"Well, I ran this stinkpot flat out the whole way across. Didn't want to have you standing out in this weather and having a heatstroke."

"Across from where?" Congreve said.

"From the Isla de Pinos."

"What were you doing there?"

"Well, it's a long story, old thing. Tell you all about it over a nice lunch up on deck."

Stoke said, "Boss, what're we going to do with this damn boat now?"

"I saw a few mooring buoys still vacant in this neck of the harbor. We may have need of the Chris-Craft again. I'm going aboard to find my son. If you and Mr. Brock would be so kind as to find a convenient mooring, we'll send the launch over to pick you up."

"You got it, Skipper," Stoke said, watching Hawke ascend the ladder as he spun the helm and steamed away.

"Luncheon is served, m'lord," Pelham said, seeming to appear out of thin air.

"Ah! Nick of time, old thing!" Hawke said. "We haven't had a proper meal in forty-eight hours!"

"You won't be disappointed, sir. Chef Auguste has prepared a feast fit for a king," Pelham said before he dematerialized.

The feast was served at a large round table on the afterdeck, beneath the vast dark green awning that was attached to *Sea Hawke*'s huge wooden boom and provided shade for those dining under the sun. It truly was a feast for sore eyes and empty stomachs, Hawke saw. Roast beef, roast chicken, and a smoked ham, for starters. Mounds of potato salad, Caesar salad, deviled eggs—the works.

"So, Alex," Ambrose said, "I'm simply dying to learn how, in a matter of hours, you managed to escape from this Cuban hoosegow fortress that the rebels threw you three into?"

Stoke said, "Tell me about it, Ambrose. Agent Brock and I were actually there, and even *we* don't know how the heck he did it!"

Hawke, serving himself a portion of roast beef, said, "Ah, therein lies the tale, doesn't it, Constable? Quite simple, actually, with bags of good luck thrown in for good measure. I've always been interested in Cuba. And Fidel, for that matter. Not at all sure of the genesis of that interest, but there you have it. Read his autobiography once and found it sufficiently interesting to visit Cuba when Alexei's mother and I were vacationing at Key West years ago.

"In his autobiography, El Jefe goes on at some length about his stay at the Presidio Modelo. As you know, I'm somewhat of a student of architecture, and whilst in Havana, we hired a car and driver to take us down to the southwestern coast, where a boat was waiting to ferry us across to the Isla de Pinos. We went to the prison for a private tour and were not disappointed. The prison is a miracle of architecture. Unlike anything anywhere else in the world."

"In what way, Alex?" Congreve asked.

"It was built in the nineteen twenties, but it resembles some kind of bizarre Flash Gordon vision of a future on Mars. Quite remarkable. I asked the guide if we'd be able to see the cell where the Castro had been imprisoned, and he was delighted to learn of our interest in his hero.

"Castro apparently feared for his life during the imprisonment. He wrote a letter to the court in which he described how he had been kept incommunicado for fifty-seven days, without being allowed to see the sun, talk with anyone, or see his family. He said he had learned with certainty that 'my physical elimination, under pretext of an escape attempt or through poisoning, is being planned.'

"The cell we had was just as he'd described it in his bio. Including the fact that Fidel, desperate now for a means of escaping a death sentence, had managed to open a hole through one of the stone walls. A hole that opened into one of the miles of tunnels that existed beneath the vast prison complex. The tunnel was also used as a way to keep Castro comfortable during his stay."

"What do you mean?" Stoke said.

"Ah, yes. Well, where to start? Women, of course. A fresh supply every week. Fat, skinny, young and old, white or black. The commandante apparently had eclectic tastes when it came to bedding the female of the species. And cigars, as he didn't trust the prison variety. And good Cuban rum. Books, books, and more books. A shortwave radio so he could keep track of world news developments. Monthly reports on what was going on in Havana, Batista's latest political maneuvers. And so on and so forth.

"That's why I requested that specific cell, obviously. I knew it was the only one with a backdoor escape hatch! And only because General de los Reyes asked me to park his Jeep at Revolution Bay did I discover the hundreds of boats kept there to ferry the rebel troops over to the main land when the invasion commences, and thus I found a way for us to get across to Havana. That's it. Rather mundane, perhaps, but good enough, wouldn't you say, Stoke?"

"More ingenious than *The Great Escape* its own self, boss, I'm telling you!" Stoke said. "That Steve McQueen? Hell. He got nothin' on you, brotha, nothin' at all!"

Agent Brock, much to Hawke's surprise, suddenly leapt to his feet and started clapping loudly, causing everyone at the table to start clapping as well.

"Hell, yeah, boss!" Harry Brock said. "All you did was to save our sorry butts! And I, for one, will get down on my knees and thank you for that for the rest of my life! Bet your ass on it, boss!"

And then he dropped to his knees on the deck and began to bow and scrape like some Nubian, fresh off the boat from Egypt.

See, Hawke thought, somewhat amused at Harry's perfomance. You just never know what people are going to do from one second to the next.

Never.

CHAPTER 28

"The sun also rises, but it hasn't appeared yet!"

Aboard Sea Hawke, *Havana*

It was the next morning, and Hawke had hardly opened his eyes when he was startled by the sudden materialization of Pelham in the quiet predawn gloom of his stateroom.

"What on earth, Pelham?" he said, sleepily sitting up and stretching his long arms over his head. "The sun also rises, but I don't believe that it has appeared yet, old goose."

"Sorry to disturb so early, sir. I'm afraid Chief Inspector Congreve is desirous of a word, sir. Most urgently, he told me to tell you."

"What's this all about?"

"Not the foggiest, m'lord. But I've never seen him in such a state of high excitement."

"All right, all right. Tell my old friend to please come down to see me."

"Indeed, I shall, sir," Pelham intoned, just before he dematerialized into thin air once more. Hawke wasn't sure, but he felt like he could see a faint cloud of pale, bluish mist now hanging in the air where Pelham Grenville had just been standing.

He'd picked up his book and was finding his place when he became aware of Ambrose lingering in the doorway. He was parked there with his great round head tilted aside, like that of a doctor listening for a heartbeat from a patient who has sustained a trauma. In Congreve's sallow temple a blue vein insistently, fearfully pulsed.

The man had plainly come unhinged.

"You're looking fit as a—if not a fiddle, then what?" Hawke said. "What on earth are you so juned up about, old sport?"

"Oh, nothing really. Just that the coup d'etat is on in earnest, that's all."

"Is it, indeed?"

"Indeed, it is."

"And how did you chance upon this realization?"

"I got a call at dawn from that Pillsbury CIA chap. It seems that, at a fundraiser for Cuban schoolchildren on the back lawn of his walled estate in the El Verdado neighborhood, President Mendez, addressing the crowd, was shot dead, gunned down by one of General Castro's rebel sharpshooters, who'd hidden himself at the top of a neighboring tree."

"And now?"

"Now it's a mad race to stop the invasion of Havana and also the southern coastline of the Cuban mainland. All those bloody boats will start departing Isla de Pinos for Cuba at any time once the sun is fully risen. And—uh, Alex? Where on earth did you go?"

"I'm in my closet, putting on some clothes, of course."

"Why?"

"Why? Because we shall sail anon, that's why. The *Sea Hawke* is bound for Isla de Pinos, don't you know. My aim is to dissuade the boaters carrying rebel forces from setting sail for Havana. We'll sink them if we have to. Hell, we'll do whatever it takes."

After breakfast, Hawke rang Stoke and Brock and asked them to meet him up on the bow in five minutes. Seeing them emerge into the sunlight, he waved them over.

"Morning!" he called out cheerfully.

"Morning yourself!" they responded in tandem.

"What's up, boss?" Stoke said.

"President Mendez was assassinated last night. Shot dead by a rebel sharpshooter at a fundraiser for schoolchildren in the country's grade schools. I spoke earlier to CIA Chief Kelly. I told him the invasion of

Havana and all Cuba is imminent. He asked me to do whatever I could to help the friendly government of Cuba to withstand the invasion and the attempted coup. I've ordered the captain and crew to set sail for Isla de Pinos as soon after sunrise as humanly possible. I plan to be waiting just out of sight offshore and sound the alarm for battle stations as soon as we catch sight of the first boats attempting to deliver rebel forces to Havana and elsewhere."

Two hours later, *Sea Hawke* hove to about three miles from the northern coast of the rebel stronghold. Hawke was glad to see that no boats had yet sailed forth from the bay he'd discovered while parking the general's Jeep. It meant his gun crews still had time to prepare for the coming battle.

They were all instructed to don their US Navy PASGT flak jackets and helmets. In addition to the laser cannon mounted up on the bow, there were two .50 cal gun turrets, each manned by two men. One turret was located amidships and the second was located at the stern. Both manned turrets rotated electrically through a full 360 degrees. It was a lot of firepower for what was basically a rich man's playtoy, but today was exactly why Hawke had outfitted his new boat the way he had. Why he'd paid a bloody fortune for her armored hull and topsides.

He anticipated return fire, most likely automatic weapons and possibly RPGs. Time alone would tell if all of his blood, sweat, and tears lost to designing and constructing the big ebony boat would pay off. His plan was not to intentionally kill or wound the enemy combatants, though some of that might occur anyway. He certainly had no problem with sending a lot of ISIS or Hezbollah bully boys to paradise. But he had no urge to kill otherwise harmless Cuban farmers, shopkeepers, ranchers—whatever. His plan was to blow their boats out of the water and let the survivors swim for shore unopposed by any fire coming from *Sea Hawke*.

After all, with all those boats gone to the bottom, the rebel troops would be going nowhere fast.

Hawke lit a fresh cigarette and looked skyward, thinking about what he would now say to all those brave men preparing themselves for battle. It was at times like this that Hawke remembered reading the words of wisdom delivered to the troops by General Douglas MacArthur and General Omar Bradley whilst completing his studies at the Royal Navy War College:

A true leader, Hawke thought, has the confidence to stand alone, the courage to make tough decisions, and the compassion to listen to the needs of others. He does not set out to become a leader, but becomes one by the equality of his actions and the integrity of his intent. And he never, ever gives an order that cannot be obeyed.

And this, too, by General Omar Bradley: We need to learn to set our course by the stars, not the lights of every passing ship!

Fortified by the recollection of the germane wisdom of both Mac-Arthur and Bradley, Hawke made his way forward along the starboard side of the ship. He'd start with the men at the bow. He'd no idea what he'd actually say when the moment came, but he was totally confident in his ability to say precisely what his men needed to hear.

Just as he was approaching the men climbing up into the cannon's turret at the bow, a young emissary from the ship's bridge hurried to his side and spoke in low tones.

"Sorry, sir. Radar ops says they've picked up a bogey approaching us from the stern. Looks like they've been stalking us for some time, sir."

"Enemy vessel? What type?"

"She's Chinese, sir. One of their big missile frigates. She's on us, sir. And closing fast. What are your orders, sir? Do we try and outrun them, sir, or stand and fight?"

"What do you think, son?" Hawke said with a patient smile at the young radar officer.

Instead of answering, the handsome youth snapped off a salute and then said, "Of course, sir! We stand and fight! I'll convey your intentions to the captain posthaste."

"We've got a situation, Chief," Hawke said to Fideo, the first engineer.

"Yes, sir! We are ready for anything!"

"We've picked up a stalker. She's a Chinese missile frigate out of the

Cuban naval base. She's on our stern and beginning to close fast. We need to take action. They've spotted us, and they may have already gotten our position to the rebel HQ. Nothing we can do about that. But we're going to surprise the hell out of them. I'll tell the bridge to execute a sweeping turn to starboard and circle back toward them. Confront the bastards head-on. Lock in the laser on them from a safe distance. Come alongside them at a twenty-degree angle. And blow the bloody bow right off that damn boat! Good timing! Now we see if this thing works as well as everybody seems to think!"

CHAPTER 29

"I have created a monster in Sea Hawke. *Woe betide the enemy who underestimates her!"*

Hawke had remained up on deck, keeping his eyes on the Chinese vessel with his high-power BinoX 4K Ultra HD binoculars. The frigate seemed to be still closing with *Sea Hawke*, but at a slower pace. The officers on her bridge were no doubt staring at him, too, trying to figure out what the hell he was doing.

In their eyes, he was probably just some filthy rich playboy with his two-hundred-foot-long nautical playtoy—an easy mark for a missile-equipped Chinese warship of the first rank. Besides, they were on a mission of their own, Hawke surmised. They'd most likely been ordered to Isla de Pinos to provide cover for General Castro's invading army as their armada made its way across the thirty-mile stretch of open water to the Cuban mainland and on to Havana.

They wouldn't see *Sea Hawke* as a threat to that mission. Just another member of the idle rich. Just another man's yacht, so common down here in the Caribbean. Of course, what if their curiosity got the best of them? If they sounded their sirens and coupled that with a hailing loudspeaker command to heave to and prepare to be boarded? Not happening. Hawke considered the fact that they were now in what could be called a state of war with China.

If the enemy did that, tried to bully them, tried to board *Sea Hawke*, his answer would be instantaneous—and lethal. He had two choices: either confront them from dead ahead or sail *Sea Hawke* right up into their faces, veer off their bow at the last possible instant, and sail down along their port side. Hit them hard below the waterline dead amidships with the laser and break the spine of their keel. Literally slice the big vessel completely in half, leaving the bow section and the stern section completely open to the onrushing seawater.

He thought the cannon was capable of doing that, but both Fideo and he himself knew that Elon's amazing weapon, for all its power, had more than a few engineering issues that frequently made its use problematic. Not to mention how incredibly vulnerable one felt staring down the barrel of an enemy weapon whilst waiting for your weapon to recharge!

Still, if it worked, the Chinese vessel would most likely go down instantly, with great loss of life. If the loss of one of their precious nuclear subs wasn't enough to give the Chinese Navy pause, maybe one more disastrous encounter with the *Sea Hawke* would cause them to treat Hawke's crew with some respect.

Surely, when word of the Chinese Navy's disastrous encounter with an Englishman's yacht reached the ears of the CCP, Chinese warships would, in future, treat Hawke's sailing yacht a bit more deferentially.

At least, for the balance of *Sea Hawke*'s voyage.

At least he hoped that might be true. But, truth be told, he didn't really care. He knew what a monster of a warship he'd created in designing and constructing *Sea Hawke*, and woe betide the enemy who underestimated her. Or, in fact, her skipper.

As it happened, the confrontation between the two mighty vessels got a wee bit more complicated than Hawke, and probably the Chinese Navy skipper himself, had anticipated.

It turned out to be an incredibly dangerous game of high-stakes chicken on the high seas—one that nearly resulted in one or both of the contestants taking a vertical nosedive straight down to the depths of Davy Jones's locker. Lieutenant Jones appeared on the run. "Sir, permission to speak?"

"Go ahead," Hawke said.

"Enemy vessel is rotating her main deck guns in our direction. Preparing to fire!"

Hawke grabbed the nearest microphone from the bulkhead and

barked into it. He said: "Bridge, ahoy! Sound 'battle stations'! Repeat, sound 'battle stations.' All hands on deck. Gun crews prepare for action at close quarters! Fire at will, all guns! Fire at will!"

Then he turned and raced up the steel staircase that led to the bridge wings, two protrusions to either side of the bridge that gave one a panoramic view of the unfolding battle. He raised the mic to his lips and said, "Helm, come right to a heading of two-two-zero. We'll go at them head-on and nose to nose. On my signal, 'Veer away,' put her hard over, port or starboard, whichever looks best to you, just before we collide with them."

"Aye-aye, sir. Question?"

"Of course."

"What if they blink? What if they veer away first? Port or starboard?"

"Take what you can get. Fall off, maintain course, and reduce speed. I want to go fairly close alongside her, say, twenty feet, port or starboard, doesn't matter, we'll hit them hard amidships and slice that damn frigate in half with the laser. They asked for this fight, not me . . . and Billy be damned if I won't sink her!"

At about two miles out, steaming toward the approaching Chinese Navy vessel, Hawke ordered the helm to steer a course directly toward the bow of the enemy warship. He wondered if the Chinese skipper would be reckless enough with government property to not give way before they got seriously close to a disastrous collision at sea.

Since they took Communism deadly seriously in that benighted kingdom, he thought the man might not risk his brilliant naval career just to find out who blinked first. Hawke was reminded of a famous story coming out of World War II that he'd heard at Dartmouth Naval College.

At the height of the Battle of Britain, an American destroyer had ventured into the Firth of Forth, an estuary in the east of Scotland. The heavy gray fog was so thick, the American skipper had said, that you could walk on it.

He kept steaming north, looking for Kriegsmarine subs or warships, which intelligence said they would find.

The American vessel's radio suddenly blared. "Ahoy, vessel steaming east north east at fifteen knots. Skipper, give way!"

The American, incensed, said, "Vessel demanding we give way, we are the USS *Abner Read*. We are a US Navy Fletcher class destroyer. Twenty tons. I respectfully suggest that you give way, Skipper . . ."

"USS *Abner Read*, give way!"

"Not bloody likely. I say again, *you* give way!"

"*Abner Read*, listen carefully. I cannot give way, Captain. You may well be an American destroyer. But, I, sir, am a *bridge!*"

Hawke raced onto the bridge. "Mind your helm, son! Steady on, lads. Steady as she goes. Remember the Charge of the Light Brigade! Half a league, half a league, half a league onward! Into the Valley of Death rode the six hundred!"

Hawke stood stock-still, his steely blue eyes riveted on the bow of the missile frigate slicing through the seas ever closer now . . .

How far? he wondered. A thousand yards and closing fast . . . He could now see the shadowy silhouettes of the Chinese officers on the bridge deck staring at the lone Englishman standing at the bow of his vessel, binocs raised to his eye, challenging their courage and their devotion to duty, no matter how unfounded it might be under these intense circumstances . . .

Five hundred meters and closing. He had the uneasy feeling the Chinese skipper believed he could plow right into the yacht's bow and sink her . . . but could he?

Two hundred fifty . . . two hundred . . .

One hundred fifty . . . *Jesus!* Hawke saw the main deck gun of the big frigate swiveling around in his direction. He knew he'd get only one fatal shot to sink this bastard. And he had mere seconds to act. He grabbed the mic and barked, "Helm! Come right fifteen degrees, NOW! Easy, easy, steer a course alongside her, twenty feet separation, dead slow approaching them amidships to fire cannon . . . Steady. Steady as she goes, lads . . ."

Hawke was calm, but beneath that placid exterior, he, too, was feeling the heat. The *Sea Hawke* could well lose the edge in this encounter if

Hawke didn't get that critical shot off before the enemy blew his bow off and sent them plummeting to the bottom!

The Chinese and their powerful deck artillery gave them a decisive edge in such close quarters. This was naval combat at its most deadly. While the *Sea Hawke*'s deck cannon was far more lethal, it was a bitch to fire and reload with any semblance of sustained warfare. He knew full well that the situation had devolved into one of great peril for his ship—and his crew. All the fore and aft deck guns aboard the frigate were being rotated in his direction. Bloody hell! He knew he had to think of something fast.

Hawke continued on the PA system. "Forward cannon crew! Prepare to fire! Below her waterline! Hit them dead amidships. Slice that bloody sonofabitch in half, boys! Send her to the bottom! And do it NOW!"

He stood at the bow rail, eyes glued to the forward turret, waiting for the green fire to erupt and end this nightmare.

Except it didn't happen. Nothing did—not a bloody lick . . .

Hawke gripped the handrail in front of him with clenched wrists. What the hell was going on with Fideo and his gun crew? The Chinese skipper's ship-to-ship missiles were useless at this close range. But, now, they started pouring machine-gun and small arms fire onto the length of the *Sea Hawke*.

He raced forward to the turret, ducking and weaving and finally yanking open the hatch door and peering up inside. The two gunners seemed stunned. Bloody zombies! Incapable of even responding to his presence.

"What the hell?" he screamed at them. "Fire the goddamn weapon!"

"It won't load! We can't get a charge, Skipper. We don't know what's wrong!"

He scanned all the illuminated instruments. He could hardly believe his eyes.

"You didn't follow procedures! Get your asses out of there! Now!"

He scrambled up inside the turret and examined all the protocols. Christ! The main power switch, the one that provided the electrical power to reload the cannon, was still in the off position! His crew had panicked, left to their own devices! It was akin to mutiny. And that was all he needed at the moment.

He considered calling the bridge and ordering the helm to bear away from the big frigate and make a run for it before they took a direct hit.

But. But, but, but! He couldn't bring himself to do it. His sense of duty to Queen and Country would not let him do it. Hold fast! his brain screamed at him. Give the bastards hell or die trying!

He threw the switch and glanced at his watch. He was charging the cannon now. Did he need full power to fire the damn thing? He had no bleeding idea! He also had no time to find out. He couldn't wait!

He knew they were taking casualties, but this action was what the hell he'd been ordered to do out here by Sir David Trulove. "Give the Chinese unmitigated hell," he'd been told that fateful day at Black's Club. The day he'd been told to use his sea voyage with Alexei to begin taking down the Tang Dynasty criminal empire. And, by God, he was doing it—in spades.

He held his breath. This was do-or-die in the most extreme sense.

Frantically, he went about following the correct procedures to arm and fire his most valuable offensive asset. His mind was racing ahead, realizing how enormous the political stakes were at this point. He wouldn't, *couldn't* fail! If *Sea Hawke* went down, so, too, did Britain and America's chances of preventing Communist hegemony throughout the world.

Even now he was seriously engaged in preventing a new Castro coming to power. A Communist overthrow of the legitimate Cuban government. And, thus, his own ongoing actions were actually stopping the creation of a new Communist World Order, with Cuba, China, and Russia as the dominant world powers and—an eerie beeping noise filling the turret alerted him that the cannon was fully powered up.

He didn't hesitate. He threw the switch that armed the sonofabitch. A moment passed. Had he not waited long enough to fully charge the damn thing? If Elon was aboard at this very moment, he would have personally thrown him overboard. He would have—there was now nothing for it.

He pulled the electronic trigger, expecting the worst.

His dismal thoughts were suddenly disrupted as he saw the brilliant green streak of concentrated light energy erupt from the barrel of the laser cannon. He stared at the multiple CCTV images of the frigate on all the monitors mounted above his head. He realized he was holding his breath!

His jaw dropped with what he saw!

He knew as soon as the smoke cleared. He saw that he had succeeded in cutting the frigate's thick steel hull in two! It had been like a hot knife through warm butter. He saw the mad panic of the Chinese crewmen as they realized what had happened to them. Some were already abandoning ship. Others were clinging to anything they thought would keep them afloat when their ship went down.

Two separate halves! Still afloat, but not for long. And both already ablaze! Now he saw that those crewmen who'd dared to leap for their lives, were, to their abject horror, even now leaping to their deaths as the huge oil spill on the surface began to spread fire across the sea.

The ship's captain, Horner, anticipating this event, had started *Sea Hawke*'s three massively powerful turbo-powered diesel engines. *Sea Hawke* abruptly veered away from the doomed frigate and went to full throttle. The boat and the crew were once more out of danger.

He realized he may have given his friend Elon short shrift. He had to admit the truth: that the ultra-high-tech weapon was bloody amazing. Given what he'd just witnessed, he realized that it might well be the most powerful military killing machine the world had ever known.

The last remaining pieces of the big frigate were already gone from sight as seawater rushed in and replaced every bit of air in both stern and forward halves of the doomed vessel. There now appeared to be no survivors, poor bastards. She'd gone down with all hands.

With a 100 percent chance that not one of them ever knew what hit them! He had a message for the Chinese Navy:

"Welcome to modern naval warfare, boys!"

CHAPTER 30

"High is the Tempest roar! High the sea-bird screaming,
High the Azore!"

I t was two days later. They were sailing in a stiff blow and making good time doing so. *Sea Hawke* was fast as hell and Hornblower had her on a beam reach. Hawke and John Paul Jones had estimated landfall in Cuba in less than two hours.

Ambrose Congreve had appeared up on deck just before sunset that day, hoping to find Hawke up here somewhere. He was. Seated in the aft cockpit all alone, appearing to nurse his second or third Dark 'n' Stormy of the day. Congreve wasn't particularly concerned about his increased consumption of alcohol—rum in particular; Goslings Black Seal, of course. Hawke had spent his whole life taking care of himself, ensuring that he was always in the pink whenever duty called.

But, just prior to leaving Bermuda, Congreve and his dear wife, the former Lady Diana Mars, had spent a long candlelit supper al fresco on the always breezy bricked terrace that overlooked the crashing rollers—high drama, courtesy of the Atlantic Ocean.

The subject of the couple's conversation had been Alex Hawke. Since they shared a deep love for each other, not to mention Lord Hawke, he was not an unusual subject for worry. He was something of a force of nature, and when his mental weather was sketchy, the chief and his bride leapt into the fray.

Lady Mars, known to Hawke as Diana, was of the staunchly held opinion that Alex needed another woman in his life. And so, in her opinion, did his son. The child's life had always been filled with a stately procession of nannies and royal protection officers from Scotland Yard. Diana did acknowledge that he'd go into London for a weekend, ostensibly, and not fooling anyone, to take his young "niece," recently arrived from Paris, to dinner at Mark's Club and, as he always added, a "show."

Ambrose had known better than to argue with her on that subject! But, privately, he had to admit that ever since the horrific murder of Sigrid Kissl at the hands of that monster Mr. Smith, Hawke had lost some of the bounce in his step, or some of his usual "zip," if that was the word. Perhaps "pep" was the word he'd been searching for. Chief Inspector Congreve had been a linguistics scholar at Magdalene College, Cambridge, but an understanding of American slang still eluded him.

He went slowly to the stern.

Hawke was sipping his drink in the here and now, but his mind was miles away in Neverland, and Ambrose had no wish to disturb him. Especially if he had come up here for solace, peace, or simple contemplation.

"Sorry, old boy," he said quietly, looking down at his oldest friend in the world. Hawke had his eyes focused on the far horizon. There were no tears, certainly, but he did appear to be somewhat sad . . . or even troubled. He was certainly drinking more, and smoking more, than was his wont. It was a bad business, all right. He was going to need all of his strength and then some for what lay ahead.

"Penny for your thoughts, Alex," he added. "You appear to be suffering from melancholia. Are you quite all right? Diana and I are concerned about you."

"For what reason?" Hawke asked, mildly miffed.

"We worry about your health, Alex. Whatever is bothering you emotionally is affecting you physically."

"You mean drinking."

"And smoking."

"Oh, come, come, Constable. You're no paragon of abstemiousness yourself, for all love! Christ!"

"Nor have I ever claimed to be," the man said, regarding him with pale blue eyes that looked positively motherly. "I'm just trying to look out for my dearest friend in all the world. And if that's a sin, well, I don't know what to—"

"Look here, Ambrose. It's quite simple, really. I only drink because I'd rather die of drink than of thirst. And as to cigarettes, it's really only that I don't know what to do with my hands."

"Very funny, Alex. Most amusing. Diana believes you need a woman in your life. Sigrid's horrific murder has left you feeling guilty, perhaps. Burdened by the fact that you couldn't save her. But, then, no one could have saved her that night, could they?"

"Only the Bermuda police, if only they'd bothered to search the cottage and grounds carefully before they left that night . . ."

"Oh, Alex, you don't know that. Perhaps they did a thorough search before they left. Perhaps, being a clever boy, Smith had gone outside into the jungle and waited for them to leave . . . then returned to the cottage."

"Then they bloody well should have searched the grounds!" Hawke said, a bit more forcefully than he would have liked.

"Alex, I think—"

"Oh, for heaven's sake, Constable. Leave it alone. It's gone. It's in the past."

"The past never dies. It's not even in the past."

"Spare me. Did you just make that up?"

"No. I'm quoting."

"Who? Never mind. We all know. Churchill. It's always Churchill, isn't it? That is, if it's not bloody Shakespeare!"

"Not this time. It's William Faulkner."

"Oh. Well, pretty good writer, that one, I have to admit."

"So. I have to repeat. A penny for your thoughts, dear boy."

Hawke paused a moment before answering. "What am I thinking about? Nothing really, I suppose. Thinking about Alexei, to be honest. Sit down and have some bloody rum or something. Light your bloody pipe. Enough of the schmaltz! What you really need is a double brandy and soda! The sun is literally right over that yardarm above your head. Here's a tumbler. Say when."

Hawke had just begun to pour the Goslings Black Seal when Congreve blurted out:

"When!"

"That's all? Oh, come, come. It's been a long day. That much rum won't even wet your whistle."

"I'm fine with this, thank you very much. So. Thinking about Alexei, eh? Good topic."

"Do you think he's all right? I mean, do you think he's enjoying the voyage? I ask because I feel I've been so busy with this Cuban business, going to prison, putting down revolutions, and things like that, that I haven't spent as much time with him as I'd planned . . . What do you think? You're the much-beloved godfather, after all."

"We've been aboard for three weeks now. You two have the whole balance of the voyage ahead of you to forge your bonds of steel. And I can tell you unequivocally that he's not the same young lad that came aboard this ship twenty-one days ago."

"He's not? Really? In what way, precisely?"

"No, not at all like that young lad. He's been stashed away at boarding school forever, remember. Cooped up inside for the most part. Studying night and day. Book learning, I'm sure you'll agree, is not nearly so good a teacher as life itself. He's opened up like some rare blossom, Alex. His latent curiosity, surely inherited from his father, has now taken control of his mind. He wants to know about everything. He's constantly asking me or Pelham or Miss Devereux about subjects he's never even considered whilst sequestered away at Eton. Nature. Marine biology. Meteorology. Astronomy. The cosmos. I could go on and on. Film noir gangster films of the nineteen forties, for all love! He's a bona fide knowledge sponge."

"Really?" Hawke said, much cheered by this news.

"Really. Want to know what he asked me the other evening on our stroll about the deck after supper? He said, 'Uncle Ambrose, which do you think was the best detective film of all? *The Maltese Falcon?* Or *The Big*

Sleep? You're a detective, aren't you? What's the secret to doing that? I'm thinking I want to be one some day . . .'

"'Ah, the secret!' I said to him. 'Well, I came upon it many, many years ago. But when it dawned on me, I knew I had it! And now I pass it down to you. I call it "the Detective's Creed": First, you find a little thread, the little thread leads you to a string, and the string leads you to a rope, and from the rope you hang the criminal by the neck.'"

"Yes. That's quite good, Constable. Never heard that before. Quite the bard lately, aren't you? So you honestly think I've been of some help to him?"

"Really I do. You introduced him to the cosmic miracle of celestial navigation that first week at sea. Well, guess what. He's absolutely mastered it. And cooking, of all things! Turns out, he loves to cook! He's already done French and Italian cuisines, and now he's graduated to Indian and Moroccan dishes. Chef Auguste—who, by the way, is teaching him to speak French—now calls him '*mon petit prodige.*' To which I heard Alexei reply, '*Mais non, Chef, vous êtes trop gentil!*'"

Hawke suddenly sat up, his steely gaze locked on something he'd seen in the red and gold skies hovering just over the horizon. He said, out of the corner of his mouth:

"All bloody marvelous, Ambrose, but—hand me those binoculars, will you? There's something about this I don't like . . ."

"Here you go. What are you looking at?"

"No idea. Three black dots on the horizon, growing rapidly larger, coming directly at us out of the sinking sun. See them? Here, have a look through these."

Ambrose accepted the offer and raised the heavy pair of binocs to his eyes. He said:

"Odd. They appear to be small airplanes, possibly fighter jets, flying in a tight V formation. Looks like they'll roar right over our heads at this rate."

"I hope that's what they've got in mind. They're definitely military. Fighter planes. I can almost make out the symbols on their fuselages . . . hold on! Coming closer now . . . diving on us . . . good God! They're North

Korean FA-50s! The new fighter bombers in the Argentine Air Force. Twelve-ton fighter jets, thirty million a pop. What the hell are they doing out here?"

Ambrose, growing rapidly wary of the developing situation, said, "There can be only one explanation, Alex. They're here to support the invasion of Cuba by the rebel forces . . ."

"But they're bloody Argentine fighters!"

"Yes, and so, too, is General Castro, as you'll recall. Little doubt the Argentine Air Force is here at his orders. Technically, he's still the ranking general in the Argentine Army. Alex, do you think they intend to open fire on *Sea Hawke*? They are behaving in a very aggressive manner and—"

At that very instant the teak of the cockpit deck, now white as a shark's tooth from seas washing over it, was ripped up beneath the men's feet and shredded with deadly accurate machine-gun fire from above. The three roaring jets had stacked up one behind the other and commenced an all-out attack on *Sea Hawke*.

"Get BELOW!" Hawke screamed at his friend, climbing up out of the cockpit and onto the deck and dragging Congreve up with him by the arm. "Stay low! We've got to make it to that open hatchway!"

The lead fighter seemed to have them dead to rights in his sights. He was firing his wing guns and ripping up yards of teak deck as he flew just above the mastheads of the huge sailing yacht.

"Go down and find Alexei! Tell everyone to stay below until the captain sounds the all clear. They'll be safe down there. But if they fire anti-ship missiles at us, it's another story. Katy bar the door, old boy. I'm going to try and make it up to the bridge. We need to initiate evasive maneuvers immediately. And where the hell is Fideo Chico and the laser cannon gun crew? I'll fire the damn thing myself if I have to! And I'll damn well fire Fideo myself if I have to! Elon gave me a Zoom tutorial just in case of screwups like this. I can bloody well do it, believe me!"

Ambrose disappeared down below.

Hawke kept moving forward, dodging and weaving his way toward the bow. He zigzagged past the steel steps up to the portside bridge wing.

He'd changed his mind. He could radio the captain from the safety of the heavy steel turret enclosing the laser cannon.

He reached the bow unscathed and climbed up inside the turret. Rounds from the lead fighter were loud twangs ricocheting off the turret. He powered up the laser and its radar-synchronized guidance systems, then picked up the mic and told the skipper to commence evasive actions and give him time to take out the three attacking fighters. They'd stopped firing now and peeled away, flying at low altitude about fifteen feet off the deck. They were getting back into the V formation again, preparing for yet another attack. This time, Hawke feared, it would probably be a bombing run.

He needed to bloody well take them out right this second!

Here they come, he thought, watching them through the range finder with his right index finger on the cannon's electronic trigger.

The warning alarm sounded. It meant that the cannon's radar-guided systems had locked onto a target—namely, the lead fighter.

Hawke waited until the aircraft was centered in his sights and pulled the trigger. It took the brilliant green beam a matter of milliseconds to hit the lead fighter. It literally vaporized in midair.

He got the second one locked in, waited a beat, and fired again. The results were identical to the first one. He bent down and put his eye to the sight. The third one had clearly not wanted to share the fate his comrades had suffered and turned tail. Hawke climbed down out of the turret and watched the jet's departure. It was clearly headed south to provide cover for General Castro's invading army.

Hawke smiled and made his way up to the bridge to assess the damage with the officers and crew.

He was pretty damn sure that Argie in the third FA-50 would not be in any mood to do another strafing run on what the three pilots had automatically assumed was an unarmed sailing yacht.

And they hadn't known the half of it!

CHAPTER 31

"And how she did fly! His boat seemed almost disconnected
from the surface of the sea itself!"

They made for Isla de Pinos, *Sea Hawke* heeling hard to port with her
lee rail buried in the frothing water. Hornblower had her on a broad
reach in a freshening breeze, en route to the small island where lay
General Castro's stronghold. And how she did fly! His pride and joy, this
lovely wind machine he'd built from nothing, out of thin air, seemed
miraculous—something, despite her gargantuan size and weight and dis-
placement, almost disconnected from the surface of the sea itself. She was
riding the wind and the wind alone, and nothing temporal, nothing else
that was of this earth.

To Hawke, it felt like she was literally flying, skimming merrily along,
above wave after wave. Going like a racehorse. Like she had the bit in her
teeth, rounding the last turn before heading into the homestretch.

They were headed for his preselected spot off the northern shore of
the island. From there, emerging vessels packed with guerrillas would
not be aware of *Sea Hawke*'s presence, just waiting to lay waste to whatever remained of the big armada. But, with their powerful optics, Hawke
and his men could track their speed and bearings and sort out the low-
hanging fruit among them.

Hawke, standing in the bow pulpit with the big black binocs to hand,
surveying the coastline, caught sight of the first vessel to emerge from the
bay and out into the sea.

Fideo Chico, who had incurred the massive wrath of the owner after being AWOL during the dive bomber attacks visited on them by the Argentine Air Force, had begrudgingly been allowed to remain on board, but only until their next port of call in Isla de Pinos.

"It's either that or keelhaul the sonofabitch," he'd said to Stoke. He and Stoke had done that once, keelhauled a Russian mafia hardass who refused to answer their questions about an impending assassination plot.

It's an old technique, but it gets results. You need a very long line, at least the length of your vessel. You loop the line at both bow and stern and then tether the miscreant dead amidships. Heave him overboard from the bow pulpit and drag him under the whole length of the boat. He's fighting for air and continuously having his battered body whipped about, slamming into the steel hull all the way from bow to stern. Then you ask your questions.

"Too good for him, boss. Up to me, we'd just throw his skinny ass overboard and sail away. I never liked him. Didn't trust him, either. Always thought he had some agenda he didn't want any of us to know about."

"You felt that? I did, too," Hawke said.

"Why didn't you say something?"

"Good question. I guess the fact that it was Sir David who suggested him, and Trulove is a man who makes very few mistakes. But when I realized Fideo recommended that pathetic little Cuban driver, Carlos, who delivered us to the rebels and prison, I figured him for a mole of some kind. Just didn't know what he was up to."

"Yeah," Stoke said. "You remember that day when Devereux and Alexei went to Vizcaya? When Shit Smith followed them there from the marina? Tried to kidnap Alexei for the second damn time? Shit."

"What about it?" Hawke said.

"Well, I remember her saying the security officer told her that Smith was seen by tourists racing out to a boat moored at the Vizcaya docks out on the bay. There was, the cop said, an accomplice already waiting in the fire-engine red Cigarette racing speedboat out there. Smith hopped in and they roared away, headed south to the Keys, most likely. Good place to hide a boat. Name on the transom?"

"Don't tell me. *Top Gun?*"

"You got it, boss. One of the crew told me that earlier that day, Fideo had told Capataín Hornblower he was, at your request, taking *Top Gun* to the yard so the mechanics could check out the timing on one of the outboards. Said it was running rough."

"Good Lord, Stoke. So Fideo was actually working with the cowboy on the kidnapping attempt? Meaning you know who else was involved with that."

"Putin, boss. Putin."

"Sure as hell looks like it. Tell your pal Harry Brock that I want him to arrange for federal marshals to come aboard *Sea Hawke* as soon as possible to arrest Fideo for the attempted kidnapping of a minor in Miami and keep him imprisoned there till we can get back and put him away for life."

"That's the way to do it, boss," Stoke said.

"Still too good for him, though," Hawke said. "I'd like to kill him with my bare hands. Maybe two or three times, just to make sure it takes."

Hawke had the comfort of knowing that Thunder and Lightning and their gang of hard-assed soldiers would be waiting for them in the dense thicket of jungle surrounding Revolution Bay.

T&L had executed a HALO drop into the deep interior jungle of the Cuban island from their old Hercules C-130, *Puff the Magic Dragon*. Under cover of darkness, they would make their way through the green hell to Revolution Bay. Two of their number were former Navy SEALs—that is, master underwater demolition experts.

It would be their job to enter the waters of the bay from the thick jungle unseen, and, swimming underwater, look for the very largest vessels first, namely two mothballed Cuban warships that Castro had recommissioned. There were also two cutters, a torpedo attack boat, and a tired old destroyer from WWII. They would then attach magnetic limpet mines to their hulls. All the mines were on wireless timers, set to explode simultaneously at sunrise, a time collected from local meteorologists.

This surprise attack would have the effect of creating a massive distraction among the rebel forces right at the outset of their planned invasion. When the besieged fleet attempted to find the attackers, they would launch a retaliatory major offensive from jungle locations all around the small bay. The Cherokee chieftain had firepower: mortars, heavy automatic weapons fire, M-60 grenade launchers, and other goodies they'd brought along for the upcoming battle to help avert a revolution in Cuba.

Thunder, a full-blooded Cherokee, whom, for years, Hawke had called Chief, was the bravest of warriors and a master of all things that go bang in the night. He had called Hawke on his radio a little earlier.

His partner in crime, Lightning by name, was a legendary redheaded Irishman who had created the "blitzkreig" approach to hostage rescue years ago, still used worldwide by HRTs, hostage rescue teams. If the chief was the muscle, the Irishman was the acknowledged brains of the outfit.

"Hey, boss," the Cherokee warrior said to Hawke. "We're on the ground, strung out around the entire bay. We've already rigged underwater limpet mines on the hulls of about fifteen or twenty of the larger vessels. The largest, fifty feet or more, are old Cuban Navy warships. There's also a big troop transport vessel where the bulk of the Middle East mujahideen fighters will make the crossing and an ancient but serviceable attack torpedo boat, plus a cutter and a minelayer. All are packed to the gunwales with guerrilla fighters from all over creation, a ton from the Middle East.

"Detonation of all the mined boats is gonna be simultaneous, as we previously discussed, triggered by a single detonation device paired wirelessly to them all. All mines have been timed to blow at five fifty tomorrow morning. Dawn.

"At that time, my guys will add to all the panic and confusion created by the mines and open intensive fire from our .50 cals, automatic weapons, and rocket-launched grenades, all from secure positions inside the edge of the jungle on shore. We will continue to rain living hell on these godless mujahideens and Chechen killers, plus a few Commie guerrillas thrown in for good measure, until the last boat is either sunk or has managed to escape our noose and is headed out to sea and your waiting monstrosity. They won't be happy to see you, either!"

"Sounds good, Chief. Just heard the newly elected president of Cuba has ordered thousands of government troops into the streets of Havana to protect the existing government buildings and personnel, as well as certain hot spots in the interior. If we get lucky, we can put down this revolution and return to normalcy by the end of this week."

"And based on what you told me earlier, blow a big fuckin' hole in the Cuban commies' top secret plans to ally with China and Russia, which I know your CIA buddy at Langley was most concerned about. Not to mention the White House, Congress, the State Department, you name it.

"The word around Washington is that Havana was going to be the future capital of the entire Communist world. It's been rumored in the espionage community that China has already approved a twenty-billion-dollar cash payment to the Castro crowd to build an entire city to be used as the capital of Cuba.

"The Pentagon, according to my sources, is in a big fat hurry to get all those newly acquired Russian and Chinese subs and warships the hell out of Cuban ports and sent packing back home, wherever that is . . . escorted part of the way by the US Navy's Southern Atlantic Fleet."

"Correct. Those first two Chinese subs in the Bahamas? I haven't told you this, but that little adventure was thanks to Harry Brock, Stoke, and me. That was the action that lit the Pentagon's candle and started this whole thing. Oh, here's an idea I had. Can you guys hang out in Havana for a few days after this is over? I'd love to do something for your troops. You've delivered for me for over a decade, and I want to find a way to thank you for your service."

"Why not? Our next op is not for a month. We're doing a little thing with Mossad in Iran. Taking out a nuclear fission operation outside of Tehran. Just between you and me, of course."

Hawke laughed. "Oh, it's a *secret*, Chief? Damn, I'm sure glad you told me before I went around shooting my mouth off about it."

"Yeah, well, you know . . ."

"Yeah, yeah, I know," Hawke said. "Good shooting, old sport. We'll see you at the after-party."

CHAPTER 32

"Open fire, lads! Give the bastards hell."

Revolution Bay

The crews aboard the sixteen steel-hulled ships that had ultimately been unlucky enough to have limpet magnetic mines attached to their hulls got a big fat wake-up call at precisely ten minutes to six that morning. No orange juice or tea and crumpets were served, no folded copy of the *Times*. None of that. Only the varied array of moored boats suddenly blown sky-high, lifting into the air due to the severity and lethality of the explosive charges the Thunder and Lightning boys had just detonated beneath them.

And the still-dark heavens above were detonated, suddenly illuminated in shades of violent orange and vicious red. From a distance, the Chief would later learn, it appeared as if the entire island had exploded upward into the skies.

When the dust had cleared somewhat, the Chief was surprised to see that the big troopship full of murderous mujahideen, including almost 90 percent comprised of former ISIS thugs, was still intact. Not only that, she'd started her engines and was preparing to get underway.

"Open fire, lads!" Chief said. "Give those bastards hell."

And as the rusty old troopship steamed out of the bay and into open waters, they did just that.

With a will. With a fury.

The most effective fire coming from the jungles that crept down to the edge of the bay's blue water came from the RPGs, the grenade launchers fired by Hawke's mercenary warriors with the big M60s.

Hawke had stationed himself outside on *Sea Hawke*'s portside bridge wing. It was the best command post available on his boat, with terrific comms abilities, height over the water, and 360-degree views of the entire ship.

He heard a brief blitz of static on the radio and put on his headset, adjusting the mic.

"Alex, it's me," Mick Hammersmith, the new chief engineer, said. "Bad news, I'm afraid."

"Go ahead."

"The limpet mine on the big troopship *El Colón* malfunctioned. It failed to detonate. She's now headed your way, steaming out of the mouth of the bay. Just a heads-up. That damn vessel full of ISIS fighters was probably our highest-value-target opportunity, and goddammit, they slipped right through our fingers. Sorry about that."

"Love and war. That's just how it goes. All's fair. Something tells me the Lord's going to give us a second chance."

"Yeah. Maybe. I don't have a whole lot of experience in the love half of that equation, sir."

"Don't worry about the troopship, buddy. We just picked them up on radar and are about to get visual contact. *Sea Hawke* has a top speed of thirty knots under power. I doubt that leaky old rust bucket can manage ten. We'll be waiting for them when they reach the end of the channel leading to the bay. One more thing. What kind of weapons did you see on that boat? Over."

"Oh, the usual. Lots of old AK-47s, light machine guns captured from various sources, recycled bazookas, stuff like that. Over."

"Roger that," Hawke said, terminating his transmission.

Hawke then got the two remaining gunnery lads in the laser turret on the radio.

"Attention, forward gun crew. We've got an extremely high-priority target emerging from the bay and steaming this way. Get your radar systems up and lock onto this vessel now. Track and lock, then wait for my order to fire. I want to get a closer look at them before we commence combat ops against them."

"Affirmative, Skipper. Roger wilco."

Hawke smiled.

During the long period of *Sea Hawke*'s construction, he'd been worried about the huge expense added to his budget with the addition of Elon's fantastic new laser weapon. He needn't have worried. It was soon to become worth every damned shilling he'd forked over. The damn thing had already helped him stymie a Communist revolution, sent an enemy submarine and a Chinese missile frigate rocketing to the bottom, and blown two Argentine fighter jets out of the sky . . . and now he was about to dispatch an entire boatload of vicious cutthroat ISIS terrorists to the bottom of the sea in one fell swoop.

Because sometimes God puts his heavenly hand on the Scales of Life and tips them in your favor.

And you really do get what you pay for.

Aboard the troopship *El Colón*, the former Cuban Navy captain was all smiles. They had, by dint of a holy miracle, avoided the fate of their comrades in the other ships, blown sky-high by the mines attached to their hulls during the night. And now he was standing on the bridge with some of his old officers, who, like himself, had been brought out of mothballs to help his country in this, their most glorious hour.

And not only that, but he, *el capitán*, Rodrigo de la Maza, now had a sturdy ship beneath his feet once more, the vibrations of her powerful engines making their way all the way up to the bridge deck. *El Colón*, "Columbus," was the ship that he had actually been the captain of back in the 1960s. Those were the salad days when he'd ferry Cuban troops all the way from Cuba to Africa and back. Those were the days when his country was fighting for the people of Angola.

El Colón had some serious fighting power back then, heavy cannon fore and aft, antiaircraft guns to port and starboard. The cannons were still operable but no one had any idea about the firepower. And the crew was well-armed, too, all to protect the ship's precious cargo, the sainted Sons of Cuba and the proud warrior class of the mujahideen, ISIS!

Most of that glorious firepower had been sold for scrap when his ship, like her skipper himself, had been unceremoniously mothballed. A sadder day there never was.

But, but, but! There was another miracle in his life that made him feel that surely God, in his infinite wisdom, had decided to right the wrongs of history: to avenge the humiliation Fidel and his people had suffered under the thick soles of the Yankee boots for far too long. Yes, now was the time! Vengeance is mine, saith the Lord!

Another military saying popped into his fevered mind, and he almost said it aloud: *Praise the Lord and pass the ammunition!*

"El Capitán!" his second-in-command said upon entering the bridge and coming to attention and snapping off a very credible salute. "Pleased to report, we have a fighter escort, sir!"

"Qué? De verdad? It's true?"

"Sí, sí, Capitán! An Argentine fighter jet appeared out of the blue in our wake as we left the bay. He zoomed in low overhead and waggled his wings at us. He's come to defend us, sir!"

"Defend us? From what? We've escaped our enemies . . ."

"Except for that big sailing yacht out there. She seems to be lying in wait for us. Something ominous about her, sir. Can't really explain it. Just a gut feeling."

"No, no! I studied her with the glasses from stem to stern. She's harmless. A sailing yacht, for God's sake. From Britain. A big yacht, but still a mere yacht, after all."

And so, one much assured, one not so much, onward they sailed, into the glorious fray once more, the captain thought, his old heart swelling with pride and joy.

––––––––––

Aboard *Sea Hawke*, his lordship was also monitoring the approach of the rebel troopship. He'd just ducked inside the bridge to the comms room. He needed to put in a quick call to CIA Chief Kelly. He wanted to apprise him of the dramatically unfolding events as regarded General Castro's attempted coup, or lack thereof.

The fact that he was currently offshore at Isla de Pinos awaiting a troopship carrying between 200 and 350 terrorist mujahideen fighters, mostly ISIS murderers, got Kelly's attention pretty quickly. What was Hawke going to do about this situation? Kelly wanted to know.

"Uh, gee, I dunno, Brick," Hawke replied, "maybe send the boatload full of ISIS fighters—America and Britain's most vicious enemies—straight to the bottom? Does that work for you? Oh, and by the way, I've been using the high-power binocs you gave me to surveil the vessel from stem to stern. And guess who I spied conversing with the captain up on the bridge?"

"I'll bite. Yogi Berra."

Hawke laughed. Brick's dry sense of humor always delighted him.

"No, not Yogi Berra," Hawke said. "Our friend the man in black himself. Mr. Smith."

"Sink that damn boat, Alex. No matter what else you do, you sink that boat! We let Smith and those vicious bastards take up residence in Havana, next thing you know, they'll show up in Miami and start beheading citizens on Brickell Avenue. Take 'em all off the board, old buddy. Not now, but right now!"

"Roger that," Hawke intoned, in a fake American spec ops tone of voice, with a slow Western drawl, the way American commercial airline pilots address the passengers.

Apparently, it worked for Brick.

He heard a squawk on the turret's radio and then a voice said, "Hawke, do you copy?"

It was his favorite Cherokee warrior.

"Hey, Chief. Read you loud and clear. It's getting pretty spicy out here. We've got the big troopship in our sights and closing. Just talked to Brick Kelly. We've got orders to sink her on sight."

"Good," the chief said. "Because I've got some interesting news for you. We captured two of the boat's crew who dived into the sea under heavy fire. During interrogation, we learned that the actual composition of the two or three hundred troops on board was incorrect for some reason. The truth, they said, was that the vast majority of fighters on board were not Hezbollah, al Qaeda, Boko Haram, or the Taliban."

"What the hell is left, Chief? You just named the usual suspects."

"Ninety-five percent of the fighters aboard *El Colón* are ISIS. Your pal Mr. Smith has seized command of those ISIS forces, and I've little doubt he's coming for you personally, Skipper."

"No doubt. I know he's aboard. I saw him talking to the captain up on the bridge. According to my guys, all these terrorist fighters were recruited specifically for their barbarism and cruelty by General Castro himself."

"And I know what a special space in your heart you reserve for those fuckin' ISIS assholes."

"Oh, yeah. Glad you shared that intel, Chief. There's a special place in hell for those vile thugs, I'm sure. All those beheadings, burning people alive . . . God. Okay. Got to jump, Chief, I have a boat to sink!"

Hawke looked out across the water and saw that the boat would soon be where he wanted it: emerging from the shallow channel into much deeper water. Brick wanted that boatful of murderous zealots on the bottom, out of sight forevermore. Nobody without security clearance needed to know about this.

He descended to the main deck and went forward to the cannon turret. He knew the laser turret boys and the two American gunnery officers still on duty with the .50 cals on the bow—without the traitorous Fideo Chico, who was stewing in the brig awaiting the arrival of federal marshals—were very capable of executing his orders. But because Brick had been so adamant about his desires for swiftness and secrecy, he would damn well sink the thing himself.

He'd gotten halfway to the bow when he caught sight of the third Argentine fighter jet. The one that got away and lived to fight another day. The fighter had obviously been assigned to escort the troopship carrying ISIS fighters all the way to Havana Harbor to ensure that *Sea*

Hawke, the warship in sheep's clothing, didn't interfere with the battered old boat's progress onward to Havana.

Well, it was going to be a very short day for Argie combatants who had no business being in this fight, no matter what that old fox Castro thought about the matter.

He reached the turret and climbed up the stainless-steel ladder high enough that his head could be seen by the two Americans up inside the reddish glow of the turret's control panels.

It was very claustrophobic inside, very tight quarters up there. Especially since, to get to the chief gunnery officer's seat, it was three steps up from the port and starboard gunner's platform.

"Morning, gents," he said, amiably enough.

"Morning, sir!" they replied in tandem.

"No need to salute, gentlemen. I'll be at the turret all afternoon. You've heard about Fideo's betrayal by now, have you? Well, I've assigned myself as his replacement, and I'm giving myself permission to come up."

"Welcome to Green Beam World, sir," said one of the younger gunnery men, whose names, as far as Hawke could discern, were Buzzy and Dizzy. The one who had spoken was red-haired and fair-skinned, with the cherubic face of the child Hollywood star of one of Hawke's favorite films in his own childhood. He had played, alongside Elizabeth Taylor, the young horse trainer in *National Velvet.*

He squeezed between the two junior officers and secured himself in the higher seat, waiting for his eyes to adjust to the darkness inside. In addition to the cannon, there were two heavy machine guns, remote-controlled from the turret and mounted on bulkheads to either side of *Sea Hawke.* Each of his two subordinates would fire these in a tight-quarters combat situation. At his seat, however, was an antiaircraft weapon that Hawke would be able to use in battle.

"You've heard by now that Fideo has been thrown in the brig?" Hawke said.

"Yes, sir, we have. We were disgusted to hear about how he'd played us all. That he was a bad actor right from the beginning. I'm sure you were aware that he was secretly trying to poison the crew against you. He actually believed he could incite an insurrection, sir. He was dead set on a bloody mutiny aboard *Sea Hawke*, sir!"

"A mutiny? Predicated on *what*, exactly?" Hawke said. Little shocked him now, but plumbing the depths of Fideo's betrayal had narrowly avoided being monumentally harmful. It had almost cost Hawke his son. And he made a vow then and there that some day, somehow, he was going to make Putin pay for his unceasing menace, his hidebound determination to cause harm to Hawke's family.

"He was a virulent Communist, Skipper. He had totally sided with General Castro's desire to retake Havana and the Cuban government in the holy name of Communism."

"And Buzzy, what was the crew's reaction to this traitor among us?"

"We all thought he was batshit crazy, sir."

"Glad to hear it. It's even worse than you know. He was a plant recruited from the highest levels of the Russian government, put onboard by Vladimir Putin himself to spy on me—and, moreover, to attempt to kidnap my son, Alexei, during this voyage. They failed miserably at both, thank God, thanks to the bravery and skills of Scotland Yard's Miss Devereux, who severely wounded the assailant and saved my son."

"Oh, my God, sir. I'm so sorry," the older of the two said.

Hawke said, "Beneath contempt. And I now know that the attempted kidnapping that happened in Miami was done with the aid and cooperation of Fideo Chico. He was working with Putin's top paid assassin, a Mr. Smith. I've remanded Fideo to the brig for the time being. But I'm turning him over to the federal marshals. Mr. Brock is going to use my aircraft to fly to Miami as the prisoner's armed escort. That swine is going away for the rest of his life. The Miami case officer assigned to his case guaranteed me of that."

"Good riddance to bad rubbish, sir. Tell you the truth, Skipper? Nobody we knew much trusted that bad actor from the very beginning. Something just didn't feel right about the guy, right from the start. When he'd told us who had recommended him for the job, no one had ever heard of him."

"Indeed," Hawke said. He had his binocs on the troopship now and saw it steaming ahead. It was wallowing somewhat in the choppy seas, but definitely getting closer. And he saw, too, the bright yellow Argie fighter jet. The pilot was flying directly above the Cuban ship, down low, about a hundred feet above the gray-white smoke curling up from the old ship's lone stack.

As he watched, however, he was deeply troubled to see the pilot suddenly execute a steep climb up to a higher altitude, leveling off at about five thousand feet. This would give him airspace to commence a steep dive down on *Sea Hawke.*

Hawke had only seconds to stop him.

This time it wouldn't be the staccato of machine-gun fire he had to fear.

No. This time, the fighter jet would be *raining bombs* down upon their heads!

CHAPTER 33

Hawke quickly elevated the twin barrels of the ship's sole antiaircraft gun as it swiveled silently toward the Argentine fighter jet's corner of the sky. He knew he had just moments before the enemy pilot initiated his dive-bombing run. Somehow, with scant seconds to spare, Hawke had to manage to get the fighter locked in the crosshairs of the gun's synchronous radar guidance systems. He applied increasing pressure to the single trigger, which fired both ack-ack barrels in tandem.

He said to himself, with squinted eyes and through gritted teeth, "Say your prayers, you son of a bitch! You're in a hot rod to hell with the top down, pal! You just don't know it yet."

"*Tora! Tora! Tora!*" Hawke shouted, making the Japanese battle cry at Pearl Harbor more than loud enough for most of the crew to hear.

He squeezed the trigger and unleashed a hail of hot lead into the glide path of the oncoming enemy plane, which now felt like it was diving straight at him *personally*. For a moment, Hawke experienced sheer dread that the Argie fighter pilot, though his aircraft was severely crippled by the furious onslaught of *Sea Hawke*'s high-intensity antiaircraft gunfire, still might, in the throes of desperation, and perhaps mortally wounded, attempt to emulate the rabid Japanese *kamikaze* (divine wind) pilots of yore . . . a looming disaster of catastrophic proportions.

"Christ," he said to himself, firing the dangerously overheated guns relentlessly. Fearing the very real possibility of a kamikaze attack, he was desperately trying to pull off what the Yank footballer fans called a Hail Mary and get just enough lead up there to blow the bastard out of the sky before he could get close enough to crash-dive into *Sea Hawke*—and send her to the bottom, along with her crew of fifty-two souls. Not to mention the two or three people aboard his ship who he loved more than anything in this world.

And just when it looked like that looming, catastrophic event might actually materialize, the doomed pilot made a fatal mistake. Hawke saw that the would-be suicide pilot was now lined up on a glide path. He would try to set the aircraft down on the water on its belly. But there was a problem with that concept, one any fighter jock worthy of the name would surely know: the wind was up. It was far too choppy to even contemplate the notion of a successful water landing.

And yet here he came waggling his wings, his powerful engine screaming, leveling off just a few feet above the wave tops and maintaining that altitude as he made his run toward the *Sea Hawke*. Hawke's only hope now was that the Argie pilot was insufficiently trained to execute the maneuver he was now attempting. Hawke said aloud through gritted teeth:

"*Come on*, you bastard. Careful, because I'm not going anywhere. I'm waiting for you right here, so bring it, damn you!"

Hawke's eyes went wide and he breathed a huge sigh of relief. It looked like they might be able to dodge this bullet after all . . . wait for it . . .

Sure enough!

The Argie fighter jock had caught his portside wing tip just inside the breaking crest of a serious wave, and his airplane instantly went spinning arse over teakettle, totally out of control, ripping the cockpit canopy off the fuselage. He could actually see the enemy pilot now, catapulting across the surface of the water until his fighter jet had expended all of its kinetic energy and begun to sink.

And, as sometimes happens in times of war, another nameless, faceless pilot and his plane slipped beneath the waves, never again to see the sun shining down from the heavens.

———————

Hawke went to the rail to assess the situation. He'd made a calculated decision as the boatload of terrorists got within fairly close proximity to *Sea Hawke*'s stern quarter.

He knew the Cuban skipper, having seen what had just befallen his stalwart fighter escort, might now want to stay well clear of the big sailing yacht. Or maybe not. If Smith was indeed calling the shots, as the captured terrorists had told their interlocutors, *definitely* not.

A yacht that clearly was not at all what it appeared to be, *el capitán cubano* now knew. What she really was, the aging captain had decided, was a warship, a state-of-the-art *destroyer*, well disguised as a sailing yacht. Obviously, he wanted nothing to do with it.

And Hawke decided to indulge him.

El Colón was far too valuable a prize. She was a public relations gift straight from heaven—and thus very much desired by Lord Alexander Hawke. This target represented both America's and Britain's enemies in many ways. Cuba? The return of Marxism and Communism to Cuba, right on America's doorstep? Political disaster for the US and her many allies in the region.

Middle Eastern terrorists? We've got those, too. In spades. Here were all those howling hyenas down there, the worst of the worst of all the terrorist armies on earth. There would be enormous positive PR value if Hawke could send all of them to a swift and watery grave.

He let the old bucket veer away and make a run for the western tip of Cuba and then Havana. He would ghost her until the timing was propitious. He'd follow her for a while, taking his time about things. Then, when the moment was right, he would power up *Sea Hawke*'s big turbo-diesels and go right for her.

Once bow to bow with her, he'd race ahead of her, then suddenly slow and wait for her to steam forward so that *El Colón*'s bow now had about a fifty-foot separation from *Sea Hawke*'s stern. And there Hawke's helmsman would make sure they remained.

Within a kill zone.

Hawke then went out on the bridge wing, where he could look down on the terrorist forces jammed up, packed inside like so many sardines on every square foot of deck. Sitting ducks, every last one of them. And, unbeknownst to them, all doomed.

Which is precisely what happened.

Almost.

Mr. Smith, as per usual, had other ideas.

Hawke went to the rail, looking down at the mash-up of swarming ISIS fighters, and waved at them, smiling his brilliant white smile all the while. Some of them, not having even the foggiest notion of who this idiot on the fancy yacht was, looked up at him and smiled in return.

Not a few of them returned his wave or raised their AKs aloft, hailing in salute, mistakenly thinking they shared a common enemy. And that's when he'd whipped out his trusty old Leica with the telephoto lens and started snapping off as many pictures of this murderous, motley, ragtag crew as he could.

The resulting ISIS photos were to be a surprise e-mail present to his old friend Brick in Virginia. One telephoto shot in particular had caught his attention. It was a face he knew well—right at the top of CIA and FBI's most wanted terrorists. The *most* wanted. He had been the head ISIS honcho during their reign of bloodlust and terror.

Witness to the beheadings, the public stoning death and burning alive of adulterous women who defied the Koran, the legions of gay men thrown off rooftops just for sport. He not only had blood on his hands; he had blood from the top of his head to the tips of his bloody toes!

Hawke had been hot on his trail a few years ago, but he'd lost the scent after Haji had taken a bullet in his shoulder at a firefight in Kabul and had withdrawn from sight.

Hawke had an idea. Pass the photo of Haji around to each and every one of his fighters. Nobody would be allowed to take a shot at this guy. He handed the photo to Stoke.

"Who the hell is that?" Stoke said.

"Stoke," he said. "Listen up. I want you to do something about this character. I want you, Chief, and Lightning to form a six-man commando squad. Use the Wally tender stowed over on the starboard side to board the ship over the stern of *El Colón* and take Haji alive. Bring Haji to me for interrogation once you're back on board *Sea Hawke*. I'll put him under guard down in the brig for now, and then CIA and FBI will send him packing to Gitmo."

Stoke found the chief firing an AR-15 from a location up high on the ship and waved him to come down. He told the chief all about Haji and the plan to take him alive. "The sooner, the better, Chief. Boss says our best shot at him right now is to board *El Colón* over her stern. That's where they're weakest. He wants six of us to go get this trumped-up dickhead. And we got to bring him back alive, for God's sake!"

Hawke radioed *Sea Hawke*'s captain to maintain current course and speed alongside the Cuban vessel while he raced down to the main deck and, thence, forward to the cannon turret, taking the measure of his crew, now at battle stations, as he advanced forward on the wide, sun-bleached teak deck.

He was pleased by what he saw.

The men aboard at the guns appeared vigilant and yet relaxed, and they would lose no time, not even one-tenth of a second, in opening fire should an attack by the ISIS fighters commence; but, like all seasoned and veteran warfighters everywhere, they were all savvy enough to know not to waste their reserves of strength and energy by staying all keyed-up unnecessarily.

The operative word was "chill."

Thunder, Stoke, Lightning, and their three handpicked commandos were all present. Their fighters were all soldiers of fortune, former French Foreign Legionnaires, and mercenaries from Europe and Asia. They were all hard veterans of war, having spent years when during any moment death might swoop down upon them from the skies. The weapons of war they handled had long been an integral part of their lives, not toys for some formal parade, nor wearisome nuisances to be kept clean and polished in accordance with meaningless and outdated military conventions.

Their guns were of the very essence of life, as had been the long rifles to the frontier pioneers, the brush to the artist, the bow to the concert violinist. In a dangerous world where the rule of law was "kill or be killed," they were determined to be the killers and not the killed—they were the tiger stalking the Serengeti in pursuit of prey; they all lived under the very same law of the jungle.

Hawke stepped out onto the foredeck. He instantly felt a cool, wet whisper of breath on his cheeks. Fog, big-time, and no advance word from his meteorologist. What the hell? He put the Leica to his eyes and stared at the northern horizon, what little he could see of it. The front was a deep, boiling purple, and it wouldn't be long before *Sea Hawke* was becalmed in zero visibility.

Stoke was on the radio to Hawke. "Boss, we're back."

"And? Haji?"

"We got his sorry ass. Already put him down in the brig with two guards."

"God love you, Stoke," Hawke said. "You're the best!"

A much-relieved Hawke, now back in his turret seat and looking at the live feed on his CCTV monitor, was observing the chaotic scene aboard *El Colón* via the tiny video cameras mounted up in the yacht's rigging. On the foredeck, a circle of fighters had formed around a group of men who appeared to be roasting a goat on an open fire, burning gaily on the worn steel deck.

There was also a group of Hezbollah fighters lined up on the foredeck, at the old steamer's bow rail, ripping up acres of bleached-out teak decking.

"What the hell do you suppose those maniacs are doing *now*, Lieutenant?" Hawke said.

Lieutenant Jones had intel from some of the ISIS captives already held down in the brig and awaiting interrogation.

"We were told that they would be erecting jury-rigged wooden boarding ladders assembled from the ship's decking. They plan to board us, sir! They're slowly massing at our stern! It's a ragged bunch of ISIS and Cuban fighters but as violently hostile a one as ever I've seen."

Hawke knew that these satanic butchers' unholy mission would be to kill every last one of the fighters in the brave legions of Hawke's dauntless crew.

After all, Hawke and company were all that stood between them and a heroic Marxist return to the glories of the Castro era, when Cuba was a beacon to the world and stood as proof that the teachings of Lenin, Marx, and Trotsky were the way forward.

Hawke, his blood aboil, grinned silently, for well he knew it did not require any great leap of intuition to know that having a craven mob of jacked-up ISIS killers on board his ship, hell-bent on a bloodthirsty rampage, running freely, killing everyone who got in their way, was no way to run a railroad, nor a valiant British warship in disguise.

They had to be stopped.

And, Hawke knew that to kill the beast, he had to first cut off the head. The head of the demented Mr. Smith in particular—an evil fiend in human form, and the man who was now leading them into battle.

Today, Hawke swore to himself, was to be the day when he rid himself of this vicious, vile monster, so mildly named *Mr. Smith*.

"Lieutenant Jones," Hawke said, "tell the lads it's time to get aloft, high up into the rigging. Instruct them to climb to their assigned positions and hold them in reserve until they hear from me—or you, if something happens to me."

Hawke smiled at his young lieutenant, then turned away and shot up to the highest yardarm at the very top of the foremast with some very Tarzan-like rope climbing in the process. He'd even shed his tunic, thinking there was an off chance that he might appear an even more lethal foe!

He was not alone up there in the stratosphere at the top of the rigging. Several of them were up here for a reason. One that could turn the tide of battle at a critical juncture.

He and a handpicked team of five had spent the night prior, in howling winds and stinging rains, practicing high in the rigging. Hawke had a plan. He had done a schematic drawing of the ship's rigging, including a series of intersecting lines hung in the proper order for his team to reach the stern from the bow in short order without ever setting foot on the decks.

Now it was time to put the plan into action.

"Think Tarzan, lads," he'd said straight-faced to his teammates. "Imagine we're swinging through the trees, through the jungle, en route to reach Jane and rescue her from the headhunters and cannibals. Are you boys with me?"

"Aye!" they all shouted in unison.

One of those present tried unsuccessfully to stifle a laugh at what their heroic commander apparently had in mind.

"You find this amusing, Jarvis?" Hawke said to him.

"The Tarzan thing? A bit rich, yes, sir, I do. But I've felt that way about many of your plans on the eves of prior battles. And the good Lord knows, you've always won the day, sir!"

"And win we shall again!" Hawke said, and, raising his cutlass in the air, he motioned for them to get aloft immediately. Battle was nigh.

And the fog was rolling in.

That wasn't a good thing. There's no way he could execute his plan if the men couldn't even see where the bloody lines were when they were sailing through the rigging . . .

———————

Lord Hawke now stood bare-chested and barefooted and balanced somewhat precariously atop the carbon fiber foremast spar some forty feet above the heaving deck below. It was going to be a dangerous business, to be sure. But he'd thought his scheme through, with input from both Harry Brock and Stokely Jones, Jr. All agreed that everything had to go off precisely as planned, or Hawke himself would face certain torture and a nightmarish death at the hands of the barbarians.

He'd faced that nightmare at the hands of a vile and cruel enemy before. Once, in a vile Russian prison called Energetika, he was fated to be executed at dawn. It would not have been an easy death. Death seldom comes easily to a man who is to be hoisted atop a stout tree, the upper part of which is devoid of all branches and the top of which has been whittled down to a hideous point.

And then the victim finds himself lowered ever farther down, inch by inch, until the spike enters his bowels and the weight of his body finds him ever more deeply impaled, his guts ripped to pieces, until, in all his agony, he's granted the relief of death.

But he wasn't fated to die then, and he wasn't fated to die now.

He was fated to kill.

CHAPTER 34

"F lock round, me hearties!" Hawke cried out to his handpicked team of five. Five aerial acrobats–cum–counterterrorist warfighters gathered round Hawke on the ship's afterdeck, his broad, confident white smile beaming at them all. Here was a natural warrior clearly spoiling for a fight. They gathered round him now, eager for any last-minute orders or instructions from on high.

And Hawke had now finally found his team, as the five men he'd been looking for had emerged up on deck and gathered at the bow—men who would spend the coming battle with their feet seldom or never even touching the decks.

They would be swinging, like so many Tarzans, through not trees but the big ship's four high-tech carbon fiber masts, swinging to and fro, fore and aft, from the yardarms of the masts marching from stem to stern, executing lightning-fast surgical attacks to take out enemy combatants beyond the reach of the crew for whatever reasons. Hawke said:

"It's high time we began ascending into the heavens and make ready to join the fray that will soon consume us all. Far too many of those sons-ofbitches over there are soon going to be getting past our defensive arm-locked cordon ranged round the stern rail. It shall be up to us to take them off the bloody board!"

"You're saying that stern measures are called for, Skipper?" the one called Tristan said, smiling broadly.

"Aye, lad, I am, indeed." Hawke smiled. "Thank you for that, old boy. Just what we needed." This kind of jolly banter was precisely what he wanted to inculcate among his five lads as they gathered their courage and their wits about them and prepared once more to go into battle. It showed confidence—yes, and courage, too.

Hawke had gathered his team of five together on the foredeck. It was nearing the critical time to begin deploying them to their battle stations aloft, each man taking his position atop the masts, out on the crosstrees.

Anticipating that, in the course of their voyage, there would likely be any number of pitched battles at sea here aboard the *Sea Hawke*, they'd been rehearsing for this high-wire act since the first day they'd boarded back in Holland.

They'd called themselves, right from the outset, "The High Five." After all, they were nothing if not an incredibly well-trained and fearless aerial acrobatic team, using their special skills to take the battle to the enemy at another level.

Acrobats carrying razor-sharp swords, mind you, for that had been Hawke's original vision for the team. They had been created to respond to any armed incursion aboard the yacht and to engage in hand-to-hand combat on the open water.

Their names were Tristan, Smitty, Antoine, Christian, and, last but certainly not least, Lancelot, otherwise known as their fearless leader. And, save for Lancelot, who was by far the eldest of the bunch, they were all in their early thirties, recruits from the French Foreign Legion, like Antoine, and the Ringling Brothers and Barnum & Bailey Circus, like Smitty. Meanwhile, Christian was a retired former member of the US Navy Seal Team Six who'd seen action all over the globe, and Lancelot was one of the most highly decorated paramilitary troopers ever to serve with Britain's SAS.

As was their tradition and custom when going into battle, they were, all five of them, both bare-chested and barefooted.

It sent a signal: Your enemy is fearless.

Each man was also armed with a razor-sharp cutlass or broadsword, now secured to his left hip inside a brilliantly colored sash now wrapped and tied round his waist.

Hawke's own sash was a bright splash of crimson that highlighted the deepwater tan he had acquired on the voyage thus far. As the fog had now

dissipated somewhat, the brilliant sun was glinting off the solid gold hilt
of his father's ceremonial cutlass.

Christian's broad chest was tanned to a deep nut brown that highlighted his snow-white sash, whilst Tristan's sash was a strong shade of
violet. Antoine of the Foreign Legion wore, logically enough, a beautiful
silk scarf done up in French blue. Lancelot wore a sash of royal purple.
And Smitty, the youngest and smallest of the lot, was resplendent in a
sash of emerald green.

"Are you ready to do your duty, boys?" Hawke said.

"Aye, we are, Skipper," Lancelot answered for them.

"Then up you go! Go! Go!" Hawke cried, and they all shot upward
with what looked like supernatural speed, moving simultaneously and
instantaneously, so quickly that it seemed they were not climbing the
lines arranged so expertly in the rigging so much as simply flying upward
on invisible wings.

"And hear this," Hawke shouted up to them, then put two fingers to
his lips and brought forth a piercing whistle that could be heard all the
way at the back of the boat. It sounded exactly like a bosun whistle and
would be recognized even above the cacophonous roar of men fighting
for their lives at extremely close quarters.

Hawke had singled out the brawny Lancelot, with his flowing dark
brown locks brushing his shoulders. He wanted this highly decorated
SAS commando to concentrate on finding and isolating the man in black.
Mr. Smith.

Hawke said, "Lance, listen up. I've ordered Lieutenant Jones to alert
me the moment Smith comes aboard. Three toots on the bosun pipe.
Now, as soon as you've cornered him and peeled him away from the
herd, Jones will sound the pipe again, and I will fly to him with the intent
to kill. Understood?"

"Aye, sir. Crystal."

"Good on you, mate!" Hawke said. "Get him somewhere apart from the
mass of the fighting, a place where there's deck room enough for a sword-
fight to the death, should that happen, Lance. Once you've got him where
you want, give a whistle, old boy, and stand back when I appear, swinging

down to the deck from on high, yes? Give that old cowboy a wake-up call. What time is it? Time to die."

"Aye-aye, sir!" the man said. "His time has finally come."

Hawke had started their training during the last six months of the completion of the *Sea Hawke*. He was now certain that, to a man, they were ready.

Ready for anything.

Thus, his High Five team would soon all be at battle stations, staring down from the yardarms at the decks so far beneath their bare feet as events unfolded, each and every one of them keeping an eye on Hawke—and an eye out for the man in black. In addition to Lieutenant Jones and Hawke's whistled signals to the team, he'd prepped them in a series of hand signals they would also use to make any adjustments to his plan as warranted by unforeseen circumstances. Trying always to anticipate any unintended consequences, that's what the skipper had ordered.

Hawke was worried about one thing, though he would never give voice to it. He worried, in the back recesses of his mind, that he might be killed before he even joined the fray.

He had worried that Smith or one of his henchmen might spot him in the rigging high above. But he now realized that, in the smoke and heat of battle, and possibly the swirling mists of fog, he would be difficult to spot. What with all the *Sea Hawke* sailors and sharpshooters above and below his station on the mizzenmast yardarm, he could probably lose himself in the lofty crowd high in the ship's rigging.

Just long enough for Lancelot to isolate him and keep the decks clear of other fighters until only Smith remained where Hawke wanted to engage him in a bit of swordplay.

Hawke's blood was up, all right, that much was sure. And yet there was an almost trancelike quality about his movements and the fearsome grin he wore on his face.

He fully intended to extract a terrible revenge on this psycho cowboy, this twisted killer who had caused such pain, heartbreak, and fear, not only to his beloved son, but also to Pelham, Miss Devereux, and Ambrose Congreve.

And so he stood his perilous ground, atop the slippery carbon spar, the yardarms as slippery from the fog as ever they could have been. He took a deep breath to compose himself. Stepping off into space when the time came, with the decks some fifty feet below him, required a bit of grace under pressure.

He had completed preparations for his mano a mano fight to the death with his archenemy. Like the five other members of what Hawke had taken to calling the *Sea Hawke*'s own "air command," he'd heaved a fifty-foot length of cordage, a halyard in fact, all the way up to the uppermost yardarm, perhaps some twenty feet just above him.

When he was a boy, his father had taken him to the art-house cinema in Soho to see an old Hollywood picture called *The Sea Hawk*. It was the inspiration for his father's naming his own new schooner *Sea Hawke*, and it starred the boy's favorite movie hero, the dashing Errol Flynn, who in the heat of battle would swing down to the deck from a halyard line tied to an upper yardarm and wound round his wrist.

If a movie star can do this, he thought, getting ready to leap into space, by God, I can do it, too!

He now held the bitter end of the halyard in his left hand, having wrapped it securely several times around his left wrist. His right hand rested quietly on the solid gold hilt of his father's ceremonial cutlass. But though his father had always liked to refer to the blade as ceremonial, it was hardly that. Over the years his dad had been honing that blade to razor-like sharpness.

Earlier, in his stateroom, he had wound a scarlet sash several times around his waist. And it was there that the cutlass was safely secured to his left hip. He was sure that—

His thoughts were suddenly interrupted by sporadic bursts of gunfire rising up from somewhere on the afterdeck at the stern. Smith and his ISIS crew had now commenced the long upward climb on the flimsy wooden boarding ladders to reach *Sea Hawke*'s stern and subsequently board the enemy vessel.

He could just make out Lieutenant Jones standing among a few heavily armed sailors who were wisely holding their fire until, as Hawke had told young Mr. Jones, they could see the whites of Mr. Smith's eyes.

Suddenly, he saw Mr. Jones whirl round and use his right arm and three-toned whistle on the bosun pipe as prearranged signals to Hawke that the battle was well nigh at hand—that the enemy would soon be at the gate, but was not yet of sufficient mass or strength and prepared to engage.

Hawke instantly flipped on his radio. His orders would now be broadcast on speakers located throughout the entire ship. He paused to keep his breath for a moment, then raised the transceiver to his lips. He then shouted at the top of his lungs:

"On my signal! REPEL BOARDERS! I REPEAT, REPEL ALL BOARDERS! HOLD FAST, ME LADDIES, HOLD FAST!"

The effect of these powerful seagoing words, handed down to generations of sailors and seamen round the world and time tested from the glorious past, on the crew was electric, galvanizing them into a cohesive fighting force with a formidable enemy. Nelson's hallowed words moved Hawke in ways he'd never imagined heretofore. This precious moment, in this now and in this time and place, was what truly stirred his soul, and what he'd always lived for. To be in the thick of it once more!

Suddenly, perched high above on his spar, he was that six-year-old lad once more! It was as if he were watching Errol Flynn, aboard his flagship, the original *Sea Hawk*, an epic figure flying through the air from high in the rigging, a halyard wrapped round his wrist just the way Hawke's was now. And, also, Flynn's great broadsword to hand, just as his lordship's was! Magic!

CHAPTER 35

Alex Hawke stood high atop his mighty perch, his feet spread wide apart to increase his purchase on the smooth finish of the spar at the pinnacle of the yardarm, his powerful arms crossed upon his broad chest, calmly calling down to the men, brave, stouthearted chaps who were even now climbing ever upward into the highest reaches of the ship's rigging like so many monkeys until they reached their battle stations and— He heard the piercing sound of Lieutenant Jones's three-note whistle on the pipe! It could mean only one thing.

Smith! The fiend in human form was now aboard Hawke's vessel! Where was he? He peered down through all the confusion of rigging and spars and cleats and halyards and stays.

And there he saw Smith, who, as luck would have it, was standing with his back to Hawke.

He stood out, even among this motley crew: a gaunt figure dressed head to toe in black, skeletal, with shoulder-length black hair and a full black beard down to his sternum.

It was him, all right, Hawke saw clearly, urging his fighters on, smiting the enemy with heavy blows . . . Hawke's heart stopped.

Smith had caught sight of the handsome young Lieutenant Jones. Jones was clearly unaware of the stealthy approach of the enemy, being consumed by fencing simultaneously with three ISIS killers armed with massive machete-like blades already dripping with the lieutenant's blood as Jones took a knee and desperately fought them from the deck!

"Lieutenant! Up here! Hold fast, boy, help is on its way!" Hawke shouted down to him. He saw the boy's face turn upward searching for Hawke's face and, seeing it high above, mustering a manly smile and shakily trying to rise to his feet once more.

Lancelot was just above Hawke. He, too, saw the young lieutenant down on one knee, bloody and wounded, with Smith advancing toward him with his blade out for a kill.

Hawke cupped his hands round his mouth and called up to Lancelot, "Lance! It's Jones! He's hurt! Go, go!"

And, so, with the inspiration of the great pirate captains of old in his heart and in his mind and the fate of the young lieutenant at imminent risk, Lancelot flew down from on high, through the smoke of battle, the powerful stench of spilled blood, and the hellish hail of lead, sailing right through hell itself, it seemed, down, down, down, and into the thick of battle.

He had timed his leap so that he could snatch the wounded officer right off the deck and into his arms before soaring upward once more to the safety of the upper rigging of the mizzenmast.

Were Lancelot honest with himself, he would have given himself perhaps a zero chance of success with this scheme. Too tricky by half, he knew.

What the hell? he thought. That had never stopped him before!

But in the event he proved himself wrong . . .

Lancelot shot out his right hand at the very instant he soared just above the lieutenant's head, grasping the man beneath his armpits and round his chest, then heaving him up mightily in his powerful arms and off the deck just as Smith lunged forward to finish him.

Hawke cheered when he saw this and realized that the High Five had turned themselves into a fighting unit of the first order and one that could easily help the *Sea Hawke* to victory this fateful day.

He glanced down at Smith, who still had his back to Hawke, thank God. It was now or never.

He flew.

As he swooped down toward the unsuspecting Smith, he raised both his powerful legs and stuck them out horizontally, directly in front of him . . .

. . . and slammed his boots viciously into Smith's back, right between his shoulders. The blow packed tremendous force and sent the cowboy pitching forward, his head striking the deck hard, blood pouring down his face from a wound on his forehead. Somehow, he managed to hold on to his bowie knife, and when Hawke let go of the halyard and dropped to the deck behind the man, he whirled and lunged at Hawke with his blade extended.

Both swords were out.

The air resounded with the deep metallic clang of steel on steel. It was nothing like the silly fighting one sees with broadswords in the cinema or on the stage. It was not even like the rapier fighting which one sees rather better done. This was all-out, real broadsword fighting. The sea air had had its usual effect on Hawke since the outset of the voyage. Despite his long hiatus when it came to the sword and its uses, he found that all his old battles came back to him, and his arms and fingers remembered their old skill.

Round and round the two combatants circled; stroke after stroke, thrust upon thrust, they gave as good as they got. Then, so quickly that no one aboard, gathered round to witness what they knew to be a fight to the death, could quite see how it happened, Hawke flashed his broadsword round with a peculiar twist of the wrist, and Smith's blade flew out of his grip and clattered across the deck.

Hawke had learned long ago, in the halcyon days on the playing fields at Eton, the fencing, and the boxing, that even the best swordsman in the world may be disarmed by a trick that's new to him.

The cowboy made a move to retrieve the knife. But Hawke stepped into him and placed the tip of his cutlass on his Adam's apple, adding pressure, drawing blood.

"You're done, Smith," Hawke said.

"You think?" he said.

"Oh, I do. I really do," Hawke said with a smile. And then, to Lancelot, "Mr. Lancelot, bind his wrists behind his back and escort him to the bow."

"Time for his farewell ceremony, Skipper?"

"It is. High time, indeed," Hawke said. "He's well past his sell-by date, don't you think?"

"What the hell are you talking about, Hawke?" Smith said.

"Purely for the amusement of the crew, we're about to reenact one of the great traditions of the Royal Navy and my own pirate ancestors whenever some sailor committed a grievous offense against an officer or fellow crewman."

Many of the crew were already gathered at the bow when Hawke arrived, Smith's knife in his hand. A fifteen-foot plank of wood had been fastened to the ship's pulpit and extended about a dozen feet out over the water at a height of twenty feet or more.

"What's this? What are you doing?" Smith whined.

"This?" Hawke said. "Bit of fun and games, that's all. Nothing to get your knickers in a twist about. It's called 'walking the plank.' Seen many pirate movies? Heard of it?"

"No, no. Please. I beg you!"

"Good! So you have heard of it!" Hawke smiled. "That will add a bit of drama, for sure. The boys will eat it up!"

"Look, Hawke, I beg you to spare me. I have access to untold billions of dollars. Mountains of gold belonging to my employer, Vladimir Putin. Stored high in the Swiss Alps in great vaults. Vaults to which I have the combination. I could make you very rich! Richer than you are!"

"Most kind, Smith. But I'm afraid it's too late for bargaining. You lost your get-out-of-jail card many years ago. When you began your efforts to destroy me and my family. I don't really—

"I beg forgiveness."

"Really? Move! Step forward!"

Hawke put a hand on the cowboy's shoulder and roughly shoved him forward and out onto the plank.

"Crewman, throw in a bit more chum. Our finny denizens of the deep are not showing sufficient excitement. They're about to receive quite a treat. Prime Texas beef on the hoof, so to speak. Well, perhaps not 'prime' exactly, but, from the looks of them, I don't think they're going to be picky . . ."

He stuck the point of the bowie knife in the middle of Smith's back and shoved him forward and farther out onto the plank. Far enough out that he could observe the chum and blood and offal floating atop the surface. It was causing a frenzy of excitement among the ten or so bull sharks and great whites, as it happened, that were now in a roiling frenzy, whipping the water into a pinkish froth . . .

"Sir Lancelot, blindfold, please," Hawke said. "And bind his hands."

"Aye-aye," he replied, and tied a ragged skein of sail that covered Smith's eyes.

"No!" Smith said. "No."

"You want me to run you through with your own blade? Because I'll be glad to do so. It will be for my son. And for my dear friend Pelham. And for the beautiful Sigrid, whom you took from me in the very worst way in my own home. Oh, you deserve this, old boy. I cannot imagine anyone more deserving of this fate . . . Now get the hell out there. Do it now!"

"No! I can't!"

"Oh, do show a bit of manly courage, Smith. You'll disappoint the lads if you start whimpering."

"You can't do this . . ." the cowboy said, his voice a tremolo.

"Oh, believe me, I can, old chap. And I will! Now! Start walking. And do not stop until I tell you to, or by God and all that's holy, I will skin you alive with your own knife before I throw you to the sharks! Start moving!"

Smith, who had little choice but to comply, began to slowly shuffle forward, pausing to use one tentative foot to see if he'd reached the business end of the plank.

"He bores me, Lancelot," Hawke said, and walked out on the plank and put his hands on Smith's shoulders, saying, "Those sharks are going to rip you to pieces and tear you limb from limb before you die. And even that's too good for you . . ."

"Oh, sweet Jesus . . ." Smith croaked.

He screamed when he felt the tip of his bowie knife in Hawke's hands pierce his flesh and start pushing him forward . . . and then he found himself pinwheeling in midair before he hit the water. The sharks reacted immediately, fighting over his limbs, his feet, his hands. He felt severe pain on his right forearm. The last thing he was aware of was the feeling of having his arm ripped from his shoulder . . .

Hawke stood and watched until the bitter end.

And then he turned his back on what used to be his vile enemy and walked away.

His death had been painful, to be sure.

But not nearly painful enough.

———————

Hawke saw that many of the men still crowded below on *El Colón*'s main deck and not engaged in the frantic work of ripping up sections of the teak decking at the stern for the boarding ladders were ogling Hawke's yacht and trying to engage some of her crew who were presently at battle stations on both the main and stern decks—and then he saw it unfolding before his eyes.

Random men in the crowd on the *El Colón* had decided it was a jolly good time to pull heavy automatic weapons from inside their voluminous robes and open fire on his crew! A number of Hawke's men were already down on the deck and bleeding . . . Three were perfectly still. He thumbed the mic on the radio and barked, "Attention, all crew. We are under attack. Fire at will!"

Then he turned to his two-man turret crew.

"This is it!" he cried out to his gunnery lads. "Open fire on those bastards over there! Kill as many as you can before they all go down as one. These are dead men walking. They just don't know it yet!"

In a fever of anger at the bloody ISIS murderers, the vilest of the vile, the two laser gunners powered up the laser cannon and prepared to fire. The blind rage of these savages couldn't leave this mortal coil too soon to suit Hawke. His two-gun crew in the turret was busily ripping the enemy to shreds. But he knew that Brick wanted them all on the bottom. Pronto.

With the possible exception of Haji Abdallah, the world's most-wanted terrorist, of course. But now they had him in custody.

Since he'd already proven to himself that he could slice a massive enemy warship in half, Hawke decided on a new approach to employ this time out.

He would pick four target areas along the hull and well below the waterline. When all systems were ready, he would fire four short bursts of energy in rapid succession. One astern, two amidships, and one forward.

Elon, in one of his infamous Zoom tutorials, had told his new customer that the directed energy beams, traveling through water, were clearly capable of burning large holes inside a ship's lower hull, all the way from the stem to the stern.

El Colón would die fairly quickly as a rush of seawater flooded inside her rusted innards, almost instantly replacing air in every cubic inch of space belowdecks with Mother Nature's good old H_2O.

Her troops, her human cargo, having witnessed the powerful directed energy bursts from the cannon, were stricken with fear as it dawned on them that they were faced with an enemy with almost unearthly powers such as they had never witnessed during the recent wars with the Americans and their hated Middle Eastern allies.

But that knowledge would go down with the terrified crew and fighters crammed together in one seething mass on the ship's decks.

And, thus, a new era in modern warfare was about to be launched.

———

Hawke knew that when he finally got around to telling the brass at the Pentagon, CIA, and State Department about the capture of the world's most-wanted terrorist and the amazing successes he'd experienced with Elon Musk's radical new offensive weapon, the balance of power with, say, the Iranians in the Strait of Hormuz, or with the Chinese in the South China Sea, or the Russian Sukhoi SU-27s and SU-30s threatening US air power off the coast of Alaska or China's nuclear subs in the Arctic Circle, would never, ever be the same.

Note to self:

Sometime prior to sunset this very afternoon, he must dash off a thank-you note to Mr. Musk. Thanks to his efforts, Hawke had single-handedly transformed his beloved *Sea Hawke* into one of the most powerful, both defensively and offensively, ships arrayed out across the Seven Seas! The time to test his theory had come at last.

―――――――――

Hawke initiated a systems program that rotated the turret 90 degrees until it was facing due west, and thus aimed directly at the starboard side of *El Colón*'s rusted hull. He then lowered the elevation of the cannon fifteen degrees and picked a point well below the waterline, nearest to the stern. He intended to fire off a burst of lethal energy and open a hole the size of a manhole cover in the leaky old ship's hull.

He triggered the Green Monster, expecting the by-now-familiar brilliant flash of green.

Nothing. No flash—nada—nothing at all!

"Bloody hell!" Hawke cried. "Lieutenant Jones! Come over here! The bloody laser's malfunctioning! And now is not a particularly timely moment for the damn thing to shut down. Get those two laser gunners up here immediately. See if they can fix the bloody thing before it's too late!"

Hawke was well aware of the imperiled *El Colón* skipper's plans to board the yacht. Even now, ISIS crewmen began laying their makeshift ladders against *Sea Hawke*'s stern, heaving grappling hooks aboard *Sea Hawke*'s stern deck and securing them to bollards and cleats wherever they could find them aboard their own vessel.

The enemy now had two choices: troops could stay aboard the old steamer and go down with the ship, or they could take the fight to the enemy on the home turf. At least there they would have some chance of survival.

Most of them, Hawke saw with visible concern, were racing forward, gathering at the bow of *El Colón* in a frantic rush to board him in lieu of a watery grave.

Why not? That's what he himself would have done. In hand-to-hand combat, at least they had some semblance of a chance of survival.

He rotated the turret counterclockwise once more, choosing as his target a spot just aft of the amidships position. Ready, aim, fire! he said to himself, burning a fresh hole in the hull as easily as one slices open a hole in a can of bloody tuna fish. And, as man has known since the dawn of time, "Nature abhors a vacuum!"

Just two holes in the hull to go, now, and the boat's stern was already visibly riding lower in the water.

The third shot. As was apparent from the expressions of panic on the faces of the ragtag mujahideen, something was gravely amiss. Ancient alarms aboard *El Colón* were sounding from stem to stern! A rumor had spread like a virus among the troops aboard—the captain was considering ordering the dreaded words, "Abandon ship!"

These guys, Hawke suddenly realized, had to be living out their last minutes in abject terror! They were, after all, desert rats, were they not? The percentage of this population who knew how to bloody well *swim*? Less than zero! Hell, their only chance of survival now was to get their skinny asses up and over *Sea Hawke*'s stern rail.

Hawke then dropped down to the deck and out of the turret. He raced aft to the steps leading up to the bridge. Arriving at the portside bridge wing, he stood at the rail and lit his fifth cigarette of the day as a minor gesture of celebration.

It occurred to him that the warm and cozy feelings he was now experiencing must be something akin to those felt by the skippers of the Royal Navy battleships *King George V* and the HMS *Romney* during World War II as they stood there and watched the "unsinkable" German battleship *Bismarck* being thoroughly pummeled, knocking its battery of guns out of action and killing most of the senior officers on board.

This happened as her two attackers closed to within three thousand meters and fired at will. *Bismarck* was afire from stem to stern and sank with all hands in 1941. Twenty-two hundred German souls were lost in this triumph, one of Britain's finest hours of the war, on a par with their victory against Nazi air power in the Battle of Britain.

Those two Royal Navy skippers, he well knew, had had far bigger fish to fry that day than the lowly owner of the yacht *Sea Hawke*. They had the

823-foot German *Bismarck*, which at the time was the largest battleship the world had ever seen. He, on the other hand, had only the sixty-foot rust bucket *El Colón* to boast about.

But, he thought, admittedly with grimmest hints of schadenfreude, his level of self-satisfaction at witnessing the current demise of the ISIS fighters aboard the rusty old barge *El Colón* could scarcely be outweighed by those of the officers aboard those two Royal Navy warships who sank the *Bismarck* that fateful day in the North Atlantic off the coast of France, May 27, 1941.

As a side note, Hawke's father had taken him, when he was but a six-year-old boy, to the Curzon Theater in London to see the picture *Sink the Bismarck!* It had moved him so powerfully that he always thought that the experience had, almost single-handedly, set his course on the life that he would lead when he became a man.

El Colón's stern had settled even more drastically. Her bow was now tilted upward at a steep angle and getting steeper. It made the ladders much closer to the *Sea Hawke*'s stern rails, but in the mad scramble to get to the top, a lot of the early boarders were being grabbed by their fiercest comrades in arms and heaved into the sea to make room for the waves of the ones climbing up and over for their lives.

They all had but one thing on their minds, Hawke imagined: all those luscious virgins waiting for the heroes to arrive in paradise.

The abandon-ship order over the static-filled PA system had now been delivered from *El Colón*'s bridge.

This naturally had an adverse effect on the mood of the swarms of desperate, bearded men crowded on the exposed decks, each and every one of them now holding a one-way ticket to paradise clenched in his gnarled hands. These were men who now knew, with total precision, how their lives would end.

The big bad wolf was at the door, so to speak, Hawke thought. Now, if only Lady Luck would hold . . . Then he lit a cigarette. One last one before he joined the fray!

Puffing away, loving the bite of the smoke as he watched the pitch of panic climb even higher, he was a man of two minds.

Although his job as senior counterterrorist officer at MI6 required him to take a man's life rather frequently, he had no taste for either blood or any loss of human life.

But for these vile enemies of the free world? Of freedom of religion? Of the sanctity of life? Of the reverence for women?

Well, what the hell else *could* he do?

He'd have to make an exception, that's all. Alas, he would take no prisoners this day. Except for the one already taken. The worst of them all.

Haji.

CHAPTER 36

"El gran problema was a massive traffic jam at the mouth of Revolution Bay . . ."

Revolution Bay, Isla de Pinos

Thunder and Lightning commandos were still hammering the vast array of all and sundry vessels and their crews and troopers all trying like hell to get out from under the withering fire directed at them by these commandos sent by God knows who to make their lives unbearable, if not over. The expeditionary force here assembled now found themselves, quite literally, sitting ducks bobbing about in a small pond with little hope of escaping anytime soon, if ever.

The chief had a plan to exploit the situation. He knew the amount of gunfire directed at his men had dropped substantially as the hours wore on. Clearly, the men in charge on the various boats were beginning to realize that, if they kept this shitstorm up, not only would more of their fighters die, but those who would arrive in Havana would arrive with little or no ammo.

El gran problema was a nasty nautical traffic jam created by Mother Nature herself at the mouth of Revolution Bay, as well as the carelessness of General de los Reyes and, to some extent, General Castro himself.

There was a little-noticed, unanticipated, nor long-remembered topographical problem with General de los Reyes's unfortunate choice to use Revolution Bay as the desired staging location for the historic seaborne invasion of Cuba—this for the manifest purposes of insurrection.

At the intersection of bay and sea, where the twain shall meet, there was a natural bottleneck. Two sandy spits of land, with abundant palms, were like extended arms jutting out into the water from the island proper, creating a narrow opening to the sea. There were, the chief thought, only about twenty feet of width between them.

So it was impossible for more than one boat at a time to exit the bay and make for Havana. And now there was another problem for the hombres so eager for depature to Havana. Since the late, unlamented departure of *El Colón*, very few boats indeed had made it out beyond the bay and to the open sea.

And it was just then that the chief saw that this was the ideal time for him to wreak a bit more havoc on these misguided, misbegotten revolutionary wannabes. He silently motioned for his two UDT guys to move up to his position hidden at the edge of the jungle.

"Sir!" they said as one. SEALs to the bone, that was for damn sure.

"Awright, listen up," Chief said, seeing them glance with approval at his favorite SEALs T-shirt from Coronado. "You can run, but you'll only die tired!" The T-shirt he was wearing today was one of his favorites, too. "If you don't sweat in training, you'll bleed in combat."

He continued, "Got this idea. Involves high-powered explosives. You two still-wet-behind-the-ears characters familiar with that particular concept?"

"Aye-aye, sir!"

"Good. 'Cause here's what we're gonna do now. You children see that big steel-hulled commercial fishing trawler out there? The one patiently waiting her turn in line? She's next. So, before she weighs anchor and makes for Havana Harbor, you two birds swim out to her and attach two of your most powerful limpets to her hull. One to port and one to starboard. Sync the detonators. Radio me as soon as I can push the bang button. Sooner the better. Now, just so we're on the same page, why the hell are we doing this? What do you two teenagers suppose?"

The younger of the two SEALs, the one called Trace, the one the chief privately referred to as Officer Material, spoke up immediately.

"Sir! There's not that much seawater under her keel. The way she's listing to starboard makes me think she's run aground on the outgoing tide. And almost no sea room to maneuver in once she floats off the shoal. We send that shrimper to the bottom and we block the only exit. Permanently. Nobody gets out. All these Cuban dudes? And their glorious revolution? They're both pretty much rat-fucked, sir. And they're not exactly Patton's Third Army, sir."

"They're not exactly Patton's anything," Hawke said. "Not even a drop of his sweat."

"No, sir!"

They snapped off two quality salutes and slipped into the water with the mines. Half an hour later, they were back, reporting mission accomplished to the chief, who was half hidden in his jungle camo paint in the dense green of the tropical jungle.

"Mission accomplished, sir!" Officer Material barked.

"Attaboy, son."

"May I?" the rugged young SEAL said, his index finger poised just above the bang button.

Chief said, "Hell, yeah, Trace. If not you, who? If not now, when?"

"Exactly!" he said, and lit the candles.

A riotous, thunderous explosion at the mouth of the bay was the last thing anyone trapped in Revolution Bay wanted. And then the crews and the fighters packed aboard *all* saw the rusted prow of the *Cuba Libre* out of Havana rise up into the air majestically, sort of, and then, all of them praying that the thing would sink back to the bottom, saw it settle in the middle of the channel mouth. An obstacle, looming up with about thirty feet of hull exposed, fifteen feet wide, and completely blocking even the slightest fevered dream of escape from this living hell.

"That oughta do it," Chief said, mildly.

"Definitely do it, sir. These troops are not going anywhere now, and they damn well know it. What next?"

"Next?" the chief said. "Their move. Entirely. We wait. See what they do . . ."

"I think they'll swim for it, sir," one said. "If we let them."

"We'll see," Chief said. "We let them do what they need to do. I don't see any point in trying to stop them from going ashore safely. They've surrendered. These are guys down from tiny towns up in the Sierra Madre. Farmers and dairymen and cattle ranchers. Schoolteachers, doctors, husbands, fathers, brothers. Men and boys who've seen their dreams destroyed today by a pair of arrogant and incompetent tyrants, ruled by the dogma of the Red Star Brigade. The impending alliance of all the world's Communist countries, whose stated mission was to shift the balance of world power away from America and her allies."

The other UDT guy, Sonny, the one from Lookout Mountain, Tennessee, the one the chief thought of as the "SEAL from the SOUTH," said, "They're kinda runnin' low on options, sir. Way I see it, Chief? Shitfire. They're either pre-dicked, or they're dicked, or, worst-case scenario? They're *redicked*."

The chief had to laugh at that one.

"Right," he said. "All three, most likely, Sonny. So, I talked with Hawke while you two mermaids were enjoying your fun-filled underwater swim. He approves of my idea of a battlefield truce. Now, like I say, we wait."

You had to ask yourself, the chief thought. I mean, what the hell did they have to gain by slaughtering a few hundred Cuban country boys? Just because you didn't agree with their politics? So far, at least, the Western allies had not declared war on Cuba, or any other Communist governments. It wouldn't look good, especially when the international newswires picked up the story of T&L's atrocity, their massacre of innocents at Revolution Bay. They'd all of them become instant pariahs, just like Erik Prince and his merry men at Blackwater.

He knew Lightning might disagree with him. He and his business partner often disagreed about all things political. But this was no time for discord in the ranks. This was the time for a man to damn well do the right thing, and only the right thing.

And then, he saw a brave young Cuban soldier do what somebody should have done hours ago. It would have saved a lot of lives and sent a lot of boys home to their mothers.

Chief watched him in great admiration. The kid shinnied up to the next-highest platform on the stainless-steel ladder, looked below at what was left of the once-shining dream of the great revolution, now in fearful tatters, and raised his AK high into the air above his head, shouting at the top of his lungs:

"Viva Cuba! Viva Cuba! Viva Cuba!" with the shining white guayabera tied to the rifle instantly catching the strong breezes in from the sea.

Armando's white flag of surrender, which would achieve great historical significance one day, now whipped about in the tropic breezes in from the sea, flapping audibly, as all eyes looked upward and saw he would be their salvation.

And cries of *"Viva Cuba!"* rose up to greet him, coming from the lips of hundreds. In only an instant, it was a *roar*. It was *thunder*.

As Chief watched, the brave boy's actions were slowly repeated like a ripple effect, aboard boat after boat as they all saw that one after another and then another patriot put a swift end to the madness of the deadly situation they'd been left in by Castro and General de los Reyes.

Chief got Hawke on the sat radio and told him what was occurring here in Revolution Bay. Hawke couldn't speak. He was so moved by what his old friends from Fort Whupass in Costa Rica had managed to achieve this day at Revolution Bay. Nothing less than the destruction of countless mujahideen fighters, but, now, the total surrender of all the rebel forces.

"God bless you, Chief," Hawke said, his strong voice wavering with deep gratitude and heartfelt emotion. "Not just you, Chief. All of you lads. You've never let me down before. And I knew you wouldn't do it this time."

"It's always our honor, boss. Every time you call on us. Is it over, now, do you think, boss?"

"Yeah, Chief, it is. Thank God. It's over."

"What's next?"

"I'm going to send a launch to the beach to ferry you guys back to *Sea Hawke*. We'll have a drink or three on board tonight. In the morning we'll weigh anchor and make for Havana. I know a seldom-used airstrip up in the Sierra Madres. If you like, you can use the radio aboard to call your pilots aboard *Puff the Magic Dragon* to come to Cuba and fetch all of you home. I think that's the safest route to evac you guys back to Costa Rica, to Fort Whupass. Agree?"

"I do."

"Good. By the way, you might be surprised to see who's driving the launch for me these days. Does all the pickups, all the drop-offs. You've met him a few times before, but you probably won't recognize him."

"Who is he, boss? You've got my curiosity up."

"Just some kid I look after now and then."

"Yeah?"

"Yeah. His name is Alexei Hawke."

CHAPTER 37

"Nobody can dance like a blind fat guy."

Havana, bound for Brazil

Thunder and Lighting decided that, tonight, rather than be the honored guests at the celebratory dinner aboard *Sea Hawke*, they would throw a surprise victory celebration dinner in Alex Hawke's honor. Over the many years, the Cherokee chieftain (Thunder) and the ruddy Irish tactical wizard (Dr. Thom Swift) had not only gained respect for Hawke, but they had, in their way, come to love the man.

The chief said to Lightning, "So I got this idea, okay? We stage a competition on board to kick off the evening. Something funny, you know, that everyone on board can compete in . . . You know, Professor?"

"Not really."

"C'mon, get in the spirit of things. Try, for once in your life, to think outside the box. So, I'm thinking a pillow fight, Doc."

"Pillow fight. Great idea. Everybody in a great big bed."

"Shut up and listen, dude. Not just any stupid old pillow fight. Two guys are facing each other, straddling a big fat spar laid across a big fat tank of water. The combatants are not allowed to lock their feet beneath the pole, see. So, both of them, whacking away at each other, usually end up pitching headfirst into the tank. You with me? It's funny, right?"

"Funny? Maybe. Question. Are they naked, these guys? One more question. What idea came in second? After the pillow fight?"

"Okay. You know what a Hornpipe is?"

"Some kind of dance. Nineteenth-century sailors in the Royal Navy used to do it when they were bored. Like I am now."

"Exactly. But here's the good part. You know this guy Beekins who works down in the engine room? Big fat guy who wears little gold glasses."

"Don't think I've had the pleasure, no. But I don't get out much anymore."

"Well, anyway, I like him. Met him on Hawke's last boat and we stay in touch. He brings his family down Costa Rica way on vacation every year. We had a little firewater around the campfire one night, and damned if he didn't get up, cross his arms, and set his legs flying. He did one helluva Hornpipe, believe me."

"Oh, I do believe you. Nobody can dance like a blind fat guy."

"So, I talked to Beekins about our victory party idea. He said there's a few musicians in the crew. Horns, accordions, fiddles, stuff like that. A bagpiper, even. He said if they all get free booze, he could get them all to play when he does his Hornpipe. How's that sound?"

"Genius."

"You're hopeless. No imagination. Not even a freakin' glimmer."

"You're not the first one to say that, believe me," Lightning said.

Hawke, for his part, and with some time to reflect, was immensely pleased with the performance of his entire crew during the last few days. And all Hawke's men aboard *Sea Hawke* were equally pleased with him. It was simple: He put them at ease with his vividly told tales of epic adventures on land, sea, and in the air. And, most especially, they appreciated his keen and sincere interest in their own individual lives, as well as his almost boyish thrill about the voyage ahead, which had won their confidence and loyalty right from the outset.

Sea Hawke's core team, composed of Hawke, Captain Hornblower, Congreve, Stokely Jones, Jr., and Harry Brock, were easily T&L's favorite clients. There was no weak link in this chain. Together with the men aboard the ship, they were a fighting unit nonpareil in international mercenary, French Foreign Legion, or any other circles.

Hawke's patronage had allowed the two men's start-up of their company, which they had called, in those very early days at least, "Soldiers of Misfortune," to gain the respect of others in their chosen field—Blackwater, for instance, among many others.

Hawke now faced a long drive, and the most unpleasant task of conveying the reviled traitor and Putin puppet, Fideo Chico, to the airfield high in the Sierra Madres where his airplane was waiting. It had been determined that having federal marshals rendezvous with the yacht was not practical. So, Special Agent Brock was to be his armed escort during a short flight to Miami aboard Hawke's Gulfstream G650. Once in Miami, he'd have Fideo remanded over to the authorities to do with what they will.

Hawke said, as they headed up a steep mountain road, "Sorry about all this, Harry. But I couldn't think of a more expeditious way to get this cretin out of our collective hair and into prison where he belongs. As a small thank-you, I've booked you a suite at the Mandarin Hotel on Brickell Key for tonight. Splendid hotel, even for Miami. The bar is a must. And so is the pool. Marvelous scenery there every afternoon. Quite well-oiled, I can assure you from experience. What's the lotion of choice these days? Ah, yes. Coppertone, I'm told, is the brand most used at the pool."

Brock was speechless. Hawke had never, ever been either so appreciative, nor as generous.

"Oh, well, that does sound pretty good gravy, as Chief Inspector Congreve says. I'll take you up on that."

"Good, good. Captain Quartermain will await your call in the a.m. as to when you'd like to return to the ship. Someone will be at the airstrip awaiting your arrival tomorrow."

"Thank you, boss. Remind me to wash my hands soon as I get myself shut of this dickless wonder."

"You won't need reminding, Harry. This little bastard is a thoroughly nasty piece of work. You'll find the stink of him on you for weeks. You hear me back there, Chico? Little Spaghetti, my ass! I wouldn't feed you to my dogs!"

"Okay, boss, I think we're good to go, here."

"Right. I'd better be getting back to the boat. A lot going on back there, as you know. I'm meeting with the captain and crew aboard *Sea*

Hawke to discuss the itinerary as we set sail for the great river down south in Brazil. Safe trip. See you tomorrow."

Hawke walked back to where he'd left his car. He didn't give a hoot in hell what they did with Fideo or where they stashed him. Just vanish him.

And vanish him he'd just done.

Hawke heaved a sigh of relief and climbed in behind the wheel of his olive green Range Rover Defender, one of the early classic editions. He made good time getting back to Havana and his boat.

After saying good-bye, Harry climbed up the steps behind Fideo and entered the plane. The jet, furnished with white leather seats and Brazilian fruitwood tables and chairs in the main cabin interior, could accommodate twenty. It was a bit pricey, Hawke admitted privately. He'd plunked down a cool sixty-eight million USD for the privilege of owning the world's most elevated mode of private aviation.

Hawke's new senior pilot, a former RAF flight lieutenant named Alain Quartermain, stepped outside the cockpit to welcome the CIA case officer and his prisoner aboard.

"Jesus Christ, Quartermain," Brock said, upon following Fideo aboard, "this is some damn hot-shit airplane." Fideo, his wrists handcuffed behind his back, started back to a curved sofa with a round table in the middle where there was an ice bucket with bottles of San Pellegrino. The trick was, how the hell was he going to open a bottle given his handcuffs?

"That chap seated at the back of the bus, as you may already know, is not an honored guest. He's the lowest form of man known to man: a traitor and a liar. Should he give us the least bit of trouble during the flight, I suggest you or your copilot show him the door, if you get my meaning."

"My pleasure, I'm sure, sir," the pilot replied. "He does look like a nasty piece of work."

"'Nasty' is a vast understatement. He's been spying on Hawke for our old pal Putin so that Putin would always know our whereabouts on this voyage of discovery and be able to send his personal assassin to lie in wait for us to arrive in each new port of call so the fiendish Mr. Smith could kidnap Hawke's son—for the second time, if you can believe that."

Quartermain said, "Good heavens, Special Agent Brock. Perhaps he should make the entire journey to Miami outside the aircraft? Strapped to the vertical stabilizer at the tail of the airplane, perhaps? Or better yet, tell the little bastard to step outside the aircraft at 30,000 feet?"

"No. The boss wants him alive. Hawke wants to be able to relish every day that this human stain rots in prison and thinks about how bloody stupid he was to bet against him."

At 3:00 p.m., Hawke called the officers' meeting in the *Sea Hawke*'s ward-room to order. He was anxious to begin. He'd been spending every waking moment thinking about the future. He saw this next chapter in the voyage not so much as a sea odyssey, but rather as an *expedition*.

"Thank you for coming, gentlemen. I know how busy you are," he said. "Now that we've finally rid ourselves of the rodent Fideo, the man whom I've begun to call 'the spy who came down with a cold'—"

There was a polite expression of amusement and he continued.

"—I intend that we make for Bahia on the coast of Brazil. There's a world-class shipyard there, and I'd like to lay up there for a few days, or at least as long as it takes to replenish what needs replenishing, resupply our stores, and have the yard perform any repairs or maintenance the ship requires—anything at all that gets her seaworthy enough to sail south of the equator and down the vast shoulder of South America to Brazil. I say, John Brown, are you present?"

"Aye, sir. Present and accounted for."

"Not at all so sure that you're 'accounted for,' but at least you're here, as requested. I need you to get on the horn with my travel specialists at Hawke LLC HQ in Mayfair, London. Tell them I shall require accommodations on Bahia for at least a week. We could all use a break from shipboard life, and Bahia will do nicely. Rooms there for myself, my son, my friends. Tell them that my first choice is the Bahia Principe Grand

Punta Cana. Been around forever and still the finest resort down there, even if they do still require black tie at dinner every night. Yes?"

"Yes, sir. They still do."

"Good. I'm a big fan of old traditions. And we'll require hired cars—or cars and drivers—whilst we're there. And while you're at it, ring up the concierge at Punta Cana. Tell him to book tee times at the hotel's Ocean Course for Chief Inspector Congreve, my son, and myself. A threesome, eighteen holes, at least every other day. We could use some golf and some rest and recuperation. They usually host a beach BBQ for newly arriving guests. Book a reservation for us. We clear?"

"R&R, BBQ, yessir. I'm on it."

"Captain, could you bring up the ship's charts on the system monitors?"

It was done.

"Well, we all know our next primary target destination. It's here—the mouth of the great Amazon River. We're going as far up the Amazon River as we have to in order to reach our destination. I'm working with MI6 via Zoom to pinpoint the location of the Dragonfire Club on the river. Our very next destination, however, is Bahia, Brazil, where we shall moor for three or four days of strategic planning and provisioning for what will perhaps be a protracted trip upriver. The Amazon, which I have never seen, extends for four thousand miles into the interior of Brazil."

"If I may, sir, a question?"

"Certainly."

"Can you tell the navigator a little about the next port of call after this one? We could use a head start on charting and navigation, sir . . ."

"Yes, I can. But I will do it privately. If this voyage has taught me anything, it's that I need to keep as many of our itinerary details as I can to myself. Understood? You'll know when you need to know . . .

"That's all, gentlemen," Hawke said, and headed for the door. Alexei was cooking with Auguste down in the galley, waiting for him. And he had a great surprise for the lucky boy.

CHAPTER 38

"Inside that box are ten ships that can carry you far, far away."

Havana, bound for Brazil

"Hi, Dad," Alexei said when he saw his father standing in the doorway of the sparkling stainless-steel ship's galley.

"Bonjour, monsieur," Auguste said, giving Hawke a subtle little bow. *"Ça va?"*

"Ça va bien," Hawke said. "What are you two pirates cooking today?"

"Soufflé Grand Marnier, monsieur! C'est très délicieux! You will taste for yourself tonight at *le dîner,* sir. *Un premier masterpiece de Chef Alexei!"*

"Alexei," Hawke said, "can you tear yourself away from your chef de cuisine lessons for a while? Your father has a surprise for you."

"Yeah, Dad, sure. Just let me add a soupçon of the Grand Marnier sauce to my soufflé, okay?"

Hawke smiled at the precocious little gentleman. *"Mais certainement, mon bon fils. Prends ton temps.* Fulfill your obligations to the soufflé above all else, above everything. Everything pales in comparison. Then, as soon as you can slip away, please come below and join your father in the ship's library, *s'il te plaît?"*

"Mais oui, Papa," was his reply.

Not ten minutes later, the young fellow appeared in the doorway of the small room, which was dominated by wall-to-wall books, vintage knotty pine paneling polished to a fare-the-well, and a well-worn but beautiful Oriental rug.

Alexei smiled bashfully and said, "It really is good, you know that, right, Dad?"

"What is?"

"My soufflé, of course! What did you think? Is it the best thing ever, Papa?"

"Oh, that. Well, maybe not the best thing ever. That essay you're writing on George Washington and the Founding Fathers? Hey, buddy, that's pretty good, too!"

Hawke laughed. "Come on in—I don't bite. I mean, unless there's one of your world-famous soufflés on the table."

Alexei strode in and collapsed into a big brown leather club chair, right next to where his father sat on the wine-colored sofa.

"What's in the pretty box with the ribbon, Dad?"

"Your surprise, of course, sonny boy."

"Show me, show me!"

"In a minute. First, I want to tell you a story, so you'll have a better understanding of my gift to you, son."

"Yes, Pop. I'm listening."

"All right. There's always a story, isn't there? We cling to stories because they are the one true lifeblood of life itself. This story is about an event in my life that occurred when I was about seven years old, maybe a year or so younger. I was on holiday up in Scotland with my parents, young Pelham, and my dog, a black-and-white English springer spaniel. He was a handsome Johnnie, I'll tell you. We were staying up at Castle Hawke—you've been there. Granddad's shooting estate."

"I love it up there. What was the dog's name?"

"Captain. But we all called him 'Cappy,' because it was easier to say. Anyway, it's always cold and raining up there, as you well know. And one afternoon, I was up in my room on the third floor, lying by the fire and reading a book, something I'd found downstairs in the library. It was written by an American. Fellow named Herman Melville. And it was about a whale."

"A book about a whale. That sounds pretty awesome. I like the story about Jonah being swallowed by one."

"Oh, it is awesome, as you say, it is. Which is the point of this story. The abiding memories that stories afford us, generation upon generation. You with me, son?"

"Of course, Dad."

"Now, I know you never knew much about my mother, your grand-mother, because you never got to meet her. But she was a splendid woman of the American South, and very kind to me her whole life. Her name was Katherine, but after she married my father, everyone called her 'Kitty.' Do you know why that's funny?"

"Sure. Kitty Hawk. The place where the Wright Brothers, Wilbur and Orville, made the first-ever airplane flight. North Carolina, I think it was."

"Wow. I'm impressed. How'd you know that?"

"I *read*, Dad!"

"Thank God. You take after your father."

"She was pretty, wasn't she? I do remember that. That picture of her over the mantel in the library at Hawkesmoor."

"Yes, she was pretty. As lovely a woman as ever you'll see. She was a movie star, you know, when she finally let my dad sweep her off her feet. And she never regretted a second over that decision. She traded Holly-wood for Sherwood Forest. But her heart was always in the cradle of the American southland. She was born in Louisiana at a plantation right at a bend on the mighty Mississippi River, which was beautiful, but without much for a young girl to do there on those long and drowsy summer days. So she started reading as a very young girl."

"What kind of books did she like? History books? Funny books? Science books?"

"No, she had no time for those. She read novels—American novels, mostly, but some British favorites. She always said to me, 'Alex, turn off that damn television! Read a book, for heaven's sake! A book is a ship that can carry you far, far away. Can TV do that? I don't think so.'

"'No, Momma,' I'd say, and pick up one of the many books she'd given me. Of course, they were American novels, because that's what she loved. She kept lists of all the books she was reading. I still have them. Top ten lists, top twenty lists, top fifty lists, and so on. Her books were always moving up or down the list, depending on how much she'd loved, disliked, or hated each one.

"So back to the day when she'd found me reading the whale book, okay? She approved of it rather heartily, as I recall. And Mother said to me, 'Alex, it's high time you started your personal library.' And so I did. I began collecting books in earnest, books given to me by my dear mother. Only the ones she and I both loved. And in this box is what I called my starter set. Now it's yours. Because in there are my top ten books given to me by the beautiful, lost Kitty Hawke. And those are all books that I think are absolutely essential to any young reader's life and appreciation for fine literature. You read them and you are laying down a foundation for a lifetime of swimming in endless pools of sublime literature. American literature, of course, because 'The heart of America is my beloved homeland,' she always said, and I just . . . I just . . ."

"You just what, Dad?"

Hawke was crying now. The tears glistened on his ruddy cheeks, and he bowed his head.

"I just . . . just loved her so damn hard, son. So hard it hurt. She was my anchor. My North Star, you see. The way she winked at me across the breakfast table. The way she smelled when she tucked me into bed. I was so lost myself when I lost her . . . I didn't believe in anything anymore. Even heaven. Streets of gold? Save me. Or angels? I never felt safe after that. Not for the longest time. I felt like I had become . . . hell, what's the word? Untethered. Until my grandfather rescued me. He was a rock, just like Mum.

"And because of Grandfather Hawke, I had Pelham to make me safe. And your uncle Ambrose. The two of them raised me. My surrogate parents, really, who made me who I am, for better or worse . . . I'm sorry. I never meant to let you see me like this."

"Oh, Dad. Please don't cry. Don't be so sad . . ."

"You see, she gave me that pretty wooden box over there on the table for my seventh birthday. She said, uh, she said, 'Inside that old box, Alex, there are ten ships that will carry you far, far away.'"

"Oh, Dad," Alexei sobbed, for he, too, was crying now.

"And, as I told you, I, in turn, am now giving Mother's box to you."

"You are? These books were your ... what ... starter set?"

"They were, indeed."

"Oh, Dad ..."

Hawke thought the boy was going to cry some more then, but he didn't. He gathered himself together. He got up and went over to his father and hugged him around the neck and told him how much he loved him. And then he went over and brought the wooden box back and placed it on the table by the sofa.

Alexei's eyes went wide as he reached inside the box and began pulling books out one at a time, inspecting each one with sheer delight before reaching for the next.

And Hawke said, "Those ten books are exactly the same books that I found inside this box twenty-five long years ago! I've read and reread them all, many times."

The books on the table included these:

1. *Adventures of Huckleberry Finn,* Mark Twain, 1884
2. *Moby-Dick,* Herman Melville, 1851
3. *To Kill a Mockingbird,* Harper Lee, 1960
4. *The Grapes of Wrath,* John Steinbeck, 1929
5. *The Great Gatsby,* F. Scott Fitzgerald, 1926
6. *Little Women,* Louisa May Alcott, 1868
7. *The House of Mirth,* Edith Wharton, 1906
8. *Gone With the Wind,* Margaret Mitchell, 1936
9. *The Secret Garden,* Frances Hodgson Burnett, 1911
10. *The Call of the Wild,* Jack London, 1903

CHAPTER 39

"Fortunately, their mutual man-crushes proved short-lived."

At sea, bound for the Amazon

Hawke, having consulted first thing that Sunday morning with both the ship's meteorologist and the ship's navigator, decided to cut the holiday stay in Bahia short by two full days. For one thing, as he'd been told by Ambrose, Lady Mars was in Bermuda, suffering from some strange new virus.

Ambrose had knocked at Hawke's door early that very morning.

"Yes, Ambrose. What is it? What's wrong?" Hawke had said.

"It's Diana, Alex. She's in Bermuda. She's been at Shadowlands for the last few weeks. Bad news, I'm afraid. She's in hospital. Our mutual friend at King Edward VII Hospital rang me up at dawn. He says she was rushed there late last night with a very, very high fever. They are working to bring it down. But he said it would be very helpful to her if I could possibly fly in as quickly as possible. Apparently with these bloody viruses, the next few days will be critical. They've put her on some kind of antibiotic cocktail. They give it a few days, then observe her in hospital for perhaps a week. The doctors say this new drug is an incredible therapeutic. Most of the time the patient recovers and goes home."

"I'm so sorry. Do they have any idea what's wrong? The kind of virus?"

"Not yet. But they did say that she was back resting comfortably in her room, no longer in the ICU."

"Well, that's certainly encouraging!" Alex said. "Now, listen to me. Once you get to Shadowlands on Bermuda, will you keep me up to speed on her health? Perhaps even daily. So I won't worry."

"I shall. And I cannot possibly tell you how much I've enjoyed this epic voyage with you—even knowing that you were thrown in prison with Stokely and Special Agent Brock. But, sad to say, I've already packed my bags and booked myself a flight to Bermuda out of the international airport on this island we're bound for. What's it called, the island?"

"Marajó."

"My flight leaves the day after tomorrow. Takes off at around noon. Will that timing work with our arrival?"

"Yes, Cap'n says we should arrive around nine that morning. I'll drive you to the airport and see you off. I'll try to find a florist in town and send Diana something to make her room a little cheery. God knows mine wasn't when I was last there, recovering from my near-death experience at the hands of that beastly Mr. Smith."

"Very kind," Ambrose said, giving his friend a quick hug. "I'm aware of the beautiful flowers you've sent her through all the years. I'm sure she'll be thrilled to receive them. Well. I'll let you get back to what you're doing. Alexei and I are having a skeet and trap contest on the stern this morning. He's getting damned good with a shotgun, I can tell you that much!"

He paused. "Alex, there's an issue come up that we need to discuss. It's rather urgent. Do you mind?"

"Of course not, Ambrose."

"Well, I know Ms. Devereux is going to discuss this with you, but I wanted to put in my two cents while I still have you face-to-face. It's about Alexei and Royal Protection Officer Devereux.

"Apparently, she was awakened in the middle of the night to loud screaming coming from Alexei's cabin just across the hall."

"Oh, God. Don't tell me it's Smith again, back from the dead to haunt us forevermore?"

"No, nothing to do with him at all. The point is Devereux thinks it's the one-two punch of the bloody encounter with Smith, and days later, when the firefight broke out, all those security forces were peppering us with high-powered rounds ricocheting loudly off the ship's armored hull and superstructure."

"So what does she want me to do?"

"She thinks he's too young for all this violence in his life. He's tired of being confined to his cabin when battles break out. She believes he's had a marvelous voyage and a glorious time being with his loving father, not to mention all the amazing things he's learned on this trip."

"But."

"But me no buts. But what?"

"She believes it's her duty as a Scotland Yard protection officer to protect him no matter what. And she knows the next stop is quite possibly the South Pole—that is, if time and tide allow. And if that should be the case, it's basically going to be fiercely cold and he will not be allowed to spend much time, if any at all, up on deck. And she knows that this will be an espionage operation. And that there will likely be skirmishes with Chinese MSS fighters, the Ministry for State Security's trained killers and soldiers. Bullets and more bullets will be flying again, and she thinks that another experience like that will be extremely traumatic for a boy his age."

Hawke said, "Ambrose, what is your honest assessment of her position?"

"I must say, I tried to disagree with her, but in good conscience, I simply cannot. Protection, after all, is her sole purpose in life. She knows whereof she speaks. My position is that the boy clearly adores this time with his father, as does his father cherish the time spent with him. But that she makes a strong case, Alex, and I think you ought to consider what she says. As the boy's godfather, I, too, feel a responsibility to keep him out of harm's way."

"I see. And what do you two propose?"

"I think the child and Miss Deveraux, as well as dear old Pelham, should all fly back to Bermuda with me on the flight out of Marajó and remain there at Shadowlands with my dear wife and me. You well know how much Diana dotes on that little boy. Plus, it would do him a world of good, spending every day out in the sunshine and fresh sea air. Nothing better. He'll have the ocean out the back door and a swimming pool where Devereux wants to teach him to swim."

"Can I come, too? It all sounds so lovely."

"Maybe next time, but for now I ask you, will you let him come with me to Bermuda?"

"Of course I shall, old fellow. Should I refuse and he get hurt, or worse, I could never forgive myself. I don't think I could go on without him, Ambrose . . . and you and Devereux should know that I'm contemplating a trip by rail to Siberia with Alexei. I've been corresponding with Anastasia lately. My purpose is that it's time for him to pay a visit to his dear mother, whom, I must say, I love still. In the event they do get along, I would consider letting him stay on for a while in her care. God knows she hasn't seen him since he was four years old."

A cloud passed over Hawke's face. It was fear, of course, because he now wondered if he could ever find a way to keep his son away from danger. He'd considered traveling to Siberia along with Alexei when they returned home to England. His mother, who missed him terribly, would adore him at this age. He was a toddler when she put him aboard the Siberian Express train when Alex was headed back to St. Petersburg.

His mother was still being held prisoner at Peter the Great's beautiful Winter Palace, now converted to a secret HQ for the KGB. He used the term "prisoner" loosely in her case. Arkady Arkov, the KGB general who ruled the prison with an iron fist in an iron glove, had been protecting Anastasia from the powers that be: the oligarchs in the Kremlin who wanted her dead.

Arkov had fallen in love with her, actually, and taken her under his protection. She had a wonderful life there. He'd given her a splendid carriage and four magnificent black horses. They were Orlov Trotters. The breed originated during the eighteenth century as a hardy harness horse with speed and stamina. These horses were generally powerful and agile, yet they were also gentle and trainable, and they were often used in harness racing as well as to pull m'ladies' carriages.

The layover had been partly about replenishing supplies and using the yard there to make any and all necessary repairs to *Sea Hawke* before he ventured upriver into the deep, dark interior of Brazil. To prepare for the trip, he'd read many accounts of explorers and scientists who'd been lost. He did not want to be underprepared for whatever they would encounter.

He imagined that any damage done to his boat would primarily be due to the attacks by the two Argentine fighter jets. But *Sea Hawke* was a very complex ship, and he wanted her systems and her mechanicals gone over by the yard's crew with a fine-tooth comb—this, before he even considered going deep into the Amazon jungles by water.

Sad to say, a lot of his thinking about the R&R layover had been because he felt like some of the closest members of his team were displaying the familiar signs of dreaded cabin fever. They'd all been aboard for the better part of a month, and, like them, Hawke felt a compelling need to get ashore and stretch his legs for a little while, preferably on a golf course. No matter how big a boat you sailed the Seven Seas on, it felt confining after a time.

He'd already booked tee times for a threesome with Congreve and Alexei, who'd been happily hitting balls off the stern with one of the crewmen who'd been a golf pro at the Ocean Reef Club down in the Florida Keys.

Unfortunately, they ended up spending only two nights instead of the four they originally planned.

The problem was the weather down around Cape Horn, in southern Chile's Tierra del Fuego archipelago.

The meteorologist said all the models indicated the tropical storm was rapidly building strength as it moved up into warmer waters. NOAA, the National Oceanic and Atmospheric Administration, was predicting that Tropical Storm Victoria would be a Cat-4 hurricane when she got up to the Horn, as sailors had labeled it a century ago.

He could not afford to have any weather conditions delay his arrival at the Dragonfire Club. He was mission-critical now and he couldn't take his eye off this weather situation.

As had been pointed out to him by his meteorologist, there was a severe tropical storm system called Victoria boiling up from the South

Atlantic. It was moving at a good clip up the eastern seaboard of South America, and that front was estimated to arrive in three days' time at the mouth of the Amazon River.

Eliminating two nights and two days at Bahia would give the *Sea Hawke* a far better chance of arriving ahead of schedule at the great river and sailing inland as far as she could to avoid being battered about by Cat-4 winds out on the open seas.

Sea Hawke sailed at first light on that clear and breezy Sunday morning in Bahia. Hawke had found the old port city both beautiful and charming. A backwater town that had long been forgotten. As rooftops and treetops slowly faded into the background in the frothy white ribbon of foam of the wake of the sailing yacht, he vowed that he and Alexei would return one day to spend a few weeks on the verdant greens of the Bahia Golf Club, swimming in the crystal clear blue waters at the hotel's beach. And he could introduce his son Alexei to the exhilaration of deep-sea fishing, the adrenaline rush one found upon hooking into a mighty sailfish from atop the tuna tower of a sleek sportfishing boat, powering through the waves.

Hawke knew that the voyage to the mouth of the Amazon would have been far shorter were it not for the continent's enormous northeastern coastline, which juts out into the Atlantic like the broad shoulder of some otherworldly god, forcing southbound ships to travel hundreds of miles eastward before resuming their southward journey.

Hawke was up on the bridge with the captain, discussing the considerable perils the upcoming journey would entail. They were all about to venture into the deepest, darkest depths of the Amazonian rain forest. History had long called it the "River of No Return" for a very good reason. A sacred and profane place, from which, for centuries long gone, countless brave explorers had never returned. Fallen victim to raging typhoid fevers, deadly insects, the green anaconda, poison dart frogs, electric eels, jaguars, and wandering spiders, the most lethal arachnids in the world.

There, in that pestilential Amazonian gloom, danger lurked round every bend of the river. Some of it was man-made (there were headhunters with blowguns with lethal poisoned darts, as well as cannibals, ancient tribes who'd little or no knowledge that civilization even existed and for whom human life had little or no meaning).

And, as Hawke had experienced firsthand, there was disease upon disease floating around in the Amazon, or, as Harry Brock had quipped, "In the Amazon, even the diseases have diseases!" And then there were the tropical flesh-eating viruses that made malaria look like a case of the sniffles, plus man-eating piranhas that could, in under a minute, strip the flesh off a full-grown man who'd had the misfortune to fall overboard.

Hawke still had vivid memories of his first visit to *el río Amazonas* and its rain forests. He had been on the trail of a terrorist mastermind by the name of Poppa Top. The man had amassed an army of over two thousand mujahideen fighters from Lebanon and planned to march them north through Mexico and across the US border into Texas. Hawke had gotten lost in the jungle, irretrievably lost, and had the terrible luck of blundering into the temporary encampment of a score of naked headhunters.

He had turned and run, but it was too late. They'd seen him and they gave chase, shouting and carrying razor-sharp spears and blowguns that used poisoned darts as ammunition. Somehow, by some trick of fate, he'd managed to avoid becoming supper for twelve starving headhunters.

Not Hawke, nor any of the ship's officers, could see the Amazon River, even though it now lay due west of the *Sea Hawke*. But even here, sailing south through heavy seas off the coast, there was no escaping the sheer power of the giant river. Hawke had been doing some heavy reading to prepare himself for his second trek into the green void. He'd read that the Amazon was a nonstop deluge that, by itself, accounts for 15 percent of all fresh water carried to the sea by all of the planet's rivers put together.

And his next destination, the width of the mouth of the river, was over 180 kilometers, or 110 miles. It is so vast that the island that rests in the middle of it, Marajó, is nearly the size of Switzerland, and the muddy plume that spills into the Atlantic reaches some hundred miles out into the open sea.

He'd also learned from his books that for millions of years, the Amazon River was a vast inland sea that covered the central part of the continent. Finally, during the Pleistocene epoch, which began approximately 1.6 million years ago, the rising waters broke through the continent's eastern escarpment and poured into the Atlantic. In their wake, the waters left behind the world's greatest river system and former inland seabed—a vast basin of rich sediments and fertile lowlands perfectly suited to support an array of plant and animal life almost without parallel on the face of the earth.

For all its exotic allure and potential riches, the great Amazon Basin in 1911 remained a vast and remarkably mysterious place, untouched by modernity and repelling all but the most determined attempts to explore its hidden secrets. Although more than two-thirds of the Amazon Basin rests within Brazilian borders, the vast majority of Brazilians in the early twentieth century, crowded along the sun-soaked eastern coast, had little interest in knowing what lay within the basin and no way of finding out even if they had.

The great river has thousands of tributaries, too, which reach like tentacles into every corner of Brazil. They are fast, twisting, and wild. Until very late in the nineteenth century, the only alternative for entering the interior was by mule, over rutted dirt roads and through heavy jungle and wide, barren highlands.

Two days later, without any serious issues, encounters, or incidences to speak of, the majestic *Sea Hawke* landed at Marajó, the island that lay at the very center of the mouth of the Amazon. Sir David had called two days earlier to tell Alex that he'd been losing sleep, worried to death about his premier counterterrorist officer venturing deep into the "Green Hell," as some explorers had described it, without benefit of a knowledgeable guide. So Trulove had taken it upon himself to find one for him. He had, he said, located a good man, a guide—but not just a guide, an explorer. He was a transplanted American bloke who lived on the island of Marajó, a chap named Colonel Peter Quint, and Trulove made it clear that he would never forgive Hawke unless he took this man up the river with him.

The forty-year-old Quint, ex–Delta Force operative, explorer by nature, and a botanist and cartographer by trade, had spent half his life exploring the Amazon and had traversed roughly fourteen thousand miles of wilderness that was not only unmapped but largely unknown to anyone save the indigenous peoples who lived there.

Sir David said that Quint, as he preferred to be called, had been on one doomed expedition when, before the men had even reached *el río Amazonas,* they were reduced to eating "nothing but leather, belts, and entire shoes, including the soles of shoes, cooked with certain herbs."

And, once finally on the river, they fought nearly every Indian tribe they encountered, eventually losing roughly a dozen men to starvation and three others to poisonous darts and arrows. Incredibly enough, Quint survived to repeat the ordeal just three years later, this time losing nearly fifty men to starvation and Indian attacks before himself abandoning the project to nurse the heartbreak he'd suffered at the disastrous collapse of his ambitions.

"Lord Hawke?" a man said to him, having strolled up to the boat just as Hawke was tying off the spring line, shirtless and sweating in the unbearable heat and humidity of the island in the stream and muttering to himself that, if it was this unbearable on an island in the onshore Atlantic breezes from the hurricane boiling up from the south, just how bloody unbearable was it going to be when he got into the thick of it upriver in a couple of days?

Hawke said, "Yes, I plead guilty to that charge, sir. I'm afraid you have me at a disadvantage. Do I know you?"

"Not yet, sir, but perhaps you will. I am the fellow Sir David Trulove told you about. My name is Peter Quint. Colonel Peter Quint, actually. Ex–Army Ranger, First Ranger Battalion, Fort Bragg. I'm called Quint, by the way."

Hawke stuck out his hand, reaching across to the man on the dock and shaking hands with this notable fellow. "I'm Alex Hawke, Quint. Please come aboard and have a good look round. I'll be with you momentarily."

Quint jammed a stubby pipe into one corner of his mouth and then went about boarding, and Hawke saw him headed for the bow, where he spent a few long moments studying the laser cannon turret. He even knelt down on the deck beneath it and tried to open the hatch. Which was, of course, always locked down tight when not in a combat situation.

Watching him, you could tell, just by his gait, by his balance, and by the way his long legs propelled him, that he was someone who had seen a good deal of the world's oceans, rivers, and then some. A man who had long ago gone to sea.

The man was extremely handsome—a dark-bronzed lady-killer with a neat mustache above the sort of callous mouth women kiss in their dreams. He had regular features that suggested Spanish or South American blood and bold, hard brown eyes that turned up oddly, or, as a woman might put it, intriguingly, at the corners.

He was an athletic-looking six-footer plus, dressed in a crisp white Sea Island linen shirt unbuttoned down to his belt to display his well-muscled chest and a pair of bleached and worn khaki shorts belted with a thick length of weathered ship's cordage. Hawke took him for a good-looking bastard who got all the women he wanted and probably lived on them—and lived well.

Maybe Hawke's reaction of Quint was colored by a pitiful, irrational tinge of manly jealousy. It was usually brought to the fore when it came to that "mine's bigger" mentality, whether it applied to women, boats or vintage race cars, pedigree—everything, basically. Two extraordinarily attractive men, both long accustomed to having the eye of every woman in the room, always seemed on the verge of throwing a punch. Even though it would behoove neither, the very idea of putting the other on his arse was incredibly appealing to both.

But the man's qualifications as a botanist and an explorer and former Delta Force made him a splendid addition to the crew. Hawke felt like Sir David had anticipated his needs. And, indeed, his notion of Quint felt like a godsend.

Ten minutes later, Pelham was serving the two of them some ice-cold beer and a good English cheddar in the after cockpit. Hawke and Colonel Quint were splayed out on the dark green Sunbrella cushions in the stern, both taking the measure of each other and both seeming, despite their unspoken rivalry, to find the other good company. Hawke said a silent thank-you to Sir David. He immediately understood why this man had been a good idea. He had vast experience in areas where Hawke had little. He seemingly had great reserves of humor and confidence. He was strong, athletic, and in very good health. And he was good company to boot.

He was a perfect fit for this mission up the river.

At least at the beginning, that is.

Their mutual man crushes fortunately proved to be short-lived, after all. As the days and weeks were left in the wake far behind them, Hawke grew to loathe this man that Sir David had sent his way, probably after one too many bottles of the Infuriator at Black's.

Hawke pondered the question of ridding himself of this pompous twit. But, short of murder, he'd not come up with a plausible excuse to make him disappear as rapidly as humanly possible!

CHAPTER 40

"My son, you must unlock every secret!"

Sea Hawke, *on the Amazon River*

The fact that the mighty *Sea Hawke* entered the world's greatest river that morning and was about to plumb the dark depths of the Amazon rain forest had had a profound effect on Hawke. He was put in mind of something his father had said to him on what he believed had been his sixth birthday—the last birthday they would celebrate together. Hawke believed his father, the Admiral, had some secret cranial storage bin where he could stow every conversation he'd had that was worth saving. This was one of them. Hawke marveled at the irony of the thing.

His father had taught him a life lesson that would serve him well many years later.

His father had said, "Alex, if you should chance upon a river, you must follow it to its source. No matter the perils, no matter those many comrades who fall along the way. You must know how things *work*, son! You must *unlock* every secret! This alone will fortify you against all the trials, tears, and sorrows that this cruel life has in store for you."

The first day, everyone tried to spend as much time up on deck as they could inhaling the fecund smells of the rain forest, the phantasmagoria of colors of birds, and the profundity of brilliantly vibrant, multicolored flowers. Hawke was enjoying the passing scenery, pleased that they were now cruising under power, the two massive turbofan diesels driving the yacht into the currents at a very good clip. Fifteen knots, was Hawke's estimate. And the crew was getting some much-needed time off from tending the massive sails and rigging day and night.

That night, in his stateroom, he picked up the book he was reading. It was called *Triste Tropiques* and was written by a French explorer of the Amazon named Lévi-Strauss. Hawke had been a veritable sponge when it came to gathering information about the mighty river.

Lévi-Strauss had written, "If the explorer and his men could have soared over the rain forest like the hawks that wheeled above them, the river would have looked like a piece of black ribbon candy nestled in an endless expanse of green. Here, at the start of one's tortuous journey, the river is so tightly coiled that at times it doubled back on itself, and in every direction the jungle stretched—dense, impenetrable, and untouched to the horizon. Even from the air, the river's path into the jungle lowlands was so capricious, and the terrain so uneven, that it frequently disappeared entirely beneath the dense green canopy, making it nearly impossible to follow."

Indeed, everyone aboard was fascinated with every aspect of this brave new world they had entered. Everyone seemed to have realized that they had entered a kind of febrile wonderland; some fantasist's dream world that existed nowhere else. The rainbow of colors of tropical birds and tropical trees was amazing. The great trees, for one thing, were magnificent. The largest of these trees, according to the colonel, was the kapok, which can easily grow to two hundred feet high and eleven feet in diameter. And the profundity of these giants was astounding.

"Truly amazing, Quint," Hawke said to his new botanist friend, both men looking up at the solid green canopy far above their heads. "They're brilliant. And I've never seen another forest where trees grow to such great heights and in such close proximity to one another."

"Yes," Quint said. "Because there are so many of them, Alex. The number is almost incalculable, but I happen to have a pretty good idea . . ."

"Really? Astounding. How many, do you suppose?"

"I don't suppose; I actually *know*. Let me just put it this way: There are more trees in the Amazon than there are stars in our Milky Way galaxy."

"Good Lord! Is that true?" Hawke said, "Quint, please, you cannot be serious."

"Oh, but I am. This is my field, as you know. One of the valuable things I can offer you on this voyage of discovery is my expert knowledge in the science of botany. I am very comfortable here. I know it like my face in the mirror. In my life, I have swallowed it whole. I don't fear it like I did in the beginning. Now I feel like I worship at its altar. It is godlike, somehow, this place both sacred and profane. A majestic green cathedral. I don't know exactly why I feel that way. The epic fecundity of this environment, maybe. Perhaps I can't even explain it."

"You just did, Quint. Perfectly. I'm extremely grateful to Sir David for suggesting you. I wonder, did he tell you the purpose of my journey?"

"No. He told me where you work, so I can make some assumptions about it, but do I know? No, I do not. I do know that Ambrose is a semiretired chief inspector at Scotland Yard, because he told me so before he returned to Bermuda. I assume you're in the espionage game. And we're going somewhere to spy on someone. Or, anyway, something like that."

"Something like that, yes. But I think I can show you where we're headed better than I can explain it. Would you mind accompanying me down to the charts room?"

"Not at all, sir. Delighted."

Hawke ordered all the charts related to his mission and took Quint through them one at a time.

"Quint, please stop me if I say something you don't agree with or if you have a question regarding something that I've said."

"Will do."

"First chart. Our present location."

Quint said, "After leaving *Ilha de Marajó*, my home port, the first village we encounter is Macata, just coming abeam of us now. Charming port town, incredible restaurants, especially one seafood joint called *Las Brujas Settantes,* or the Seven Witches. Certainly one of the best, if not the best restaurant in this region of Brazil. I still recall my first glimpse of Macata. Bathed in the late-afternoon sunlight, the red-tiled roofs and whitewashed walls were in pleasing contrast to the rich green of banana trees and the fronds of waving palms."

"You make it sound lovely, Quint," Hawke said.

"Well, it is, Alex. If we should live long enough to get back here, I'll treat you and your friends to a memorable celebratory dinner there— whatever it is that we're celebrating at that moment."

"Done and done," Hawke said with a broad smile. "What about these three coming up at the first bend we've encountered? Santarém, Alexquer, and Óbidos?"

"Not a dime's worth of difference between them. Small fishing villages. Easy access to the Atlantic is the reason they're there. The first truly interesting destination is the port city of Manaus. Tourists and first-time visitors think they're dreaming when they see such an impressive city here in the rain forest. A major metropolis. Skyscrapers galore. I call it 'the Chicago of Brazil.' It's a major interior port city and well worth a visit to let everyone disembark and walk around for an afternoon. Unless you're in a hurry, of course."

"I could spare us all an afternoon. I've built in a comfortable margin of time to the scheduled arrival. Assuming, and it's a big assumption, that we don't run into any difficulties."

Quint laughed. "Alex, c'mon, mate. You know that you never go up the Amazon for any distance without encountering difficulties. It's already pitch-black, and the sun is still setting. The canopy up there changes everything, you know. Even at high noon, it's pretty dark below. Let me ask you an important question, if I may?"

"Of course."

"How much does *Sea Hawke* draw, exactly? I need to know that going forward. You don't want to run aground in a big boat like this one. The last thing we need is to broach her in this kind of current. I've seen men go down in boats much smaller. There's no time to leap to safety."

"I understand. She draws fifteen feet."

"Good. Less than I thought. But, still, we need to talk to your helmsman and navigator, because in random spots lying beneath this river is extraordinarily rugged vegetation. I've known divers who dove too deep—who got a foot or an ankle caught up in a vicious tangle—who died because they drowned trying to cut their way out of the stuff.

"Because of all the nutrients the river carries, such underwater plants grow to within ten feet of the surface. You will require a lookout stationed on the bow who knows the clues to look for when approaching an area with thick vegetation."

"What are the clues?" Hawke said.

"Not many, I'm afraid. He might be able to spot a large tendril or two, waving away a few feet below the surface, as if beckoning a sailor to plumb the depths."

"Like the Sirens of Greek mythology."

"Precisely so. Or a lookout may spy plants on the riverbanks that disappear beneath the water and continue to grow to dangerous heights. Things like that. Don't worry, I'll have a chat with him."

"Thanks. What's the worst that can happen?" Hawke said.

"You foul your props and your very expensive engines burn out, for one."

"She has automatic cutoffs if the props stop turning."

"Good. But I'm not at all sure those cutoffs were designed to deal with the Amazon. We just need to be careful. Sailing at night in utter blackout conditions is problematic for me, Alex. This can be a dangerous place at night. I know you are aware of the presence of unfriendly, some say murderous, Indian tribesmen who still practice headhunting for trophies. They shrink the heads, which are locally known as Tzan-Tzas. Right now, we are passing through the lands of the Shuar tribe, who are still fighting for their old way of life and keeping their lands away from the white land-grabbers."

"I understand what you're saying. But we lost a lot of time bucking these currents all day. I'd like to get a little farther upriver before we shut down the engines and throw a couple of hooks over the side."

"How much longer do you need, Alex?"

"A couple of hours would help."

"Too dangerous. I'll give you one."

———————

Not half an hour later, Hawke heard the alarms wailing down in the engine room. *Sea Hawke* slowed perceptibly and then quickly drifted to a stop, dueling with the fierce Amazon currents. No question about it, he thought, racing three decks down to the lowest deck. She'd run afoul of the thick vegetation the colonel had just warned him about.

Christ!

Arriving inside the cavernous and incredibly noisy engine room, he was at least relieved that the chief engineer had manually shut down the massive engines.

He raced over to the chief.

"Chief! Any damage to the turbofans?"

"Negative, sir. But I'm glad you gave me that heads-up about the underwater vegetation. I had my hand on the cut-out switch the instant she got fouled."

"Good man. So let's send a couple of divers under the hull to clear the fouled props? Yes?"

"No, sir. I wouldn't advise it, safety wise. They'd be dealing with those powerful currents in total darkness, above and below the surface. If you like, I'll put a ringer around two of our best divers and tell them to be ready to go down at first light in the morning. Luckily, our turbos didn't sustain any damage at all. We'll be ready to resume the voyage with no problems in the morning."

"Sounds good. I appreciate what you do, Chief. Just want you to know that. Always have. How long have we been together? And how many bloody boats have we run through?"

"Going on fifteen years now, sir. And, by my count, five boats, starting with *Warrior*, I believe."

"Sounds right, Chief. Well, I'm for bed. Tomorrow's going to be a long day."

"G'night, sir."

"G'night."

CHAPTER 41

"Was Alex Hawke now the Marlboro Man?"

Sea Hawke *heads up the Amazon River*

awke was having one of his bad nights. He tossed, he turned, he tossed once more. His thoughts wouldn't turn into dreams, then his dreams turned into thoughts, and his mind was chattering away up there about all things great and small, keeping him awake deep into the wee hours. Things he needed to worry about. Things he needed to do. But the worst of them was the memory of when, at Black's, Sir David had told him his mission was to sail up the Amazon to the Dragonfire Club and shut down the Red Star Alliance foundational conference with the top twenty-five Communist and socialist nations in attendance.

All right, it had certainly sounded fairly straightforward the way he put it at the time, anyway. The way he'd explained it oh so simply. But, once more, for the second time this week, he'd been wrestling with finding a way to follow orders without killing a whole lot of people who had different ideas from his own. He had, he admitted to himself, managed to come up with a fairly boffo idea to deal in a humane way with General Castro's people's armada, but maybe one good idea was all he could summon per week . . . Damn it all!

He swung his long legs over the side of the bed and climbed out. He pulled a T-shirt over his head, zipped up his favorite faded pair of boat trousers, and grabbed his Marlboros from the bedside table. He bloody well *had* to come up with something, because sometime tomorrow afternoon they would arrive at their destination. And if he didn't come up with something before then? C would have his head if he failed him on this critical mission—one that could save the whole world if they were successful up the river.

Not to mention the American president, the prime minister of England, and the king of Spain, all of whom had a huge stake in his impending success.

Or lack thereof, as the case may be.

He suddenly got a notion to go up on deck. Stroll about the quarterdeck whilst wringing his hands. Clear his head in the cool night air. Take a tumbler of best brandy along and a pack of his new favorite brand of cigarettes—Marlboros. Bloody Americans. They always, despite their insufficiencies in many areas, managed to come up with the best of the best. Was the Amazon rain forest truly Marlboro Country? Was he now the Marlboro Man?

Well, at any rate, they certainly were now.

He went up on the main deck via the aft staircase. Weary, he was going to collapse in the stern's crescent-shaped seating area, drink his firewater, and smoke his damned Marlboros. But on second thought, maybe not. He had an urge to secure the boat, at least visually, before he went back to bed.

First, he would inspect the four anchors they'd used to secure the big yacht in the middle of the fast-moving river, hell-bent for the sea. He wanted to ensure that the currents were not causing *Sea Hawke* to "drag" the anchors along the bottom and possibly reposition her in a dangerous way, like perpendicular to the land, which could result in her decks being awash with muddy river water and the deadly possibility of broaching.

He padded forward on bare feet, wearing only an old Royal Navy T-shirt, the one that said "You can run, but you'll only die tired!" and a pair of faded Nantucket Reds, trousers he bought at his favorite men's clothier on the Gray Lady, as he was wont to call that favored isle, Murray's Toggery at the top of the avenue. He paused at the rail and lit his cigarette. Stokely appeared at his side.

"Every little thing A-okay, boss?" his friend said.

"I think so. But I've got this feeling. Not sure how to describe it. Uneasy."

"I know that feeling. General Custer had it, too, at Little Big Horn. He said, 'It's quiet out here—too quiet.' Remember that?"

"Every schoolboy, even in Britain, remembers that one. But, it wasn't Custer who said it, Stoke. It was actually Mr. T in one of the first episodes of *The A-Team*."

"Really, boss? Mr. T? That dude was something else entirely. I can see him saying that. Yeah, sure."

Hawke lit a Marlboro and stared out into the darkness. But of course, he saw nothing in the deep velvet cosmic blackness only found in an Amazonian rain forest in the darkness before the dawn.

The hair on the back of his neck suddenly tingled, causing him to shudder involuntarily. He thought he'd heard something out on the river, and not too far away, either. What was it? He knew how the darkness amplified and distorted sounds. Like what he thought he'd heard: the gulp of dipping paddles or oars? The knock of a wood shaft against the gunwale?

He wasn't at all sure.

"You hear that, Stoke?"

"Oh, yeah. I think we might be having a Custer moment here, bossman. But damned if I see them out there in the dark."

He and Hawke stood stock-still and concentrated on the night sounds all around them: Insects. Laughing monkeys. Nothing. Fish, maybe that's what it was, Stoke thought, surfacing to feed on mosquitos. Piranhas, even, surfacing and splashing about. Relieved, the two of them started forward again.

All was well aboard the *Sea Hawke.*

Until they reached the bow.

There was an inert body lying facedown on the deck, just beneath the cannon turret. And even in the darkness, they could see that it wasn't moving.

They raced over to the figure, whom both men now recognized as Butch Barker, the young American crewman who'd been assigned to the bow as the night lookout. Stoke bent to one knee and felt for a pulse. Nothing. Hawke pulled out his Zippo and lit it, passing it over to Stokely. Stoke examined the boy's body from the feet all the way to his—whoa— something was sticking out of his back! An object, right between his shoulder blades.

It was a poisoned dart, he knew instinctively. Hawke had seen it, too. And Hawke, too, knew what it was, all right. He'd seen them before, up close and personal, when he was running for his life after having been attacked by a mad horde that was quite literally out for his head.

The Shuar tribe of headhunters.

He was once more passing through their lands.

"Stoke," Hawke whispered, "you know where the exterior illumination switches are? Inside the control box on the turret?"

"Yeah. Want me to light this damn boat up like daylight?"

"Yeah."

Stoke quickly ducked down out of sight beneath the turret and held Hawke's lighter up to the panel of switches that dealt with on-deck illumination as well as the powerful searchlight on a swivel mount. He swung the powerful spotlight around to starboard, where the noises had come from. Then he saw the mobile in its charger on the turret and grabbed it.

"Light 'em up, boss," Stoke said. "I'm getting the captain on the radio. Something tells me we're going to sound battle stations again."

Hawke rotated the darkened searchlight. First he hit the switch that illuminated the underwater hull lights that turned the water around and beneath *Sea Hawke* a luminous green; then he switched on the searchlight and slowly swung the piercing blue white beam back and forth from bow to stern . . .

Jesus.

The entire length of the boat was surrounded, on both sides, and off both the bow and stern, with at least fifty dugout canoes, each dugout carrying five naked, face-painted Shuar headhunters armed with poisoned spears, arrows, and blowguns with poison darts. Two hundred and fifty of them? At least.

"Weapons," Hawke said, under his breath. "Right now!"

Hawke took the mobile from Stoke and raised it to his lips, watching Stoke racing aft to grab a couple of the machine guns down in the armory, the ones favored by the Delta Force at Fort Bragg.

"This is Alex Hawke up on the foredeck, Captain Hornblower. We got a problem up here. Get the damn officer of the deck to sound battle stations! And get the ship's surgeon up on the bow immediately! We've got a man down up here. Poison dart in his back. The ship's surrounded with canoes and batshit crazy Indians with poison blowguns and spears. Some of them are already trying to climb up the transom and board us over her stern. Over."

How long had they been sitting out there on the dark river in utter silence? he wondered. Had they been out there waiting for all the large vessel's belowdecks lighting to be extinguished as the crew turned in for the night, whereupon the Shuars would all scramble up over the stern and the bow, board his boat, and take a whole bunch of heads as trophies, trophies known as Tzan-Tzas?

When the lights exploded inside the darkness it had rocked the men in the canoes. Suddenly, these jungle warriors were all in mass confusion, shouting, pushing and shoving, and generally raising hell. They were also starting to try to climb up over the transom and board *Sea Hawke*. Same thing at the bow, where the canoes were coming right up under the pulpit, a lot of hands grasping at the rails, so—

He was interrupted by the sounding order of battle stations all over the ship's exterior on the interior communications system. Almost immediately the topsides were full of running feet and the rattle of machine guns and small-arms fire from one end of the boat to the other.

The headhunters weren't taking it sitting down. They were on their feet now, making good use of their blowguns and hurling poison-tipped spears up at the men who were at the rail pouring fire down upon them.

Which gave Hawke an idea, thank God.

He knew a faster, easier way to make these crazy bastards run—or, even better, swim—for their lives.

He reached up and opened the turret hatch. Then he reached up with one hand and pulled himself up and inside. Flipping on the interior lighting, he climbed into his seat and powered up the laser cannon.

The tribesmen in the canoes to starboard appeared in front of him.

He thought for a moment. He had clearly mastered the laser cannon well enough. He could now use it like a surgeon's lancet to slice a Chinese missile frigate neatly in two. The mean green beam's current setting had roughly the same circumference as a basketball. But he had been practicing. He could now narrow the laser's beam down to something fine and sharp, approaching the razor-sharp blade of a Coldstream Guardsman's Sheffield Steel sword. That was the ticket for this moment.

He sighted in on the lone dugout off the starboard bow. There were blowguns to the fore, and the five tribesmen were firing a hail of poisoned arrows, trying to pick off members of Hawke's crew, who were shooting mere bullets at them.

He put the laser's crosshairs on the dugout's V-shaped bow, but aimed it about one foot aft and fired.

He'd neatly sliced off the whole front of the canoe. Water poured in, and the headhunters went berserk as their dugout began to sink. Worried about the piranhas, Hawke assumed. He hadn't even thought about that. Too late now. He moved on to the next target.

And the next. And the next. And the next.

All of the warriors who could manage it turned back for the shoreline to starboard.

They all swam for their lives.

Hawke and Stoke stood there and watched them scramble up the muddy banks and disappear into the dark jungle, swallowed up by nature herself.

Hawke sighed and dropped down to the deck from the turret. Then he and his old friend walked aft, both of them stopping to talk to his men along the way, comforting the wounded waiting for sick bay to have room for them and the boys who had so bravely fought to defend the mighty *Sea Hawke* and her crew.

The sick bay called him a little later and said they'd suffered three casualties. Two were severely wounded, but their injuries were not life-threatening. The third, a young sailor named Johnnie Hardesty from Boothbay Harbor, Maine, who'd taken a poison-tipped arrow in the center of his chest, had died on the operating table. He was the affable lad, a former lobsterman, whom Hawke had appointed as the bow lookout, helping the captain and crew to navigate the twisty turning paths through all the perils the river ahead offered.

The arrow, five feet long and with a ten-inch macaw feather, was split in two on one end, and a serrated, curare-coated tip on the other was still buried in his chest when they committed his body to the deep.

RIP.

Johnnie, we hardly knew ye.

CHAPTER 42

"Small yachts. The new curse of the Communist working class."

Sea Hawke *upriver, off Dragonfire*

It was shortly after two in the afternoon on Sunday. They'd now been out on the "Big River" for almost a week. Hawke felt himself growing more and more apprehensive as the *Sea Hawke* got to within a few more miles downriver just east of where the Tang Brothers had built, according to Quint anyway, one of the most dramatic and beautiful of their infamous Dragonfire clubs.

The problem was this: Hawke still had not a clue what he was going to do when they arrived at the bloody resort. He'd been up all night, feverishly jotting down ideas, but none of them had seemed to be anywhere near what was going to be required to take down the entire Red Star leadership and organization and all their new bullyboy Communist allies from around the world.

He could only imagine the vast numbers of armed security guards surrounding all those Commie bigwigs! Their Praetorian guards, so to speak.

Quint had told him at breakfast that, just before they came to the next sweeping bend in the river, it would be the last river bend before they got close enough to actually see the much ballyhooed Dragonfire Club up ahead. It would be, he had said, on the right bank of the Amazon heading west. Hawke and the colonel were standing at the starboard rail near the bow so they'd be the first to see the complex hove into view in the near distance.

As the morning wore on, tired of listening to Quint expounding on every bird, every fish, every snake, every bloody topic under the sun, Hawke had told the semi-world-famous-foremost-authority-on-just-about-everything botanist all about his mission and the new Red Star Alliance. And the coming change in the world order. But this would only happen if the newly united Communist powerhouse was actually allowed to exist by the Allies, mainly Britain and the United States, and the majority of the European democracies.

That, Hawke had told the botanist, was the weight he was now carrying on his weary shoulders. And he would appreciate the man shutting the eff up for a couple of hours at least so he could think straight.

That shut him up for at least ten minutes, maybe nine.

"So, old man. What's the plan?"

Hawke stiffened and said, "I've been wondering. About the attendees..."

"What about them?"

"I've been wondering how the hell they get to and from the resort. They are all far from their home countries. I mean, there are no roads. You can't walk. They can't land a helo here because of the solidity of the rain forest canopy. There are no trains ... So, how do they do it?"

"You're about to find out, Alex. Matter of fact, the answer lies just around the bend, as they say."

Ten minutes later, when Alex Hawke, who was now up on the bridge, standing at the helm, saw what lay ahead of him, he exclaimed, "What the *eff*?"

The colonel laughed. Sir David had warned him that Hawke was just a bit tetchy when it came to the random use of foul language, especially the formally forbidden four-letter expletive that had now become about as common a word as "darn" or "shoot" or even "jeepers." Trulove told the botanist that Hawke had never been known to utter that one word aloud, although on many occasions, he had been clearly on the verge of thinking about saying it.

Quint smiled and said, "Quite something, isn't it?"

"Something?" Hawke said. "I'll say, something! It looks like bloody Palm Beach meets Disney World during the snowbird season! That bloody marina out front takes up a third of the river! So that's how our Communist comrades travel these days. I might have known it. I seriously doubt there's a boat in that marina under a hundred fifty feet. Small yachts are the curse of the modern socialist working class, it would appear. How did all this grandiosity come about?"

"As it turns out," Colonel Quint said, "I was one of the first contractors the Tang Brothers hired when they began construction of the complex. They wanted me to consult on the landscape design. They wanted me to tag all the trees and plants they should keep and offer ideas on creating a lush jungle garden feel to the whole property. Fountains, exotic birds, antique garden statues, black swans on the lakes, the whole kit and caboodle.

"This was all years ago, of course, but even then I had a most enviable international reputation, and I recall that the marina was the first thing the boys wanted built. I had pointed out to them that if they wanted exotic plants, trees, and flowers, they'd have to provide some way for the nurseries in Manaus to transport the stuff up here. And, I reminded them, unless they provided a very high-end dockage situation for the whales, which is what the Las Vegas casino operators call the high rollers, the cream of the cash crop, they'd not attract the international mega-yacht crowd."

"Are they receiving hotel guests during the conference?"

"No," Quint said. "Neither are there any staff remaining. And, according to what his insiders said, Red Star bigwigs, including foreign ministers and high-ranking military officers, have zero tolerance for witnesses to their secret meetings and speeches and manifestos and so forth and so on. So the Tang Brothers shut the hotel down for anyone, save for attendees and their support staff, now that the big kahunas were in the planning stages leading up to this Commie powwow in the jungle."

"How many attendees inside, do you imagine, Quint?" Hawke said, in his most impatient verbal coloration.

"Let me see," Quint said as they edged closer and closer to the resort proper, cruising at idle speed, with the crew having been ordered to keep their voices down. There were sentries on both sides of the river, hidden in the jungle.

Hawke said, "I guess we could just count the yachts. I see a helluva lot of flags I don't recognize on the sterns of those things. But I imagine there would be at least one, maybe two representatives from each invited country. So that would be roughly fifty of them. Plus support staff and security who would have traveled upriver commercially."

Quint, never one to keep his two cents to himself, said, "I sure as hell hope you came up with a plan. Do you have one?"

"I do now. I just came up with it."

"Which is . . ."

"We'll start with all these bloody yachts."

"And do what with them?"

"Sink them all, of course."

"Sink them all? Are you crazy? You cannot be serious, Alex."

"You just watch me. I'm going forward to deal with this. Would you mind taking the helm?"

"Love to. What do you want me to do?"

"Lay offshore a good distance, keeping her bow into the currents. And give her just enough throttle to keep her stationary. If you position us dead center in the river and at the center of the entrance to the docks, I'll be in good shape."

"You got it, Skipper," the man said, and snapped off a piss-poor imitation of a Royal Navy salute.

———————

Hawke strode forward and climbed up into the turret. His two young gunners were there, as ordered, sipping Diet Cokes with wedges of lemon through straws. Americans. Who could explain them? Although, Hawke reflected, they probably feel precisely the same way about us. Hawke said:

"Hello, boys. Ready to get busy?"

"Born ready," the older one said, never at a loss for words. Sometimes on this voyage, Hawke had felt surrounded by wankers with an attitude. And now he had Quint, the bloody Wanker-in-Chief!

"If the Tang Brigade or anybody else shoots at us, we shoot right back," Hawke said, powering up the laser cannon and its attendant GPS guiding and firing systems. "There's a lot of security on the property, even though they're not making themselves obvious. The only reason we haven't seen hide nor hair of them is that they're oh so busy trying to figure out how to rule the world. And I'm sure they're all heavily armed, so keep your eyes open and your wits about you!"

"Aye-aye, sir! You're the boss!" Quint chimed in over the radio.

Who even says that tired old phrase anymore? Hawke had been quite taken with this chap upon first meeting. But there was something a bit off about him. Or maybe a bit too on. And Hawke was beginning to tire of his pompous, cheeky personality. He certainly didn't intend to have him aboard for the downriver sail to the Atlantic.

Looking at the live feed video systems looming above his head, he saw that Quint had positioned him perfectly for what he was about to do. "Right on the money, Quint," he said. "Just keep her right here until I'm done."

"Roger that. Steady as she goes."

Hawke centered the cannon's crosshairs on the yacht farthest to his left. He'd never seen her before, but he knew who she belonged to. This fire-engine red monstrosity, name of *Chop-Chop*, belonged to the infamous Tang Twins, Tiger and Tommy. Hawke and Stoke had already sent one of their boats to the bottom—a beautiful Wally boat, the tender to *Chop-Chop*.

Seeing no one aboard, he squeezed lightly on the trigger and the pulled it. He saw he'd opened a hole in the big navy blue Feadship yacht's hull about two feet in diameter, just below the waterline, and then he moved on to his next target. Before he'd acquired the yacht in the firing system, the blue Feadship was down by the head and sinking fast.

Quint's voice suddenly squawked over the radio.

"What the bloody hell are you doing, old boy? Have you lost your effing mind?"

"I'm sinking yachts, actually. I should think at least that much must be apparent even to the likes of you."

Irritated, he was pulling the trigger and blowing the bow off of the numerous Feadships, Benettis, Lürssens, Fincantieri, and others. And another of these, and then another one of those after that. He'd sunk boats both by firing below the waterline and by blowing their bows off. One, he'd sliced in two. The bow shots sent them to the bottom almost instantaneously. He'd decided bow shots suited his needs best. Time was of the essence.

He'd half expected the Chinese cavalry to show up after learning five or six mega-yachts, now ridiculed as "MAGA-yachts" by the left-leaning media in the States, had mysteriously disappeared. But, no, they were nowhere to be seen. Even as, one by one, Hawke continued to send the hefty boats to the muddy bottom.

He believed this lack of awareness at the massive destruction he'd caused at the marina was because everyone—the ministers, the generals, the support staff, and, yes, the security guards—was hermetically sealed underground, inside the great Marble Hall immediately below the beautiful glass pyramid. This was probably on orders from Putin and Xi Jinping and maybe even the Iranian Ayatollah Ali Khamenei and Little Rocket Man himself.

And all of them wanted anything having to do with creating Red Star out of whole cloth to be the best-kept political secret on the planet.

Until, of course, they were all quite ready to unleash the force of the Red Star Alliance on an unsuspecting world.

Putin and Xi Jinping had probably ordered them to "Lock yourselves inside a secure location and don't let anyone leave until you have finished your heroic agenda completely!" Or something to that effect.

———————

Hawke now began firing in earnest, methodically and rapidly, to great effect. Another good thing about this cannon, aside from its stealthy, silent operation: Since Elon's tech team had totally revamped the power supply, you never had to stop and reload the bloody thing! You were moving instantly from one target to the next, firing, and moving on, not waiting around to watch them go down. He sank a huge German yacht, a Blohm+Voss in matte silver. Then a Dutch beauty, a forest green Heesen yacht from the Netherlands. Then there was a magnificent Lürssen from

Germany and another Dutch boat from the famous Oceanco yard—precisely the same yard where *Sea Hawke* had been constructed.

But when he'd finally finished up with the last few remaining yachts in the marina, when the last one floating floated no longer, he had to say that his favorite boat of all had been the *Sistine*, from Fincantieri, in Italy, of course. No one built beautiful machines like the Italians. Just look at the Ferrari or the Lamborghini, the early Alfas. Michelangelo-level masterpieces on four wheels—that was his view.

He got the *Sistine* in his crosshairs and applied a light touch to the trigger, the delicate but longing touch one might apply whilst stroking a beautiful woman's swanlike neck.

He inhaled, then exhaled like a sniper, preparing to shoot.

His trigger finger would not obey his brain's command. He couldn't in all conscience consider sinking that wonder of naval architecture, that Italian masterpiece.

"Sinking all those beautiful yachts to what end, may I ask? Jesus Christ!" Quint squawked over the radio speaker in the turret. "This is a suicide mission!"

"I'll explain all that when I'm quite good and ready."

"No need to get pissy, old boy," this fiend in human form said in his damnably cheeky fashion. He was the kind of fellow who showboats his way through life; a paper tiger. A man who boasted about himself because he had so little to boast about! Rampant insecurity.

Hawke had no reply for his question. He didn't have time for jousting with this self-described man of action genius, this self-absorbed, jumped-up hero of his own life, but nobody else's. Self-important people, especially men, grated upon his nerves like no other. He just couldn't abide all that vainglorious crap.

Like some Americans who'd attended some very snooty Ivy League universites, perhaps one in particular, who all had the overwhelming desire to tell you, within mere moments of being introduced to you, that they'd gone there by name-dropping some line like, "Well, I agree with you. But, you know, back when I was at *Harvard, don't you know.*" (Or fill in the blank with many another alma mater.)

Had Quint really called Hawke "pissy"? And not so subtly ridiculed his Britishisms, with his pompous and sarcastic use of the quintessentially necessary phrase "old boy," which was about as ubiquitous in the UK as "dude" was in the US?

How on earth had Sir David Trulove come up with this American menace to sanity and polite society? Probably whilst having the barman uncork a second bottle of the Infuriator over dinner in the dining room at Black's!

There could not possibly be any other explanation!

CHAPTER 43

"I'm at war. It's what I do. I eliminate enemies of my Queen and Country!"

Sea Hawke *upriver, Dragonfire Club*

Sea Hawke ghosted and drifted at idle speed forward, her mighty engines and massive props burbling at the stern, sending rippling waves toward the muddy riverbanks. Lord Hawke, standing on the port bridge wing with his binocs, kept his finger on the focus ring. He was finally able to get his first really good look at what the Tangs had wrought here in the deepest part of the jungle.

It was a large complex, architecturally diverse, and far larger than the one where he'd stayed in the Bahamas whilst looking for Prince Henry, the Queen's favorite grandson. He hated to admit it, but it was quite striking. The great Palladio himself would not have been amused—it was bordering on the bizarre, downright silly in some ways, almost Disneyesque, especially in this prehistoric jungle setting.

For starters, the huge central structure at the epicenter of everything was an exact, though much larger, replica of the *Pyramide du Louvre* in the main courtyard of the museum in Paris, the beautiful glass-and-metal pyramid designed by Chinese-American architect I. M. Pei. Hawke, seeing one of his most favorite works of art standing there in the midst of one of the world's great jungles, wholly lit from within, made this mission of his one to remember.

He hated to do it, but his never-idle curiosity drove him to radio the bridge, and to the man banished to the bridge for the duration, standing at the helm.

"What's that huge glass pyramid used for, Quint?"

"Well, first of all, you should know that it is a perfect replica of—"

Hawke, quite rudely, in his own opinion, slyly interrupted him in a condescending tone, saying the following:

"Ah, but of course! The *Pyramide du Louvre* at the *musée du Louvre* in Paris, *mais oui?*" Hawke said rather curtly. "Designed to copy the exact same proportions as the pyramid of Cheops, if I'm not mistaken. You know, the world's oldest surviving site of the original Seven Wonders of the World. Yes?"

"Um, yes. That's the one. It's primarily used for reception, concierge, staff offices, that sort of thing. But the vast marble halls below the pyramid are used for banquets and conferences like the one today. It's a favorite for weddings for couples in Manaus who want to stay close to home. My wife and I were married there. Juan Carlos, the king of Spain, was a guest. Friend of my father's, actually."

"Ah, fascinating," Hawke said, pretending to have been listening to the man. "And to the left, that twenty-story citadel, that's the hotel?"

"Yes, but the most desirable, and the most expensive, rooms are not in the main building. Those are tree houses, actually. They're the small white British Colonial–style cottages built in the trees, with interconnecting rope walks. Guests abandon their mega-yachts to spend a few nights up in the trees."

Hawke asked, "And what of the other buildings, the beautifully imaginative modern-bells-and-whistles architecture? What purpose do they serve? Reminds one a bit of Disney World, to be perfectly honest."

"Well, let's see . . . Three of them are restaurants. One Chinese, obviously, designed to resemble the famous Grauman's Chinese Theater on the Hollywood Walk of Fame in LA. That silly Leaning Tower over there is called Armando al Pantheon, in honor of the chef du cuisine— Italian, of course. And the beautifully illuminated one, a smaller version of Pei's *Pyramide*, is the glorious French restaurant where my beautiful wife and I have celebrated our last ten anniversaries!"

"And the large building at the edge of the gardens? With the giant revolving gold coin bathed in blazing light high on the roof? That has to be the casino."

"Of course."

"Probably empty now, until they wrap things up at the end of the meeting tomorrow."

"Certainly empty now."

"Good. I'll start with that one."

"What? What do you mean, 'start with that one'?"

"Watch me," Hawke said, then leveled the casino with three consecutive brilliant cannon bursts of green fire. The building fell into itself, collapsing in the blink of an eye to the jungle floor.

"Jesus Christ!" Quint said. "You really are insane! These Tang Brothers? You don't want to get on the wrong side of the road with them, trust me."

"Hmm. Not really insane, old boy. I'm at war. This is what I do. I eliminate the enemies of my Queen and Country. She's grown rather fond of me, actually. She's my son's godmother, you know. His godfather was the late Lord Mountbatten, bless his soul. Perhaps you've heard of him? Old friend of the family, don't you see."

"How very interesting," the man said, in that ironic, condescending way he had with people. "Listen, I've just had what I perceive to be a brilliant idea. Can I tell you about it?"

"Of course. But don't take it the wrong way if I don't share your notions about what is and is not brilliant, old boy."

Quint smiled, feebly trying to deflect Hawke's ironic treatment of him. He knew he was in over his head with this Hawke. And he wisely kept his own counsel in the heat of the moment. After all, he was going to need a lift home. This was the genesis of his genius idea.

"So, here goes nothing," he said to Hawke. "As I've mentioned, I am very well known and respected by both of the twins and pretty much all of their staff here at Dragonfire."

"Yes?" Hawke said impatiently, as he wasn't really listening.

"Well, it's a very straightforward notion. My presence ashore would not be taken as anything but normal because of my close relationship with the family. Right?"

Hawke had no reply.

"Well, here it is. I could take the launch over to the club docks, have a casual stroll about ashore, and just do a recon. Assess the situation and identify the threats we might face, what unpleasant surprises may be awaiting us, that sort of thing. What do you think?"

"I'm sorry," Hawke said. "What did you say?"

"I'll take the launch to shore and do a complete threat assessment and recon so we'll know precisely what we're up against over there."

"Hmm. Whatever floats your boat, old boy," he said, not really caring about what the fellow could or could not accomplish, and frankly, very happy to have him the hell off of *Sea Hawke* for the rest of the afternoon.

For the next half hour or so, emanating from the bow turret aboard *Sea Hawke* came bursts of highly energized bright green cannon fire, streaking across the water and throughout the Dragonfire Club, devastating everything in its path. Everywhere you looked were mounds of ash and smoking embers, fireflies of flaming wood floating up into the darkness and up into the green canopy over two hundred feet in the air. Remnants of fire and destruction lent the whole scene a fearsome and eerie quality.

It was at that precise moment that Alex Hawke saw a few of the armed Tang security forces emerge from the vicinity of the *Pyramide du Louvre*. They were in no big hurry, these guys. This was, after all, more than anything, a military operation, and these guards were unaccustomed to a firefight with this level of violence and destruction.

The pyramid was the only building that remained standing untouched. Hawke had deliberately left it so. He had done so for the sake of Art itself.

The truth was, he didn't much mind destroying physical structures that had no inherent value. But he would never in his life destroy what he considered to be art, in its many forms, including poetry or music, or any beauty in a physical form, for instance.

"Hawke," the radio squawked. It was Captain Hornblower up on the bridge.

"Hawke here, Cap'n."

"Sir, radar confirms we have just picked up three bogies. We've been sat-tracking them ever since they first entered the river. Now all three are traveling east to west on the river at very high speed. A crewman just got eyes on them coming around a bend maybe fifteen miles from our current position. Radar says, 'What we've got here are three heavily armed Chinese Navy warships, with a design very similar to that of the American patrol torpedo boats in the Pacific theater during World War II and also down in the Mekong Delta during the Vietnam era. But our intel says the Chinese versions are built wholly of carbon fiber. Still lightweight, but much stronger than the old World War II American versions."

"What kind of armaments do they have, Captain?"

"We did a zoom down on one them. There are what appear to be four very modern live torpedoes visible on the stern decks of all three vessels, both on port and starboard sides of the identical boats. We think word of the attack on Dragonfire Club has somehow gotten out and that the chief of Tang security is now fully aware of what has transpired in his absence. The chief, whose name is Kris Wu, is no doubt highly motivated now, sir!"

Indeed, the proof of that motivation was suddenly a reality. The jungles surrounding the Chinese complex were now alive with combat troops, heavily armed and ordered to destroy the invaders with their superior firepower. Already, patches of thick green jungle were alive with fiery bursts of heavy machine-gun fire trained on *Sea Hawke* and her complement of sailors.

Hawke stared at the scene in disbelief.

It was just possible that such a force as this could overrun them. And, backed up against the river, there was no chance of escape!

CHAPTER 44

"When the battle was joined, there you'd find him!"

Sea Hawke *upriver, Dragonfire Club*

The oncoming thug army, as Hawke thought of them—because that's exactly what they were, the lowest order of murderous thugs—came racing en masse toward the marauding invaders who were now storming the marina. The Resistance, this fresh crop of Red Star storm troopers, were half Russian and half Chinese military primarily, but with a salting of Cubans thrown in for good measure. But they were paid killers all the same. On the Russian side, they consisted of the washed-up and preternaturally drunken OMON troops in their infamous blue and black camo, the Chechen death squads that the Kremlin had sent to do savage killing, scorched-earth style, inside the ravaged Chechnya, killing any and everyone in their path: men, women, and children—even stray pets.

On the Chinese side were remnants of the troops that had rounded up millions of the Uighur Muslims, forced underground into concentration camps for "political education" and used primarily as slave labor and/or subjected to genocide.

Still, Hawke suspected in his gut that, despite this, Wu must know it was far too little, far too late for him. Basically, Wu was, as the Americans say, "dicked and redicked."

The Tangs would hang him, Kris Wu knew that, if he didn't by some miracle take out this enemy who had the temerity to enter their jungle cathedrals and destroy what the twins had poured millions, if not billions, into.

Hawke told Stoke, "Had to be Wu who ordered up the three Chinese Navy patrol torpedo boats now racing to reach the resort in time to blockade us inside the confines of the marina. Then, if they can muster enough Tang security personnel, they can attack both of our flanks from the rear in a pincer attack. We gotta bust out right now, dammit! Now! Seconds count! You men do what you gotta do to slow them down, and you do it now!"

"We don't need the laser on the river yet, boss. I'll go turn the bloody laser on 'em—that'll slow their asses way down!" Stoke said.

"Yes! Get up to the turret and make that happen, Stoke! Start firing both barrels! We need cover fire to get the hell away from here!"

Hornblower on the bridge radioed Hawke as the numbers shifted and the situation seriously deteriorated out on the docks. Stoke was saying, "We gotta get outta here, boss, else they're going to trap us here! Now! Or we never get out of here!"

Hawke barked back, "Aye! Captain Hornblower, order all hands on deck! Power up the turbofans, free all mooring lines, and swivel the ship one-eighty degrees in place so that her bow faces open water. Soon as you got her out in open water, put her effing hammer down! Full speed due east! Sound to battle stations! All hands on deck! Battle stations!"

Hawke radioed to helm, "Get us the hell out of this bloody mess. All ahead full! Helm hard over to port! Now! We're getting this ship the bloody hell out of this Chinese amusement park, no matter what."

"Aye-aye, sir. What about our ship's launch? The guest named Quint who took it ashore an hour ago has not yet returned. Should we duck inshore and try to rescue him and the launch?"

Hawke looked at the sailor incredulously. "*Quint?* Is that what you said? Screw Quint and the horse he rode in on, son. And the loss of that launch is of no consequence to me. Let him find an Uber around here if he's in such a hurry to get home. I've got one more launch just like it. I see the loss of that boat as a very small price to pay for getting rid of that dim-witted sonofabitch."

Hornblower shrugged his shoulders and turned away. He'd learned long ago that there was simply no accounting for the ways of the vastly rich!

Hawke now had a P226 Sig Sauer handgun jammed inside the waistband of his long khaki trousers and an M-240 belt-fed machine gun in his right hand and a bullhorn in his left.

And Stokely Jones, Jr., right behind him.

"Stoke, thanks for jumping in, but I've got this," he shouted above the raucous, rattling thunder of the marina firefight. "Get back to the stern! I'm putting you and Mr. Brock in command of our guys back there! Coordinate the battle for getting the ship to safety and the hell out of this inferno.

"Stoke, you and Brock, you have to cover the battle with the Tang forces racing out onto the docks. You two have to mount the defense! Defend the boat against these land forces. Don't let any of them get too close to the boat. They mean to board us! If you have to, use the bloody laser on them. It tends to give one pause. And I don't want to see what close-in hand-to-hand fighting looks like aboard my boat!

"You got it, boss! Brock and I, we eat these kind of soldiers as a midday snack. We're all over this damn thing."

Stoke turned away and raced aft to find Brock.

Hawke turned round and shouted after him, "Listen! Belay that order! I'm going to need that laser turret myself to take out those three bloody PT boats before they unleash those torpedoes. Do the best you can with what you've got!"

Hawke watched warily as fresh Chinese and Russian security forces, all in camo fatigues and Kevlar body armor, were now emerging en masse from three unseen jungle locations as well as from some hidden location at the rear of the pyramid. He told Hornblower, "I am commencing return fire from our stern and amidships turrets. Instruct the forward turret to commence firing on the PTs as soon as they've got a shot. Use the laser and the big guns, and .50 cals. Give 'em everything we've got!"

"Aye-aye, sir," Captain Hornblower said. "We're taking heavy fire from onshore forces, headed for the docks to surround us once we're trapped inside. We've got seconds to decide, mate! I'm going to get the ship the hell out of here, sir! Now! Over."

Hawke never heard that last bit. Some of the Tang boys were already getting into firing position out on the docks, and more were coming fast. But the vicious fire coming from *Sea Hawke* was equal or better than the incoming they were getting. Which was precisely what it should have been. She was a warship, built from the keel up for just this kind of extreme combat situation.

It was then that Hawke saw Stokely and Brock up on the twin bridge wings using the radio to communicate with the troops fighting below. Good move, you guys, Hawke thought. Now that they were up there on the high ground, they had good visibility of the various fields of fire and the advantage of height over the enemy with views to the whole of the ship. Hawke saw Stoke catch sight of him with his binocs down on the deck and gave him a salute and a thumbs-up.

Hawke smiled back up at him and was about to return the salute. But just before racing forward to his bow gun turret (he now thought of it as his own), he heard a muffled shout from high above. He looked up at Stoke. The man was screaming as loud as he could . . . It was hard to make out, but ". . . BEHIND YOU! BEHIND YOU!" reached him. He whirled around just in time to see a figure, an Iranian storm trooper, climbing up over the starboard rail, followed by another man right behind him.

It was Quint, armed with a pistol! The two of them had clearly come for Hawke. Coming to kill him.

"Hey, Quint, you bloody traitor. Look what I've got!" Hawke said, pulling his Sig Nine, firing into his chest, and sending him pinwheeling down into the water below. He struggled to keep his head above the surface, but after a few seconds, he slipped beneath the waters of the river.

He would not be missed.

"Nothing to worry about here, sailors," Hawke said. "Just a little unfinished business between two old enemies."

"You sure 'bout that, sir?"

"Oh, sure," Hawke said. He'd caught eye of Stoke racing down from high above.

Hawke then disappeared up inside the turret and rotated the cannon into the dead aft firing direction. Just in the nick of time, too, because he could now see that the two Chinese PT boats were getting close.

Hawke flicked on all the relevant exterior monitors, then zoomed in on the four torpedoes on each boat. They were the real McCoy: Black Shark torpedoes, also known far and wide as the world's deadliest torpedoes. He did a mental calculation. Four Black Sharks were plainly visible. And there were at least two Black Sharks already loaded into the forward torpedo tubes of the other boats. Six per boat; eighteen bloody Black Sharks. These boys like to play rough. But he'd show them what rough was if it was the last thing he did.

When battle was joined, there you'd find him!

Hawke could only imagine how the Tang security forces on the ground must have thought they were dreaming as they raced out toward the steep riverbanks. They now had to come to grips with what they saw. And that was the fact that the entire marina, to their utter disbelief, was now . . . simply gone, save for great broken slabs and ragged bits of concrete and twisted rebar sticking up out of the water at odd angles. Standing around scratching their heads, the enemy was seemingly unable to deal with what was now a destroyed marina completely devoid of *any* vessels at all!—save for the big white sailing yacht with its majestic bow projecting out over the rapidly rushing river.

What they had to face, Hawke knew, wasn't exactly a morale builder!

After all, where the hell had all the damn owner's yachts gone to? Not to mention this scorched-earth attack on the entire dock complex itself. And if they turned their attention to what was left behind them, they would see that the entire resort complex had now been reduced to piles of burning debris and thick gray smoke. It was as if a massive nuclear device had been detonated. Nothing else could have wreaked such destruction.

Or could it?

Hawke knew that the Tang security heads would certainly be blamed for this outrage and would soon be facing the wrath of the Tangs, if not a firing squad. And that was never a happy fate. One thing must have particularly shocked the men in charge of security during the conference:

No one sequestered belowground in the Marble Hall would have heard a thing from the outside world! There'd been no explosions, no rattling sounds of automatic weapons or shots fired or engines being started on the mega-yachts and heading out to the river to escape! And, if there had been, they'd be wondering just who the hell had taken all their boats and where and *how*? Had they been taken for ransom coming from Red Star?

Hawke did not envy the Chief of Security. The really bad thing for him, whoever he was, was that, here at Dragonfire, he had rejected most of the delegates' pleas to, at bare minimum, leave a squad of men patrolling the marina to safeguard all the expensive yachts out there, not to mention having a squad patrol outside the pyramid to engage with any enemy forces attacking the resort proper.

The arrogant Wu, whom Quint had described to Hawke, and who now knew that he was in a very precarious position here, would likely come to regret it.

Where the hell is everybody? Hawke wondered. He could only guess!

Based on what he'd learned from Quint, he knew that the most likely scenario was this: that the attendee yacht owners, not to mention their support staff, their private security, and their convivial hosts, Tommy and Tiger Tang, were still all locked away and insulated well belowground and, in the political fervor of the moment, totally oblivious to what was going on outside in the real world. They were all belowground, down in the Marble Halls listening to endless speeches about the joys of being a Communist bigwig. The money. The power. The glory.

Then there was the huge white sailing yacht anchored in the center of their marina. She was motoring away at dead slow, her sails were furled, and she was headed bow-on toward the opposite shore of the Amazon. Her props turning, she was whipping up a large, frothy white wake at her stern, all ahead half, now hell-bent on escape from the Dragonfire's wrath.

Hawke had to smile at what he had wrought deep in the Amazonian jungle!

But, Hawke thought, beware! Aboard our gleaming white sailing vessel with its soaring spars stand our armed Yankee and mercenary fighters, standing shoulder to shoulder all along her rail, from the tip of the bow to the stern. It was as if a wall of heavily armed men had been erected like fortification castle walls to defend this ship against all and any who threatened her.

Hawke suddenly leapt up onto the top of a capstan, raised his clenched right fist, somewhat in the manner of Robin Hood alerting his Merry Men, and cried aloud, "Ahoy, Lads! Let's show them our true colors. Hoist the Jolly Roger, Ensign Jones!" Hawke shouted to John Paul Jones, the young Royal Navy midshipman he'd become so friendly with on the voyage, and suddenly the Skull and Crossbones was fluttering, being hauled aloft, then snapping at the masthead in a stiff breeze!

Suddenly, the Tang forces all saw the Jolly Roger now hoisted aloft to the top of the mainmast! The infamous pirate flag of the Skull and Crossbones was not a sight any of them welcomed.

And also, hidden gun emplacements aboard *Sea Hawke*'s massive superstructure were now unveiled high above the decks, but still the question remained unanswered: However the hell had these few men managed to make an entire marina, along with perhaps thirty mega-yachts, simply disappear into thin air?

In total silence?

It defied belief! For the Tang Twins, who even now were being informed of the utter disaster aboveground, it was a gut blow, delivered by the same English Devil who'd defiled them so horribly at Dragonfire in the Bahamas:

The infamous Lord Hawke and his lethal legions of fighters.

It would not take long for the Tang Army, as the twins called their ragtag brigades, to come to realize they suddenly had a significant problem on their hands. They opened fire as one, charging forth in a crouch toward what little was left of the marina to join their comrades already out on the smoking docks.

All this in a feeble attempt to wreak havoc on this mystery ship, a ghost ship perhaps, which was even now trying so desperately to escape the confines of the marina before the steaming Chinese PT boats, summoned all too late by Tang security, arrived in time to entrap them. Whoever the hell "them" was, anyway.

Up on *Sea Hawke*'s bridge, standing alongside the bosun's mate, the good Captain Hornblower took control of the conn, saying, "All ahead half until her stern's well clear of the breakwater and the boat's fully out on the river. Give her enough sea room to maneuver," he said, to the men at his side. "But, listen up, the skipper has altered our plan of attack for the coming conflict on the river. We're swinging due east for the Atlantic, mind you, not going farther upriver into this stinking jungle. The boss wants to stand and fight, always.

"So once we're out in mid-river, we'll swing the old gal hard to port and race eastward all ahead full toward the three approaching enemy vessels. And then, damn the torpedoes! And then, all ahead full! We'll bloody well take them head-on, goddammit. Tell sonar to be in constant contact with the bridge, on the lookout for incoming torpedoes in the water from the forward tubes when we get closer to their position."

And so what would come to be known as the great riverine battle between *Sea Hawke* and China's three enemy PT boats had finally commenced in earnest. Little did Alex Hawke know at that point, but he would soon find himself outmanned and outgunned. But, as Hawke always liked to think, or at least to reassure himself whilst trembling on the brink of battle, never outsmarted!

CHAPTER 45

The oncoming trio of torpedo boats was continuing westward toward him at a very high velocity, their sleek prows slicing through the oncoming chop. Eastward bound, *Sea Hawke*'s radar and sonar were now monitoring the PT boats' speed over ground, all the while bucking those intense eastward currents of the world's greatest river. Hornblower's estimate of the time until the actual confrontation varied as the enemy vessels, probably well aware of the fact they were being tracked electronically, were swerving this way and that, changing their speeds constantly, making it as difficult as possible for the opposing forces to determine for sure exactly when and where the actual encounter would actually happen.

Watching them on the radar, Hawke saw that the speeding PTs would periodically just go dead in the water to confuse *Sea Hawke*'s pinpoint tracking systems.

Two hours later, Hawke was asked up to the bridge by Cap'n Hornblower. The mood was palpably tense, and Hawke felt it wash over him like some kind of a curse. Something was not going right. Cap'n Hornblower was bending over the chart table, inspecting one with a large magnifying glass.

"Sir," Hornblower said, "do you mind stepping over here? I need to make you aware of something."

"What is it?" Hawke said. "More bleeding sea tendrils to foul our props? I'm of a mood to exchange this bloody river for the Danube or a barge on the Mississippi. I think I'd find either of the two much more copacetic than this Green Hell of a nightmare."

"No, no, nothing like that. Have a look at the chart."

Hawke did. And said, "All right, I give. It's the bloody Amazon. What about it, Cap'n?"

Hornblower replied, "We now verge on approaching that tight bend in the river, the one a famous English explorer named Benson gave a name that stuck for a century or more. He named it 'Benson's Big Bend.' Clever, what? Here is where it begins and where it ends, in a section of the river known as the Narrows, as I'm sure you'll recall. It's actually the deepest section of the Amazon as well as the narrowest. Soundings from the earliest expeditions have posited two hundred feet or more beneath their keels."

"Yes, I recall. It does get very narrow there. And deep. What about it?"

"Well, here's the thing. If I was going to ambush an eastbound enemy vessel, this is precisely where I would lay my trap, no question."

"Because?"

"Because as soon as we round Benson's Big Bend and have shown our true colors to the enemy, we will basically be a sitting duck. We'll be heading straight for them, the three torpedo boats carrying twelve of the most lethal weapons known to man. We'll have no chance of escape if they should instantly launch two or three fish at us, followed by more."

"Why is that?" Hawke said.

"Well, normally we would take evasive action against inbound torpedoes. But you've just seen on the chart just how narrow the river is at that point! And it remains like this for a good two miles. We can't evade laterally, and we certainly can't back away, because there's no sea room to turn this leviathan around. So we cannot just turn her around and run. And the three Chinese PTs facing us, lying in wait, three abreast, four fish apiece, will certainly block our path forward and steaming eastward for the Atlantic Ocean . . . that's why it's the ideal spot for an ambush. Well, you see the issue, I'm sure."

Hawke said, "I do, Cap'n, I certainly do. In your view, we've just escaped one trap by a hairsbreadth, only to be caught in another. But we do have an advantage over them, don't we? The green-eyed monster. I'll fire at the middle one, sinking it in an instant. Then we go damn the torpedoes, firewall the throttles, full speed ahead. I could use a football analogy. After the snap, the running back takes a handoff from the QB and goes straight up the middle for the touchdown! So, in essence, the *Sea Hawke* will run for daylight. We race like hell, right between the two enemy linesmen, raking them with stiff-arms, etc., and breaking free of them and sailing beyond into clear air! Still racing for daylight full speed ahead so that they won't possibly be able to give chase or manage to reload their forward tubes in time to sink us first before a shot is fired. Yes?"

"Yes, yes, but . . ."

"But what, Captain?"

"The timing of the thing must be absolutely perfect! Down to the second!" Hornblower said.

"Indeed," Hawke replied. "But, remember, unlike a torpedo boat, we don't have to reload our primary weapons systems, do we? Torpedoes are a bitch to reload in battle, believe me! The enemy will be reduced to opening fire with small arms and probably a couple of .50 caliber machine guns mounted on the foredeck while they scramble to load fresh fish into the forward tubes. And by the time they've rounded up on us, by the time the tubes are fully loaded? We'll be well beyond them and headed at last for the wide-open seas! They can give chase, but they can't catch us. Not with our big turbofan engines cranking out a thousand horsepower each."

"Hmm," Cap'n Hornblower said, thoughtfully stroking his goatee as he mulled the thing over. "Well, you do make a good case, sir, I'll give you that. I just hope they don't have any surprises waiting for us, any dirty tricks up their sleeves, that's my only concern. For all we know, they could have mined this entire stretch of the river during the night just past."

"Hardly plausible," Hawke said, "highly unlikely. There was not enough time for them to do that and still reach the marina in time to block us in!"

"True enough, sir, true enough," Hornblower said.

"I want to round that bend dead slow, Cap'n," Hawke said. "Center the boat mid-river, bow on, to minimize the target's physical presence—and then a full stop. I need all the time I can get to lock onto the torpedoes and stop them. I'll blow the center boat to smithereens before they can blink an eye. Then, once their bow tubes have been expended, it'll take a goodly amount of time for them to reload fresh fish, as you so aptly call them. And, during that fevered period, that's when the good ship *Sea Hawke* shall be running hell-bent for daylight, all ahead full, putting as much distance between us and the two flankers as we possibly can."

"Done, sir," Hornblower said. "I take it you've played war games like this before."

"Oh, you have no idea, Cap'n," Hawke said, jamming a Marlboro in the corner of his mouth and flicking his Zippo lighter. "Not the damn foggiest idea, Sunshine!" he said, in his best Marlboro Man accent.

Unfortunately for Captain Hornblower, Lord Alex Hawke, and the beleaguered, battle-weary crew of the *Sea Hawke*, dirty tricks were precisely what the three Chinese PT boat commanders lying in wait did have up their sleeves. And, to make matters even worse, they were very dirty little tricks indeed!

CHAPTER 46

C ap'n Hornblower had his blood up. He knew he should get down on his knees and kiss Hawke's Royal Navy ring in gratitude. This was the man who'd restored him to the glorious, adventurous life he'd once loved—being in command of a great warship and engaging the enemy at every turn. He felt like his very soul had shed a good twenty years, and that was a conservative number. Hawke was a born warrior. And now another warrior, by the sainted name of Hornblower, had been reborn.

It was time to bid fond farewell to the embattled Red Star conventioneers, still haggling over how to divvy up the spoils of the free world once Red Star's glorious plans were revealed in all their splendor.

"All ahead half!" Hornblower shouted. "Take her out to mid-river and put her over hard to port, bearing ninety degrees, due east! We'll engage them in the Narrows downriver, just after we exit the bend. We've got strong sunlight in their eyes right now, Bosun. So post a lookout on the bow to watch for those bloody underwater plants that fouled our props on our westward journey into the heart of the jungle."

Sea Hawke surged forward and began steaming downriver at an amazing clip for a big sailing yacht.

She was making good headway toward Big Bend, at barely idle speed. Sometimes the helmsman would give a little bit of reverse to counteract for currents and windage.

As Hawke had seen for himself on the overhead monitors inside the cannon's turret, it wouldn't be very long before they were entering the huge snaking bend in the river. It wouldn't be long now, perhaps three-quarters of an hour, he thought, until he found out if his grand scheme to escape this new trap the Chinese Navy had set for them would work. He felt the boat slowing gradually, to the point where she was barely moving at all, save for the stiff currents.

They had finally entered Benson's Big Bend.

Hawke said, "You gunners know the battle plan, correct? You were briefed as scheduled, yes?"

"Yes, sir! Radar and sonar gave us a sitrep an hour ago and brought us up to speed, sir! Our mission is to suppress fire from the two flanking patrol boats. You're taking the center boat head-on, sir."

"Aye. As soon as we've got eyes on those three torpedo boats, you lads open fire with all you've got. I've also ordered the M60 gunners to fire multiple barrages of RPGs at the flankers. Rocket-propelled grenades were just what the doctor ordered when one is trying to sow fear and confusion, a sense of impending chaos aboard a pair of enemy vessels."

Hawke continued, "We'll need as much distraction as we can get out of those Chinese sailor boys. Keep their attention off the primary job at hand. Namely, keep those deadly Black Sharks out of the water—and persuade them to keep their bloody heads down or get them blown off.

"And, when we've sunk the middle PT and the path ahead is all clear, we make a run for it straight up the middle, between the two flanking PTs, and that is precisely when you two gunslingers give 'em everything you've got! Understood? Don't leave anything on the playing field! As the Yanks are so fond of saying, 'This is for the whole ball game.' Or is it the whole shooting match? Anyway, you get the idea."

"Yes, sir!" they said. And they meant it. The radio squawked, and the closest crewman yanked it off the hook and handed it to Hawke. "Sir, it's Cap'n Hornblower on the bridge. We're near the end of the bend and just about to round the corner and pull fully into plain sight of the enemy. Everything up there battle ready? Cannons fully powered up? Are you shipshape, sir?"

"Indeed we are, Cap'n," Hawke said, with a wide grin. "We're as ready as we'll bloody ever be, I'll warrant! I've got two good men up here with me, as you know. We'll get the job done, come hell or high water, or bloody well both!"

"Good on you all, then, sir! Good shooting," Hornblower said, and signed off.

The next thing Hawke heard was the call to battle stations, sirens wailing from speakers scattered throughout the *Sea Hawke*. She'd now been thoroughly battle-tested and had definitely gotten the upper hand of the enemy back at the Dragonfire Club. Now, as the tension mounted, he had but one regret. The true speed of the Black Shark torpedoes was highly classified by the Pentagon. But his job today would have been considerably more doable had he thought to get those classified numbers from Brick Kelly at CIA.

Hawke had decided to enable the AI-assisted seek-and-destroy mode. With it, he could fire the laser at much quicker intervals because he wouldn't have to acquire the targets himself and aim the cannon. The AI-assisted mode would do all that for him!

Hawke caught sight of the three dull gray-green enemy patrol boats, rafted together head-on and stretching from one bank of the river to the other—completely blocking out safe passage to the east. He was staggered to see that, with their broad beams, together the three enemy warships formed an almost solid wall of steel across this narrow span of the Amazon River.

From the bridge, the blare of the captain's voice rang throughout the length and breadth of the ship.

"Battle stations! Battle stations! All hands to your stations!"

The instant those words pricked his ears, Hawke's blood was up full steam. He was fever-pitch excited, down to his bones, as he always was just prior to engaging with an enemy in combat. He could recall with ease the adrenaline rush he often got whilst serving as a combat pilot with the Royal Navy.

Whenever the opportunity for a real bang-up dogfight had presented itself in the skies over Kabul, Afghanistan, he found himself to be more alive than at any other time in his life. There was simply nothing else on earth to match that rush, that high, that soaring feeling when you had bested the enemy and had him squarely in your gunsights.

But this tricky situation had most certainly gotten his blood pumping . . . and not a shot had been fired. Yet.

"All hands on deck," he heard the bosun's mate repeat over the ship's radio. "And give 'em hell, gentlemen!"

Secure inside the forward gun turret, Hawke couldn't see what was happening out on deck all round him, but you could almost feel the hum and drumbeat of the *Sea Hawke* coming to life, gearing up and preparing for a battle that would decide their fate this day.

"Focus!" he admonished himself. "Quit your bloody daydreaming and focus on the forward tubes of the center patrol boat!

He needed to lock in the cannon on those Black Sharks seconds after the launch sequence, but when the deadly fish were not yet fully out of the tube. In other words, he had to shoot before he'd even seen a trail in the water. That's why he had, at the last minute and despite the enormous expense, decided to incorporate the cannon's AI target acquisition/ fire mode and try to take the powerful torpedoes off the game board while the evil black snouts were just emerging from the tubes. If successful, their own torpedoes would send them to the bottom!

It was a little combat maxim he liked to think of as "Maximum Damage Possible."

The power of his laser cannon added to the huge payload of high explosives in the torpedo's warhead would blow away half the bow section of the boat and render the Chinese warship sinking and fundamentally useless in the fight. And there would certainly be collateral damage to the ships to either side!

And she'd sink fast, too, what with that onrush of river water pouring into her at hundreds of gallons per second and— Holy hell! Automatic fire had broken out close by, and rounds were ricocheting off the armored turret with deafening twangs . . . in other words . . .

Showtime, lads!

––––––––––

Hawke had invited young J. P. Jones up into the turret to witness a demonstration of the firepower. He now had his finger on the cannon's manual trigger system. Not to shoot, not just yet, but as a backup, to be ready to immediately fire the cannon manually in case of any AI glitch or malfunction. One thing he'd learned about himself in combat: There was nothing artificial about his intelligence.

If they launched a speeding lethal torpedo at him, or even two, he could still eliminate both manually with the laser cannon. One way or the other. What he liked about Elon's addition of AI to the suite of functions the laser could employ, especially in such delicate situation, was that it eliminated the negative potential of the flawed human brain from the equation.

He smiled to himself, remembering a conversation he'd had with Elon months ago when the cannon was being integrated into the ship's defensive and offensive array.

And the doomed crews aboard the three Chinese PT boats? Well, their fate had already been sealed by the ingenious Mr. Musk. Hawke knew full well that the Chinese Communist Party had every intention of conquering the world in the twenty-first century. These were the resurgent and very determined legitimate enemies of the freedom and democracy enjoyed by the Western allies. And, as such, it was Alex Hawke's sworn duty to defeat them at every turn. Including Benson's Bend.

Most, if not all, of the enemy combatants aboard the three patrol boats would perish, of course—and instantly.

Atomized, as it were.

"Let's score one for Queen and Country, Mr. Jones!" Hawke said, smiling at the kid.

"Aye-aye, sir!" John Paul Jones, the recently promoted young second-in-command barked back. He, too, had had his blood roiled up in the midst of hot-leaded combat with a determined enemy!

Hornblower, glancing around at the state of battle, smiled to himself. How things had changed!

He'd thought, in the very beginning of this bally voyage, that it was going to be some kind of leisurely cruise down to Rio along the coast of South America—a rich man's yacht and his rich friends along for the ride, out for a bit of leisurely cruising and shrimps on the barbie!

Alex Hawke, Hornblower was delighted to say, was having absolutely none of that cruising bullcrap! He still remembered what Hawke had said to him after he'd finally described *Sea Hawke*'s real mission:

"China has been spoiling for a fight with the Western Allies? Well, we'll bloody well give them one to remember, Cap'n Hornblower! And give their new allies, the Russians and the Cubans and the NOKOs, all something to think about as well!"

Hawke had preprogrammed the laser cannon to automatically lock onto any torpedo that was launched and emerged from the tube and then fire at the optimum moment during that launch, when half the fish was still in the tube! The US Navy's second- and third-generation land- and ship-based laser weapons were capable of acquiring any incoming ICBMs launching from enemy missile silos half a world away when the missile was only partway out of the silo and destroying it while it was still moving slowly. Missiles, just like torpedoes, are always traveling at their slowest speed at the earliest moments into the launch sequence. That is the critical moment when guided missiles of all kinds are the easiest to take out: when they are traveling at their slowest velocity and, thus, at the single most vulnerable stage of the flight.

"We're about to find out if these damn things work, Skipper!" the sonar man squawked on the radio. "In my sights, sir. The AI targeting systems are locking on, to eliminate any chance of human error . . ."

"Yeah, sonar," Hawke barked back. "And my targeting sights are locking on to eliminate any chance of AI error, goddammit!"

The radio squawked. "Torpedo fired, Skipper! Torpedo away! One fish is wet, launched from the center boat!"

Hawke had kept his eyes glued to the monitors above as the Black Shark raced toward the *Sea Hawke*. The AI had failed! So much for human error! So much for destroying the torpedo whilst it was still partly inside the tube!

"Christ!" Hawke said, on automatic pilot now, furiously disarming the AI function and putting his own human finger inside the electronic trigger guard, squeezing it ever so slightly . . .

Take a deep breath. Expel it slowly. Squeeze the damn trigger and don't bloody miss!

Hawke estimated the time till impact was less than ten seconds. Nine. Eight. Seven. Six ...

He saw the tracking crosshairs on the weapon's scope begin flashing red, zooming in on the torpedo now at speed, racing toward him, leaving a foamy white trail in its wake. He fired the cannon. The green beam impacted the torpedo at the moment it broached the surface. It was still way too close to the hull of the PT boat.

He held his breath.

But maybe not ...

"Five. Six. Seven ... Laser direct impact!"

He could feel the massive torpedo's explosion shock wave move up through the soles of his shoes on the steel deck.

He quickly rotated the turret and elevated the muzzle of the laser cannon and sighted in on the bridge atop the superstructure of the Chinese torpedo boat at the center of the river. Kill the snake at its head.

The Black Shark had been simply and unceremoniously obliterated. Seconds later, the other PT boat to port began listing heavily to starboard as the result of multiple RPGs, powerful grenades fired by the topside gun crews into her hull just at the waterline. But the Shark on the right was getting dangerously close to launch.

He had flicked the laser's AI tracking system back online, and just in time! Sonar was saying it was now locked on, the screws were turning full crank, and yet the fish was still partially inside the hull of the enemy boat. Time to bloody fire! Hawke screamed at himself, his eye glued to the scope ... He saw an ugly black bulging shape protruding at the mouth of the tube ... two ... three ... four ... Christ! ... Where the hell was that bloody AI?

The ugly black snout protruded farther, moving now ... shark on its way ...

And suddenly the AI systems kicked in. And fired the cannon instantly.

The resulting explosion was a detonation of epic proportions.

The sky itself detonated, revealing a wide gap of daylight, opening up a clear sea lane between the two remaining patrol boats, both of them wounded badly but still narrowly afloat and still putting up a fight from either bank of the river.

Sea Hawke would still have to run their gauntlet, still have to make a dash for it, shoot it out with the two remaining enemy boats to either side to get to the safety of the big river that would carry *Sea Hawke* to the sea. But Hawke had little doubt that *Sea Hawke*'s firepower vastly outgunned that of the Chinese vessels. And he knew the Chinese officers on the bridge would underestimate the speed the *Sea Hawke* would be capable of when she finally made a run for it. She was nothing but a bloody yacht, after all!

Hawke made a decision and issued one last command to the sailors on the bridge: They would make a run for daylight, all right, but they would make it with all guns blazing, giving them all the old girl had left to give. He said, "And, by God, she's still got a hell of a lot left to give, lads!"

He then shouted into the ship's PA for all to hear, "*Sea Hawke*, damn the torpedoes, lads, all ahead bloody full! Commence firing at will, boys!"

Sea Hawke surged ahead with shocking ferocity, her massive prow lifting proudly into the air and throwing off huge torrents of boiling white water to either side of her bows.

Words to live by, "all ahead full." Hawke chuckled to himself as he felt the sheer thrust generated by those bloody turbos kicking in! "All ahead full" is not a bad life motto, he thought. No, not a bad motto at all!

CHAPTER 47

"A Chinese nuclear submarine? Chasing him all the way up the Amazon River? Madness, I tell you, sheer madness!"

Aboard Sea Hawke, *the Amazon River*

A nd still the battles, which Hawke would later recall as "The Riverine Wars," raged on in the heat of day, far beneath the high canopy of green blotting out the blue skies hundreds of feet above. They were still taking fire from machine gun nests hidden in the jungle on both sides of the river. But it was fundamentally harmless.

It would be safe to say that Hawke did not have time to rest on his laurels, nor did anyone else aboard the embattled *Sea Hawke,* for that matter. There was still a vicious firefight going on, with *Sea Hawke* still taking incoming and more withering fire, caught in the cross fire between the two flanking torpedo boats—wounded, yes, but still struggling valiantly to give chase as chase could.

The rattling sound of automatic weapons, punctuated by great booming noises from the rocket-propelled grenades slamming with a *whoomph,* penetrating into the hulls and superstructures of the two patrol boats, was deafening inside the forward turret. And it was hot as the hellfires of Hades in here now, Hawke realized, wiping the salty, stinging sweat from his eyes so he could bloody well see what was happening on the flickering monitors.

And then he saw something that had to be an illusion, or, at the very least, something that made him quite sure that he was actually losing

what was left of his mind! He was reminded of the early explorers who'd
ventured deep into the far reaches of the Amazon and how many of them
had never made it out because they'd been driven stark raving mad by the
horrors they'd been subjected to.

Now, he began to understand the process of the descent. If the burning sands of the Sahara could drive strong men round the bend, so, too,
could the oppressive confines of this green hell make the strongest of
men doubt their sanity.

Get a hold of yourself, damn you! People are counting on you!

Something passing strange was moving upstream toward them. It was
traveling in the dead center of the river. It was moving forward at about
five knots, and leaving behind it a frothy white wake. It was—no, it
couldn't be that. Just an illusion. At first, Hawke thought it must be some
rare breed, a snake that swam upright, using its tail for propulsion, its
triangular head held high, its forked tongue slithering in and out of its
mouth, swimming with its lower body concealed beneath the muddy water, looking every which way for prey.

Or, on second thought, perhaps it was one of those jet-black seabirds
that swim along like ducks or swans, madly paddling beneath the surface
with their webbed feet, whilst their heads, atop long slender necks, undu-
lated about a foot above the surface. He knew the name of that bird, but
at the moment could not recall it.

Where was that bloody Quint when you actually needed him? Sitting
forlorn in the smoking ruins of the Tang empire, bemoaning his fate? No,
feeding the fishes on the muddy bottom of the world's greatest river,
that's where. All of them left there, bereft of even the most basic elements
of survival, without food or water or shelter, and all wondering how the
hell, after the devastating loss of all their yachts, they could ever get out
of the impinging jungle alive. Their mobiles were useless here. They had
no method of communicating with the outside world.

Like the rest of the survivors, the Russians, the Chinese, the Cubans,
the staff, and what was left of the security forces were utterly forlorn at
this point. Hell, all of them standing there in the midst of the smoking
wreckage? Dragonfire offered them no shelter from the elements. And,

with their multimillion-dollar mega-yachts sent to the bottom by some mad English yachtsman, their Grand Alliance was now in tatters. And from the deepest depths of the jungle, there was no visible means of escape! They'd probably run out of food and water within a matter of days.

Hawke's plan, which seemed insane to some, had gone off just the way he'd intended.

So much for Red Star and their glorious dreams of worldwide supremacy, now a pile of smoking rubble! Hawke took pleasure in that dire image. He'd told Sir David he'd be the death of the Red Star movement in its infancy, in its nascent moments.

And, by God and all that's holy, he'd done what he'd said he'd do. He could return to England a man of his word. And Britain and her many allies might rest a little easier this evening . . .

Hawke's attention reverted to the river. He stared at the apparition in the middle of the river. He still had no bleeding idea what it was. Some kind of bizarre turtle or fish? But upon closer inspection, Alex Hawke saw that this apparition was neither fish, nor fowl, nor duck, nor any living creature.

It was, clearly, a periscope! Traveling at a pretty good clip up the Amazon River, saints preserve us!

A submarine periscope! Here? A submarine transiting in such shallow waters, plowing through underwater jungles that could reach out and wrap their tentacles around a bloody periscope? They could get themselves tangled up and never get out!

Insanity. Sheer insanity!

What the bloody hell was going on here? A submarine was one thing. Not just that. Oh, no. But a submarine this far up the Amazon?

Sheer madness!

He blinked his eyes once or twice, thinking he had to be hallucinating . . . He raised the palm of his hand to his forehead. He felt as if he were burning up with fever. And the fever was impairing his thinking.

And still the bloody periscope! Leaving a tiny wake behind it, it drew ever nearer to the *Sea Hawke.*

He got on the radio. Were they seeing this up on the bridge?

"Hornblower, this is Hawke. Is anyone seeing what I'm seeing out there on the river?"

"Yes, we are. Sonar just picked up the screw signature. We've got a goddamn Chinese nuclear sub on our doorstep and knocking on our front door."

Like Hawke, Hornblower was having a hard time accepting what he was seeing. He, too, thought he might at long last be going mad. Had they all gone mad? A nuclear sub? This far from the Atlantic? This far up a bloody river? The Amazon? Jesus, Mary, and Joseph in a wheelbarrow!

It was sheer insanity.

But, then, if the world had learned anything at all in the last year or two, it was that the CPC, in its new quest for power and world domination, was capable of just about anything. Make that anything at all. Order a nuclear sub to venture up the world's greatest river. Find and sink the big white yacht with the name *Sea Hawke* emblazoned on her transom. And sink it!

"Ahoy, bridge, this is sonar. She's coming up, sir! Surfacing now. She's blowing her ballast tanks and coming to the surface!"

"Here she comes," Hornblower cried.

Hawke still couldn't believe his eyes. It occurred to him then that the Tang Brothers were behind this madness.

The Tang Twins, as they were known, were vastly powerful within the Chinese military, the government, and the Chinese Secret Service. And when the Tangs, Tommy and Tiger, had just borne witness to the utter destruction of their crowning achievement, their grand design, the Dragonfire Club, and, along with it, the ruination of their cherished Red Star Alliance, they'd gotten on the wire with Beijing and demanded some kind of retaliation for the havoc a certain English spy had wreaked on their property. Given their agenda . . . well, he wouldn't be surprised if that wasn't exactly what had happened.

A Chinese nuclear submarine, lurking off the coast of Brazil, letting their presence be known in order to intimidate any and all of the Western countries who still favored the Americans in the coming war for world dominance.

That's when Hawke saw the sub's great rounded bow suddenly break free of the surface and rise majestically skyward. She was still rising at an impossible angle when Hawke decided to take action. If he let the sub get fully out of the water and onto the surface, it might be too late to counter her many forward torpedo tubes!

He reached out and hit the switches, taking the AI systems instantly offline. The cannon was where it belonged, goddammit; she was in manual mode now. And Alex Hawke's trigger finger had suddenly gotten quite itchy indeed!

Only now did he recognize the sub. Yes! She was the identical sister ship of the two boomers he and Stoke had discovered and sunk in the Bahamas at China's secret underwater sub pen at the Dragonfire Club! Once they had gotten inside, they saw that there were three submarine mooring slips in all. Two of them had subs moored in the slips. But the middle pen had been empty. And this boomer? Very likely the one that had been out on patrol when he and Stoke had explored the secret pen!

And now this.

Here she was now, directly in his crosshairs.

It seemed as if she would never cease her upward surge.

But then, almost imperceptibly at first, her momentum slowed, and she began at last to pitch forward . . . the bow falling slowly at first, bowing like the devout faithful, lowering their heads in prayer.

And when the bulbous steel hull finally came crashing down, and when the huge bulk of the great death machine slammed down onto the surface of the river, she created two tsunamis, one to either side. Hawke watched in wonder as the massive waves rolled toward the gravely wounded Chinese PT boats, already taking water and listing over dangerously on either side of the river.

It looked as if the waves created by the explosion of the massive Chinese submarine would swamp the badly damaged patrol boats, finishing the job Hawke and Co. had started.

A certain irony there, he thought to himself.

Hawke radioed the bridge.

"Hornblower, Hawke here. Can sonar pick up the screw sounds of a torpedo in the seconds prior to launch? Torpedoes still inside the tubes?"

"Yes. We can, but only a few seconds after activation. Over."

"Good! That's enough. The only way we can ruin this fat bastard's day is to hit them where it hurts. Sink them with their own bloody torpedoes still aboard the sub!"

This, Hawke knew, was making history. Never before in the epic history of naval warfare had anyone ever had the wherewithal, much less the technical ability, to take out a giant nuclear submarine by firing a single shot!

He smiled to himself as he fully shut down the AI once more and took manual control of the Green Monster.

He knew torpedoes were forthcoming, he just didn't know when.

The turret speaker squawked.

"Hawke, sonar! Getting two torpedo screw signatures inside the port and starboard bow tubes! She's launching a pair of fish any second now, sir!"

That did it.

Now!

The laser's crosshairs, now flashing red, were already locked onto the sub's forward tubes. He knew one green blast to the starboard tube would probably be more than enough to blow the whole damn bow off the damn sub. Period. But, on the other hand, he could not rationally take the chance that the port torpedo had been fired mere seconds prior to the fatal destruction of the starboard tube.

So he split the difference, and thus put the blinking red crosshairs right in between the two forward tubes.

Seconds counted now. He was sweating heavily, not just with the fever of the rising heat inside the turret, but from the heavy drama of trying to keep his crew and his friends safe from instant extinction.

He did his slow breathing, calming his nerves with brief moments of meditation.

And now he flicked the firing trigger with the light touch of a master violinist drawing his bow across the taut strings of his Stradivarius. He saw the twin instantaneous flashes of green, an action that produced a massively loud explosion that was, to Hawke's ears, music sent from heaven. The impact of his two laser strikes had brought twin violent explosions. Surely the backbone of the submarine had now been broken in two. There would be no survivors this day.

And the resulting twin explosions had sent massive shock waves hurtling toward *Sea Hawke*, rocking her to the core, as if she'd suffered taking a monstrous rogue wave broadside. He was confident that the Chinese boomer had been mortally damaged. But, at this point, he was in no mood to take chances.

He fired a quick green burst once more, sending what was left of the rogue sub plummeting to the muddy river bottom some two hundred feet below the surface.

The lads had opened the sweltering turret's hatch, and suddenly he could feel the fresher, cooler air wafting up inside the steel oven they'd been locked inside for the better part of an hour. The boys lowered the stainless-steel ladder for him and he climbed down to the deck. Breathing the air still redolent of cordite and death and destruction was still preferable to the stifling smell of sweat and fear inside the gun turret. He was glad to be shut of it.

He worked his way aft to find Stokely, the two of them stopping to talk with the crew. Both he and Stoke thanked them each and every one for their courage under fire and their stalwart resistance in the face of overwhelming odds. He stopped to talk to the wounded, trying to comfort them until the orderlies took them belowdecks to the sick bay. There were more casualties this time: three seamen killed, five severely wounded, and ten or more badly wounded, and still more with non-life-threatening injuries.

After they'd done the best they could to comfort his somewhat shell-shocked men, Hawke had come to a conclusion: Enough was enough! He'd done the very best he could do. And now it was over, he was hell-bent to get out of this Green Hell and back to the open seas, where the *Sea Hawke* could spread her big white wings and *fly, dammit!*

He ordered the captain and crew up on the bridge to make for the Atlantic full speed ahead and take no prisoners. They were bound for Marajó once more and beyond.

Hawke got up early the next morning and had a scrumptious breakfast. He realized he hadn't eaten in days! He'd been way too busy to waste time chewing on some bone or other. And why, pray tell, was that?

It had been, he admitted, a good deal spicier than he'd first imagined. He'd had no way of anticipating the degree of violence or danger that they'd encountered on the river. And he was sorry for that, he said. But, still, it was mission accomplished. A blow had been struck for sanity among the nations of the free world. And for freedom. And faith. And democracy.

And for that, he would be eternally grateful.

His thoughts turned to his dear son. In his mind's eye, he could see Alexei and Devereux splashing about in the surf, both brown as berries with huge white smiles. He could see Ambrose sitting on the beach beneath a bright yellow umbrella (his favorite color), polishing his new novel to a fare-thee-well. And he could see dear old Pelham, materializing out on the terrace and serving Ambrose and his wife, Lady Diana, Pimm's Cups before dematerializing and ghosting back to the kitchen ...

He was not embarrassed to feel the hot tears flooding his eyes and spilling down his cheeks.

These were the people he loved most in all the world.

And, God willing, he would be laying down his sword and carefully making his way down to the beach to join everyone in the joy of the Bermuda sunshine ... and the rolling blue Atlantic.

CHAPTER 48

"The polar ice pack is still too thick for us to be able to get anywhere even near the South Pole."

Aboard Sea Hawke, *across the South Atlantic*

The next day, the sun shone brightly down upon them, the wavy seas were of a deep blue hue and rolling gently. And the big white-winged *Sea Hawke*, under full sail? Why, she was flying homeward, battered but unbowed and unbeaten.

Hawke and Stoke remained up on deck for most of the day, talking about all that had transpired on the voyage, the good, the bad, and the ugly, but mainly just enjoying the blue of the sky, the puffy white clouds in the heavens high above, the iodine smell of the salty air, and the cooling spray coming over the bow and washing over their salt-encrusted bodies was akin to heaven itself. Hawke said:

"Change of plans you should know about, Stoke."

"Talk to me."

"The final chapter? The Antarctica mission? Suspicious Chinese military activity at the South Pole. MI6 wanted us to go have a look-see. But I got a telex from Sir David Trulove, and it's been canceled, apparently because of unusual weather down at the pole. The spring thaw is late this year, and the polar ice pack is still too thick for us to be able to get anywhere near the South Pole. We'd most likely get trapped for months in the ice pack. Hell, we'd need a nuclear-powered icebreaker to even consider trying it."

"So where to now, boss?"

"Bermuda, of all places! Doesn't that sound good? I mean, after the rumble in the jungle?"

"Bermuda? Hell, yeah. Sounds too good to be true to me. Can I come along for the ride?"

"Ha. I was hoping you'd ask. Yes, you are more than welcome. I'd love to have your company sailing across the Atlantic once more."

"I'm in, boss. Looking forward to it. Fancha's still up in Philly nursing her mother. So, I'm good, I'm good to go."

After luncheon up on deck, Hawke had decided to go below and just hole up in his stateroom. He was reading a good book by an American author whom he'd come to love.

The book, part of a trilogy, was called *All the Pretty Horses*, and the author was a fellow by the name of Cormac McCarthy. The tale was working wonders in his brain, pushing out the blood-drenched images of violence and war and replacing them with golden visions of the Old West.

He must have dozed off.

He heard a rapping at his door and assumed he was dreaming. But the knocking continued. He got up and padded over to the door, swinging it wide.

It was Stoke.

"Come on in, Stoke. What's going on?"

"Call for you on the radio telephone up in the comms room. From Bermuda. It's Chief Inspector Congreve."

"Congreve? What's the matter? Is something wrong? Is Alexei okay?"

"Oh, yeah. Ambrose sounds fine. Apparently, some kinda package for you was delivered this morning over at Teakettle Cottage. Special delivery. Pelham thought you should know about it, so he just dropped it off at Shadowlands."

"Okay, thanks. Wonder what it is?"

"We all do."

"Please go tell him I'll be right up, soon as I put on some jeans and a shirt!"

"You got it, boss!"

Up in the comms room, Hawke got on the radio telephone.

"Ambrose. It's Alex. Tell me what's going on."

"A special-delivery packet arrived at the cottage this morning. It's postmarked from somewhere in Siberia. Pelham thought you should know about it. So he brought it here."

Hawke's heart froze. A mysterious package from Siberia? Could Mr. Smith actually send bombs from the grave? Or, more likely, was Putin behind it? Jesus! Does this crap never bloody end?

"Siberian postmarked?"

"Yes. About a week ago. What would you like me to do? Just hold on to it until you arrive?"

"No. It can't wait that long."

"Well, if you'd like, I can open it and read it to you . . ."

"Yes. Please do that. Is it ticking?"

"All right, opening it up . . . It appears to be a handwritten letter. Quite long. Four or five or more pages. A few scattered photographs. All taken in the snow. Skiing. Horse-drawn carriages, things like that."

Hawke felt he might be on the verge of tears.

"It's from Anastasia, Ambrose. Good Lord. I haven't heard from her in so many, many years."

"Would you like me to read it aloud?"

"Indeed. Let me sit down and get someone to bring me some hot coffee . . . Okay, please go ahead, Constable."

"All right. It looks to be a very personal love letter. I hope I can do it justice. At any rate, here we go."

Ambrose began reading Anastasia's letter aloud:

My dearest darling, Alex. First, I send all my love and best wishes to both you and my darling Alexei, my precious son, whom I've missed so terribly much, lo these passing years. I'm writing to you both to tell you my news. Late last week, my beloved benefactor, protector, and savior, General Arkady Arkov, who has supported me for the duration of my many years of splendid solitude here inside the walls of Peter the Great's former Winter Palace, went to his reward.

The general passed away, peacefully in his sleep, two nights ago. He had just turned ninety-eight this last month and seemed, for all intents and purposes, to be in quite good health. He had written me, according to his nurses and the physician, a lengthy farewell note just before he went to sleep that night. Apparently, the doctor said, he'd written it after having had some kind of foreshadowing, or even foreboding about his immediate future.

Arkady, now having little or no family to speak of, has bequeathed to me his entire fortune, which I must say is more than generous of him, as it is an exceedingly large sum. I must say that I, as one who has long considered herself the "Penniless Princess Romanova," am staggered by the amount of it. In addition to providing for my financial well-being for the balance of my life, he said that, after months of correspondence and lengthy negotiations with the Kremlin, he had finally reached an agreement with President Putin that, henceforth, I will no longer be subject to arrest by FSB, or, as I still call it, KGB. Henceforth, I will be able to travel freely throughout Russia, and, indeed, throughout the world, without fear of harm from anyone, either from within or without the Russian government. The late general has left me with certain documents, including a bill of guaranteed safe passage, issued by the office of the president, and personally signed and sealed with wax by Putin himself.

So I find myself, previously a penniless pauper, now seated here all alone by the crackling fire in the palace's great library, suddenly a woman of means. And one with a great future ahead of her at last. I have to say that my first thoughts were of the two of you. My two darlings, the younger of whom probably has no recollection of me at all. And the other, you, my dear Alex, who knew and knows me better than anyone else on earth. I've been thinking these last few days of what to do with myself. Paris? Rome? Capri? Sorrento? I considered, and ultimately discarded them all.

I decided to follow the murmurs of my heart and see where they would lead me.

And, unsurprisingly, my heart, in its abundant wisdom, leads me to you both.

Thus, I've booked train passage on the Trans-Siberian Express, the "Iron Rooster" from Tvas—Alex, you'll recall the little station here in Siberia, where we last said good-bye. And thence to Odessa, where I'll board a flight bound for London Heathrow, connecting to a British Airways flight to Bermuda, which still holds a special place in my heart. I shall be arriving in the early afternoon, the fifteenth of September. I doubt my longing for Bermuda will come as any great shock to you, dear Alex.

I'm sure you remember our first meeting on that beach, you in the altogether, having swum three miles in open ocean, then sunning yourself to sleep on the beach and me emerging from the sea in the bottom half of my bikini with a bag full of seashells and finding a naked man asleep on my towel! It was at that precise moment, staring down at the most beautiful man I had ever seen, that I decided to do a life-size nude portrait of you. You were plainly terrified at the prospect. You believed me when I said you would hang in London's National Portrait Gallery for all of London to behold!

An auspicious beginning to our whirlwind courtship and subsequent relationship, was it not?

Do you still remember my father, the late Count Romanov, and his lovely estate on Bermuda? It is still there. It's called "Faraway," the name I gave it as a young girl, all those many years ago. It still belongs to me, and, over the years, I have funded its upkeep, landscaping, and maintenance, in the hopes that one day, I might be lucky enough to find myself washing ashore on the beach at Faraway once more with the rising tide.

And so I shall, my darlings, and so I shall.

I am breathless with anticipation, and my poor heart is all aflutter at the mere thought of seeing you both after all this time. I'm sure I will not even recognize my darling son, who you'll remember was less than three years old when I handed him up to you, even as the train was chugging away from the little snowbound station at Tvas that frigid afternoon so many, many years ago.

My thought then, at that precise moment, and even now, never expressed to you, was that, since I myself could not be with you, that all I had to give you in this world was our beloved child.

Just the very idea of the three of us in the same place, together again, in sunshine and in rain, a real family once more . . . I hope you share my delight, dear Alex, at this prospect.

I shan't breathe until I am in your strong arms once more, feeling your breath on my cheek, hearing your soft-spoken words of love in my ear . . .

With all my love, all my prayers, and all my bright hopes for all of us, for Alex, Alexei, and Anastasia, for all of our collective peace and happiness, for the balance of our days, I send you both this letter of love straight from my heart . . . And I hope you don't mind, but I've attached a poem by my newly discovered favorite poet.

Anastasia Romanova Hawke

EPILOGUE

*"I'm no pill popper, Pelham, but I daresay I could murder
a Goslings rum and tonic if you have one handy!"*

Teakettle Cottage, Bermuda

The day was shot through in shades of azure blue. So it was only fitting that Alex Hawke's disposition that afternoon was a bright and sunny one. Still, and he could not tell you why, he was feeling just a bit insecure, yet still full of joy, whilst excited to the point of irrationality. He'd never been happier, but he'd never been so plainly terrified. What if she didn't love him anymore? What if, what if, what if?

All these bloody what-ifs!

He was now, along with his valet and favorite octogenarian, Pelham Grenville, waiting in the glare of the sun at the airport's gate out on the tarmac. Flight 132, a British Airways flight nonstop from London Heathrow, was scheduled to arrive at Bermuda any moment now.

Hawke, who was plainly beside himself, was even getting on Pelham's nerves. And that is saying something, because as Hawke often said, this Pelham person simply had no nerves at all.

Pelham had accused him of being far too nervous, or, at the very least, exceedingly jumpy, during the drive out to the airport at St. George's parish. And, although Hawke could scarcely credit it, he supposed he was a bit of both. What he wished for, above all, was simply the happy reunion of mother and child, their having not seen each other for nearly a decade.

"M'lord," Pelham had admonished him, "you really must calm down, or you'll scare the poor woman away! She'll take one look at you, turn around, climb right back on that airplane, and fly straightaway back to London. Get your nerves under control, m'lord! She's due to arrive at any minute! The last thing you want to do is scare the poor woman to death."

"Me? Nervous? You must have me confused with one of your other m'lords. I don't get nervous, Pelham. I make *others* nervous. You know what they used to say about me when I first joined the Secret Service?"

"Tell me again, sir."

"They would say, as I'll remind you, 'That Alex Hawke is one hard case, mind you. When he dives into the sea, the sharks get out of the water!'"

"Quite right. But. *Not* nervous, did you say, sir? Not nervous? Why, you're as nervous as a long-tailed cat in a room full of rocking chairs! As it happens, I've brought along your silver pillbox. The one where you keep your nerve pills, sir. Perhaps you should take one now . . ."

"Me? Take a nerve pill, just because some woman from my past is arriving for a little visit? What do you take me for? Do you know that, precisely two weeks ago today, I was on the Amazon River, staring down a Chinese nuclear submarine! And guess who won the day!"

"The nuclear submarine, of course."

"Hardly. Only one of us remained standing when the dust cleared. And that would be he who stands before you now. In other words, your employer!"

"How marvelous for you, sir! Now, will you please take one of your nerve pills!"

"Never. I'm no pill popper, as you well know, Pelham. However, I could murder a Goslings rum and tonic if you have one handy!"

————————

Pelham had driven him out to Bermuda's airport in the Locomotive, his old gray Bentley. Hawke had ordered that the car be shipped from the stables at his ancestral home, Hawkesmoor, in the Cotswolds. The only other mode of transport he had available to himself nowadays was a vintage Norton Commando motorcycle and a vintage Morgan 3-Wheeler.

SEA HAWKE / 331

Neither very suitable for collecting fabulously wealthy Russian princesses from airports.

But, at the last minute, he'd been notified that the big gray Continental had indeed arrived on the island. The car had already been unloaded from the ship, and the Locomotive had been washed and waxed to gleaming perfection, her tank fully topped off with petrol, and she was now waiting for him out at the Royal Dockyards.

Back at Teakettle Cottage, his son, along with many of his friends, would be waiting.

Hawke had decided that the little welcome celebration he'd planned and arranged for Anastasia should take place out on the terrace overlooking the Atlantic at Teakettle Cottage, his logic being that, as this was, after all, Alexei's home turf, his son would be far more comfortable meeting his long-lost mother here. This would be, in effect, the first time they'd actually met since his infancy.

He'd also invited Chief Inspector Congreve and Lady Diana for champagne and caviar, as well as his good friends Malcom Gosling, chairman and CEO of Goslings Rum, and his lovely wife, Caroline. And, at the last minute, he had hired a Bermudian string quartet to provide a bit of entertainment for the happy occasion.

Anastasia was first to emerge from the plane, appearing at the top of the staircase in a splendid bright yellow skirt and a snow-white linen blouse. She stepped out into the brilliant sunshine, raising her right hand to shield her eyes as she surveyed the group waiting down at the gate. Hawke began to wave like a madman.

She spotted him instantly.

She had only her carry-on bag, containing the novel she was reading, *Pale Fire*, by her favorite Russian author, Vladimir Nabokov, and all of her other necessaries for the long flight from Heathrow to Bermuda. Once she had boarded the plane, and after a glass of champagne, she realized how conflicted she was by the warring emotions in her heart and on her mind.

On the one hand, she was exhilarated by the notion that, after nearly a decade's absence in her life, she was about see her darling boy at last, not to mention the man who'd won her poor heart a decade ago, then lost it to the only man in Russia who could keep her safe and alive, even if it meant spending the rest of her days as a "prisoner" in the secret KGB headquarters at Peter the Great's Winter Palace.

A moment later, she was in her lover's arms.

"Anastasia," he whispered. "You're lovelier now than ever. God, how I've missed you. How haunted I've been by the conviction that we'd never be together again . . ."

"Oh, my darling," she said, looking up into those unforgettable, arctic blue eyes of his, "I've missed you so terribly. I, too, began to believe I'd never see you again!"

"But here you are, my love. Here you are at last where you belong. In my arms!"

"Alex, really, we're making a scene. You should let me walk under my own power the rest of the way. Who is that man waving at us?"

"That, dear girl, is my oldest friend in all the world. He is my valet, my cook, my driver, my confidante. When my parents died, he stepped in and, with the help of Chief Inspector Congreve, raised me to be the man I am today. I've been talking to him about you all morning, and he's desperate to meet you."

"You mean the man I thought was your partner when first I called you at Teakettle Cottage and he answered the telephone?"

"Yes, that's him all right. My partner. We still haven't quite figured out who is the wife and who is the husband, however."

"I forgot. You're funny. I forgot all about that."

"Is that a good thing or a bad thing?"

"Good, silly! Arkady was kind and dear and generous. But he was *not* funny! You told me once you thought that humor was the answer to everything."

She squeezed his hand and walked ahead to introduce herself to the old gentleman.

"How do you do, sir? You must be Pelham. Alex has been telling me all about you and I couldn't wait to say hello!"

"Welcome to Bermuda, ma'am. I must say, the whole household, if not the entire island, is agog about your arrival. It's my very great honor to meet you. And, should you ever be in need of anything, please consider me always at your service. Oh, m'lord, let me help with all that luggage!"

Half an hour later, having managed to avoid the all the rush-hour traffic streaming out of Hamilton by taking the back roads, Pelham steered the big Bentley into the sandy drive, quite hidden from the road if you didn't know it was there. It wound through thick green jungle all the way up to Teakettle Cottage, which perched atop the hill. The white-washed roof and the pink structure did indeed bear a striking resemblance to a teakettle. This, all because of the dome-shaped main room, as well as the attached chimney always threatening to topple over, which gave the appearance for all the world like the spout on a kettle.

Hawke and Anastasia waited until Pelham had taken the last of the luggage inside the house before they stepped up to the door.

He smiled at her, his hands on her hips as he lifted her easily from the ground. Then he rapped smartly on the door to the terrace. When Pelham swung it wide, he stepped through the doorway and into the living room with Anastasia cradled in his arms. He carried her all the way through the house to the Monkey Bar and the terrace beyond.

Lady Diana was first to see them emerge into the sunshine. She shrieked loudly, surprised at the sight of a smiling Alex Hawke stepping out onto the sunny terrace with a gorgeous young woman in his arms. She leapt to her feet, clapping loudly, as all the other guests got to their feet and gave the happy couple a standing ovation, swarming around them.

Alex lowered Anastasia gently to the terrace floor and turned to face the little gathering.

"Ladies and gentlemen, may I present to you the love of my life, and the mother of my child, Alexei, the beautiful Anastasia Romanova! I think she has something to tell you. Anastasia, you have the floor."

"Hello, all, hello," she said. "What can I tell you? He swept me right off my heels!"

Everyone laughed, and then made way for Alexei, who was shyly making his way over to his parents.

He stopped and gazed up at Anastasia.

He raised his right hand for her to shake, and she shook it warmly, her big brown eyes overflowing with love as she looked down at him adoringly.

"Hello, darling Alexei," she said, still holding his hand.

"Hello, and welcome home," he said, as he'd been taught to say by his father.

"Home. What a lovely word. Perhaps the loveliest of all."

"May I ask you a question?" he said.

"Of course, my darling. Any question at all!"

"Are you really my mother? I mean, um, my real mother?"

She threw her head back and laughed, saying, "Yes, dear, I am. Now come here and give your poor mother a great big hug! I've been very lonely without you all this time."

She bent forward and beckoned him with wide-open arms. She felt her beloved son cling to her, and it opened her heart as wide as it would go . . .

"Yes, Alexei, I am really and truly your real mother. And, may I say, I always thought you'd grow up to be a fine young man who looked exactly like his father. And I'm delighted to say, after all these years, that I see I finally got one thing exactly right!"

It was at that precise moment that Pelham floated out onto the terrace, searching for Hawke.

"Oh, m'lord," he said in a low voice. "Sorry to interrupt, but I'm afraid there's a call for you in the library."

"A call?"

"Indeed, sir. A priority-one call."

"Really? I'm with my family. Can you not take a message? Who on earth is calling, Pelham?"

"Buckingham Palace, your lordship. Most urgent, sir."

"Who at Buckingham Palace, Pelham? Who has the nerve—no, not the nerve, the unbridled temerity—to call me now, when I'm finally with my family?"

Pelham rose up on his toes to whisper in Hawke's ear.

"That would be Her Royal Majesty the Queen, sir. She says she must talk with you at once. She says it's most urgent!"

Hawke stifled a stern response, got to his feet, and went over to the Monkey Bar to take the call.

"No rest for the weary," he muttered to himself after hanging up the phone and then padding back out to where everyone on this earth he loved had gathered happily at the edge of the sea . . .

"Who was it, Alex?" Congreve said.

"Oh, no one you'd know. Just an old acquaintance. Down on her luck, it seems. Wants to borrow a few quid, that's all."

ACKNOWLEDGMENTS

I would like to thank, first of all, the lovely Victoria de la Maza, who gave me the gift of time to finish this book and the encouragement to make it as good as I was capable of. And then try to make it better than I was capable of.

I would like to thank Tom Colgan, my editor at Penguin Random House, Berkley, for his belief in me and his willingness to take a chance on not only me but on Alex Hawke as well. His guidance all through the process is deeply appreciated.

I would also extend my gratitude to all the wonderfully talented folks at Berkley. They were always there for me and they always delivered.

And last, but hardly least, I thank my agent extraordinaire, Mr. John Talbot, who has steered this old ship of mine through sunny days and stormy days, for his vast knowledge of the book world, his acumen, and his very positive outlook on life.

And a big shout-out to my lifelong friend and Hollywood star John Shea. For years, John's incredible talents were on display with his dramatic portrayals of all seventeen of my books. John's use of characters and his uncanny ability to make the listener see what they're hearing is unparalleled in the audiobook world.

And I cannot forget the lovely Cynthia Hornblower, known to one and all as "Lady Hornblower." She handles all of my media and PR needs and is utterly fantastic at what she does, with style and aplomb that helps me put my best foot forward! Thank you, Cynthia, for all your diligence and hard work. It means everything to me!